BANNON
BROTHERS
HONOR

Also Available by Janet Dailey

LET'S BE JOLLY
HAPPY HOLIDAYS
MAYBE THIS CHRISTMAS
SCROOGE WORE SPURS
EVE'S CHRISTMAS
SEARCHING FOR SANTA
MISTLETOE AND MOLLY
AMERICAN DREAMS
AMERICAN DESTINY
SANTA IN A STETSON
MASQUERADE
TANGLED VINES
HEIRESS
RIVALS
TO SANTA, WITH LOVE
BANNON BROTHERS: TRUST
BANNON BROTHERS: HONOR

From the Calder Series:

SANTA IN MONTANA
SOMETHING MORE
CALDER STORM
LONE CALDER STAR
CALDER PROMISE
SHIFTING CALDER WIND
GREEN CALDER GRASS

BANNON BROTHERS
HONOR

JANET DAILEY

KENSINGTON BOOKS
www.kensingtonbooks.com

KENSINGTON BOOKS are published by

Kensington Publishing Corp.
119 West 40th Street
New York, NY 10018

All Kensington titles, imprints, and distributed lines are available at special quantity discounts for bulk purchases for sales promotion, premiums, fund-raising, educational, or institutional use.

Special book excerpts or customized printings can also be created to fit specific needs. For details, write or phone the office of the Kensington Special Sales Manager: Attn. Special Sales Department. Kensington Publishing Corp, 119 West 40th Street, New York, NY 10018. Phone: 1-800-221-2647.

Kensington and the K logo Reg. U.S. Pat. & TM Off.

ISBN-13: 978-0-7582-7834-0
ISBN-10: 0-7582-7834-9

First Trade Paperback Printing: June 2012

10   9   8   7   6   5   4   3   2   1

Printed in the United States of America

BANNON
BROTHERS
HONOR

CHAPTER 1

An immense oak shaded the Maryland mansion beneath it, casting sun-dappled light through thousands of leaves. The tree and the house were the same age, survivors from a vanished and more gracious past. The lowest branches of the grand old oak arched down to the green lawn, providing an ideal backdrop for informal photos of the Bannon wedding party.

It was a perfect fall afternoon. The landscape was touched here and there with the scarlet and gold of sumac and native creeping vines, bright dashes of color against the shimmering water in the near distance. This late in the day, the blue sky shaded to indigo where the slanting rays of the sun had begun to retreat across the vast expanse of the Chesapeake Bay. The plantation estate that had once surrounded the mansion had stretched to its shores, lined with marsh grass turning green into gold.

Linc Bannon, the best man, and his brother Deke, the grooms-man, took their places and followed the photographer's directions. Turn this way. Smile. Best foot forward.

"Excellent," the man said, nodding to his assistant, who dashed off to fetch the next group to pose. "Thank you, gentlemen. Very natural. You two could model."

Linc shot Deke a doubtful look. "Him? Seriously?"

His younger brother chuckled and slipped off his jacket, throwing it over his shoulder. "That's what I was going to say about you."

The resemblance between them was unmistakable. They both

had dark eyes and dark brown hair that the breeze was ruffling, and both were tall and well-built, with a rugged physicality that the formalwear didn't hide. But the faint scar on Linc's face was one difference that stood out. His authoritative stance marked him as the more responsible of the two. At the moment, Deke had other things in mind.

"Here come the bridesmaids," he said, looking at several young women in taffeta whose gowns brushed the lawn as they ran over it to the oak.

Linc glanced at them. "You can turn on the charm."

"I may be younger than you, but you could learn something," Deke said solemnly. "Observe the master."

A lovely brunette reached them first and singled out Deke with a flirtatious look. The shawl she'd thrown on over otherwise bare shoulders slipped down a strategic inch or so. She adjusted it with a graceful touch of her hand. "Hi, Linc. Are we next?"

Deke smiled down at her. "I believe you are. We're heading back to the party."

He nodded toward the striped tents set up for the reception where more than two hundred guests were circulating, eager to enjoy the social event of the season.

An hour or so later the celebration was in full swing, kicked off with several toasts. To the newlyweds, Erin and RJ Bannon. To the Montgomerys, Erin's family, reunited at last. To RJ's two brothers and their mother Sheila. To true love.

Waiters dashed around with artfully composed plates and napkin-swathed bottles of champagne while guests chatted animatedly and laughed and flirted and caught up on old times. Then the dancing began.

Linc leaned back in his chair and watched, fiddling with the stem of his narrow glass and thinking about who he wanted in his arms right now.

Kenzie, of course. Not that she was here. He wondered where she was and what she was doing. Not that it was any of his business.

At the moment, she considered him a friend. He was working

on an upgrade, but she'd been busy lately. He'd invited her to the wedding as his guest, but she'd begged off, saying something vague about a previous commitment on the day. Professional, not personal. That was something. Anyway, he had no intention of giving up. She was definitely worth waiting for.

There was no shortage of gorgeous women at the reception, but not one was in her league, in his opinion. Kenzie was his definition of perfect. Smart. And sexy, with a super-fit, petite body that looked fantastic in a plain white T-shirt and camo cargos—her version of fatigues, now that she was no longer a soldier. Although Uncle Sam wanted her back.

A female guest strolled nearby, trilling a hello to a friend a few tables away. Linc looked idly at them as the woman stopped to chat, then realized she was holding a tiny dog wearing a ruffled collar in the crook of her arm. He'd taken it for a purse at first. Her pampered pet blinked and yawned as the woman moved away.

He shook his head, amused. Not Kenzie's kind of dog, that was for sure.

She'd been a K9 trainer for the army, on a fast track right out of basic. Kenzie wasn't one to brag, but Linc had been able to fill in the blanks from the bare facts she'd offered. Her knack for the work had gotten her quickly promoted to a position of critical importance: training military handlers assigned to new animals and developing new skill sets for the experienced dogs to keep up with what was going on in country.

Then something had happened—she wouldn't say what. She didn't seem to want to reenlist. She didn't seem to want to do anything but work. A lot.

Which was why he was solo on his brother's wedding day.

Two weeks ago he'd stopped by the JB Kennels and seen her out in the field with a half-grown shepherd. Their jumps and leaps looked like pure joy, but he knew she was testing the pup's reflexes and instincts. In time, under her tutelage, the young animal would learn to turn play into power. The sight of the two of them, twisting and turning in midair in mock battle, was something he would never forget.

Hell, Kenzie looked good even in thick bite sleeves and padded pants. But he let himself imagine her in something close-fitting and classy, her hair brushed to a silken shine and her head tipped back to gaze up at him as they danced to a slow number. Like the one the band was playing right now . . .

"Linc. You with us?"

He snapped out of his reverie and looked up at his younger brother. "Just thinking."

Deke took hold of a bentwood chair, spun it around with one hand, and sat on it backward, resting his arms on the curved top and stretching out his long legs.

"About what? Or should I say who?" he asked shrewdly.

"Give me a break, Deke." Linc took a sip of champagne and set the glass aside.

His younger brother wasn't done ribbing him. "You've got someone on your mind. I can see it in your eyes."

"What are you talking about?"

"That moody, romantic, distracted look is what I'm talking about."

"You're imagining things, Deke."

His brother only laughed. "Am I? Just so you know, one wedding per year is all I can handle. I'm not ready to see you walk down the aisle."

Linc smiled slightly. "If I found the right woman, why not?"

Deke was tactful enough to quit at that point. He surveyed the crowd. "Look at all these gorgeous babes. How come you're not dancing?"

"I'm waiting for a song I like," Linc parried.

Deke gave up, shaking his head. "Okay. Have it your way." He returned the inviting smile of the brunette on the other side of the dance floor. She brightened, but stayed where she was, smoothing the brilliant folds of her taffeta dress. "There's my girl. I think she likes me."

"Go for it. You're not taken."

"Neither are you."

Linc only shrugged.

Deke turned his head and studied him for a long moment. "C'mon, bro. You can tell me. What don't I know?"

"Nothing."

Deke didn't seem to believe that reply. "Wait a minute—there was someone. Her name was—it's coming back to me—Karen, right?"

"Who?"

For a second, Linc drew a blank. Then he remembered. Months ago Kenzie had used that name when she'd showed up at Bannon's door with a guard dog to loan him as a favor to Linc.

"Karen," Deke said impatiently. "You know who I mean."

Linc smiled. "Oh, yeah. Her. Ah, we're just friends."

Deke shot him a knowing look.

"If it changes, I'll let you know," Linc said calmly.

His brother lost interest when the brunette seized her chance and swept across the dance floor as the band paused. "I do believe she really is interested." Deke ran a hand over his brown locks and asked, "How's the hair?"

"Looks great. Very natural," Linc teased, echoing the photographer's comment.

"Shut up." Deke straightened his lapels.

The two brothers rose at the same time, but Linc turned to go before the brunette arrived.

A group of younger guests, including Deke and date, decided to keep the celebration going when the reception formally ended, paying the limo drivers to take them to a nearby hotel for an impromptu after-party.

Linc took the red pickup he'd had since forever. He was sentimental about it, though his brother had nixed the old truck for the procession from the church. The car he drove every day was sleek, black, and not particularly noticeable.

Everyone except him headed straight for the noisy lounge to dance into the wee hours. He wandered away down a carpeted corridor, feeling a little lonely. Without intending to, he ended up in the hotel's bar. It was mostly empty. There was only one other customer, an older man having a beer, but no bartender. The pounding music in the lounge was barely audible in the dim, luxuriously furnished room.

He slid onto a stool, folding his arms on the counter and looking around idly while he waited to be served. The liquor bottles arrayed in ranks behind the bar reflected blue light coming from an unseen source. The bar was dark otherwise, but he didn't mind.

The bartender appeared from a door at the end of the polished counter and took his order, exchanging a few words with Linc as he put the drink on a napkin. Then he turned away to set up, setting clean glasses of various types on trays and filling up a compartmented container with slices of lemon and lime and bright red cherries.

Linc barely noticed. He took one sip and set the drink down, intending to make it last. He had nothing to do and nowhere to go except back to the lounge.

Later for that. He was truly tired, and it was catching up with him. Being the best man was serious work. Linc had rolled out of bed at six A.M. and barely had a chance to catch his breath since.

Zoning out over a cold drink felt fine. The TV over the bar offered the usual ten thousand stations via cable. Right now it was tuned to local news, on low. Good. He didn't really want to listen. The weatherman was saying something about clouds rolling in.

So be it. The perfect day was over.

Linc undid his black silk bow tie, taking a deep breath or two as he eased the collar button open next. He wasn't made to wear a monkey suit.

He half heard the reporter going on and on about an accident just outside of a town with a name he wasn't going to remember. Not a pile-up, not a jackknifed semi, just a solitary car.

Filler. News shows made a huge deal out of a fender bender when there wasn't anything else to yap about.

Then the live feed crackled and filled the screen behind the guy and Linc winced. The accident wasn't minor. It looked like a rollover. Smashed frame, crumpled black chassis scraped to the gray undercoat in a lot of places, back wheels high in the air.

Linc could just make out an ambulance, a red and white blotch in the background, and activity around it, a stretcher being loaded. He got a glimpse of what looked like a head-and-neck stabilizer frame attached to the stretcher.

Fatalities got a body bag, not that rig. He automatically wished the injured person well—he or she was lucky to be alive.

He scowled when the cameraman evaded the highway patrol officer's gaze and moved around for a close-up of the nearly totaled vehicle. The reporter on the scene dogged him, trying to stay in the frame and not always succeeding. They both knew what would get on TV: a dramatic shot, preferably with blood.

Good thing there were a few seconds of lag time before any broadcast, Linc thought. Imagine the shock of recognizing a victim of a bad accident or seeing some identifying detail—

He pushed away his barely touched drink. Apparently that rule didn't apply to the film crew of this two-bit TV station. Linc knew that license plate. There was only one word on it.

KENZYZ.

Jesus. The realization that he was looking at Kenzie's crashed sports car hit him like a hammer blow. He'd parked next to it at her apartment more than once. The yellow racing stripes on the damaged black paint were half-hidden by wisps of smoke, but he could just make them out now. His glimpse of the license plate clinched it.

That had to have been her on the stretcher. Right now she must be inside the ambulance. He heard the siren kick up to a wail as the reporter kept on talking, one hand placed awkwardly on a back wheel, spinning it until a highway patrolman yelled at him to stop and got in front of the lens. A dark blue uniform filled the frame and someone at the TV station cut to a commercial.

Linc swore under his breath. He yanked a ten out of his wallet and tossed it on the polished wood of the bar, running out of the hotel to the parking lot.

Trying to think.

He'd only seen one stretcher—she must have been alone in the car. How bad were her injuries? He had to find her, and more importantly, help the cops and hospital personnel get info they might need.

Where the hell had he parked? He stopped, looked around wildly, and finally saw his truck, half-hidden by a catering van. He raced to it, unlocked the door, slid behind the wheel, and started the engine, shifting rapidly into reverse, backing out a little too fast. Somebody honked.

He didn't care. He had to do something. Talk to the cops, find out who'd been notified. Her folks, of course—they'd make that call first. He could get the word out to others. After he was sure she was in a hospital with a top-notch trauma team.

His thoughts were spinning faster than his wheels. It came back to him that Kenzie's parents were in Germany, her dad's last posting before retirement; they'd just moved into base housing. The new phone number might not be in her emergency contacts. She had no brothers or sisters. He only knew a few of her friends. By name. Not well.

Linc found his smartphone and jammed one end of a charger into the cigarette lighter and the other end into the phone so it wouldn't die on him.

The name of the town—the reporter had said it. He cursed himself for not remembering. Summerton. Summerville. Something like that. It hadn't rung a bell.

Then it came back to him. Summer River. Yeah, that was it. It sounded small. He hoped it wasn't too far away.

Once he was west of the bay and back on roads he knew, he pulled over for a few seconds to get a locator app on his phone and tagged the nearest big hospitals to Summer River that qualified as trauma centers. With mangled wreckage like that, she could be critically injured.

Setting the phone to GPS mode, he gunned the truck out onto the road again. Navigating the turns at top speed took concentration, but it still gave him too much time to think. He and Kenzie had barely gotten to know each other in all the months since they'd met. The universe wasn't fair.

He drove faster, keeping an eye on the rearview mirror for following cops. The federal ID he carried would get him waved on about an instant after it was requested, but he didn't want to waste even that much time with John Law.

Where had she been going?

She never was home much, out of town on training gigs more often than not while he'd been cooped up in a featureless building near Langley. His CO had him tracking a worm inside a secret government blacknet. Some hacker five thousand miles away didn't like democracy.

He'd gotten rid of it. Damage repaired and bait left for the perpetrator. The free world would never know, but a couple of four-stars had come over from the Pentagon to personally shake his hand.

All that time. Gone. He shouldn't have been so patient. He shouldn't have waited for her to make the first real moves.

A few drops of rain hit the curved glass of the windshield by the time he raced down the bay road that would take him to I-95. Five minutes later, it was pouring. The glass was obscured by thick, spattering drops that made everything blurry.

An eighteen-wheeler overtook him on the left, throwing blinding spray back against his windshield. Linc swerved to the right, wondering if a rig that size had done in Kenzie's car. Could be. But she'd been driving under clear skies.

Just let her be all right. That didn't seem like too much to ask.

Merged into six fast-moving lanes, he headed straight for the largest hospital of the four he'd tagged, a few miles from the highway. The emergency room entrance was brightly lit, marked by a red sign. He screeched the truck into a parking spot and jumped out, barely noticing the pounding rain.

The ER didn't seem busy. Talking into a slotted metal circle set into wire-mesh glass, he gave the intake clerk a basic explanation and got the runaround.

"The paramedics had her on a spine board before they lifted her into the ambulance. B. MacKenzie. Anyone by that name brought in?" He knew his voice was agitated, but he couldn't control it.

"I just started my shift, sir." She pursed her lips and looked at him disapprovingly, safe in her cubicle.

"But you have to have the admit list for today and tonight." Linc pushed his wet hair back with one hand, aware that he looked like he'd been rolling around in an overflowing gutter. No doubt that was what she was thinking. He didn't give a damn. But he had to be nice.

"I'll look." She began to shuffle through papers on her desktop. Very slowly.

"Maybe she went straight into surgery. How about the ICU? Help me out here."

The intake clerk shook her head. "We don't give patient information to anyone who asks. As a general rule, family members are allowed to visit patients, but you said you weren't family."

Next time he would lie. The clerk hadn't said in so many words that Kenzie wasn't there, so maybe she was. Right now he was ready to slam through the swinging doors that said Staff Only and find out for himself.

A clipboard landed on the counter next to Linc's elbow and he turned to see a youngish woman wearing glasses. The tag pinned to her jacket said her name and under that, *ER Supervisor*.

"What seems to be the problem here?"

The intake clerk slid a disdainful look at Linc to indicate that he was. The ER manager peered at him through lenses that made her eyes wide and owlish.

"Can I help you?" she asked him crisply.

"Sorry to bother you. I'm looking for someone who may have been in an accident—"

"And you are?" she interrupted him.

"Her, um, friend." He couldn't suddenly turn into Kenzie's brother in front of the unhelpful clerk. "My name is Linc Bannon—"

She interrupted him again. "And your friend's name is?"

"Her last name is MacKenzie."

"You don't know her first name?"

"She goes by—never mind. Tell me something. How many MacKenzies do you get on an average night? Ten? Fifteen? Is she here or not?"

The supervisor kept her cool. "I'm trying to help you."

She was. Linc collected himself. "Sorry. Look, I know I saw her crashed car on the news. Live on the scene—ambulance, highway patrol, the works. I couldn't see her on the stretcher but they showed a close-up of the plates. It was a rollover. Maybe on 1-95 or a connecting highway."

"Can you narrow that down a little? You're talking about a lot of road."

"Somewhere around here, I think. The reporter said Summer River."

The ER supervisor nodded. "That's not far from us. Let me check the admit list." Linc noticed that the clerk ducked her head down when she heard that and got busy with the papers again. "Sorry. No one by that name has come in."

"Oh, *here's* my copy," the clerk muttered behind the glass. "The day person keeps moving my files."

The supervisor frowned at her and turned to speak to him. Linc was getting the feeling that she was on his side.

"So—you said you recognized the car and the plates, but you didn't see her. Is it possible that she wasn't driving?"

Her remark startled him. "What?"

"A teenager could have swiped her car for a joyride. Unfortunately, they often wreck what they steal. So do car thieves, though they're a little more careful. Anyway, we get both now and then."

Linc blew out the breath he'd been holding.

"Try calling your friend first, just in case. Then try the Summer River police department. They wouldn't necessarily have been the first responders, but they can run her name through a statewide database, and also connect you to the highway patrol."

The voice of sanity. It worked. Linc got a grip. "That makes sense. Okay. I'll do that. Thanks."

She nodded to him as her pager went off. "I'm sure you'll find her." She walked quickly away without a backward look.

Linc caught a glimpse of himself in the wire-mesh glass around the clerk's cubicle. His hair had turned into a scruffy mess and dark stubble was putting in an unwanted appearance. The damp, wrinkled tuxedo jacket and the dangling ends of his silk bowtie didn't help.

The intake clerk had her head down again, ignoring him. He jammed his hands in his pants pockets and walked quickly toward the wide double doors. The steel-framed glass panels opened with a hiss and out he went into the sluicing rain.

Chilled to the bone, he got back into his truck and slumped in his seat, reaching wearily for the smartphone, not seeing any messages on the little glowing screen.

Apparently his absence hadn't been noted. No one who knew him had seen him enter the bar or leave it. No texts, no e-mails. He found Kenzie's number and tapped the screen.

His call went straight to her voicemail. Maybe she'd shut off her phone, maybe her battery was dead. Given the uncertainty of her whereabouts, that didn't reassure him.

Linc gave it a minute and tapped her number again. The recorded message was twice as irritating the second time around. The hell with it. He was going to drive to her place and see for himself if she was there or not.

He entered her address into the GPS search bar. It wouldn't take that long to get there, unless the highway was under water. He sped out of the parking lot, spraying through puddles on either side.

Not slowing down until he went down the exit ramp, he pulled around the back of her apartment building a few minutes later. Her spot was empty. No surprise. The wreck wouldn't have been towed here. He craned his neck and looked through the windshield. Her windows on the third floor glowed amber.

Maybe the ER supervisor had guessed right. But he hadn't seen or talked to Kenzie yet.

He got out and made his way to the rear entrance. If she was there, he wanted to actually set eyes on her.

There was a long rectangle of opaque glass just above the entrance, meant to illuminate the stairwell during the day. Right now it was lit up, but not brightly. He saw a shadow move quickly down from the third floor to the second, then disappear.

No one came out.

He didn't think too much about it. Linc pushed open the door and glanced at the security camera, an old clunker, positioned high in a corner. It didn't move. The lens was flat black, with no gleam to its glass. Painted over, he thought distractedly, taking the stairs two at a time. No one was going to see him, as if that mattered.

He reached her floor and opened the fire door onto a long hall. Another shadow appeared at the other end, then vanished so swiftly he thought he'd imagined it.

He was dead beat by now. Tired wasn't the word. The mad

dash down too many roads and the stop at the hospital had disoriented him. Linc didn't like feeling so off balance.

There were no more shadows. The fixtures in the hall provided even light. He heard nothing except the faint sound of water running somewhere in the building. Linc walked halfway down the hall before he realized that her door was ever so slightly ajar. A thin slice of golden light edged it.

He tensed. Had someone else noticed it was unlocked and tried it from the outside, then run away just as he'd opened the stairwell door? No telling.

His hand moved automatically inside his jacket for a weapon that wasn't there. His fingers brushed the smooth lining of his tux. No gun, no nothing.

And no sound from inside. Linc shoved the door open.

He choked as an unseen arm shot around his neck and pressed against his windpipe. Linc felt like someone was climbing his back, fast. He reached up to yank the arm away but in a split second his wrist got grabbed and forced behind his back.

Gasping, he arched his back until he broke free of the steel-strong hold and—damn. Cracked his head against the door. The pain was blinding.

He whirled around, dizzy, and swung a fist. Didn't connect. Something wet slapped his arm . . . long, wet, whipping hair. His attacker was on the small side and had ducked the roundhouse punch. He stared at her, collecting his wits.

"Kenzie?"

She immediately straightened, standing with her arms akimbo and her clenched hands braced against her hips, her breath heaving in her chest.

"What the hell do you think you're doing?" she snapped. "Did you pick my lock or something?"

He sucked in air, his throat swelling from the pressure she'd applied, raw on the inside.

"No. Door—was open. Thought I—saw—" He gasped the words, recovering slowly. "Somebody out here." He waved at the hall. "Maybe running away."

Her green eyes widened. "What?" She moved to look down the hall for herself, both ways. "There's no one there."

"Hope not."

She came back in and shut the door hard, then slid the inside bolt into place. "Sometimes it doesn't latch unless I kick it. Are you all right?"

"Maybe."

Kenzie kept her distance, but came a little closer. He noticed, vaguely, that she was wearing something white and short. "You scared me half to death."

He patted her shoulder, which seemed to be bare, for some reason. She smelled awfully good, but it didn't seem like the right time to nuzzle her or anything like that. At least she didn't pull away or whack him.

Reassured by the thought, he stumbled to her couch and dropped down heavily. "Had to come. Too bad I didn't know your first name." He looked up at her, still not able to think straight. His head hurt like hell where he'd cracked it. "*B* is for—?"

"Babe," she replied. "My dad thought it was cute. I can't stand it, never could. So don't switch."

"Okay, okay. Sorry, Kenzie."

"Why are you even here?"

She seemed more mystified than angry.

"For a very good reason. I saw the accident on TV."

Someone who kinda had it coming, a car thief or a stupid punk, had been taken away on that stretcher. Not Kenzie. She was right here, real as could be. He felt relief wash through him.

"What accident? You're not making sense." She came over and sat beside him, her bare arms folded across her chest.

Linc took a deep, rasping breath, then another. "Don't you ever answer your phone?"

"Not in the shower."

He finally figured out that she was wearing only a terry wrap thing tied in a knot above her breasts.

Shower. Right. So that was why she hadn't heard him.

But that didn't explain why the door had been cracked open. Her explanation—that it had to be kicked to latch right—didn't do it for him. Kenzie wasn't an airhead.

But everybody made mistakes. He'd spent most of the last hour doing just that.

Ow. He was hurting way too much to form a coherent thought. And he was distracted. The wrap was extremely short, at least from where he was sitting. Out of respect and the growing aware-ness that he'd made a world-class fool of himself by coming here unannounced, he did his best not to look too long at her bare legs, as slender and shapely as her arms.

No fluffy slippers for her—her feet were bare too. And recently pedicured. Golden bronze toenails, polish flawlessly applied, not a chip to be seen.

That could be why she hadn't kicked the door. He told himself not to ask if that was the reason, for fear of sparking her self-protective instincts a second time. He forced himself to look up, all the way up. Her dark, wet hair trickled little rivers over her shoulders. Linc felt weak.

"Kenzie—ah—you do have a helluva chokehold." His voice was coming back but he stopped to breathe. She was alive, even if she'd half killed him. That was good. "I seem to remember you telling me you aced hand-to-hand back in basic."

"Yes, I did. And I still practice."

"Good for you." Linc coughed. "But you need to work on rec-ognizing friendlies. Make yourself a chart or something."

She got up again and tugged at the wrap. Was it slipping?

"How was I supposed to know it was you, Linc?"

"God, I'd hate to be your enemy." He blinked. "Now I'm seeing sparks." He forced his eyes closed, but the sparks didn't go away. "Blue sparks. Wow."

She seemed unimpressed. "How much champagne did you have at the reception?"

He didn't answer the question. "It was fun. But I kept thinking about you." He rubbed his eyes, then his neck. "Ouch. Those nerves are waking up. You know how to hang on."

Bare, bronze-polished toes tapped impatiently on the carpet. "I'm waiting for an explanation. Right now would be a good time."

"You bet. Here goes." He launched into a fast recap of his search for her, starting with the news report.

"That can't be—" The rosy glow left her face and she stopped him before he could finish. "Linc, I loaned my car to my friend Christine."

"What?"

He could see her struggling to stay in control. What was going through her mind right now, he couldn't imagine.

"You heard me. That was her you saw on the stretcher. Unless—"

She didn't crack. But she avoided his eyes. "Damn it, where's my cell phone?" Suddenly she was frantic, searching over and under every surface. He didn't see a landline.

"I left mine in my car." He got up, feeling rocky.

Ugly twist. Not a joyrider, not a thief—a friend of hers had been at the wheel. Another possibility that hadn't occurred to him, and he had been trained to think outside every box there was. But Christine had survived. As far as he knew. "I'll go get it."

"No! Stay here!"

She grabbed a pair of jeans that had been slung over the flatscreen TV and shook them upside down. A small cell phone bounced on the carpet and she scooped it up, flipping it open and staring at the messages listed on the tiny screen. "Two texts. Nine voicemails. Oh no."

She pressed the key for call return and got one of Christine's parents almost immediately. Linc saw her shudder and dash away tears. She turned away from him after that. "Critical condition—I understand—Mrs. Corelli, I am so sorry. I just found out—no, from a friend—and picked up your message. Where is she? Where are you?" She grabbed a pencil and notepad and jotted down the replies. "I'm on my way." Then she looked at Linc. "Yes, I have someone who can come with me."

"She's so pale," Kenzie whispered.

Christine's mother smiled sadly and didn't respond right away. She sat at the head of the bed where her daughter lay unconscious, her husband standing at her side.

"Thank you for getting here so quickly," Mrs. Corelli finally said. Her voice was no more than a whisper. "The police called us from the scene. They told us it was your car. I was worried when you didn't answer."

"I—I was working with a new client and I went out for a run when I came back. Then I took a shower. My cell was in my jeans. I didn't even look at it."

"You didn't know," Mrs. Corelli soothed.

"I just wish I had. How long have you been here?" Kenzie asked the Corellis.

"Since . . ." The older woman looked up at her husband. "When was it, dear?"

"We got here after dark," Alfred Corelli said.

Linc took Kenzie's hand and gave it a comforting squeeze.

She was fighting back tears as she looked at Christine's badly bruised face. Her friend's eyes were shut and her lashes were wet. There were wires connected to her scalp and neck, running to machines that registered her every breath and heartbeat.

A doctor came in, glancing first at Christine, then at her parents. Then at Linc and Kenzie. He got the idea instantly: They weren't supposed to be in the ICU. The doctor didn't make a point of saying so.

"Kenzie, this is Dr. Asher, Christine's neurologist," Mr. Corelli said. "Kenzie is Christine's best friend. They're like sisters. I'm sorry, young man, but I don't know your name."

"Linc Bannon."

"Thank you for bringing her," Mrs. Corelli said simply.

The doctor acknowledged both Linc and Kenzie with a slight nod and a brief hello as he studied Christine's charts and the readouts, swiftly absorbing information. "No substantial change."

"Is that bad?" her mother asked almost inaudibly.

"It means her condition has stabilized. Considering the severity of her injuries, that's a good sign."

Mrs. Corelli looked anxiously at her daughter. "Can she hear us?"

"Actually, she can," the neurologist replied in a measured voice. "But the heavy sedation makes it impossible for her to respond or remember. However, her reflexes are there—pupil function, touch sensation—and she reacts to the usual stimuli as well as can be expected."

Linc knew the drill. The motorcycle accident that had left him with no more than a scar on his face had been a lesson learned the hard way. He'd been lucky, relatively speaking. Christine seemed much worse off.

"The immediate problem is controlling brain swelling." The doctor addressed both Corellis as he spoke. "Her CAT scans show a skull fracture, and right now we can't predict exactly what will happen. The next twenty-four hours are critical."

"I see." Mrs. Corelli's voice was dull.

"How long will she be unconscious?" Christine's father asked bluntly.

"I can't give an exact date. But we will bring her out of the deep sedation as soon as we can safely do so, Mr. Corelli."

The older man looked down at his wife, then back at Dr. Asher. "We're going to stay here with her."

The doctor nodded. "Someone on staff can arrange for cots and other things you might need. There are different support services and groups to help—one of the social workers will have a list for you. Family involvement is important, particularly in cases like this."

Mrs. Corelli took the last comment more stoically. She reached out a hand and smoothed a lock of hair away from Christine's forehead. "We're right by your side, sweetheart," she murmured.

"It's going to be a long process." There was sympathy and understanding in the doctor's voice. "Again, the sedation is necessary. The admitting neurologist may have explained to you that patients with head injuries can become extremely agitated at any time, to say nothing of the pain they may experience."

Pain. He didn't soften the word. The Corellis flinched visibly.

"Right now, she isn't feeling any, as far as we know," the neurologist assured them. "She's getting the best possible care. Everyone in the ICU is committed to her pulling through. You have my word on that."

"Thank you," Mrs. Corelli whispered. He wrapped up the consultation in a few more minutes and left the room when a nurse came to get him.

Kenzie went to Mrs. Corelli and bent over to give her an awkward hug, murmuring a few words of encouragement as she straightened. The older woman patted her arm.

"She won't be alone," Christine's mother said. "I'm so glad we can stay in the room. I really think it will help."

"Yes," Kenzie said softly. She looked around at Linc. "I—I guess Linc and I ought to go. They don't usually allow visitors in the ICU."

"Once I knew you were coming, I told them to make an exception," Mr. Corelli replied. "Glad I did. It's good to see you, Kenzie."

"I wish there was something I could do. Do either of you want anything?" she asked in an unsteady voice. "I mean, like coffee or a sandwich? The hospital cafeteria is open twenty-four hours."

"No, honey. Not now. Alf or I will run down later." Mrs. Corelli rose and made an infinitesimal adjustment to the blanket that covered Christine.

There was nothing more to be said. Kenzie took a last look at her best friend and turned to go.

Linc offered her his arm and she took it, leaning on him as they walked out into the corridor to the elevators.

She let go to jab at the button panel once they were inside the car, then leaned against the back wall. She avoided Linc's gaze. "What time is it?"

"Two, maybe three A.M.," he said. "We were in there a while."

"I'm not going to be able to sleep."

Linc nodded in understanding. "Do you want to get a bite to eat?"

"Probably a good idea." She straightened away from the wall and pressed the button for the cafeteria. The doors opened at the lobby, then closed. They went down one more floor.

The cafeteria was far from empty. Looked like mostly staff refueling for long shifts. Scrubs predominated, with the occasional white coat. There was a scattering of civilians. Linc suspected that he and Kenzie looked just as forlorn as they did.

She didn't even step out of the elevator, just shrank back. "Too many people," she said in a whisper. "I can't deal. Let's go someplace else."

"You got it." No one looked their way as the doors closed again. He knew the reality of the accident was sinking in. They walked quickly from the gleaming lobby to the parking lot.

"She's stable," Linc said quietly as he slipped behind the wheel. "Focus on that."

Kenzie stared straight ahead. "Stable but still critical," she amended. "And in a drug-induced coma."

Those were the facts. Linc turned the key in the ignition.

"She's in good hands, Kenz. Guilford General is an excellent hospital."

Kenzie didn't reply.

"Where to?" he asked gently.

"The diner on Third," she answered after a beat.

When they entered they got a few curious looks from long-haul truckers getting started on giant platters of bacon and eggs at the counter. Linc put a hand at the small of her back and walked her to a booth that was more private.

"Thanks." She clasped her hands together on the printed paper tablemat, not saying a word. An older waitress came over with a fresh pot of coffee and didn't say anything either.

Linc was infinitely grateful for the woman's instinctive tact. No cheery small talk, no rattling off the specials of the day. She turned over the coffee cups on the saucers with her free hand, poured, reached for a cream-and-sugar stand from the next table, and left them alone.

Kenzie circled her cup with both hands, just for the warmth, he suspected.

"Just like that, your world gets turned upside down," she sighed. "Christine and I really are like sisters. Mrs. Corelli wasn't wrong about that."

Linc nodded.

"I wish I knew what happened with the car. Maybe she swerved to avoid hitting an animal. That's what she would do."

"Could have been that or something else. Mechanical failure, maybe." He didn't want to say what he was thinking. Another driver could have caused the crash.

She fell silent for a while, then sipped her coffee. "She can't talk. She can't tell us anything." Kenzie shook her head. "I guess I should go look at the car today."

"Whoa." Linc wasn't so sure that was a good idea. Not just yet. "You don't have to inspect it. Let the insurance adjuster do that."

"He will anyway. I want to see it for myself," she insisted.

Linc knew better than to argue with her. "Then I'll go with you when you're ready."

"After I drink this."

"Kenzie, you haven't had any sleep."

"I don't care."

The impound lot was a depressing place. The wrecks were in a separate area from cars that had been towed for other violations, and they were the only non-uniformed visitors in it. There was an inescapable smell—part metallic, part scorched plastic—that made him feel sick to his stomach. He had to wonder how many people had crawled out alive from the twisted frames and shattered windows.

In the opposite space, about fifty feet away, Linc glimpsed a man who seemed somehow familiar. Not a friend. Then he remembered the TV reporter's face. He picked up on the guy's surly remarks to an impound clerk. Seemed that the reporter's car had been towed from the scene of the accident and the nosy bastard was out several hundred in fees. Tough luck.

Kenzie was silent as they walked, concentrating on finding her car. She finally spotted it in a corner and headed that way. It was right side up now, but crumpled, the roof caved in and the windows reduced to pebbled fragments. He guessed at a glance that the steel side frames had been strong enough to keep Christine from being crushed, but they too were bent.

Kenzie walked around it, studying the wreck from several angles. Linc let her think, looking at her more than the car.

There was a fierceness in her beautiful eyes that he'd never seen. Then her mouth tightened into a frown that tensed her fine jawline.

"That's a sideswipe," she said, pointing to a deep, irregular dent that ran the length of the driver's side of the car.

"Could be."

She shot him an angry look. "Think I'm wrong?"

He held up both hands in a peacemaking gesture. "I didn't say that."

"I have a feeling this was a hit-and-run," she said with low fury. "A drunk driver, or maybe some kid who just got his license. Someone who had a reason to drive off."

"What did the cops say?"

Kenzie shrugged. "Nothing about that. I didn't speak to any of them directly. They left several messages about the wrecked car. The last one gave the location of this place."

"So there is no investigation—" He broke off, feeling the impact of her glare. "I mean, no investigation yet," he finished.

"Not as far as I know," she snapped.

Linc looked at the car again. The damage was so extensive it was hard to make out anything definite. A utility pole could have made that long dent in the side if Christine had lost control and careened against it at high speed. That was a reasonable guess. There would be others. He knew zip about accident forensics.

"Kenzie, it's been less than twenty-four hours," he said. "Give it time. Let the experts figure it out."

"Oh, yes. The experts. They know everything. I'm just a girl," she said mockingly.

"Take it easy, Kenzie. I'm on your side. All the way." He kept his tone as calm as possible. She was beyond exhausted at this point. He intended to get her home and see that she got some sleep. If she let loose with a few jabs at him, so what? He had a thick hide.

She turned her back to him, walking away from the car as if she'd seen enough. Linc followed a few steps behind. Her body language conveyed a clear message. Hands off.

The clerk was talking to some cops about departmental business and didn't see them go.

Kenzie reached his truck and got in before he could open the door for her, slamming it hard. He went around to his side and slid in, glancing at her profile. Her features were composed, but he sensed that she was ready to blow from a volatile mix of nervous exhaustion and fear. She had to have been afraid when she'd examined the wreck.

It could have happened to her. It had happened to her best friend.

One reassuring touch might get him a wildcat scratch in return.

They drove back to her apartment without either of them saying a word. As they entered her building from the parking area, Linc cast a glance toward the door to the stairwell, remembering the shadows he'd seen for a second or two, then dismissing the thought.

The day had dawned bright and clear after last night's rain, and the morning light brightened the interior. She headed straight for the elevator.

Linc hesitated. She hadn't asked him to come in, but he was reluctant to leave her alone. He knew she needed someone with her even if she didn't.

Kenzie punched the Up button and waited until the single door slid open. She entered without looking back at him—but she did hold the door with one hand to keep it from closing.

The gesture was all the invitation he needed. He set his hand higher than hers on the elevator frame and she let go of it. "Got it. Thanks."

Kenzie folded her arms over her chest and leaned against the elevator paneling without looking at him. Linc pressed Three.

They got off on her floor and went down the hallway together in silence. She opened her door with her key just as the cell phone in his pocket sounded the ring tone he'd assigned to Deke.

His brother was probably going to give him hell for disappearing last night. Too bad. Deke would have to wait longer for an explanation.

"Go ahead and answer," she said.

"Not necessary."

She shrugged and he entered with Kenzie, looking around her apartment but not following her into the kitchen. He heard the clink of ice cubes falling into a glass and water running over them. Cabinet doors opened and closed. She was probably looking for aspirin.

"Who was it?" she called. "If you don't mind my asking."

"My brother Deke. We usually text."

"Go ahead. I just want to sit by myself in the kitchen for a little while."

"I understand."

Linc took the phone out and tapped at the screen, reading Deke's text message.

So u took off. NQA.

That was brotherspeak for No Questions Asked. Good, because Linc didn't have answers.

Newlyweds deploy to paradise at 0900 hours.

Right. Big brother RJ Bannon and his bride were headed for Hawaii. Also good. They didn't need to know about the accident and Christine.

Going back to sleep.

Not alone, Linc was sure.

Over and out.

He slipped the phone back in his pocket without texting back, settling down on the sofa. His sleepless brain was beginning to race. To calm himself, he started putting the few facts he had about the accident into a mental grid to look for connections, a habit of his.

The first responders had been focused on getting the victim to a hospital. Skid lines, debris from the chassis or hubcaps—had any of that been obtained on the scene? Thousands of cars and trucks must have driven down the highway since then. Vehicular accidents weren't Linc's area of expertise, and he didn't have a right to put questions to the cops, but he could speculate.

In his head. He didn't think Kenzie wanted to talk.

He marshaled a few more facts, visualizing the aftermath. It hadn't been raining during the brief broadcast, but it was more than likely that the TV reporter and camera crew had been all over the road asphalt and the shoulder. So had the paramedics and the police.

With all that commotion and the downpour somewhat later, most if not all of the on-scene evidence had most likely been trashed.

That left the wrecked car at the impound lot. It wasn't like he could go back there and gather evidence for himself. There was one witness—so far. Christine. She might not remember anything about the crash, if and when she returned to full consciousness.

Linc looked up as Kenzie came into the living room. "You okay?"

She shook her head. "Not really."

"What do you want to do now?"

"Stay focused and not think." She gazed at him steadily. "I told Mrs. Corelli that I would contact SK Corp—that's where Christine works—and tell them about the accident. But I don't think they're open yet."

SKC. The initials rang a faint bell. Military suppliers, he thought. Of what, he didn't know. "Probably not."

She wandered around her apartment, lost in thought, for another minute or two. "I'm not going to work today, that's for damn sure."

"You should rest."

"Yeah. As if I could."

"Try."

Kenzie turned suddenly to face him. "Linc, can you stay here for a while?"

He hadn't been expecting her to say that. "Ah—sure. If you want me to. I can make a few calls and explain that I'll be working outside the office for a few days." He stretched out his hand and indicated the cushion next to him. "This is fine."

"I meant stay here in Ridgewood," she said hastily. "Not here in my apartment. I only have one bedroom. And I—I have to have some downtime. By myself."

Linc could have kicked himself for instantly assuming he'd be on the couch.

"There's a motel about five blocks from my building," Kenzie ventured. "It's right on the main road, but—"

"I'll check it out," he said. He wasn't committing to a plan of action when she didn't have one.

"Sorry. I should have been clearer," she said politely.

"Don't worry about it."

Kenzie began to pace. "I'll wind down. Might take me a while."

He was curious. "How do you do that? Seems to me that you don't have an off switch."

She smiled faintly. "It doesn't work too well. I usually exercise until I'm ready to drop. Or watch TV. Right now, I don't want to do either. So let's talk."

Another request he hadn't expected. He nodded, though. "All right." He'd let her start the conversation.

"What do you do, Linc?" The question came out of nowhere. "You never really told me anything specific."

It was a hell of a time to get into that. But she'd asked, so he'd answer. She didn't need the details about Project 25, though.

"Special projects, technical, out of Fort Meade. Usually classified. Mostly army. Sometimes they send me over to Langley."

"Oh. The agency."

He nodded again. He knew she understood. Army intelligence maintained a major presence in Fort Meade, Maryland, along with the National Security Agency, and they had an off-and-on reciprocal arrangement with Central.

"I've done investigative work for both. The world got a lot more complicated ten years ago and it isn't getting any simpler. We do what we can."

She moved over to the couch and sat down on the farthest cushion from him. "That doesn't tell me too much."

"Sorry. That's all I can say."

Kenzie kept her voice level when she turned to him. "Think you can take a short leave?"

"Excuse me?"

"I want to know what the hell really happened on that highway."

"That's what the police are for, Kenz."

She dismissed his reply with a slight shrug. "How long will it take for them to get up to speed?"

"I don't know." He was doomed. He knew what she was going to ask next. He couldn't say no.

"You in?" she asked abruptly.

He sighed and shook his head, meeting her look of fierce determination. "Yeah, I'm in."

"Good." She folded her legs and rested her chin on her knees. "I think I'm going to need someone like you."

After she'd sent Linc on his way, Kenzie headed for the couch. Not to cry. To think.

She had to find out who had smashed into Christine and driven away. She took the corner away from the lamp and curled up, holding a pillow.

She'd been the type of kid who fought hardest for a friend, and that hadn't changed. Christine had been her best pal since Kenzie had been an army brat without one.

Fortunately, she didn't have to go it alone. There was Linc. Kenzie marveled that he'd dropped everything to come and find her when he thought she'd been hurt—and felt a tiny flash of guilt for turning down his invitation to accompany him to the wedding. Appearing in public as his girl or anything close to it—she just hadn't been ready.

Kenzie had been too startled to wonder why a guy in evening wear had just stepped through her door. React first, think later.

Like a tall, strong tree, he'd withstood her attack—but his reflex reaction might have taken her out if she hadn't dodged in time. Hell of a way to say hello for both of them.

Linc seemed to know when she didn't want to talk, and she had to admit that she found his presence comforting.

Truth told, more than comforting. The big, muscular body under the fine suit, the tousled hair and handsome face, right down to the scar on his cheek and especially that soft but tough smile he flashed occasionally got to her.

Kenzie stretched out and put the pillow under her head, looking at the ceiling. It was going to be tough to ignore all that.

CHAPTER 2

He turned the key in the ignition and headed away from her building, memorizing the streets of Ridgewood along the way. Nestled in rolling green hills that were typical of Virginia, it was a pleasant town, a bedroom community just far enough away from DC and the tony suburbs of Maryland to be friendly.

Exhaustion had hit him at last. He hoped she'd gone to bed. Their parting had been matter-of-fact, but he'd been surprised by her rising on tiptoe and pressing her lips to his unshaven cheek in a ghost of a kiss.

Just before she closed the door on him.

He'd heard the latch click from where he stood in the hall, then left.

The motel wasn't hard to find. He noted that a letter on the neon sign was out of commission. It couldn't get worse than staying at the D-Light Inn.

Even with a name like that on the sign, Linc got the hairy eyeball from the desk clerk, who surveyed him and, through the window, his car with equal suspicion. Linc knew he looked like a refugee from an all-night stag party.

Oughta fit right in here.

But the clerk slid over a thick metal key to a room as soon as the card reader hummed its approval of whichever piece of plastic he'd handed him. He climbed metal stairs to the room, on the side of the building that faced the road, and walked in.

It was dismal. Noisy too. Linc was too fried to care. He sat on the edge of the bed and set the alarm on his phone for two hours ahead. He shrugged out of his wrinkled tuxedo jacket and flung it across the room onto the floor.

Hard to believe he'd had it on for more than twenty-four hours. He slipped off his shoes and threw them too, earning a barely audible grunt of protest from some guy in the next room. The walls must be made of cardboard.

Then he fell back without turning down the grimy coverlet or taking off the rest of his clothes. Linc unbuttoned his shirt and fell sound asleep.

He woke up feeling awful. A glance in the motel's cheap mirror told him he looked worse. However, it was nothing he couldn't scrape or shower off. And he could buy a few basics in terms of clothes and drop the monkey suit off at a dry cleaner's later today.

Linc made himself a cup of instant, making a face when he took the first sip. Nasty brew. But it was hot and it would help him get out the door and focus on what needed to be done.

He drank the rest of the coffee, thinking about Kenzie's question and how quickly he had said yes. She'd asked for help. He would give it. Explaining that to the commanding officer of his operations group would be lots of fun.

He told himself to make the call and get it over with.

Turned out no one had a problem with his announcement. Good enough. Putting on the tux shirt and pants from the crumpled formal suit, he drove out to the mall and bought some ordinary clothes, jeans and polos, a couple of flannel shirts, socks and briefs, and a jacket. Nothing remotely memorable.

Next up, discount sneakers to replace his gleaming black dress shoes. He tossed the box when he was in the parking lot, then rubbed the tops and sides with a little dirt from the planted median strip so they didn't look so new, covering his action with his opened car door.

A quick stop at a drugstore for manly essentials like disposable razors and shaving cream and he was done. The clerk at the register barely looked at him, which was good. Linc didn't want to be remembered, he wanted to be invisible. The agency encouraged it anyway. He went back to the motel and got cleaned up and headed out again.

To Kenzie's apartment.

"Come on in. Have you had breakfast?"

Her welcoming voice took the chill off the fall morning. He almost wished he hadn't eaten.

"Diner delight, four bucks. The hash browns were great."

"So you're fueled." Kenzie scrutinized him. "New clothes, huh? Guess you really are in."

He inclined his head in a brief nod. "I could use some more coffee."

"Be right with you. Just have to finish making my bed."

She must have just rolled out of it. Her dark hair was tousled and he could see the impression of a pillowcase hem ever so faintly on one cheek.

"It has to be perfect," she threw over her shoulder.

"Mind if I watch?"

"No."

He followed her and stood in the doorway of her bedroom, watching her tuck in the corners with military precision. Her vigorous reaching and stretching pulled her sleep tee out of her pajama bottoms. Linc tried not to stare.

She was done. A few final tugs and yanks and a sergeant could have bounced the legendary quarter off the top blanket. He'd bet anything she'd done that correctly from her first day as a soldier.

Kenzie straightened and looked at him a little sheepishly. "I keep telling myself not to obsess."

"Doesn't seem to be working," he said gently.

She walked past him out of the room. Maybe *prowl* was a better word for the way she moved. He felt a distinctive electricity raise the fine hair on his body in the split second it took her to go by him. "Well, that's because I got a call from a police lieutenant just before you got here. Mike Warren. From the Ridgewood PD. He said, quote, that he's working with the other jurisdictions, but he's the main man on this."

That meant an investigation had begun. Linc raised an inquiring eyebrow. "What did he say?"

She shrugged, sitting down on the couch and motioning to him to do the same. "Not much. He asked if I could stop by the impound lot again, look at the wreck with him. Today or tomorrow. I said I'd let him know."

"Mind if I come along?"

Kenzie shot him a look. "Of course not."

"Do you want me to act like your friend or identify myself as a federal op?"

"Is that what you are? Ready to admit it?"

Not yet. He shrugged. "It's close enough."

"Hmm. Well, I'll just introduce you as my friend for this go-round. Let's see what he has to say before you pull rank," she said mockingly. "I assume he's going to give us the bare minimum on what he thinks happened."

Her instincts were good. It was always better to let the other person do most of the talking.

"You're probably right." Linc had grown up with the unwritten rules of police. Protect and serve—and cover your ass. His late father, a lifelong cop, had made sure his rowdy teenage sons knew how law enforcement really worked.

If, as he'd thought, evidence had been skipped over or trashed in the confusion around the accident—especially if the crash turned out to be more than an accident—guess who would get blamed for it. He suspected Mike Warren would do his best to keep that from happening. So would Linc, in his shoes.

"Did you set a time to meet him?"

She nodded and flipped open her laptop. "An hour from now. But I want to show you what Mrs. Corelli did before we go. She called first thing this morning to update me. From Christine's apartment."

Linc had figured one of the Corellis would be there occasionally, when they weren't at the hospital. "Where do they live, by the way?"

"Not all that far from you, actually. In Hopkinton."

He sat down beside her, watching absently as she pulled up a Facebook page. "She used Christine's laptop to post an announcement about the accident. Look at all those responses. Everyone really wants to help."

"Good idea to get the word out."

Kenzie clicked over to her own page. "Mrs. Corelli wanted me to reply to the people I knew. Maybe later. Not quite up to that at the moment." Her fingers moved briskly but Linc heard the catch in her voice. "That's Christine," she said, pointing to a group of photos.

Linc leaned closer to the screen. The young woman's vibrant expression was a far cry from the pale, battered face he'd seen at the hospital. "She looks a lot like you, Kenzie."

"People used to say that. The Corellis thought it was funny, because she's an only child and so am I."

"They're really nice people. They seem to know you pretty well."

She seemed flustered. "Yeah, they do. When I was a teenager I didn't exactly get along with my parents. So I hung around the Corelli house whenever I could, pretending I was one of them."

"Like sisters." He repeated Mrs. Corelli's comment to the doctor. "What did her mom say today? Update me."

Kenzie brightened but just a little. "That the brain swelling has diminished. They're thinking of taking her off the critical list—but she's still in the ICU," she added nervously. "And she's going to be there indefinitely."

"Then all we can do is wait."

"Yes," she said with a soft sigh. "I don't want to think about it."

Distracting herself, Kenzie scrolled rapidly through posted photos on different pages as Linc tried to take in the details. There were several of Kenzie and Christine partying with friends in various nightspots, clearly having a great time.

Then she clicked a larger shot, taken during the day, of the two of them posing by alert-looking, big-eared puppies with smooth coats the color of dark honey and black muzzles. Belgian Malinois. The girls were at the JB training compound—he remembered it. He noted a beefy guy in camos in the background, grinning at both of them.

Click. Click. Click. She moved right along, too fast for him to memorize the guy's features.

He glanced at outdoorsy shots of a camping trip. Tent, backpacks, firepit. Then Kenzie paddling left, Christine paddling right in a canoe on a quiet river. Who had taken the photo? He wasn't going to ask.

Then he zeroed in on one of Christine standing by a black sports car with yellow detailing, her hand resting on the hood like it was hers.

"You never did say why she borrowed your car."

Kenzie sighed. "Hers was in the shop. She'd always wanted to drive mine and there was a big sale at the mall. So I got out of the session with the new client a little early, picked her up at her place, and she dropped me off here. You know the rest. It seems like a hundred years ago."

Linc gave a slight nod. "Accidents put you in a time warp."

She clicked around on her page, moving the cursor over the messages on her wall without reading them.

"You're right about that. And I can't seem to concentrate. On anything. I still haven't notified SKC."

"Has to be done."

"I'm not looking forward to it." Kenzie frowned. "I never met any of the people she worked with, but I do know she wasn't happy there."

"Why not?"

"Not any major reason. She didn't like her new boss, though. And there was an outdoor equipment firm opening an outlet three towns over. She was going to apply there, then quit SKC."

"Was she that sure she'd get the job?" The question was idle.

Kenzie adjusted the laptop's screen position and looked up at him. "You don't know Christine. Everybody loves her and she never gives up." She paused. "I know exactly what she'd tell me. It's like I can hear her voice. *Make the freakin' call, Kenz, get it out of the way.*"

"Right," Linc said.

Kenzie gave a ragged sigh. "Maybe I'll do it from her apartment. Mrs. Corelli asked me to go over there and look for Christine's insurance documents and health records. She's sure the SKC human resources department is going to want something they don't have. Bureaucracy. I hate it. But I have to do something to help or I'll go nuts."

Linc took a few seconds to reply. Kenzie waited, glancing again at the messages on her wall.

"Go," he said simply. "It'll help you, too."

"Hang on," she replied. "Incoming. Haven't heard from her in a while." A new message appeared at the end of the ones she'd been scanning. "My friend Donna."

He looked at her inquiringly.

Kenzie's expression was brighter when she glanced up again. "She's a surgical nurse at an overseas base hospital. Wicked sense of humor. I need a shot of that." Her hands hovered over the keyboard. "Do you mind?"

Linc tsked. "You going to remember the call? And don't forget about meeting Mike Warren, by the way."

"Oh, him. Yes. No. I won't." Distracted, she glanced down at the message from the nurse as Linc read over her shoulder.

Did you hear about Frank Branigan?

"No, I didn't," Kenzie said out loud, turning to look at Linc. "Okay. I know you want to know who Frank Branigan is."

"Not really."

She clicked around on her page and located a photo of a grinning, handsome soldier in camo fatigues and a maroon beret with his unit's insignia on the front. "That's him."

Somehow, Linc didn't feel reassured.

"The army sent Frank to Big Dawg to train as a K9 handler before he was deployed to Afghanistan last year."

"Whoa. Back it up. Who or what is Big Dawg?"

Kenzie smiled faintly. "He's my boss. Guess I never told you his nickname. Also known as Jim Biggers."

"That I remember."

"He's a Gulf War vet, married, six kids."

"More than I needed to know, but okay."

She tapped at a photo on her page. "And that's Jim."

Linc noticed that Big Dawg was fit but somewhat thick in the middle, and going gray. Pretty wife firmly attached. Good, he thought.

Kenzie went back to the previous subject. "Anyway, Frank's an experienced K9 handler. He was heading out to his second deployment to Afghanistan and I got him up to speed with a new dog. Chili."

Linc nodded, letting her chatter away.

"They clicked right away. A true team from day one."

So the handsome soldier was a dog lover. And rugged. On the front lines too. The kind of guy who'd probably punch Linc in the arm and call him Desk Boy. Linc wasn't seeing a reason to like Frank Branigan.

He glanced at the clock in the living room. "Do you want to answer Donna before you get going?"

"Yes. I really do."

Her eyes widened when she looked back at the screen. Another message from Donna had popped up under the first one.

So sad. I cried when I heard.

Kenzie sat straight up and typed a question at top speed.

What happened?

Her friend responded almost instantly.

He died in Kandahar. Routine patrol. Ambush.

Kenzie gasped and rocked back in her chair. Linc felt ashamed of himself. His work for the army kept him away from the front lines, but he had the utmost respect for the soldiers who were doing the actual fighting in Afghanistan and elsewhere. The province of Kandahar was notoriously dangerous. He looked away from the photo of Frank Branigan.

Tears welled in Kenzie's eyes as she began to type again. One word.

How?

There was a pause, not long. The reply was blunt.

Shot in the chest.

Kenzie glanced up at Linc with fierce puzzlement, then back at the screen. She scrubbed away her tears and focused hard on the screen as her friend typed.

I'm sorry, Kenzie. I saw his name on the casualty list for the region and I thought you knew—it was a few days ago.

Linc understood. Those lists got read all over the world, wherever there were service members. You never knew. A buddy could be on it. You prayed your friends wouldn't be—and you prayed for the men and women you didn't know who were.

Heck, I just got beeped. Back in a bit.

Kenzie didn't reply, just sat where she was for a little while. Eventually the screensaver appeared, a moving design that made her blink. She clicked on a key to get the page back, staring at the message space as if she could will Donna to come back.

For a few seconds, Linc rested a reassuring hand on her shoulder and was surprised that she didn't brush it off. He could feel her pulse racing faintly under her silken skin.

Suddenly more words appeared. Unconsciously, Kenzie turned the laptop away from him, hiding her grief as best she could.

She had moved to her desk to sit in a swivel chair. With a touch to the keys, she shut down the laptop after the silent conversation was over.

Kenzie heaved a raw sigh, then pressed her lips together before she spoke again. "Apparently Frank had more than one wound." She swallowed hard before she summed it up for him. "Handguns, close range. Could have been more than one shooter. They cleared out. The two soldiers with him did what they could to help."

He nodded.

"The body armor's supposed to be better than it was in Iraq. But it makes you wonder."

"Sounds like the odds weren't on his side."

"No. They couldn't save him. The field surgeon found a rifle bullet in his chest too. Most likely from a Dragunov. Does that mean anything to you?" She fell silent.

"That's a sniper weapon. Russian design, probably made some-where in China, popular in Afghanistan. Depending on the bullet, it can kill from a mile away."

She shrugged. "Nobody knows exactly which shot killed him. Casualty of war, no more, no less. Not the subject of an official in-vestigation."

Something in her tone made him ask more. "But he could be."

Kenzie paused. "Donna knows a medic on his evac team who told her the vest was shredded, looked like bad gear. Maybe Frank didn't have to die."

The thought rocked her. She sat very still, as if she would fall to pieces if she breathed.

"Are you all right, Kenzie?"

"Right now I'm just numb. First Christine and now this."

Linc forced himself to keep his distance, guessing that reaching out to hold her wasn't something she wanted.

She cleared her throat. "Linc, I know you wanted to come with me, but I'm going to postpone the meeting with the lieutenant. Right now I just want to be alone."

He hesitated. "I can make that call for you."

"Thanks. No."

She rose from the swivel chair she'd been sitting in and grabbed a brush she kept on the desk, using it to scrape her hair back into a tight ponytail. That, and the white T and the baggy canvas pants she wore made her look like she was headed back to boot camp.

The suck-it-up toughness she'd learned there was about to trip her up, in his opinion.

"You shouldn't be by yourself," he said. "Not at a time like this."

"I have to think. And I can't do that with you around being

helpful and nice and solving problems for me." She moved away from him, rubbing her upper arms as if she felt a chill. "I'll be fine. What about you?" she asked absently. "Don't you have to check in with your office or something?"

"I did already, at the motel. I got an okay to come and go from my department chief and CO. Right now, I'm officially gone."

"Okay." She wandered away from him and came back when he gathered up the few things he'd had with him and headed for the door. "You leaving?" she asked distractedly.

"You just asked me to." He wanted to stay more than anything.

"Right. I can't think straight. Linc—" She paused and he saw her eyes were shimmering with tears she would never shed in front of him. "Just so you know, I—I like knowing you're not far away."

Rather than letting him respond verbally, she put her hands on his shoulders and lifted herself up to press her cheek to his for a fraction of a second. Not a kiss. Better somehow.

Then she stepped back, her arms folded across her chest.

"Don't think too much about it." He meant Frank Branigan and she knew it. "And stay off that laptop for a while," he said.

"No to both." She reached around him and turned the doorknob. "But I appreciate the thought."

He had to step over the threshold to avoid being whacked by the door. Not that the hollowcore would hurt that much. He could probably put his fist through it. Linc wished he could replace the cheap door with solid steel.

"You and doors are a dangerous combination," he said softly. "Lock it behind me."

She frowned. "Okay, okay. I will."

"And make sure it's really locked."

She held on to the doorknob as he turned to walk down the hall. "Did I tell you yet how much I hate good advice?"

"No. But I hear you."

"Good. Then go."

She watched until he reached the stairwell. A moment later, Linc just heard a tiny click. At least she'd listened. But he hated the idea of her crying it out alone.

CHAPTER 3

Kenzie didn't do much of anything after he left. Just looking out the window at the changing fall colors made her feel sadder than before. She rolled down the translucent shades to block some of the afternoon light, then went to sit on the sofa. A golden glow filled the shaded room, bouncing off walls she'd painted amber several months ago to contrast with the ivory of the upholstery material she'd chosen. The color was on the wild side, but the effect was cozy. She hugged a pillow to her chest and rested her chin on it to think.

Two friends, thousands of miles apart, both trapped by fate in the wrong place at the wrong time. One was gone; the other barely alive. And here she was, unable to do anything. Safe and sound. It seemed wrong somehow.

She even had a protector.

The way Linc had showed up and stuck around impressed her. And he wasn't playing the hero. He was just there when you needed him, rock solid and built to last.

True, he wasn't very communicative about what he did, but her army background and work with special ops soldiers meant she could figure it out to some degree. She was beginning to think she'd underestimated the second Bannon brother.

The oldest, RJ, had cracked the Montgomery kidnapping case and married the long-lost daughter. He'd had his moment of fame—she'd followed the story like everyone else. But Linc didn't seem like he was in anyone's shadow. He was very much his own man.

Right now she wasn't up to guessing where it could go with him.

After a while she set the pillow aside and dragged over the laptop she'd moved to the end table. She'd managed to ignore it for an hour. Good enough.

She opened her Facebook page and followed the tag on Frank Branigan's photo to his, thinking that it was probably still up. One of his friends or a family member might have set up a memorial page as well, but she could go to that later. Something about the photo was nagging at her. She was hoping to find an explanatory caption on his side of the send.

Kenzie clicked into his page, looking at many more photographs than just the one she had on hers. He had lots of friends—but besides Donna and Christine, they had none in common. Christine had dated him.

But other faces were familiar. And so was the military camaraderie.

Family—she could guess at his cousins from the look-alike grins, and that had to be his mom and dad. No brothers or sisters as far as she could tell—apparently he was their only child. Mr. and Mrs. Branigan had suffered a devastating loss.

She studied a shot of a pretty woman she was sure was his wife. His widow, Kenzie silently corrected herself. The photo tag said Sofia Branigan.

The woman was alone in the photo and looking sideways at something unseen, a coldness in her expression. Kenzie reminded herself not to judge. Character couldn't be defined by one image. She wondered why Frank had kept the photo posted when he listed his status as single. Not a lie and not quite true, either.

Official story, according to Frank: He and Sofia were working toward a friendly settlement with a mediator. No kids—he'd mentioned once that he'd wanted to have at least two; the wife, not.

Kenzie hadn't really wanted to know about all that. Being married—well, you were or you weren't, that was how she saw it. Semi-divorced men weren't worth getting hung up on.

Christine had thought differently. They'd agreed to disagree on that subject. Kenzie had left out that part of the story when Linc was looking at the photos.

It would be up to Kenzie to tell Christine about Frank's death, once her best friend was on the road to recovery. That was going to happen. Kenzie would do everything she could to make it happen.

She had no idea if Frank had been seriously interested in Christine or not. And now he'd never get another chance to figure out what he wanted from life.

Kenzie clicked on the photo of Frank showing off his just-issued combat uniform and gear, clicking again to enlarge it before she read the caption.

The body armor he wore was different from what she remembered from her army days—that was what had bothered her. Cut higher here, lower there, and not as bulky. She clicked back to read his comment.

Here I am, folks, wearing the latest in tactical. New vest, same chest. I'm off to Kandahar. Hope this gear stops bullets.

It didn't look that different from the older gear, except for the high collar to protect the neck. Gray multi-camo shell, Improved Outer Tactical type. Without a vest, it might only take one shot to kill a man. He'd been hit multiple times, according to Donna.

She looked at the old comments posted on his wall, rereading with a pang a few lighthearted ones from her from about a month ago. None from Sofia, she noticed. His about-to-be ex would make out all right with the army death benefit.

Kenzie moved to the searchbar and typed in *memorial page* and his name.

It was already up. The large photo posted above his dates of birth and death made her heart constrict with pain. One of his army buddies had contributed a shot of Frank Branigan's battlefield cross.

His dusty boots were placed together. His rifle, unloaded, was thrust into one boot upside down, the stock supporting his helmet at a tilt. His dogtags hung from the trigger. Someone had stuck a couple of wallet-size photos into the boot's laces. She couldn't make them out—they were dusty, too, and curled from the heat of that distant land. There was a bottle of beer, left there by a pal.

She knew the temporary memorial would be removed eventually. His tags and a few other things would be sent to Sofia, who would probably chuck them into a drawer and forget all about them. It didn't seem fair to his parents at all.

Would they even receive the folded flag that had covered his coffin? Didn't that go to the widow too?

Kenzie felt a flash of guilt that she knew was irrational. She'd never had to risk her life—her skill at training K9 handlers had simply been too valuable to the army for her to deploy to the front lines. Frank, who was older than her by at least seven years, had been one of her best students. He learned fast and he'd gone away without saying good-bye.

Donna hadn't mentioned the dog he'd trained with, a female shepherd mix, but then Kenzie didn't remember if she'd told Donna about Chili.

She knew that the dog would continue working, rather than get sent back stateside. Their training cost a fortune and the animals were in high demand. The army program at Lackland in San Antonio only graduated a hundred dogs a year, though private contractors like her boss added more.

Chili would go right back on bomb-sniffing patrol once she adapted to a new handler. There wasn't time to grieve on the front.

She thought about contacting Frank's parents. They didn't know her. She didn't know too much about their son.

I was so sorry to hear . . . if there's anything I can do . . .

The routine words of condolence had an empty ring.

Her gaze moved to the wall of the memorial page. Slowly, Kenzie began to read the poignant comments and brief tributes to a man who'd been a brave soldier and a true friend to people she'd never met.

Then a new post appeared. With her name in it. Her eyes widened as she read the blunt words.

Hello to all. Randy Holt here. Not a friend exactly—I was one of the flight medics on the Kandahar evac for Frank.

The one Donna knew? The nurse hadn't given a name. Kenzie would have to ask. She read the rest.

Wish he'd made it. We did our best. Am looking for Kenzie or Kenzy. He said her name.

A pause. No one replied or commented. Kenzie didn't either. Was she the only one on the page? It was possible. The medic posted again.

Maybe I spelled it wrong.

Kenzie bit her lip. Randy Holt had been with Frank in his last hour of life. Why was the medic looking for her?

Anyone know her?

She typed a response.

Hello. I'm Kenzie. Can we e-mail later today, not on FB? Let me know.

She wasn't going to post her schedule for all to see. She hoped Randy would say yes. The medic answered swiftly.

Here you go.

A contact e-mail address appeared on the wall and she copied it. Then it disappeared, deleted by Randy or so she assumed. She figured the medic was taking it on faith that she actually was Kenzie. Clicking out of Facebook and opening up her e-mail, she typed in the medic's address and sent her phone number for good measure.

*   *   *

Somewhere else, someone else copied the e-mail address too. Then he leaned back in his swivel chair, clasped his hands behind his head, and put his feet up on his desk.

Tough luck for Branigan, whoever he was.

There'd been reports of sporadic problems with X-Ultra body armor. He'd picked up e-mail on it using a tracking worm he'd slipped into a Department of Defense server account reserved for military suppliers. No one had noticed.

It was a useful, unobtrusive worm that didn't take down systems or make itself known in any way, unless an experienced IT person was tipped off and went after it. That hadn't happened.

All it did was follow things. He'd programmed it to locate mentions of X-Ultra, mine data, and report what it found. So far, not much. A few conscientious procurement sergeants had filed reports on X-Ultra here and there, classified but not top secret. A few negative comments from medics had been scraped from the web. Only a few. The consensus, if there was one: The new type of armor worked well most of the time.

Just not all of the time. Failures in the field noted. No fatalities until now.

Luck of the draw, he thought idly. But not for Frank Branigan. No big deal. The guy was only a private. Expendable, basically. But he'd still been monitoring the guy's Facebook posts and the separate memorial page. The photo of the battlefield cross was over the top.

Give it a rest, patriots, he thought, loosening the knot in his silk tie. Soldiers died every damn day of the week. Branigan was a statistic, nothing more. But he was one that didn't make X-Ultra look good.

He'd monitored all the heartfelt posts from Branigan's friends—boo hoo hoo. Did they think combat was a walk in the park? Not one asked questions about the soldier's body armor.

Then that smarty-pants medic popped up. Posting daily, asking if anyone knew a girl named Kenzie—and then deleting the posts when no one answered right away. What was Randy Holt afraid of?

He swung his feet off the desk and leaned forward over his keyboard, jabbing at the keys until his favorite photo of Kenzie filled his screen. He'd tracked her down easily enough. The name wasn't common, and the Facebook connection was easy to make. Practically no one seemed to know that a whole lot of the photos they posted had hidden geotags.

He didn't need a worm to follow hot women without them knowing it, and Kenzie qualified as very hot.

Good thing her pal Christine hadn't bothered with the most stringent privacy settings on Facebook—a lot of people didn't even know how to use them since the rules had changed. Plus the new face recognition software on the site made it super hard for anyone to hide.

He'd lurked on her page, visited links to her friends' pages to steal more photos—of both of them. He knew where they worked, had figured out where they lived.

One at a time, he told himself.

Like Christine, Kenzie was the active type. Outdoorsy. Athletic. Looked like she'd put up an exciting fight if it ever came to that.

His curiosity about her had gotten the better of him. He'd hung out in one of his cars at her building's parking lot just for the hell of it that one time.

He'd needed some fun, needed to blow off the tension after that incident on I-95. First he'd swapped cars to get rid of the banged-up one. It hadn't taken more than one good hit to force Christine off the road. Her fear of him had made her swerve too hard.

Coming around for a second look had been fun. He'd covered up the damage to his right front fender with a can of spray paint. He'd covered his hair with a quality rug and hidden his eyes with a pair of wraparounds.

That car had gone straight to the back of the garage belonging to a house he owned but didn't live in. Nondescript one-story, sketchy lawn, curtains always closed. If the neighbors only knew what he kept in the living room and parlor . . . His own arsenal. Disguises in the closet. But they kept to themselves. The tenants in Kenzie's building were kind of the same.

He'd scoped the windows, figuring out which one was which.

A nearly invisible mist had drifted out an opaque little window, open at the top.

He could almost smell her taking a shower. He'd gone up the back stairwell and tried a slim tool he kept in his pocket for just such occasions. The lock was easy to pick—but then that guy dressed for a wedding had run up the stairs and interrupted him.

He grinned. He planned to go back.

Maybe he could pay a call on the kennels, schmooze with her boss, one ex-military man to another, get to know her professionally, gain her trust. Although he didn't like dogs. And the animals she trained knew the stench of fear.

He had to wonder why Kenzie hadn't answered the medic's posts sooner. Apparently she hadn't been on the memorial page before. It seemed she didn't check her own page too often—he hadn't noticed new posts from her while he'd been lurking here and there. She didn't seem to waste time on other people's pages.

Not a problem. Now he had an e-mail address for Randy Holt. He typed it in and introduced himself as a friend of Frank Branigan's. It bounced back.

Mailer Daemon unable to deliver.

Randy Holt must have canceled the account and used another one to e-mail Kenzie. Covering tracks. As if the medic knew someone was spying.

Good guess.

He swiveled around in his chair until he was facing the window. All that plate glass and nothing to see. The nondescript office park that housed X-Ultra might as well be invisible. Worked for him.

Kenzie forced herself to call Mike Warren and postpone the meeting at the impound lot. He was nice enough about it.

First she wanted to get to Christine's apartment and make sure Mrs. Corelli had everything she needed. She would phone SK Corp from there, give someone in charge the basic info on Christine's accident and offer herself as a contact.

Barely seeing her surroundings, she drove to Christine's, maneuvering the car through the narrow streets that led to the other side of town.

Life went on.

The ordinariness of that fact was small comfort. She was still numb. She happened to drive past the motel that Linc was staying in, wondering if he was there. She caught a glimpse of a red pickup. Confirmed.

She pulled up in front of Christine's building and parked. Her friend lived in a second-floor apartment. Its curtained windows had been left closed, Kenzie saw. She got out and looked up at the semi-sheer panels. For a second, she imagined that they moved. No. The closed windows were reflecting the autumn sky. A cloud had moved across the sun, that was all.

Locking her car, she took the key to the apartment from her purse. She hadn't had to ask Mrs. Corelli for it. Since forever, Kenzie had had Christine's key and Christine had hers. There were no secrets between them. But she felt a little funny about rummaging through her friend's papers. It had to be done, though.

She squared her shoulders and marched up the exterior stairs to the second floor.

The key turned soundlessly and the apartment door swung inward. Kenzie hesitated on the threshold.

It was as if the place had never been lived in. At least not by Christine. It was immaculate, not how her far-from-organized best friend kept it.

She told herself not to be silly.

It probably looked like that because Mrs. Corelli had put things away and tidied up when she was here. Christine's mother was as neat as her daughter was messy.

Kenzie smiled to herself. She owed it to her best buddy to disorganize it again. Closing the door and setting down her purse, she took another look around, trying to remember where Christine kept bills and documents. Her gaze stopped on a tall, modern-style hutch that held family photos on its top shelves, with two roomy cabinets behind closed doors below.

She walked over and kneeled in front of it, pulling the doors open as slowly as she could. Despite her carefulness, a heap of miscellaneous papers slithered out, tilting the laptop they'd been stacked on. Kenzie steadied it with one hand and gathered up the papers with the other. Some of the bills had the logo of a health insurance company. Christine had even scrawled "paid" across a few.

Kenzie repositioned the laptop, a slim model with a pearly cover and kittycat decals. She smiled. Christine liked girly stuff and decorated her laptop like an old-fashioned diary.

The laptop was warm to the touch. It must be plugged in somewhere—she'd figure that out in a minute. First she checked the dates on the bills. They were current. Excellent. Christine wasn't so disorganized that she didn't take care of the copays for her health insurance.

She set those aside and sat cross-legged on the floor, going through more paperwork. Looked like everything they might need was here, though not, of course, in order.

That wouldn't take long.

Taking out the laptop to get to the box beneath it, she followed its cord to an outlet strip snaked through an opening in the back of the hutch. Christine had probably left it there to recharge the afternoon she'd borrowed the sports car. Kenzie lost her hold on the smooth cover and the laptop slid from her fingers, landing on the floor and partly opening.

She set it flat and put the screen at a right angle. A pink-purple screen flickered into life. If Kenzie spotted any unicorns on it, she was going to give Christine a hard time, for sure.

There weren't any, just vibrant colors that swirled. She set the open laptop to one side, clicking the menu to shut it down. She just didn't feel like leaving it here, and the Corellis might need something on it.

Kenzie got up to stretch and wandered over to the window, peeking out through one side of the closed curtains. The street was quiet, lined with parked vehicles underneath trees that were beginning to let go of their leaves.

A black car with tinted windows cruised by slowly and disappeared. She let the curtain fall and went back to the laptop, seeing the same colors. A whirling-wheel icon in the middle was still going.

Okay, it was slow, she thought absently. Christine liked to download stuff and there were tons of videos on her hard drive.

Kenzie had time. She settled down on the couch, not minding the few extra minutes to think.

About Linc.

He'd stood by her. After all his support, she didn't feel like being so damn skittish anymore. She'd kept him at arm's length for months, for reasons she wasn't ready to explain to him.

He maintained his own distance, but somehow, every time they got together, he seemed to be just a little closer. Patient guy. It was kind of funny the way he dodged questions about what he did. Obviously he was Special Ops. She just wasn't sure exactly what kind. They came in a lot of interesting flavors.

A few had gone through the giant base in Europe where she'd trained war dogs and their handlers. Not for SO, though. The super-secret elite of the armed services trained their own. Human and animal, they were a breed apart. Linc seemed more down-to-earth than that. Though he definitely looked like he could scale an enemy wall in full kit with a grenade in his teeth and live to tell the tale.

No, not tell. He would neither confirm nor deny. That was the phrase.

Still, he looked more like a thinker than a fighter. The army wasn't going to throw him into the maw of a faraway conflict to get chewed up. They needed brains just as much as brawn—and they must want him stateside if he was working out of Fort Meade and getting loaned to the agency in Langley.

Which meant he wasn't going to be deployed any time soon. If ever.

Restless, Kenzie got up again when the screen flickered, then glowed more brightly than before. She sat down in front of it and tapped the touch pad. She'd use the cursor and pulldown menu to force quit. She didn't have all day.

The screen changed in an instant from pink-purple to white. Then nothing happened. The empty white screen faded away and a few icons popped up. The small whirling wheel disappeared.

Kenzie knew better than to tap impatient commands that would confuse a slow hard drive. She set the laptop aside again and concentrated on sorting papers.

A faint but familiar bar of music interrupted her. Not her cell—

her ringtone was completely different. Christine must have forgotten her phone, in a hurry to get to the mall.

Kenzie scrambled to her feet, trying to locate it by the sound. The ringtone repeated several times. At the last second, she glanced toward the top shelf of the hutch and saw the small phone half-concealed by a framed picture.

It went silent and the screen flashed a number. She looked to see who'd just called. Someone who didn't know about Christine's accident, obviously. Or—

Kenzie saw three initials come up. SKC. Christine's employer.

Wanting to know where she was, no doubt. Kenzie's stomach tightened. She wasn't comfortable calling back on Christine's phone, but she kept it in her hand so she could read the number on its screen. She went to her purse and found her own cell, enduring an irritating voicemail menu that went on forever. SKC was a big company.

Finally Kenzie got fed up and pressed a random number. An actual human being in an unknown department answered.

"SKC. This is Terri Novik. How may I help you?"

"Oh—hello." Kenzie had been expecting to get another automated message. She had no idea who Terri Novik was. "I need to speak to someone about Christine Corelli."

"Okay. Just give me a sec." There was a pause, as if Terri was looking something up. "I think she's Melvin Brody's assistant. I'll transfer you to his extension."

"Thanks." Kenzie vaguely remembered Christine telling her the name of her new boss. That was it.

A few seconds later, a man's loud voice hurt her ear. "Mel Brody here. Who is this? Make it short. I'm busy."

Brody had a smoker's rasp and a Maryland way of slurring his words. She knew what he looked like from a company picture Christine had showed her, taken at a motivational meeting.

Paunchy. More than middle-aged. A lump for a nose and a receding hairline. White shirt stained from eating lunch at his desk. You had to wonder how he'd ever gotten the job.

She took a deep breath before she spoke. "Mr. Brody, I'm a friend of Christine Corelli."

He paused. "That's nice. Where the hell is she? I got quotas to fill."

Kenzie frowned but forged on. "Her mother asked me to call. Christine was in an accident."

"What?" Brody growled. "You mean, like a car crash? What next?"

The unexpected news seemed to make him angry. Kenzie didn't feel like telling him that Christine had nearly died in a rollover. She certainly wasn't going to mention who she was or that Christine had been driving her car.

"Yes, a crash. A serious one." She spoke quickly, her tone clipped. "She's in Guilford Hospital. In the ICU."

"Bad off, huh?"

No concern. No sympathy.

"She's critical," Kenzie snapped. "But that may have changed."

"I'll call the hospital." Brody hung up on her.

No thanks, either. Kenzie realized that the man had to have her number on his phone's caller ID, even if she hadn't given him her name. Did it matter? She didn't think so. When she got the paperwork together, she would be dealing with someone in human resources, not Christine's obnoxious boss.

No wonder her friend had wanted to quit.

It occurred to Kenzie that Christine had brought project paperwork home now and again. What if Brody wanted stuff like that back? She sat back down and riffled through what she had, then looked at the crammed lower half of the hutch.

The question was where Christine had kept it. Kenzie thought that if she couldn't find it, she couldn't return it. Which would prevent an in-person encounter with that loudmouth.

She heard a ping coming from the laptop and turned her attention that way.

The pink-purple screen was gone. It flashed pure white again— and then a stranger's face filled it. A man. Not all that young, but not middle-aged either. Regular features and oddly colored, staring eyes. He was half in shadow but somehow very real. Kenzie jumped back as if he were actually in the room with her.

"Hey there. Finding everything you need?" he asked softly.

She gasped. "Who are you?"

He moved closer. His eyes filled the screen. Burning. Staring. Filled with hate. "I hear that bitch Christine is still on life support. Too bad."

Kenzie slammed the laptop shut.

CHAPTER 4

Kenzie kept her hands on the closed laptop, swallowing a scream. After a few seconds she pushed it away from her.

How had the man with the burning eyes known she was there—or that she was about to look into Christine's laptop? She looked wildly around the room for a discreetly placed camera and saw nothing.

None needed, she thought, feeling like a fool. The laptop's webcam must have been turned on, though she hadn't noticed its tiny light at the top of the screen. Kenzie wished to God she'd been able to get a screen grab of that face. The shadowy light had made his features indistinct.

She scrambled to her feet and paced, staying far away from the shut laptop. At least, she hoped desperately, he couldn't see her now. She tried to remember details of the hack attack.

He'd seemed to be around thirty. Nothing very distinctive about him. His bland voice didn't sound like he came from anywhere.

It was calm and uninflected. And somehow . . . dead. Despite the hate in his eyes.

Whoever he was, he was after Christine and Kenzie was in the way—or a target herself. How in hell had he known she was here?

Without knowing it, she'd been followed and watched. The image of her wrecked car filled her mind. She was alone—she could be the next victim of an accident. Kenzie wasn't staying in Christine's apartment a second longer than she had to.

She had to reach Linc.

Was it even safe to leave?

Jumping up, she ran to the door and tested it to make sure it was locked. She pressed her ear to it, listening for the faintest sound in the hall. Footsteps. Breathing. Was the man there?

She heard nothing. Sliding her sweating hands down the door, she stepped back from it. Then she took a chair and wedged it at an angle under the doorknob.

Shaking, she returned to the couch, trying again to remember the man's face and drawing a blank. The shock of seeing him pop up had obliterated her ability to recall.

Except for the way he'd stared at her out of the shadows. The hot intensity of his gaze was totally creepy. He must have leaned in toward the camera lens, as if he knew exactly which angle was the most frightening.

She got up and paced. If only she'd had the presence of mind to hit the right key for a screen grab and get him. Linc might even be able to match that face on some database—stop it, she told herself. Wishing and hoping weren't going to cut it. She'd screwed up.

Kenzie stopped and slammed her open hand against a wall and didn't even wince. The hutch rattled. She looked down and scooped up the insurance papers and records, stuffing them into her purse. She had to get out of here. The cops couldn't do anything about an online call she had no record of. She had no proof of anything.

But she knew without a doubt the car crash that had left Christine fighting for life was intentional. Her best friend was being stalked by a psycho who meant to hurt or kill her—and Kenzie had just seen his face. Somehow he'd found out that Christine was alive and hacked into her laptop. Waiting for her? Why, when he'd known she was in the hospital?

What was he looking for? The laptop was Christine's, a personal thing, hidden away. It didn't matter. Kenzie had opened it. As good as invited him in.

Kenzie was afraid to open the door, but she wasn't about to stay and wait for a sicko to pounce.

Hell no. Not here and not at her apartment either.

She was moving out of there as of tonight.

As to where she could go, she'd have to hurry up and find temporary accommodations online—oh no. Absolutely not. She wasn't opening her own laptop either.

She heard giggling in the hallway and several pairs of high-heeled shoes clicking by. When the group of young women had passed, Kenzie turned the door latch and looked. All clear in the hallway. The exterior stairs were too open to hide anyone. She ran for it.

Kenzie checked the rearview mirror again and again. Rattled as she was, she'd pulled over to phone Linc on her cell before she merged into traffic. He hadn't picked up.

She'd left a message. No details. Just that something strange had happened at Christine's apartment and would he meet her at her place or call back, pronto.

Over and out.

What she'd wanted to do was wail like an ambulance siren and beg him to take out the invisible bad guy with a top-secret weapon, but that would have hurt her pride. However, it didn't seem too much to expect that Mr. Super Crypto Classified Tech Wizard would remember to charge his cell phone and keep it with him. Evidently not.

Linc didn't love bunking down in a two-bit motel, but for right now it was home base. Speaking of home, he'd made a mad dash to Clearston to trade the red pickup for the black car in his garage. Before he'd left, he'd checked the steel tool case back of the cab for anything he might need—nothing much in it but his tacklebox and a battered, wide-brimmed hat. Linc had slammed down the heavy lid without removing either. He wasn't going to have a chance to go fishing for a good long while.

He drove back a little too fast. Good thing he hadn't gotten a speeding ticket. He was hungry as hell and the bag in his hand held the fix for that problem.

He pulled up a chair to a small table whose varnish had worn off at the angles, and tore the bag down one side, removing a takeout container that held his lunch: a split roll heaped with pulled pork barbecue, with sides of coleslaw and mac-n-cheese. The ramshackle roadside joint it came from didn't look like much from the outside, but the crowded parking lot and lines of customers were his idea of a recommendation.

He didn't like to eat alone either. Linc reached for the remote he'd left on the table and switched on the TV, keeping the volume low. A news announcer nattered on about this and that. He wasn't really listening. The sloppy but delicious sandwich got most of his attention.

Linc devoured it, then used up about five napkins to wipe his hands. He picked up a plastic fork to get started on the sides when a photo appeared onscreen. He'd seen it before. On Kenzie's laptop.

"Next up," the announcer intoned, "a local hero will be remembered today. We'll be right back with the story of Frank Branigan."

The soldier's face filled the screen for a few seconds before several commercials played. Linc finished his lunch and cleaned up before the anchor started off with that faked business of stacking papers and laying them down without even looking at them.

Linc listened. He wondered if Kenzie was too. She might have switched on the TV to keep her company over at Christine's empty apartment. He could call her there, but he'd taken the hint about her needing downtime. Besides, she might be at the hospital or keeping one of the Corellis company.

The screen insets showed Frank Branigan in uniform, then a few family snapshots. Then a photomontage.

His coffin, arriving at Dover Air Force Base in Delaware, carried down the ramp of a C-17 by a team of soldiers in white gloves. A waiting mortuary van. The family, standing at a distance on the tarmac near the huge plane, too far away for their faces to be identifiable.

The process of a dignified transfer—the official term—had begun. No newshounds allowed close in, no live footage of the transfer permitted at all. The privacy of the grieving relatives was well-protected, Linc knew.

The army mortuary would prepare and dress the body for burial. Then Branigan's remains would be taken by hearse to a private funeral home. Kenzie would go to the funeral, he expected. He didn't know if she'd want him there.

He clicked off the TV to observe five minutes of silence for a man he'd never known.

It wasn't enough to show the respect that Frank Branigan deserved.

It was some time later when he turned on CNN. They were featuring new developments in the ongoing conflict, explaining the terms of unconventional warfare, including rapid deployments of smaller units, improved equipment, and so on.

Different talking head, same war. Soldiers got shot no matter who was talking. Linc wasn't cynical about it. The dangers the armed services faced weren't abstract.

He watched the broadcast, mentally filling in the inevitable blanks. Project 25, his current assignment, involved developing relational matrixes for ground intelligence gathered on multiple fronts. It just might get the GIs and the generals out of there and back home sooner than anyone seemed to think. However, it didn't qualify Linc as a hero, local or otherwise.

Which was okay. Being more or less invisible suited him fine.

Linc got up and switched off the report, tossing the remote onto the bed. It slid off, landing on the formalwear that still lay sprawled on the floor like a body outline at a crime scene. He reached down to grab it, and gathered up the clothes while he was at it, slinging them over the back of a chair.

Enough housekeeping. He needed to check in—that wasn't optional. Project 25 personnel had some leeway in terms of where they worked, and face time wasn't that high a priority. Still, everyone's hours and output got tracked, and he wasn't exempt from performance reviews.

He'd brought in a laptop from his car, a good one that looked ordinary but wasn't. He kept it stashed inside a hidden compartment under the backseat, along with a specialized toolkit that held a lot of useful gizmos.

One was a bug sweeper. Not for the kind of bugs that went

splat on the windshield. He would need it to check Kenzie's rental car and his own. Twice a day.

Linc tapped the side of the laptop cover. It opened at a touch, keyed to his fingerprint. Anyone else trying to use it would trigger a failsafe self-destruct.

Checking the encryption out of habit, Linc logged in at a workplace about a hundred miles to the north and joined a bull session at the digital water cooler for several minutes. Then he settled down, ready to immerse himself in work.

Out of habit, he glanced at his cell phone. The small screen showed black. He didn't check the call log, not expecting Kenzie to check in. For one thing, she prided herself on not seeming weak, which was a word that didn't describe her at all.

He pushed the phone aside, not noticing that it had gone dead.

Kenzie was still in her rented car when her own cell rang and she snatched it up, pulling over again. Not Linc. One of the Corellis.

Christine's mother sounded weary as she said hello and gave Kenzie an update. Dr. Asher had discussed the latest round of tests and assured them that their daughter, though still unconscious, was doing relatively well.

Kenzie heard the doubt in Mrs. Corelli's voice on that score.

"Anyway, dear, how are you?"

She managed not to blurt out what had just happened, though the Corellis would have to know, and soon.

"Oh—okay, I guess. I think I got all the paperwork."

"Good. I'll look at it tomorrow. Thanks so much for all your help."

"If you don't mind my asking," Kenzie said quickly, "are you staying at Christine's apartment tonight?" She had no idea how to forestall either of the Corellis if the answer was yes.

There was a pause on the other end. "No," Mrs. Corelli said finally. "Being in her place with all her things, remembering how happy she was there, just hurts. That was Christine before the accident."

Kenzie swallowed hard. "I understand."

"I'm going to my sister's house instead. Alf will bed down on the cot in the hospital room."

So neither of them would be going back to Christine's apartment tonight. That was a relief.

She wanted desperately to talk to Linc about how to tell them. He had damn well better return her call or show up at her place per her message. If he wasn't quick about it, she'd be gone for good when he got there.

A strange sensation of calm descended on her as she drove the rest of the way. She didn't recognize it as shock. Her perceptions felt heightened, her nerves stretched taut.

Kenzie scanned the parking lot behind her building. There were no cars she didn't recognize. Even so, she was on the alert until she was safely behind her own door.

Once inside, she dumped the purse stuffed with documents and ran to the closet. In a frenzy, Kenzie yanked open the sliding door, dragging out the nylon-web tote bags she'd bought at a dollar store.

Preferred by homeless people everywhere, she thought, raging inwardly. She was now one of them. She threw a bulky jacket into one and several pairs of sneakers into another, then pulled out her wheeled carry-on to fill that too.

A knock at the door stopped her cold. Kenzie straightened without responding, trying to think of a weapon—hammer, wine bottle, anything that she could reach in time to whack the stalker with. A plastic hanger wasn't going to do it.

She stayed where she was, listening. The doorknob didn't start to turn. The locks didn't rattle. There was no slasher-movie creak of the hinges. But that didn't mean she was safe.

"Hey. It's Linc." His deep voice made her breath catch. Her blood flowed again, warming her.

She walked noiselessly to the door and looked through the peephole. Fast and from the side, just in case.

It was Linc. Kenzie opened the door and stood there.

"Got your message. Sorry it wasn't sooner—my phone wasn't charged and I didn't notice."

"Brilliant."

"Yeah, well, I do stupid things. Anyway, I chose the come-on-over option," he said lightly. "We need to talk about some stuff." He glanced down at the filled nylon bags and open but empty carry-on behind her. "What are you doing?"

"Packing."

The curt answer seemed to startle him and he looked at her curiously. "Oh."

Her relief at seeing him opened up the floodgates to a whole lot of other feelings. One was anger. With him, even though she knew it was irrational. If he'd gone with her in the first place, picked up when she'd called afterward—don't, she told herself. He couldn't read her mind. He didn't know about the man with the burning eyes.

Linc kept his tone casual. "Want to tell me where you're going?"

Actually, she didn't. Right now she wanted to crawl into an armor-plated bunker and keep her head down. "I don't know. Anywhere but here. I just came from Christine's apartment."

"So you said. Did her mother call you there?" He looked at her intently. "Tell me right now if Christine took a turn for the worse."

"No. I talked to Mrs. Corelli on the way home. According to the doctors, Christine is doing somewhat better. But her mom didn't sound that sure."

"Why not?"

"Probably because she's too exhausted to think straight," Kenzie answered bluntly. "She's going to stay with her sister tonight instead of at Christine's apartment."

"Sounds like a plan." He looked at her warily. "Back to you. Are you all right?"

"Not exactly," she answered in a monotone. "I have to get out of here. Now." The last word hung in the air.

"Okay."

He took a slow step toward her as if he intended to touch her and she took three fast steps back.

Confusion clouded his gaze.

She forced her breathing into a nice, slow pace. Linc stayed silent.

He looked around at her immaculate apartment, analyzing every object in it with his eyes, searching for something that he couldn't find.

"Something bad happened. You won't say what and I can't see it." He studied her, from head to toe, almost clinically. "And you look the same but I think you're in shock."

"Why?"

"You tell me. Wait a sec. I'm going to sit over here"—he took an armchair across the room and pointed to the couch—"and you can sit over there, and when you're ready, then tell me."

"Go to hell." She was trembling.

"That's a start. Now sit down. Give it to me. Both barrels."

"Where were you? What were you doing?" There was a thread of panic in her voice.

"I drove all the way home to Clearston to get my car and my work laptop. On the way back I stopped for barbecue—"

"Of course. Barbecue does dissolve brain cells. That is a scientific fact."

He thought he detected a fractional softening. Maybe not. Either way, it didn't seem like the time to ask her if she'd seen the Frank Branigan coverage on the local station.

"Kenzie, you must have really wanted to talk to me. I'm here. I'm listening."

She finally sat down, clenching and unclenching her hands. "There's not much to say. I went to Christine's, found her stuff. Then—" In a raw voice, she told him every detail she could remember of her brief time in the apartment, ending with the terrifying face on the screen.

When she was done, Linc nodded soberly. "Got it. And now you want to get out of here."

"Yeah. I do. I'm not waiting for Mr. Evil Eyes to knock on my door or show up on my laptop screen."

He leaned forward, his hands clasped in front of him. "Christine's laptop is still there, right?"

She swore. "I was thinking of taking it. But I slammed it shut and left it on the floor."

"I'll go back for it tomorrow," he said.

"What for, Linc?"

He smiled slightly. "Because I don't want someone else to take it. Does that make sense to you?"

"Nothing is making sense right now."

He raised his hands in a conciliatory gesture. "Just trying to think this through. I hate to see you on the run."

"I don't see an alternative."

"Kenzie, this is your home." He waved a hand at the amber living room.

"Those are walls and that is paint," she snapped. "It comes in a can. The hardware store has lots of it."

"Okay, okay."

"Linc, home is where you feel safe. Right now I don't. Not anywhere."

"I hear you."

"It's not a big deal to just go, you know. Don't forget I'm an army brat. Pick up, pack up, and start over—I did it all my life with my mom and dad."

He held up his hands in a gesture of surrender. "Dial it down, okay? I'm on your side. All the way. I just wish I lived closer to Ridgewood. You could—"

"Oh no," she burst out. "I'm not going to leave the Corellis to deal with everything at the hospital and—what? Stay with you at the motel?"

"I didn't ask you to," Linc said in a reasonable tone. His comment seemed to irk her. She got up again, walking quickly around the apartment.

He watched her for a while. Her restless, almost instinctive movements reminded him of a sleek, nervous cat. Not a housecat, though. Something more like an ocelot. Or a smallish panther. His nature-show thoughts were interrupted by her whizzing by to grab more stuff out of a closet. She slammed open the sliding door so fast it bounced off the track.

She actually didn't have that much stuff, he noticed. And what she had was organized to the nth degree.

"Slow down," he said in a measured tone.

"I can't. I get kind of hyper when my friends and my life are in danger. I'm funny that way."

Linc got up. He kept his distance. The shock waves were still hitting her. They'd come and go. And eventually wear off, but maybe not tonight. He could deal. He was fairly sure she couldn't do him any serious damage.

"Make yourself useful," she said curtly. "You can box up the blender and the stacked plates. Get started."

A blender. The china. She was irrational, no doubt about it. But he still didn't like being ordered around. "You eat off plates?" he responded. "You mean someone just doesn't poke meat through the bars at sundown?" Maybe a joke would get through to her. If not, he was in for it.

Kenzie stopped in her tracks and dropped the box she was holding to the floor. Faster than he could imagine, her hand came up—and he felt a stinging sensation in his cheek before he realized that she'd slapped him.

Gently but quickly Linc grabbed her wrist on the way down. "Don't do that again," he said pleasantly. "I'm not the enemy. Get that straight."

Kenzie broke free with a tremendous effort. She stood there for a few seconds, rubbing her wrist and breathing hard. "If you're here to help, I guess I could be a little more grateful," she said at last.

Linc suppressed a faint smile. "Fine with me. Just remember I can take you in a fair fight."

"Maybe." She picked up the box and shoved it at him. "Put this in the car."

He took it and set it by the door. "How about here?"

Kenzie stopped rushing around and gave him an odd look. "Are you trying to tell me something?"

"Yeah. Tearing out the door with half of what you own is not a good idea. You have to calm down."

"I can't." She glanced at the random belongings she'd already stuffed into the nylon bags as if she had no idea how they'd gotten there.

"Then pack what you need for a couple of nights, no more than that, and I'll come up with a plan."

Kenzie stared at him. "Excuse me? Did I ask you to take charge?"

"No."

"Next you'll be telling me where I should go. Got any ideas?"

"Not yet."

She poked him in the chest. "Then don't distract me and don't get in my damn way."

"Kenzie, you're too scared to think straight."

"No, I'm not," she said in a clipped voice. "Stop lecturing me. Get out of here. Just get out."

"I'm not leaving you alone."

She brushed past him and Linc caught her arm.

"Let go," she snapped, twisting out of his hold.

He tried another tack. "At some point, we should contact Lieutenant Warren. You canceled that appointment with him, right?"

"I did, and I told him I'd call soon."

"Okay. You're in no shape to do it now, but when you can—"

Kenzie turned to face him. "What good will it do?"

"Look, I don't know what he's going to say and neither do you, but he has to know about this. Just call the nice policeman." Linc was losing patience. "Let someone help you. It doesn't have to be me."

"I told you I didn't get a screen grab and I don't really remember what the guy looked like," she burst out.

"Even so. Kenzie, if you could just settle down—"

She waved away what he was going to say and drew in a shaky breath. "The face I saw—that's gone."

She pressed her lips together, hard. The brilliant shimmer of tears in her eyes told Linc how afraid she was for her friend. And herself.

Linc chose his next words carefully. "You might remember more about him than you think. Trust me on that."

She shook her head. He didn't know which statement she was saying no to.

"While it's still fresh in your mind—when you're ready—if you could describe exactly what happened again and I could ask a few questions—"

Kenzie closed her eyes and leaned her head back. "Oh hell. Go ahead."

"I don't think it was a coincidence that he was onscreen when you got back to the laptop," Linc began. "You said you were waiting for it to shut down by itself, right?"

"Yeah. It didn't. Tell me why."

"Probably because he'd gained remote access to the hard drive. My guess is, he was watching you through the webcam with the on light shut off."

"What a fun game. Red light, green light. Kenzie gets stalked."

He looked at her steadily. "That's right."

She fell silent for several moments. "Was he far away?"

"It's possible to activate a webcam or control a hard drive from thousands of miles away or right next door. It's not that complicated."

She shuddered.

"Draw a circle on a mental map. I just did. Everything is happening within a fifty-mile radius. He's not in another country. He's here."

"Do you think he followed me to Christine's apartment?"

"Yes."

"Then what?"

Linc explained it as simply as he could. "He didn't have to break down the door. All he had to do was hack into her laptop, and there's a million ways to do that. He knew the second you opened it."

"It fell on the floor. I actually didn't open it."

"He got lucky with that. But he did know you were there. He could have been in a car on the street. How would you know if you weren't looking for him?"

"I was, though. Right and left."

"Look, it's clear to me even at this stage that this guy is good at his game."

Kenzie's eyes flashed with angry fire. "That laptop has Christine's whole life in it, just about. Photos, web bookmarks, browser history, her documents—can he get into everything?"

"Yeah. Most likely he already has. Which is another reason I want to get it back and look at it, run some scans. I should be able to find a few digital footprints."

Kenzie raised a hand to her neck and slowly rubbed the tense muscles. "Do you think he followed me here?"

"Definitely a possibility and no big deal for him. It's safe to say that he knows where you live."

She straightened and walked away from him. "I kept checking my rearview mirror on the way home and I took different streets. I didn't see anyone behind me."

"Doesn't mean he wasn't there."

"True." She sank into an upholstered chair and clutched the padded armrests, drumming her fingers on the taut material.

"Getting back to what we were talking about—what exactly did you do with the laptop? Before you ran out, I mean."

"I slammed it shut and left it on the floor."

Linc frowned. "So it's in standby mode."

"What of it?" she asked. "I'm not going to give him a second chance to trap me."

Linc nodded in agreement. "Good. Me neither."

She cleared her throat. "Hey, you can be my hero." He didn't miss the ironic edge in the comment. "And by the way, I assume you have a gun."

Linc knew that was about as close as Kenzie would come to actually asking him for help. "I do."

Her gaze moved over him. He patted the left side of his shirt. Fall weather and flannel shirts made concealed carry easier.

"First things first," he said. "Maybe we can set a trap for him, lure him into showing his face again. Getting a visual on the guy is key."

"Well—yes."

Linc pointed a warning finger at her. "That's going to be my job."

"Be my guest," she said with feeling.

"Your job is to be extra careful from now on. He definitely knows how to stay out of sight, Kenz. And he may have been following Christine around for a while."

Linc didn't want to get into the possibilities as far as her best friend was concerned. Around meant everywhere. All over town. Lurking online when Christine was, trolling sites she visited.

The guy could be someone who no one noticed much. Crazy in a quiet, unassuming, lethal way. But most stalkers got bolder over time. Linc kept the thought to himself.

"Why didn't either one of us notice?"

"Because you didn't, that's all. Look, Kenz, my dad was a cop. He used to say that stalking cases were one long nightmare. And it was tough as hell to bring charges unless the guy made contact, and even then you couldn't get them behind bars for long enough."

She bit her lip, struggling for self-control. "I would have remembered those eyes if I'd ever seen them before," she said softly. "He's a killer. I know it."

Linc let her talk.

Her fear, her anger, her desire to get even—it all tumbled out in a rush. He couldn't argue with any of it or discuss it rationally. So he listened. It was one thing he could do. His first concern was to guard her tonight and get her out of here tomorrow. If she'd let him help.

Kenzie rested her head against the back cushions of the couch, seeming overwhelmed by sudden exhaustion. He didn't say anything, just watched her. She let her eyes drift shut as she fell silent, forcing herself to breathe slowly.

"Feel better?" he asked after a while.

"A little. Sorry." She sounded embarrassed.

"For what?"

"Being scared. Giving you hell for it."

Linc shook his head. "It's okay. Don't apologize."

She rubbed her forehead. "I should get to bed. What are you going to do?"

"Sit up. Stay awake."

"Oh," she said faintly. "And watch over me?"

"Yeah. You mind?"

"I'm beginning to think it's a good idea. Temporarily, anyway." Kenzie eased forward to a straighter sitting position. "I have to work tomorrow." She stood up, lithe in jeans and sweater. "But I want to ask for time off."

"You going to tell your boss what happened?" Linc asked.

"Some of it. Not everything. Jim can be kind of overprotective. They don't call him Big Dawg for nothing."

Linc shrugged at the comment. He'd judge for himself if the guy deserved the nickname when he met him. Right now every male in Kenzie's life and Christine's was on the suspect list.

"Whatever. So where do you want me tonight?"

The remark got him a quelling look from dark green eyes. "Stay right where you are. I'll be in the bedroom."

Thanks for the hospitality, beautiful, he wanted to say. He hadn't meant the question the way she seemed to be interpreting it. Linc settled down and watched her go into her bedroom without another word.

Kenzie slept only fitfully. Around four A.M., she gave up trying, too restless to stay in bed. Maybe a cup of something hot and herbal would help. She threw back the covers and stood up, pulling down her tank top over the knit short-shorts she wore to bed.

She peered around the open door of her bedroom, trying to catch a glimpse of Linc. He wasn't sitting up. That left the couch or the floor. Kenzie craned her neck to see better and realized he was curled up on the couch when she spotted a large, sock-clad foot extended over the arm. She stood still, listening to his deep, regular breathing.

Out cold.

She wished she could say the same. Kenzie stepped quietly into the living room, looking sideways at him as she made her way to the kitchen. He'd folded a fancy pillow in half and tucked it under his head.

Some hostess she was. Kenzie hadn't even thought to give him bedding for the night. But he had given her the impression he wouldn't shut his eyes.

Nice to know he was human. And, she reminded herself, it was very nice of him to stay when she'd been so irrational at first. Linc Bannon was a good guy.

The dim glow of the night-light was enough to see by. She wasn't going to wake him up with a blast of white from the overheads. Kenzie put a cup of water in the microwave and took it out a second or two before the loud beep went off. There was a box of herbal tea bags in the cabinet and she tossed one into the cup, watching delicate spirals of color appear.

Her hands curled around the smooth porcelain as she waited for it to brew, letting herself be soothed by the heat.

She didn't usually slow down this much. Christine used to tell her to often enough. *Just be. Just breathe.*

Not her thing.

Linc was doing a good job of it. His solid chest rose and fell under the strong arms crossed over it. Unbuttoned, his shirt revealed a blue tee underneath.

She took a sip of tea, studying him. Nothing would feel better right now than to curl up against the warm softness of flannel and knit material over all that hard muscle beneath. The body heat of a sleeping man beat the hell out of herbal tea, that was for sure. Given what had happened, the urge she felt to join him there surprised her.

He seemed comfortable. At home, even. Well, he was the first. The apartment, her sanctuary, hadn't had a man in it since she'd moved in and done the decorating exactly the way she liked it.

Linc didn't stir. She drank most of the tea and set the cup on a side table, then went back into her bedroom for a light blanket, throwing it over him as gently as she could, only half-hoping she wouldn't awaken him.

It settled over his body in soft folds and she glanced down, wondering if she saw a faint smile appear on his drowsy mouth. She had. It touched the scar on his cheek, an old one. She never had asked him where he got that. Kenzie shifted position a bit—then stiffened when his hand brushed against her bare leg.

He hadn't done it. Her movement had brought her into accidental contact with his hand. But the brief, inadvertent touch caused a sensation to race through her that could only be described as erotic.

She stepped back and stumbled, banging her heel painfully. Linc half opened his eyes.

"What time is it?"

Flustered, Kenzie glanced over her shoulder at the clock and told him. Did he take the chance to look her up and down in the abbreviated sleep shorts and tank? She couldn't tell when she turned back to him.

"Too early. Mind if I go back to sleep?" he asked a little groggily.

"No. That's fine. I got up to make myself some tea, that's all." She picked up her cup from the side table and headed to her bedroom. She could have sworn she felt his eyes on her. If he'd been asleep, he was awake now. But she didn't look back.

Kenzie rested a hand on the steering wheel as she waited for the traffic light to change. She barely saw the fall glory of the trees blazing scarlet and gold all around her. The drive to work was something she could have done in her sleep anyway. The man in the car in her rearview mirror was very much on her mind. Through the tinted lenses of her sunglasses, she saw Linc nod to her and smiled to herself.

The green light appeared and she went a few more blocks, feeling a pang when Linc turned off on the street that would take him back to the motel.

Although they hadn't discussed it, it was probably best that he keep the anonymous room if he was going to stay in Ridgewood. Just that one accidental touch made her very sure of that. Her reaction to him was a little too physical for her peace of mind.

She was still racking her brains for other places to bunk down temporarily and she didn't need that kind of distraction, not with the danger she was now in.

Linc had helped her store some valuables and lock up, telling her to make the place look like she hadn't left for good. Apparently that meant leaving a few dishes in the sink, the bed unmade, and an open magazine on a side table, all of which bugged her but were not worth arguing about. She'd made the bed anyway. Fast.

He seemed to think he knew what he was doing and was willing to stick around to protect her. But when she put in her two cents, he had to agree that neither of them should stay in her apartment.

Which opened up the big question of where she would go and for how long. Good thing she didn't have a dog to worry about— she hadn't gotten another since fostering Tex for intensive train- ing and deployment in Afghanistan.

Six weeks in country and Tex had been killed by a grenade thrown in among the sleeping soldiers he guarded, with only a few seconds to alert the men he saved. One of the great dogs, bar none.

She hadn't wanted another.

Her apartment had become her retreat once she'd returned stateside. She'd felt safe enough there. Not anymore. Right now, she had to focus on protecting Christine and herself, and get the hell out of harm's way.

No way would she risk anyone else's safety and ask a girlfriend if she could stay for a while.

At some point she would have to be a good little girl and tell her parents what was going on. Not today, though. If they hap- pened to call from Germany, no problem—they'd reach her cell. She didn't have a landline anyway. Besides, she wasn't ready to tell them everything when she really didn't know much herself.

Something would turn up. She was somewhat less nervous today, in part because she'd forced herself not to obsess.

And as for Linc, when he was wide awake and buttoning up his shirt, he didn't unsettle her the way he did when he was half- asleep and stretched out full-length on her couch. Although he was incredibly sexy with his hair messed up and that twinkle in his dark eyes. He looked rumpled but well-rested.

She wasn't. But the morning sunshine worked to dispel the last trace of the sensations he'd accidentally aroused. Sticking to the practical task of making breakfast had helped too.

They'd shared a platter of eggs and toast. He'd done the cook- ing, she'd washed the dishes and cups. They hadn't rehashed last night's discussion, just agreed to talk later. He seemed to under- stand that she needed time and they both had a lot to do.

She turned off onto a road that brought her into a more rural part of the county, and soon was driving through the gates of the JB dog-training operation. Kenzie pulled up next to a white van painted with the company logo, and gave herself the luxury of a few minutes to think. She didn't see Jim Biggers's car in the parking lot, but there were several others. The employees who cared for the dogs and maintained the kennels came in early.

Breakfast over, the dogs were revving up. Their yelps and barks reached her even with the car windows rolled up.

A rubber toy bounced off her windshield and a dog's eager face popped up next to her. It had wide pricked ears brushed with black and a black muzzle, with golden brown everywhere else.

"Hello, Bogie."

Before she could roll down her window to pet him, a distant whistle summoned him and the dog ran off, its tail high, a flash of enthusiasm against the dull asphalt of the parking lot.

Kenzie's spirits lifted a little. She opened the door and got out, breathing the country air. The nip to it invigorated her—and took her back. She leaned against the car, remembering the day she'd started working here.

Jim Biggers had hired her sight unseen, on the basis of a recommendation from the kennel master of a military police detachment based at Darmstadt in Germany, where she'd been a Specialist 1st Class.

With an active social life at first, she thought wistfully. Unlike now. Back then she hadn't wanted to bother with a serious relationship, and most of the men she'd met were raw recruits or career army.

She honestly hadn't wanted to get involved with someone likely to deploy at any time. Her parents had lived with that worry hanging over them from the day they'd married, and Kenzie knew how glad both of them were when that stage of her father's career was over.

But there had been that one soldier. Dan Fuller.

Dan fully expected to be tapped for a Special Ops team. There seemed to be no fighting skill he couldn't master. He was smart and rugged and too brave for his own good. Her kind of man. She'd known that right away. Hadn't told anyone but him, though.

And then—only five weeks after she'd met him—Dan had died in combat, unable to escape the cab of an up-armored vehicle when it had rolled over a roadside bomb.

She'd kept her feelings for him private in the first place and skipped the sympathy, counting the days until she was sent home.

The Darmstadt base had been on the verge of closing, per government orders, after going strong for something like sixty years. She'd only been there for two. The last two, as it turned out. Her friends there had begun to scatter to other postings and new lives all over the world, but she'd hung on to the end.

Burying herself in work was as good a way as any to forget. Kenzie had taken on the complex training of bomb-sniffing dogs and guard animals. Their unique abilities could never be equaled by machines. War dogs were increasingly important in Afghanistan and elsewhere.

Not every dog completed the rigorous program. But they could move on to other responsibilities if they didn't.

She'd also served as liaison to stateside kennel masters who came through Darmstadt on occasion, looking for high-quality animals for specialized army missions. There simply weren't enough to go everywhere they were needed. She had learned not to get too attached to the dogs she worked with. Or to anyone else.

Losing Dan had underscored that.

Once she was stateside again, she'd done the same thing, kept a protective distance from just about everyone. And then she'd met Linc. A true-blue guy who made her want to change her mind.

She reminded herself that he wasn't likely to be deployed. Not if he was needed at Fort Meade and Langley.

But . . . one thing she'd learned was that there were no guarantees. She straightened away from the car with a sigh. Kenzie headed through the parking lot and past the kennels, empty for the moment. The dogs wouldn't return to them until around noon, exhausted in a good way from their play and training sessions. She looked around for Truck, who had the run of the place.

So named because Jim had found him chained to an abandoned pickup as a half-starved puppy, Truck was huge now, a shaggy black-and-white ball of energy and canine smarts. Jim Biggers insisted Truck was the best damn dog he'd ever had.

The mutt was nowhere to be seen, but she knew he'd show up soon.

Sometimes he trotted over to the kennels by himself from the Biggers farm a mile away, going through the woods on a trail only he could follow. Suddenly she heard a noise behind her and turned to see the big dog emerging from the underbrush. He bounded over to greet her, metal tags jingling loudly.

While she and Truck were saying good morning, Jim swung into the parking lot, calling to her through the open window of his jeep. "Kenzie, what a surprise. You're here on time for once."

"Yes," she called back. "It's payday, right?"

Jim laughed and pulled into his slot. He gathered up an armful of file folders and paperwork from the front seat and got out, heading for his office. "Dogs out?"

"All the kennels were empty when I got here."

"Good. First drills start at nine sharp."

She found a tennis ball to toss for Truck for a while, giving Jim time to get inside, drink a cup of coffee, and plan the day's training schedule at his computer.

Over and over, Truck dropped the grubby ball carefully into her palm as if entrusting her with a priceless treasure. After twenty minutes or so, she threw it for the last time, hard and far, giving him a good run. Then Kenzie gave the big dog a farewell pat, sending him off on his customary patrol of the perimeter. He jingled away, eager to get to work.

She opened the steel doors of the low building and walked through the cinder-block corridor that led to Jim's office.

He believed in order. There wasn't a speck of dust or scrap of paper on the floor. Heavily padded bite sleeves hung from a rack on the wall and other training equipment was stored in lockers. Each trainer had their own—Jim allowed a certain amount of leeway for individual approaches. Training combat dogs was part science and part instinct.

Playing with Truck in the fresh air had cleared her mind and helped her think of a tentative plan. She was going to ask for unpaid time off and limit the explanations to a short version of Christine's accident.

She memorized her talking points. Best friend. Bad accident.

Seriously injured. Facing a long recovery. Naturally, Kenzie wanted to help however she could. That was enough.

She peeked through the open door of her boss's office. Jim Biggers glanced up at her over the half-glasses perched on the end of his nose. They didn't go with his military-style haircut, but he was of the age where they were necessary.

"What do you want? I don't sign payroll checks until the afternoon," he said sternly.

She knew he was teasing, though not about when he did the signing. But Jim, a former supply sergeant, was a stickler for routine. He believed fervently that time was money, and he valued both equally.

"I know," she replied, glancing at the framed diplomas and citations hung on the wall behind him. After many months of employment, they still impressed her. Jim Biggers, a decorated Gulf War veteran, was a bona fide good ol' boy, but he had a doctorate in biochemistry.

He'd founded the kennel operation in between that war and the next, in Iraq. As Linc had said, the world was a lot more complicated than it had been back then.

JB Kennels was a thriving business. He insisted on giving her credit for the recent uptick in profits whenever he had the opportunity.

"Sit down. Talk to me," he said, gesturing to a chair. He closed out the spreadsheet he had pulled up.

After working with Kenzie for over a year, he was fairly good at reading her mind. Plus he had five kids and was impossible to lie to.

Kenzie took the oak armchair across from his desk and sat, then turned when she heard the jingle of Truck's tags. One of the trainers must have let him in—sometimes it wasn't clear who was training whom. A moment later the dog was asking silently for permission to lie by Jim's side.

"At ease, Truck." Her boss pointed to the floor and gave the dog a few seconds to settle down before he nodded to her to begin.

It didn't take Kenzie long to explain. Per plan, she didn't tell him everything. His thoughtful gaze on her face didn't waver and his mouth tightened in a fierce scowl when she told him about the sideswipe.

"Hit-and-run, huh? No witnesses?"

"Not that we know of."

One thick eyebrow went up. "We? Who's on the case?"

"Ah—the police, of course. And a friend of mine. You don't know him." She returned his interested gaze with composure.

"I see. Well, I hope like hell they get the bastard. Take all the time you need, Kenzie."

"Thank you. I mean it."

His tone turned bluff. "Not a problem at the moment. I can spare you. Bottom line is looking good, real good."

"The new clients?"

"One in particular," Jim said. "Just signed a contract with a billionaire who wants canine protection. Got the wife and kids tucked away at a mountain estate and he's nervous."

"Doesn't he have bodyguards?"

Jim grinned. "Several. But JB dogs are a status symbol, apparently. He insists on paying top dollar."

"How much are you charging him?" Kenzie asked curiously.

"I suggested fifty thousand and he raised me to one hundred thousand. Per dog. For three dogs. I didn't say no."

"You're bad." Kenzie laughed.

"Hey, he started it. Three hundred thousand is small change to the guy. He wants to brag about how much his animals cost, I say let him."

Kenzie shook her head with amusement. "No harm in that. He's getting good dogs. So who's doing the training?"

"Buddy and Wells. They can't believe the money they're making for the gig."

He pointed a pencil at her and sounded stern again. "And by the way, you can forget about that unpaid-time-off crap. Your salary is direct deposit, and that's not going to stop. You earned it, you need it."

"But—"

"Just check in now and then," he interrupted. "That's an

order." His voice was gruff, but she knew that he didn't show his soft side. "I want updates."

"I will." She smiled at him. Jim was army all the way. *Never abandon a fallen comrade.* He knew Kenzie wouldn't have requested time off for a trivial reason.

"Wait. Before you go," Jim said as she rose to leave. "Think you could get my gun back for me? I left it with Norm to have the firing pin fixed."

"Sure."

"I'd do it myself but I'm up against a time crunch today."

Kenzie smiled at him. "No problem." She wouldn't mind a quick stop there. Norm Hamill's firing range was where she'd learned to shoot before she'd enlisted and still went sometimes for target practice.

"Great. That's one less thing to check off my list." He pretended indifference. "Okay, I have work to do. Scram."

"Yes sir." Her tone was gently teasing. "And thank you again."

"Stop saying that."

She moved to leave and Truck half rose until Jim's hand stopped him. He sank his big fingers into the dog's ruff as Kenzie raised a hand to wave good-bye. There was a wistful quality in her gaze, and it puzzled the man.

"Should I close the door?" she asked him.

"Please do." Jim and Truck watched Kenzie walk away on the other side of the glass panel.

"You thinking what I'm thinking?" he muttered to the dog.

Truck gave him a soulful look in reply and thumped his tail on the floor.

Jim Biggers knew in his bones that Kenzie wasn't telling the whole truth. He threw his pencil down on the desk and watched her as she went down the hall. "Yeah. She left out about half that story."

The question was why. He supposed Kenzie had her reasons. Jim shook his head and returned his attention to the computer screen in front of him

*   *   *

Outside in the parking lot, she walked quickly to her car, glancing at Buddy and Wells without saying hello. The two men were working with several new dogs, running them through simple commands that would become increasingly complex in the weeks ahead.

It was good to know that there were no urgent army orders right now. Landing a rich non-military client definitely took the pressure off Jim. She didn't feel too guilty about not coming in. Kenzie took out her car key and unlocked the doors from several feet away.

She took one last look at the new dogs through her windshield as she got in. Good group, she thought. They were off-leash, but not one had diverted its attention from the trainers at the sound of the key beep.

Kenzie heard her cell phone chime and scrambled to find it in her purse. The screen indicated a missed call from Mrs. Corelli, who hadn't left a voicemail message.

She frowned as she dialed the number, hoping Christine's mother would be able to pick up. After the fourth ring, she did.

"Oh, Kenzie. I'm so glad you called back." Her voice was shaky.

"What's the matter?"

"I'll tell you in a minute. I want to text you my sister's phone number before I forget. So you have more than one way to reach us. It was such a relief to be with Ann last night."

"That's good. What's going on?"

"She really wants us to take turns staying there when we're not at the hospital. Alf thinks it's best. Now—oh, I can't text and talk at the same time, can I?"

"Nope. Just talk to me. The phone number can wait."

Mrs. Corelli took a breath. Then another. Kenzie's heart sank. Her fingers clutched the small phone.

"The neurologist came around on morning rounds—not Dr. Asher, someone else. Apparently she is still stable, but—"

Kenzie stiffened in the seat of the car, braced for bad news.

"She's been so quiet all this time. But now—" Mrs. Corelli was silent for a few seconds. "She was moaning today, Kenzie. Like

she's in pain. He told us and the doctors with him that she probably isn't, but I—I don't know."

"Did they say anything else?"

Mrs. Corelli thought for several seconds. "There's concern
about the sedation. Dr. Asher approved a change in it and it is
lower, but she still needs careful monitoring. The neurologist
mentioned possible problems with clots—fluid in the lungs—
things like that. Alf and I were so worried, but we weren't sure if
he was speaking generally or what."

"I can come. Right now. Let me help, however I can."

"Thank you, Kenzie." Mrs. Corelli whispered the reply. "We
really appreciate it."

"I'm on my way." Kenzie turned the key in the ignition.

"Before you hang up—"

"Yes?"

"Is it possible for you to pick up Christine's laptop and bring
it in?"

"Ah—I could," she stammered. "Why?"

"All her photos are on it."

"You're right about that," Kenzie answered, still puzzled.

"I'm not making myself very clear, am I?"

"Well, no, but it sounds like you have a lot on your mind." And
Kenzie wasn't going to add to her worries, either. Not yet.

Mrs. Corelli went on, "One of the neurology residents brought
up post-trauma memory loss in brain-injured patients and ways to
treat it, including visual aids. I caught her in the hall, asked for
more information."

"I see."

"Anyway, when Christine regains full consciousness—"

She broke off. The aching hope in the older woman's voice was
heartbreaking. Kenzie waited. Mrs. Corelli had said *when*. Not *if*.

"They expect that she will, then," Kenzie prompted.

"Yes."

"That's good news." But it didn't explain away the changes in
Christine's behavior that had upset her mother. Maybe there was
no explanation for the moaning.

"It is. But not a guarantee of anything." Mrs. Corelli's voice cracked a little. Kenzie waited while she composed herself.

"Anyway, going forward, it's likely to be a while before Christine can talk to us or even form words. But she should be able to recognize images she knows. So I thought perhaps you and I could use the laptop to put together a slide show of family and friends—especially you, Kenzie—and her favorite activities, things like that."

"Oh. Sure." Stall for time, she told herself. "Um, when would you want to do that?"

"We could get started on it today or tomorrow. What do you think?"

"I'm all for it. I have to call you back, though. Soon—I promise. I'm in the car right now." Not driving it, but she would be. Kenzie looked around the JB Kennels parking lot. A couple of fancy cars had come in. Clients, most likely. She wanted to get going.

"Of course, Kenzie. And thank you again. You've been so great—I hate to ask you to do anything more."

"Don't say that. I want to."

Kenzie tossed her cell back into her purse as she backed out and headed down the county road. She heard the incoming text a minute later.

Christine's parents didn't have to know about the hacker right this second, not with their daughter in such bad shape. Once she told them what had happened, they would have to stay out of the apartment permanently.

Linc's comment about someone stealing the laptop before he could retrieve it came back to her. The idea stoked fresh anger. She struggled to control it by driving at a steady fifty-five.

Bad enough the stalker had hacked into it. He wasn't going to get his actual hands on the thing. The thought made her flesh crawl. Homicidal bastard. If he appeared in the road right now, she wouldn't swerve. She'd—she'd—

She would do the obligatory right thing and call Linc before going back to Christine's apartment. He had thirty seconds to answer and five minutes to return her call if he didn't pick up at once. Tough luck otherwise.

Kenzie kept driving as she formulated a plan. Christine's building had seemed to have a lot of people coming and going, tenants or whoever. She'd scout out the exterior stairs, get to the second-floor apartment, and stand back when the door opened, then get in and get out, fast.

But she wasn't going to risk her life if anything seemed wrong. Kenzie pulled over on the shoulder, raising dust, and dialed Linc.

No answer. She let it ring just long enough for the attempt to register as a missed call and hung it up. He couldn't say she hadn't tried. That was as virtuous as she was going to get.

The phone fell toward the back of the car when she took off again, gunning the car onto the empty road.

Suddenly she was a lot less afraid. If the hacker showed up again on the laptop, it would be a second chance to get a screen grab. More than one if she could.

Face. Eyes.

If only she could reach through the screen and haul him out for an appropriate punishment. Total fantasy, but what a fantasy. Kenzie's foot pressed down on the accelerator.

Linc saw her number on the call-waiting box. One ring. Two. Three. His commanding officer was on the line. Hang on, he told Kenzie mentally.

"So. You staying down there another week, Linc?"

Four. Five. "Yes sir. With your permission."

"What was the name of that little town again?"

"Ridgewood."

"Never heard of it." The officer chuckled. "I guess it doesn't matter. By the way, your coworkers on the project don't seem to miss you much."

It was protocol to keep specific information out of phone calls, which were ridiculously easy to intercept. There was only so much encryption could do.

The call-waiting box disappeared and Linc swore silently. "I check in every day."

"That's what I hear. Keep it up," the other man said affably. "So long."

Linc looked at the phone screen and jabbed the message icon. There weren't any. He called her. No answer.

Damn it. What could he do? He had no way of tracing her, and he couldn't just jump in the car and chase her around.

Then again, he could be overreacting. Maybe she'd called to tell him what a great guy he was, but hadn't wanted to say that to voicemail.

He wished.

CHAPTER 5

He left the motel to get something to eat, not forgetting to bring the phone in his pocket. It stayed silent as a rock.

It occurred to Linc that she might have called to let him know she'd rescheduled with the lieutenant. Somehow he doubted it. He wondered why she was leery of the police—she had to have worked with cops now and then, unless JB Kennels only trained military working dogs.

Could be just her natural impatience, combined with her army brat's sense of superiority. But she was right about how long it would take the police to get an investigation under way. That didn't mean he was going to brush them aside. He was curious about what the lieutenant would have to say.

Of course forensic analysis took forever. But there was no other way to amass the kind of evidence that could put the stalker behind bars. Conjecture wouldn't do it.

He wouldn't let that stop him.

Linc got in his car, taking his time and eventually finding his way to the road that led past the Arlington military cemetery. The rows of white markers standing sentinel passed by in a heartbeat, but made him think.

Never forget. It was that simple.

He focused on the road again, seeing the Washington Monument, the highest point in DC, alone against the blue fall sky. Standing tall.

He drove farther into Arlington proper, heading for a side

street lined with ethnic restaurants. Unfortunately, none were open. He settled for franchise food from a drive-through and tossed the takeout bag into the front passenger seat, then headed back to the motel.

The parking lot was just about empty by the time he pulled back in. Linc unlocked his door and sat down to feed himself. He wouldn't call it a meal.

In five minutes, he finished the tasteless sandwich he'd bought and got rid of the wrapping. Then he rolled up a magazine and used it to sweep the others off the motel table so he could put his feet up on it.

He leaned his head back on scratchy metallic upholstery that hadn't been cleaned since disco died. He wished he had earphones and a decent playlist to blast into his brain.

There was nothing to listen to but the drone of a vacuum in the next room. He'd hung a Do Not Disturb sign on his door. The housekeeper would have to come back later.

He entered points on his mental grid.

Girl A. That was Christine, the stalker's first target, although Linc was keeping an open mind on that. There were other possibilities.

She and Kenzie, Girl B, hung out constantly, did a lot of things together. Neither had been aware that someone was watching.

Linc tried to think like the stalker.

If he'd ever spied on Kenzie in action at the kennels or a local event that featured the JB dogs, he knew how tough she was. Her best pal Christine was easier prey.

Everyone loves her. Kenzie had said it.

The line from A to B had proved to be short.

Had he hoped for a two-for-one when Kenzie loaned Christine her car? He must have been disappointed when Christine drove off alone, but he hadn't wasted any time.

Stalkers could be methodical and remarkably patient. But obsessions had a way of intensifying. Demons had to be fed. Voices got louder. *Harass, hurt, kill.*

The creep had followed Christine, then forced her off the road on a lonely stretch of highway. Maybe he'd intended to rape her or worse—other cars or trucks could have driven by, not stopping, not seeing.

He had to have a self-protective streak. He hadn't chanced it, just taken off. Leaving Christine unconscious and badly injured, trapped in a car that could have exploded in flames at any second.

Just thinking about it made Linc want to slam the stalker's face into something hard, like a concrete wall, repeatedly.

Uncivilized. Illegal. Effective.

He kept on thinking. About the shadows he'd seen in Kenzie's hall. Linc hadn't imagined them. Done with Girl A, Evil Eyes had doubled back to Girl B's building for more sick fun.

Picked Kenzie's locks. Or simply pushed in her half-latched door. And got scared off by Linc.

It bugged the hell out of him that he remembered so little. The stalker remained a shadow, tantalizingly out of reach.

Unless . . .

A fair amount of time had elapsed between when Linc had glimpsed the aftermath of the accident on TV and when he himself had ended up at Kenzie's building.

The stalker could have sped away seconds after the crash. And done a U-turn in the next minute, come back around, rubbernecking before the cops took over. *Keep going. Nothing to see here, people. Move it.*

The cameraman might have filmed that when he and the reporter were warned away from the wreck.

Even with live feeds, someone at the station controlled what got on the air. There had to be outtakes—the stalker could have been recorded. Driving a car that could be ID'd. A visible face in the window that Kenzie might recognize.

Time frame—he needed one to mesh with the grid in his mind and pin the stalker to it. The news footage was digitally stamped down to the second, if he could get a look at it.

Did the first responders actually get there first? How long was it before Christine was pulled from the wreck? Linc didn't know but he could find out, if he could get Kenzie to play nice with the police department. It would have to be her. It was her car that had been wrecked and her friend that had been hurt.

Besides, a beautiful woman had a definite advantage, if the officers she was dealing with were male. The broadcast, if he remembered it right, confirmed that the Ridgewood PD and emergency response team didn't seem to have heard of affirmative action.

If Kenzie didn't see the need to cooperate just yet, he knew a woman who could help.

Linc swung his feet off the coffee table and reached for his cell. Time to make some calls. His younger brother had to have a phone number for Kelly Johns, star reporter. RJ had said something about her being interested in Deke.

He remembered vaguely that she'd come up through the ranks, going from smaller stations to larger. The sleazy reporter who'd covered the accident looked like he'd stayed stuck in the trenches. Still, she might know something about him or know someone who did. He figured Kelly would be happy to give him the skinny.

He speed-dialed Deke.

Not too long after that, Linc was having a cup of lousy coffee with the reporter who'd covered the crash. Gary Baum had arrived within minutes of Linc's call, but they were getting nowhere.

The guy liked to whine. "I have no idea why they towed my freakin' car—I mean, I had every right to be on the scene of the accident and I showed my press pass. But whoa, I touch the wheel of the wreck and the deputy acts like that was a felony or something, reams me out. The station had to cut the live feed and blast a commercial."

"I remember it."

The reporter gave him a disbelieving look. "You do? Nice to know someone pays attention to my broadcasts once in a while," Baum said sourly.

"You do a good job," was Linc's bland response. If he had to stroke this guy's ego to get a look at the footage, he would. Gary Baum was self-absorbed to a fault. No wonder he hadn't noticed Linc at the impound lot.

Baum glanced up at the monitor positioned high on the coffee shop wall. "I'm just a lowly reporter. There's our star anchor, Mark Huxley."

He pointed and Linc looked too. "Uh-huh."

"With a late-breaking update," Baum mimicked the anchor's deep voice, "on the pothole crisis in downtown Ridgewood." He watched as the anchorman positioned himself in front of a large crater in the street. "Two steps backward, he falls in and gets mud all over that expensive suit. Okay with me. I want his job," he sighed. "Then I could afford a suit like that. Around the station my nickname is Baum the Bum."

"That's not nice."

"Ambulance chasing isn't either." Baum's eyes narrowed on Linc's impassive face. "Are you going to tell me why you're so interested in that particular accident?"

Point scored for Baum. Maybe he was smarter than he acted. "I'm an investigator," Linc said.

"Private? Police department? What?"

Linc shrugged. "I freelance, let's put it that way."

"How's the money?"

"Depends. Sometimes it's pretty good."

"Maybe I should change jobs," Baum mused. Several teenaged boys eased into the frame with the handsome anchor, smirking and mugging behind his back. "Go get him, punks. Time to wrap it up, Huxley," he said to his onscreen rival.

Linc shrugged. Maybe it was time he wrapped up this conversation. There was a limit to how straightforward he could be with the reporter.

Gary Baum leaned forward, his hands cupping the coffee Linc had bought for him. "So is there a bigger story here? I'm getting that idea. My sixth sense is highly developed. What can you and I do for each other, Linc? And are you related to that other Bannon guy who broke the Montgomery case?"

Now they were talking. Linc sized up the man across from him and answered the second question first. "He's my brother. But that case is closed. All I'm interested in is seeing the footage from the accident, start to finish. Unedited."

"Yeah, yeah. You paying?"

Linc had expected that question. He studied the other man for a few moments before he answered. "I don't know. Depends on what you can get me."

"Give me a few days." Baum went off on another tangent. "Hey, before I forget to ask, how well do you know Kelly Johns?"

"I've met her." That was true enough.

The reporter didn't drop it. "What a babe. And what a nose for news—it was awesome how she got that old kidnapping story to go viral. Isn't she up for some award for that? National or local?"

"Local," Linc bluffed. He had a sudden feeling that Baum was testing him.

Apparently not. The reporter took his answer for the truth. "You going to the ceremony?"

"Can't say."

Gary Baum sat back and looked at him enviously, then took a long slurp of his coffee. "You lucky dog." He set down the cup. "Okay. Nice talking to you, but I gotta get back to the station."

Linc wished he had a nice crisp hundred in his wallet for encouragement, but he didn't. "I understand. You have my cell number. Let me know when you have something."

"Sure thing."

Kenzie had gone back and circled Christine's block several times, acting like she was hunting for a parking space—fortunately, there weren't any—and looking around intently.

No homicidal maniacs with glowing laptops in sight. The nearby parked cars were unoccupied. None had tinted glass. She knew her recon was kind of pointless, but she had to do it. Finally she pulled up in front of the building again, backing into a just-opened spot with a single swoop.

Get in, get out.

She reached under the passenger seat and took out a weapon. Not one with bullets—it was a curved slab of iron made to fit her palm. Meant for fighting dirty. A ring, the only part of it that showed, slipped over a finger.

Better than nothing.

Kenzie got out, moving fast, uneasy because there wasn't any-one else around. She went up the exterior stairs.

The hallway was empty. She pressed her ear to the door to Christine's apartment, hearing nothing. Quietly, she stepped back a bit and turned the key in the lock, pushing it open and staying to the side.

No sound. A faint smell of closed-in air. Her instincts told her that no one was there.

Kenzie moved to the open door and saw the laptop on the floor where she had left it. Glancing around the room and through the open interior doors as she dashed in, she yanked out the cord and scooped up the laptop.

Mission accomplished. It hadn't taken more than a few sec-onds. Kenzie closed the door, then locked it.

She got back to her car and slid behind the wheel, the laptop on the seat next to her. She steadied it when she drove off, going a little too fast for the residential neighborhood. She'd put it in the trunk when she got to the hospital.

No way in hell would she take the laptop into Christine's hos-pital room until Linc had gone over it thoroughly. Maybe not even then. They could put all the stored photos on a couple of CDs and have them printed out at a drugstore.

A few fall leaves whirled red and gold in the air as she zoomed away. In another minute, Kenzie reached a wide cross street that would take her to the interstate and the hospital. Going through the intersection, she took off the palm iron and tossed it into the passenger footwell.

She didn't notice the black car idling near a hydrant.

Later, much later, sitting in the hospital parking lot after her visit, she bit her lip to the point of pain. Sometimes that little trick worked to keep back tears. Not now. Kenzie scrubbed the hot drops away.

She found it hard to believe the doctors' prognosis—Christine seemed worse, not better. She was moaning again and restless, even with her mother's soothing care. Her hands found the tubes and pulled at them until a nurse was summoned.

Restraints or sedatives. What a choice to have to make.

The Corellis opted for the latter. A nurse came in to administer them intravenously, per Dr. Asher's orders. The drug was something new, not as strong as what she'd been on previously, they told Kenzie.

She'd waited with them until Christine was calmer and Alf finally insisted that his wife go to her sister's house. The woman, who seemed kind but careworn, had driven in to pick her up.

That was one less thing for Kenzie to worry about, at least for a little while. She hadn't said a word about the laptop and Mrs. Corelli hadn't asked.

Kenzie popped the trunk and got out to make sure it was still there. She lifted the cover over the spare tire.

There it was, held in place with a bungee. She touched it to make sure it was still secure. The pearly surface was cold. How long had she been in the hospital?

She wiped her hand on her jeans when she straightened, as if she'd made contact with the stalker. Weird. She hadn't felt that way when she'd whisked the laptop from the apartment. Maybe the adrenaline served as an antitoxin.

Kenzie replaced the spare tire cover.

She slammed the trunk closed and got back into the driver's seat, reaching into her purse for her phone. There were several messages from him. The last one gave the address of his motel just in case and the room number, which she didn't know.

It didn't take her long to get to the motel, which wasn't far from her own apartment building. For some reason she'd forgotten how seedy it was. The main sign flickered intermittently and under it was a neon triangle that said Vacancies. Only a few of the windows were lit up. Kenzie squinted up at the room numbers from her angled space, looking for Linc's.

With the laptop under her arm, she went up the stairs and knocked. He opened it before she could blink.

"Come on in," he said, cheerfully enough. "My motel room is your motel room. Sorry about the mess."

"I don't care about that." She edged past the TV and the crumpled bags of takeout food on the table next to it. "Where should I put this down?"

Linc glanced at the laptop she held. One thick eyebrow went up but he said nothing. She didn't offer an explanation.

"Here it is." Kenzie cleared a space on the table. She set down the slim machine well away from his. Linc glanced at the kittycat decals and pearly cover.

"Anyone see you get it?"

"I don't think so. Didn't take me long."

"I was on the phone with my CO when you called. Couldn't blow him off in time. Sorry about that."

She felt a flash of guilt for not waiting. Linc accepted what she'd done without knowing the reasons for it.

"Mrs. Corelli asked me to get it—and no, she still doesn't know." She explained why and what was going on with Christine. "It was so hard to see her like that."

He knew better than to hug her. "Kenzie, there's nothing worse than seeing someone you love in pain and not being able to do a thing about it. But I think you have to trust the neuro team."

"I know. We all know that. Me and the Corellis, I mean. They're patient people. But I can't stand doing nothing." Kenzie sat down on the couch and rubbed her upper arms as if she was cold. The sound of her cell phone ringing deep inside her purse claimed her attention but only for a second.

Linc raised an eyebrow when she ignored it. "You going to answer it?"

"Every time I do, it's bad news."

He sat down on the couch but kept a reasonable distance. It made her want to jump into his arms and get held right. For a long time.

The phone stopped ringing, then started again in another minute. Kenzie swore and searched for it, looking to see who it was, then shaking her head.

"Oh no. Not him."

Linc refrained from satisfying his curiosity, looking elsewhere as Kenzie pressed the icon for forwarded e-mail.

"If you want to know, and I know you do," she said, "it's from Randy Holt."

He turned toward her. "Who?"

"He's a medic—he was with Frank Branigan when he died." She stopped, unable to say more. "Randy posted on the memorial page, looking for me. I don't know why. We were going to e-mail. But I can't. Not now."

Linc nodded.

She switched to the tiny keyboard screen and typed a fast reply, sending an e-mail instead of a text to avoid confusing abbreviations and to make sure Randy could get it. Linc couldn't see what she wrote. Kenzie filled him in.

"I told him it would have to wait," she said when she was done.

Holt responded right away. Kenzie's eyes widened. She held the phone so Linc could read the message on it.

Short furlough. Have to talk to you. Confidential. Urgent. Heading home in two days.

Linc hesitated for a bit before asking a question she might take the wrong way. "You sure about this guy?"

So far he'd listened to what she knew about Randy Holt without interrupting. That the medic was suddenly heading home was a game changer.

Kenzie shrugged uneasily. She didn't want to tell Linc that she'd sent him her phone number just in case. "I guess I should vet him with Donna."

"Do that," Linc said. "Before you answer him."

She sat up straight on the couch, firing off another e-mail from her phone. How secure it was, she couldn't say. But the stalker had hacked Christine's laptop, not hers. Yet. She couldn't give up all forms of communication.

There was no reply. Kenzie got up and paced, her arms crossed over her chest, looking around the motel room. "Yikes. This place is kind of a dump," she said, not rudely. "Sorry you had to sleep here."

"It's okay. Seen worse."

Kenzie noticed the formal clothes he'd been wearing the night of the accident, still slung over a chair. "At least you got to see your brother get married before all this happened." Absently, she smoothed the satin lapel of the jacket. "How are the newlyweds?"

"On honeymoon. No one in my family knows I'm here."

She gave him a rueful look. He stuck to the business at hand.

"So. Do you want me to open up that laptop while we're waiting?"

"It's password-protected," she said ironically.

The corner of Linc's mouth twitched but he didn't say anything.

"Nothing you can't handle. Go for it, super spy."

He unzipped a small duffel bag and took out a pair of transparent exam gloves, pulling them on.

"Are those necessary?"

"Your prints are on it. Christine's too. If anyone else touched it, the police might need those. Not mine."

She knew he meant the stalker. Something else she hadn't thought of.

He went over to the laptop and plugged in the cord, then lifted the top. Kenzie looked away. The screen stayed dark.

She looked back when she heard a jingle. Linc had taken his car keys out of his pocket.

"What are you going to do with those?"

"Not those. This." He separated a flat, three-inch gizmo from the keys and held it up for her to inspect. "Ten bucks at any office supply store."

"Do you expect me to believe that?" she asked scornfully.

He grinned at her. "No. You're too smart. I invented it. Among other things, it cracks passwords."

"That's nice," Kenzie said without much enthusiasm. She picked up her cell phone to make sure she hadn't missed a text from Donna and set it down again.

"I take it you don't want me to let the genie out of the bottle."

"No," she said flatly. "I don't."

"Can't blame you. But do you think you would recognize him if you saw him again?"

"Maybe. Why?"

Linc replied in an even tone. "While you were gone, I got hold of the TV reporter who was on the scene at the accident." He left out Kelly's part in arranging the meeting. "His name's Gary Baum. There's always extra video that doesn't get on the air. He said he'd look into it."

"And?" she asked.

"Whoever forced Christine off the road might have come back around to enjoy the commotion. He'd be a face in the crowd, but it was digitally recorded. If Gary Baum comes through, we might have something. There are a lot of ways to enhance video."

"Oh."

She actually seemed impressed. But he wasn't going to get her hopes up. "It's a long shot, I know. Thought I'd try. This creep isn't going to walk up and knock on the door."

He put the keychain gizmo into the USB port and waited. "I can pinpoint when this was accessed remotely without going into Christine's personal files or anything like that. At least we'll have a time line."

A minute later, he was into the hard drive and checking recent activity. "Someone got through the firewall an hour before you arrived at Christine's apartment."

Kenzie stared fixedly in the other direction. "Don't turn that screen in my direction, please."

"I'm not going to," Linc said. "He's not inside. But I'm looking for traces of his visit."

Kenzie seemed curious. "Does that count as evidence?"

"It could. Everything adds up. Slowly."

"That's the part I don't like."

"Get over it, Kenzie. Due process means something. The law is the law." He felt compelled to make the point. Right now Kenzie was relatively calm. Angry, she was an unstoppable force.

But this evening, she'd run out of steam and she looked exhausted. There were faint circles beneath her beautiful green eyes and her petite body was rigid with tension.

"I'm tired of thinking about it," she said finally. "What now?

Looks like Donna's not going to get back to me, and I don't want to watch TV."

There seemed to be an unspoken agreement that she wasn't returning to her apartment tonight. Linc was fine with that.

"Get some sleep." He gestured toward the bed. "Take the right side. It's less lumpy."

She didn't budge.

"That doesn't mean I'm sleeping on the left side," he added quickly. "You can have the bed all to yourself."

"Don't be so noble."

He pointed to the laptop. "I'm not done with this. It takes a while to explore an operating system, and I'm not even sure what I'm looking for."

Kenzie looked at the bed, frowning. "Okay. I guess I could lie down and look at the ceiling."

"Good enough. And hey, don't forget to call Mike Warren in the morning."

Turning her back to him, she scrambled onto the bed without pulling down the coverlet and stretched out, her feet on the pillows and her dark hair streaming over the end. Linc knew when he was being ignored.

"Kenz, you should stay on track with the investigation."

"I didn't know there was one," she said to the overhead light fixture.

He rolled his eyes, glad she couldn't see him. "There is. That's why a police lieutenant was assigned to the case."

"Hmph."

Linc returned his attention to the pearly laptop, clicking around. What he needed to do would take a while.

Kenzie didn't make a sound.

After a solid forty-five minutes of following faint, very faint tracks buried deep in the drive, he rubbed his eyes and turned around again.

She had curled up in the middle of the bed, her head resting on her bent arm. Out cold. It would do her good.

He had to wonder why she was so eager to connect with the medic concerning Frank Branigan. He knew Kenzie had never dated the man, but the strength of her reaction and the way she clammed up about it made Linc think something similar had happened to her.

Kenzie had been stationed overseas for two years. A beautiful girl like her must have gotten a lot of attention. And she worked closely with the soldiers she trained as dog handlers. Maybe one she'd loved hadn't come back.

He put that on the list of questions he wasn't going to ask. If she wanted to tell him, she would. In her own sweet time.

Hours later, Linc was still at it. An indeterminate light filtered through a gap in the curtains, making him look up. Almost dawn. He went back to what he was doing.

He'd taken a break from his poking around to copy every single photo onto CDs for Mrs. Corelli and Kenzie. A couple of them made him chuckle, forgetting she was asleep so close to him. The sound woke her up. She came over for a look at the laptop.

He clicked on slideshow, the fastest way to display them.

Some of the photos brought a wistful smile to her lips. "Thanks, Linc. It's nice to see them all again."

"You're welcome."

She straightened and turned toward the bed.

"Wait. I had a question," he said. "Do you want me to include one of Frank Branigan?"

Kenzie dragged a hand through her tangled hair and thought it over. "Yes."

"Will do."

She took a circuitous route around his stuff and her overnight bag on the floor and climbed back into the bed. This time she got under the covers.

He added a photo of the smiling soldier that he'd held back. Kenzie was right to include it. Frank was part of Christine's life. The visual memory therapy made intuitive sense.

He'd heard that musical memory was even more powerful. Once Kenzie was asleep again, Linc went ahead and copied all of Christine's music files, adding a separate list of titles by track.

Then he poked around in the laptop's operating system for a

while, examining apps and things like that. No alarm bells rang. But deeper down, there were blind alleys in the coding that didn't belong there, not in this make and model of laptop. If he had to guess, he'd say they'd been deliberately created and left open for someone to wander into, just for the hell of it.

Traps. He stayed out of them, not wanting to trigger a total patty melt that would destroy the hard drive.

There were signs that everything on it had been copied. Recently. Cleverly hidden malware he could have found but didn't want to deactivate just yet.

Christine could have downloaded it inadvertently or it could have been added. He wasn't going to blast it out. Not if he could use it as a tracer somehow.

Cat and mouse. Back and forth.

There was no doubt in his mind that the stalker was viewing whatever he saw, simultaneously.

Linc leaned back in his chair and thought for a moment. Then he picked up the laptop and turned it over, looking carefully at the thin plastic feet attached to the bottom of the case. He tested each, not surprised when one of the four gave slightly in his grip.

He used his car keys to pry it loose.

Interesting. It held a microtransmitter, not a type he'd seen before. It probably sensed electronic pulses from tapped keys. Had to be GPS enabled.

Linc pressed the plastic foot back into place. He wouldn't mind if the stalker paid him a personal visit. Kenzie wasn't going to be here after tonight.

CHAPTER 6

"You swear not to tell the cops everything?"

Kenzie and Linc were polishing off a fast breakfast in a room off the lobby. It was the usual setup for a budget motel: watery coffee from a large urn, powdered creamer in a jar. Do-it-yourself waffles. He dragged his last bite through the syrup on his paper plate and forked it into his mouth. The waffles were actually okay, considering the wafflemaker had an inch-thick crust of fossilized batter on it.

"Hadn't planned to," he said thickly.

"I just want to hear what Mike Warren has to say first. Then you and I can talk it over, see if what they say connects with what we know—"

"Damn little, so far." He hadn't told her about the blind alleys hidden in the laptop's code. Too hard to explain.

The microtransmitter, she knew about. She was fine with the photo CDs—they held everything Mrs. Corelli wanted to use. The music files were a nice bonus.

"You finished?" she asked, licking a drop of syrup from the corner of her pretty mouth.

Weary as he was, he smiled at the sight. "Yeah. Let's go."

Kenzie stayed a few feet ahead of Linc, walking with the lieutenant.

"The insurance adjuster contacted me," she was saying. "The company is sending a check for the replacement value of the car, and another for Christine's medical expenses so far. And they're covering a rental for me for the next few weeks."

"Good. Glad to hear it," the lieutenant said.

They came to the car, which Linc noticed had been moved to a different spot and cordoned off.

The other man gestured toward the wreck. "Here it is and here it stays. Not going to the scrapyard, in case you were wondering."

Linc was still several steps behind as they surveyed the black-and-yellow wreck for a few moments.

"I completed a preliminary examination of the car," the lieutenant said. "That is, what's left of it. Your friend was lucky, very lucky. In a strange sort of way," he added awkwardly, seeing Kenzie flinch.

Linc caught up with them.

"Hi there. I'm Mike Warren. Didn't mean to ignore you." The officer extended a hand as Kenzie moved aside. He seemed to assume they were a couple. She'd been too preoccupied to introduce them and shot Linc a look of wordless apology.

"Linc." He left off his last name on purpose. "Nice to meet you."

They shook hands. Mike Warren struck him as capable and intelligent at first glance. He was older, with steel-gray, close-cropped hair and blue eyes that didn't miss much.

"Okay. Let's get a better look at the vehicle, you two. I'll explain as I go. If you have any questions, just ask." He squatted by the wrecked car. "We look at the obvious things first. See the long dent on the driver's side?"

"Yes," Kenzie answered flatly. Linc sensed what she didn't want to say out loud. *Tell me something I don't know, Lieutenant.*

"That's a sideswipe. Now, that could have been an accident, but this one was a hit-and-run. If we can catch the driver, he or she will be charged for leaving the scene."

"And what if it wasn't an accident?" Linc asked.

"Off the record, someone may have tried to run Christine Corelli off the highway."

"Road rage?" Linc posed an obvious question.

"Maybe. Or something else. Let's say that he—for now I'll assume the other driver was male—spotted her at the wheel and deliberately caused an accident."

"Why?" Kenzie asked.

"To force her out of her car. A woman on a lonely stretch of road at night is an easy target. But these guys can be brazen. We've had victims taken from mall parking lots in broad daylight. A staged bump, an argument, and it only gets worse from there."

Linc and Kenzie exchanged a look. "Go on," she murmured.

"Getting back to Christine, we figured she couldn't call for help—there was no cell phone in the car or at the scene. We searched twice. Once on the day of the accident and once the day after."

"With the rollover and the crash impact, it could have landed away from the car," Kenzie said.

"True. I plan to send a couple of officers back, maybe go myself. Third time's the charm sometimes."

Linc knew that Kenzie had found the cell phone in Christine's apartment, but it wouldn't hurt if the police kept looking. There could be other clues awaiting discovery.

"Fortunately, the young lady had the presence of mind to trigger the GPS emergency alert in the car just before the crash. That's how the EMTs and the patrol cars got there so fast. I checked the reports and arrival times."

"No one's come forward?" Kenzie asked. "No witnesses?"

"None, sorry to say," the lieutenant cut in. "Outside of the TV crew, there was no one but us at the site until the rubberneckers showed up."

"How can you be so sure of that?" Linc asked.

The officer cleared his throat. "Okay, maybe not a hundred percent sure. But our cars got there first, plus first responders from other towns, in what, seconds? Then the TV crew. Damn reporters are all over our radio frequency. Sometimes I think they hack into our computers too."

"Anything for a headline," Linc said.

"Yeah, that's right. You in the media?" Mike Warren asked him.

"No. I have a couple of friends who are, that's all."

"Oh. Well, maybe you noticed that the story got dropped pretty quick. Not exciting enough, I guess."

Linc heard Kenzie draw in her breath. In control. She generally was. You had to know her to see her vulnerable points. He was getting a little better at it.

The lieutenant looked sideways at Kenzie. "I did have a couple of questions for you."

"Go ahead."

"Did Christine ever mention someone bothering her, being followed or harassed, anything like that?"

"No. Never. And we talked almost every day, saw each other often."

"How about an ex-boyfriend?"

"She was on good terms with him—his name's Geoff Chase. The others too. Not that there were that many," she added.

"Jealous pal?"

Kenzie shook her head. "Everybody really liked Christine."

"Any problems with male or female coworkers?"

"Not so far as I know," Kenzie said thoughtfully.

"That brings me to another thing," the lieutenant said. "We found her wallet, but there was no company ID in it or business cards. Just her driver's license, cash, and a couple of credit cards."

That was an interesting detail. Linc filed it away.

"I can tell you why. She had this funny little ritual," Kenzie said. "She would take stuff like that out of her wallet on Friday and put it back in on Monday. She used to say that the company didn't own her on weekends."

"What company was that again?" the lieutenant asked.

As if he didn't know. Mike Warren was playing by the rules of official question-asking.

"SKC. She was an administrative assistant," Kenzie said.

"Oh, right. The big military supplier."

"That's the one. Could we get back to the accident?" she asked.

The lieutenant didn't seem to notice who was directing the conversation. "Sure. Where were we?"

"Was it random or planned?" Linc said.

"Right." Mike Warren studied the wrecked car for a few more

moments. "Honestly, at this point it's impossible to say with absolute certainty. Keep in mind that the evidence hasn't been analyzed."

The equivocal reply seemed to irritate Kenzie, Linc noticed.

"However, if I had to call it, and believe me, we're weeks away from doing that"—he straightened and stood by the wreck—"I'd categorize it as an attack."

"Why?" Linc asked.

"Similar cases, no survivors," the lieutenant said simply. "We know what to look for. If that's what happened, the charge will be vehicular assault with deadly intent."

The lieutenant didn't add anything to that. He surveyed the car again and shook his head.

"Well, that about wraps it up for today. We're definitely on it," the police lieutenant assured her. "I'm coordinating the case."

She looked at her car.

"We're starting with the wreck. There are paint flakes all over that scrape and a whole bunch of dings. Sometimes we can match those to a particular finish or type of trim. Just so you know, we've got a couple of officers checking repair places and junkyards. That kind of grunt work often pays off."

"Any tips come in?" Linc asked before he remembered that Kenzie had ventured essentially the same question.

"Not yet. Keep in mind that finding solid clues and following up on leads could take weeks."

He hesitated, looking at Kenzie for a long moment, then spoke again.

"There were no witnesses that we know of, unless someone comes forward. And the victim—your friend, I mean—isn't able to help us."

Kenzie seemed lost in thought. "No. I saw her yesterday."

"We'll be talking with her parents at some point," the lieutenant said. "And some of her colleagues, of course. Anything you think of, just shoot me an e-mail or call. Everything helps to fill in the picture. We don't expect civilians to get into the nuts-and-bolts investigative stuff. That's ours."

"Right," Linc said noncommittally.

"Guess that it's for today." He addressed his next words to Kenzie. "Thanks for coming in. And please let me know if you or your friends think of other names. We have your contact info on file—and here's mine." He reached into his shirt pocket and pulled out a business card, handing it to Kenzie. "Nice to meet you both."

"Thanks." Linc said the one word for both of them. He put an arm around her shoulders and walked her away.

Kenzie shrugged off his light hold when they reached the impound parking lot.

"He didn't tell us anything."

"Don't assume that he has to," Linc replied. "It's an active investigation now. He seemed like he was on the level to me."

Kenzie picked up her pace. He lengthened his strides to stay at her side. He heard her cell phone ring and wondered who it was this time. She didn't dodge the call.

"It's Donna," she said, tapping the screen to pick up the forwarded e-mail. She turned the phone away from the sun's glare and read it. "Okay. She says Randy Holt was on that medevac. So he's confirmed as a good guy."

Kenzie was on her way to deliver Christine's insurance paperwork to SKC. She could have just mailed it, but she wanted to be sure it was with someone she could call, not lost in one of many mailrooms. The company was huge.

Linc had insisted on sweeping her car for bugs and other hidden things before they left the motel for the impound lot, using a radio-wave interceptor that looked like a glow-stick without the glow. His invention, of course.

Give her a smart dog any day.

But it was nice of him. He hadn't found anything and seemed surprised. Which didn't mean the stalker wouldn't try to plant a bug some other time, who knew when. Still, when Linc was around, Kenzie had to admit she felt a little safer.

Maybe Linc was everything she needed right now. She smiled to herself. He still got under her skin. In a good way. She had to admit it, if only to herself. Kenzie knew a good man when she saw one.

As far as what had happened two years ago—she couldn't live in the past. Not with Linc doing everything he could for her in the present.

She pushed her sunglasses up higher on her nose and turned off at the ramp. A windowless gray block, SKC headquarters came into sight over the top of distant trees. Even from here, it seemed immense, towering over the forested land that surrounded it.

Closer, she couldn't see where the complex ended, catching glimpses of many similar buildings from the road, clustered around the tower.

Kenzie almost drove past the guarded entrance. She hadn't made an appointment.

She pulled to an abrupt stop just before the guard station. Quickly, she flipped down the driver's side sun visor and ruffled up her hair in the mirror and bit at her lips to plump them. Confused and pretty—she could play that. All the guard had to do was call Melvin Brody's office and get her a pass.

He leaned out of the guard post as she approached, waving at her to stop before a striped bar swung into action. She came to a halt with the bar down across the hood of her car.

"Oh my gosh. I am *so* sorry," she squealed. "I didn't see that thing."

"Back up."

"Of course." She put the car in reverse and rolled it back a foot or two.

"Do you have an appointment?"

"Yes. With Melvin Brody."

The guard checked a small handheld. "You're not on the list."

"I should be," she said anxiously. "Could you call his office, please?"

"Just a minute." He seemed to be listening to someone on his earphone. "Can I see some ID?"

She moved the gearshift to park and scrabbled around in her purse, making him wait while she pretended not to find it at first. "Here it is!" she crowed, handing over her driver's license.

The guard went back into the post with it while Kenzie stared straight into the surveillance camera. She uncapped her lip gloss and used the driver's side mirror to apply it.

Slick and slow.

Kenzie capped the tube and pouted at the mirror—and at the security team with the cushy indoor gig watching the monitor feeds from the entire complex. They might even beg this guy to let her in.

He came back. "My supervisor said for you to wait at reception. Mr. Brody isn't in his office. But his temp assistant can talk to you." The guard handed back her license and a temporary pass with her name on it.

"Oh, okay. Thanks *so* much for checking." She smiled at him, sincerely.

A faint noise issued from his earphone. The guys must be razzing him. He didn't soften. "Park over there." He pointed to an area by the main entrance. "Fifteen minutes. Then you have to go."

"I appreciate it." Still in park, she put her foot on the accelerator and revved the motor. "The gate?" She pointed at it with one finger and winked at him. "I don't want to take it with me. I actually have done that a couple of times."

Which was true. He didn't have to know it wasn't because she was stupid.

He went back to push the button that lifted it and she drove through, bumping over three rows of tire-stabbers and past a Do Not Reverse sign. SKC was serious about physical security.

The fences surrounding the complex were twenty feet high, only partly concealed with greenery and topped with razor wire that glinted in the sun. The posts were topped with metal balls with dark glass lenses. More cameras.

Come on in. We're watching you, she thought. To be expected.

Kenzie was glad she wasn't going to be here long. She hoped Christine would never have to come back to this place. Kenzie only had to duck in and out, but even that seemed like a chore.

Kenzie got out of her car and walked quickly toward the entrance, stepping through steel-framed doors that whooshed apart, then closed behind her.

The receptionist looked up from a phone console and stretched her lips into a smile. She gave Kenzie a cool nod, indicating the chairs in the waiting area with a slight gesture. "Good morning. Please sit down. Brenda will be right out."

She went back to her work, fielding calls and talking into a small microphone attached to a headpiece.

Kenzie settled down, setting the tote with the papers and her purse in another chair. There were promotional brochures about SKC and its many subsidiaries on a low table in front of her, and military-interest periodicals. Casually, Kenzie leafed through the SKC material, sliding a few brochures for Lieutenant Mike Warren into her purse. It would give him something to do.

She picked up a company magazine that had fallen onto the floor and looked at the cover.

The stylized company initials took up most of it, fitted into a gray, blocky shape that looked like the main building's tower. No visual to show what SKC actually did or made.

Kenzie flipped to the first inside page, catching buzzwords in the introductory letter.

Diversified. Full-service. Steadfast commitment in a changing world.

Her gaze moved to the photo of the CEO, Lee Slattery.

White-silver hair and bright blue eyes. Impeccably groomed. Plausibly tanned.

His signature took up the whole lower half of the page. But then he didn't have much to say. Some publicity person had written the intro for him. She put the magazine in with the brochures as someone spoke behind her.

"Ms. MacKenzie? I'm Brenda White." She extended a hand as Kenzie stood up and turned. "Nice to meet you. I'm covering for Christine Corelli while she's in the hospital—I understand you're a good friend of hers."

"Yes, that's right." Kenzie responded to the genuine warmth in the other woman's voice.

"Mr. Brody explained about the accident. I hope she's doing better."

"Her doctors think so." Kenzie evaded a detailed response by bending down to pick up the tote bag.

"That's good to know."

Kenzie gave an acknowledging nod and didn't volunteer any more information. "Her parents wanted to make sure that her insurance paperwork got to the right person."

"I'll see that it does," Brenda assured her.

Kenzie slipped the paperwork out of the tote and handed it over. Brenda clutched it with both hands.

"It's nice of you to do that for her."

"Well, I'm the go-to gal for the little stuff," Kenzie said. "Her folks are doing the hard work. They're with her in the ICU every single day."

"Please let them know that SKC wants her back," Brenda said.

"I will. Thanks again."

She clutched the empty tote bag in her hand and slipped her purse strap over her shoulder as she turned to leave.

"Take care, Ms. MacKenzie." Brenda got a better grip on the sheaf of papers before she headed back to the unseen office.

The women exchanged farewells and Kenzie walked past the receptionist, who was engrossed in a call. With a brief wave, Kenzie exited through the steel-framed doors, moving quickly toward her car.

She drove out, ignoring the guard at the gate when he requested her pass. He came out of the post and watched her drive off, but he didn't shout. The pass was only good for one day. He wasn't going to come after her.

To her surprise, Linc was waiting around the first curve on the road, listening to the radio. She could see his hand tapping a beat on the back of the other seat. Kenzie slowed her car to a stop when their windows lined up.

He rolled his down. "Hey. How'd it go?"

"No big deal. I handed the papers to his temp assistant. What the hell are you doing here?"

Linc studied her face. "I wanted to see if the beacon I put on your car was working."

She should have known. "Is that necessary?"

"The readout is on this." He tapped the face of his watch.

"I can't see. And I don't believe you." Kenzie put her car into park, got out, and walked around.

He turned his wrist to show her. "Check it out. Your dot merged into my dot."

"Isn't that sweet."

He grinned. "It's not a problem to remove the beacon if you don't like it."

"No. It's all right. You're the only person who knows where I am most of the time now."

That didn't seem to have occurred to him. "Really?"

She nodded.

"So where are you off to?"

Kenzie shot him a mocking look. "You don't have to ask, do you?"

Linc laughed. "The beacon can't read your mind."

She rolled her eyes. "Thank God for that. If you want to know, I was heading to the drugstore to print out some of the photos for Mrs. Corelli. Where are you going?"

"Just running errands," he said. "Need anything from the electronics store?"

"I don't think so."

"Okay. I'm just picking up a couple of components."

Kenzie gave a little yelp. "Yikes—that reminds me. Yesterday my boss asked me to pick something up for him out in the boondocks. I forgot until you said that. So if my dot falls off your watch, you'll know why."

He smiled at her warmly as he bent his arm and rested it on the bottom of the window frame. The bicep under the flannel rounded up very nicely as he lifted a hand and chucked her gently under the chin. "Funny."

The friendly touch was unexpectedly intimate.

In fact, it triggered a dangerous sensation of giving in. She smiled at him, feeling weak. His brown eyes were dark and warm. She felt herself blush under his steady gaze.

Linc was the real deal. Maybe she didn't have to be so tough all the time. It was okay to be protected. More than okay.

Back when she'd had Tex at her side, she'd actually liked the feeling. Like all military working dogs, he'd been trained to maintain an invisible six-foot circle around her, and woe to anyone who crossed into it without her permission. Including guys she was dating.

"Kenzie?"

She snapped out of it. "Sorry. You knocked on my stupid spot."

"I'll have to remember that."

She shook her head in mock dismay. "Please don't. Let's touch base around four or five o'clock."

He nodded and turned the key in the ignition. "Works for me." His gaze stayed on her a moment longer. "Call me if you need anything."

"I will. Thanks." She glanced back at the gray monolith a little distance behind them and her mouth tightened. But when her green gaze met Linc's brown eyes, she managed a quick smile.

He raised his left hand in a quick good-bye wave and eased his car ahead of hers, rolling up the window again. She watched him go, then got back into hers and drove on, turning off on the road to the firing range.

Kenzie pulled into a gravel driveway and parked in the customer area, leaving the engine running. She took her chiming cell phone out of her purse, reading her boss's reminder to please pick up his gun and responding with a brief text.

At Hamill's now.

Jim didn't text back. He trusted her to get things done in her own time and her own way.

She scrolled through the messages, checking for a response from Randy Holt. Maybe he hadn't received her reply. Playing phone tag. Then she told herself he could be in transit, enduring a long flight home in a troop transport.

Kenzie tossed the phone back into her purse and put the car in gear again, swinging around to the back where the employees parked. The front lot was full. Norm Hamill's firing range was popular with law enforcement pros from several counties around plus the states bordering Maryland, along with federal officers of every stripe.

It was a big place, about a hundred acres all told, and the owner lived there, in a house adjacent to the main building, which housed his repair shop and retail business.

She got out of her car and looked into the near distance at the shooters who stood in a row, ear and eye protection worn per Hamill rules, their feet apart in braced stances as they fired off rounds at paper targets. Kenzie headed for the shop.

Norm Hamill smiled broadly when he saw her come in.

"Kenzie! Nice to see you."

"Hi, Norm. It's been too long. You look great."

He did, in a bearded, ball-capped, wrinkled way. He was a character and always had been.

"Liar. But thanks." He rested his hands on the glass cabinet in front of him, its shelves neatly laid out with various small items. "What can I do for you?"

"Jim sent me to pick up the gun you repaired."

"Of course. It's done. Good as new. I e-mailed him the specifics so you don't have to remember them."

"Good." She smiled back. "I don't think I could. Life's been crazy."

"Oh? Why is that?" But Norm didn't wait for her answer. Another customer stepped up to the counter and Kenzie realized that he'd been waiting since she walked in.

She moved aside to let him talk to Norm. A black, very interested nose appeared where the proprietor had been standing and sniffed. Kenzie leaned over and saw the rest of Beebee, a black Lab she'd trained for guard duty, wriggling with happiness.

The dog put his enormous black paws on the glass and rose to give her an enthusiastic welcome. Kenzie laughed and took hold of his collar. "Get down, Beebee. That's not allowed and you know it."

Obeying her, Beebee dropped to the floor and trotted around until he was on the customer side of the case and next to her.

He sat, motionless and solid as a boulder.

"That's better." Absently she stroked his big head while she looked at the contents of the glass cabinet. There was a selection of folding knives, and next to that, a tray of enamel tiepins in the shape of fish.

Leaping trout. Fighting muskies. She made a mental note to buy one of each for her father's upcoming birthday. He'd like them and her mother wouldn't shudder.

Kenzie's gaze moved to a wall plaque of a proud stag with antlers out to here, surrounded by a harem of adoring does. Definitely man stuff.

She wondered idly if Linc had anything like that around his house and decided that he probably didn't. He had an outdoorsy look, though—he just wasn't ridiculously macho.

"Sorry, Kenzie. Let me get you what you came for," Norm said to her before heading to the back room.

"Thanks."

He returned with a classic army-issue pistol in one hand and its removed barrel in the other. Then he set both on the counter and reached into a shelf she couldn't see, puffing when he straightened up with Jim's gun case.

"Don't know why this got put down there," he grumbled. "Ever since Adam went off to college, I can't find a darn thing."

"You must miss him." Norm was close to his son, his only child, and Adam had always helped with all aspects of the family business.

"Yes, I do. It was nice having him right there in his two rooms up above the shop, even with that awful music he played so loud. Now that they're empty, there ain't nothing but echoes. It's not like I can rent them or would want to—"

Kenzie wasn't really listening to the rest of it. "Empty? Really?"

"Not quite," Norm corrected himself. "There's his bed and a table and a chair and an amp." He gave her a curious look. "Why, Kenz? You looking for a place?"

"No—well, sort of."

"It's nothing fancy."

She took a breath, about to tell a fib that wouldn't hurt anyone.

"That's not important. There's a plumbing leak in my building. I was told the ceiling could come down at any time."

"Why now, you can bring your things and stay here until it's safe to go home," Norm said with spirit. "Carol will be thrilled. I warn you that neither of us will have a spare second to sit and chat with you, but it'd be a roof over your head for as long as you needed it."

More than a roof. It would be a safe haven, probably the safest she could find. Norm Hamill's shooting range was surrounded by a high fence topped with barbed wire, security-patrolled, and locked up tight at night. He and his wife Carol lived on the property and so did one or two of the staff. The longstanding customers tended to be protective of Norm, Norm's family, and Norm's friends.

And then there was Beebee. One hundred pounds of unconditional love with very sharp teeth. She'd missed having a dog in her life. "Let me think it over," she said, laughing.

"Don't," he said quickly. "Just come. We'd be glad to have you."

"I can give you an answer tonight. How's that?"

Norm shook his head. "It'll have to do."

She signed the invoice for the gun repair and left while he turned to another customer. She would call Linc first and ask his opinion.

Silence.

"Hello? Linc?"

Kenzie moved the cell phone away from her ear to see if she'd accidentally switched it off. It was on. Someone had picked up.

"Linc, are you there? What do you think?"

He finally answered. "Yes, I'm here. Sorry. I was—trying to think of something to say."

"Norm and Carol are really nice people. I've known them for ages and he happened to mention the room was empty. Stroke of luck, isn't it? Private entrance and everything."

A pause.

"What can I say? If you want to hide out at a shooting range, I guess it's a good idea."

The bad news, in his opinion, was that she'd be surrounded by men. Other men.

"Look, can you meet me there in an hour? I'd like you to meet Norm and his wife."

Sounded like a done deal. She wasn't really asking his opinion.

"Okay." He took down the directions.

Linc stood in the room that Norm's son had vacated, done with the grand tour. There was a nook with a microwave and a dorm fridge and a folding table, and she had her own bathroom. All she needed, really.

He cast a glance at the heavy-metal posters on the walls. One was peeling off at a corner and another had been torn and taped back together.

"Norm said I could take those down," Kenzie told him.

"You don't like them?" he asked dryly.

She only smiled and sat down on the platform bed. It held a sagging mattress covered with a black sheet with a few holes.

"He also said I should go pick out a new mattress and bedding. He gave me enough cash for both."

Linc shot her a look. "Sounds like you're settling in."

"No way. This is temporary."

"Did you tell them why you needed to stay here?"

"I will. Norm was busy with a customer in the shop. I couldn't just blurt it out."

"He and his wife oughta know."

"I'm going to tell them!" Her forceful answer had a defensive ring.

Linc figured that Norm wouldn't be shy about saying hello with a sawed-off shotgun if the stalker showed up. But if the gun-store proprietor didn't know there was one out there, he'd be in trouble. As far as Kenzie was concerned, she'd be better off if people she trusted knew what was going on.

Granted, it hadn't been that long since the accident and since she'd seen the frightening face. But Kenzie's go-it-alone approach wasn't the right way. And the man with the evil eyes wouldn't disappear if she pretended he didn't exist, even for a little while.

Linc folded his arms over his chest. "All right. Let me know when you do."

"Get off my back. And don't you dare tell them for me."

Misplaced belligerence. He could deal. "Fair enough. So, what can I do to help around here?" he asked.

She stood up and yanked the black sheet off the bed so hard it ripped at the holes. "So much for that," Kenzie muttered. She threw it on the floor, then bent down with a swoop and balled it up, stuffing it into an empty shopping bag.

"Anything else?" he asked pleasantly. "Want to make a Destroy list?"

She threw him a fierce look. "I know you won't believe me, but you wouldn't be on it."

Her way of saying he was right. Linc couldn't mess up that small victory with some stupid comeback.

She spent several more minutes investigating the small clothes closet and the tiny cabinets above the microwave, then disappeared into the bathroom and shut the door. He heard the sink faucet running and sloshing sounds.

When she came out, her dark hair was damp and pushed back behind her ears. The cold water she'd splashed over her face put color into her cheeks and wetted her lashes to spikiness. Without a trace of makeup, she looked fantastic. And a lot more composed.

"I was wondering," she began as if the argument hadn't happened. "If I went to buy the new bedding, would you pick out the mattress? It would save time."

"Huh?" His eyebrows went up.

"I don't need to test it," she said hastily.

"Well, I'm not going to be sleeping on it."

Kenzie didn't respond directly to his faintly mocking comment. "Let me explain. You're a guy. You don't know what it's like to lie down on a mattress with a store salesman grinning at you."

Linc could see her point. It was all too easy to imagine her stretched out on a satin-topped, brand-new double. Fully clothed, of course. But even so.

"It's on Norm." She reached into her pocket for a handful of hundreds. "Just get whatever mattress seems reasonable, so long as it's in stock and they can deliver it today."

His arms uncrossed but he didn't take the money. "Did I say yes to this? I don't think I did."

"Please, Linc."

He studied her, making her wait. The room was nothing to write home about but she seemed happy here and, all of a sudden, a lot less tense, judging by her body language.

He gave in. "All right."

Claws retracted, Kenzie patted his cheek. "Thank you so much."

A while later, he was tying a plastic-wrapped mattress to the top of his car. The deliveryman at Sammy's Sleepy-Bye hadn't returned from lunch and Linc didn't feel like waiting around.

The salesman who'd helped him get it outside dragged the hand truck back to the store.

"Come again!" he called and disappeared through the doors before Linc could say thanks.

He tugged at the last knot in the taut web and slammed the door on the cord that ran through the back. Should hold.

He went around to the front of his car and took his phone out of his shirt pocket to call Kenzie.

"Where are you?" she said when she picked up. "I got back from the mall an hour ago. I'm ready to make the bed."

"On my way. See you in a few." He'd just wanted to make sure she was there. He hung up before she asked questions about the delivery. Kenzie would have to ask someone there to help him with it.

She called again just as he pulled in and parked.

"I can see you from here. How come you brought it?"

He explained about the deliveryman.

"Okay. I'll be right down."

She ran to the exterior fence and unlocked the high gate as Linc waited. He went in and she relocked it behind him, waving him into a parking space nearest the side entrance that led to her hideaway.

Plenty of room. Most of the slots were usually taken. The place seemed quiet.

He got out and started to cut the cords with a pocketknife he kept in the car, then slashed through the plastic wrapping where the side handles were and yanked them through.

Kenzie looked on. "You didn't lift that on top of the car by yourself, did you?"

"No. The salesman helped. But I could if I had to," he added.

Unwisely.

Linc looked at the shooting range. There was no one out there. His gaze moved to the wide windows of Norm's shop and stopped on the Closed sign.

"Where is everybody?"

"They went over to the gun show at the fairgrounds," she explained. "Norm decided to take the rest of the afternoon off and go with them."

Linc groaned.

"I can help you," Kenzie insisted.

He gave a nod. "Let me get it down on the ground. Stand back."

Kenzie moved away from the car and watched as he took both handles and dragged the mattress off the top of the car. It landed with a soft thump.

"How heavy is it?" she wanted to know.

"Not too. More like awkward. And floppy." He put a hand on it to hold it in place. "The hard part is going to be the turn on the stairs."

"We can bend it."

Linc looked at the mattress. "Think so? With all this stiff plastic wrapping?"

"A friend and I did it once. The plastic helps it slide."

"Okay, I'm game." He turned and grabbed both handles. "Lead the way. I really can carry it myself. You get the doors."

She went ahead of him. Linc lifted the mattress with a grunt. He could feel his shoulder muscles protest but he managed. The asphalt was too rough to drag it. He rested it on the sill of the side door that Kenzie was holding open, then lifted it again to set it at an angle on the stairs that led to her room.

"I'll guide it," she said.

She actually seemed to like moving big stuff. But he was still doing the heavy lifting. He pushed it up several feet and stood on the entry mat, letting the door close behind him as she scampered up to the top of the mattress.

"Ready?" she asked.

"Let's do it."

At either end, she gripped and he shoved. The stairs were un-carpeted and the mattress did slide. She looked at him over the top of it, her green eyes bright.

"Told you it was easy."

The turn proved to be no problem. They used the same method to get the mattress into the room.

Kenzie gave it a triumphant pat, but Linc frowned when he looked at the platform.

"What's the matter?"

He rested, bracing the mattress against his shoulder. "Are you sure it's going to fit? You told me to get a double."

"I did?" She glanced at the platform. "I meant a full. That's a lit-tle narrower, isn't it?"

"I don't know. I hope they're the same. Measure twice, move once."

Doubt flickered across Kenzie's expression. "That's not how the saying goes."

"It'll do for now."

"Let's just try it." She curled her fingers around a handle and dragged it onward. Linc reached for the other one and helped her flip it down.

It hollowed in the middle and hung over the edge. "I'm guess-ing I got suckered," he said with annoyance. He looked at the label sewn into the side. "It isn't a national brand—the measure-ment sure isn't standard. The damn thing is about three inches wider than the platform."

"The length is correct," Kenzie said helpfully.

Linc lifted it back up again and leaned it against the opposite wall. "Yeah. Great."

"Sorry," she offered.

He bent over and ran a hand along the platform's edge, pushing gently on the long wooden bar that kept the mattress in place. It gave at one corner.

"Stapled. Not exactly quality construction." He thumped at it with a closed fist to pry it loose and did the same thing at the other end, straightening with the bar in his hand. He handed it to her.

"This can go in the closet. You get to explain to Norm."

"He won't care. You're a genius."

Linc hoisted the mattress and flipped it down again. "If you say so." He grinned. "At least the bed's flat."

Kenzie rested the bar in a corner and got busy stripping off the plastic while he watched. The luxurious satin top gleamed softly—he'd spent what she'd given him. When she was done, she had an armful of plastic that she stuffed into a bag on top of the crumpled rock-star posters.

With a sigh of happiness she sat down on her new bed. "Thanks so much. You really came through."

"I like protecting you from lecherous mattress salesmen. You don't need to thank me," he joked.

"How about a kiss instead?"

Linc was taken aback. He opened his mouth, too surprised for a second to say yes.

No never entered his mind.

Kenzie's slender arms twined around his neck and she raised herself up on her sneaker toes to make good on her offer. Linc let his hands slide over her body, stopping at the sweet curve of her jeans-clad hips. She flexed, catlike, arching her back to bring herself more tightly against him. Her moves were playful, feminine to the core, instantly arousing him.

He kissed her back, gently at first, then with searching strength. She didn't seem to want to stop. She nipped at his lower lip, then moved back a little, looking up at him with half-closed eyes as her hands moved into his hair.

Linc stood his ground, enjoying the stroking caress. One hand moved down to his jawline. Soft and tender. He wasn't used to her being this gentle.

"Nice," she said softly.

He tried to remember how to talk. Too complicated. He hadn't let go of her waist, but there was more air between them than he really needed.

"And enough for now," she added.

He came to his senses. She stepped away from him, not looking at the new mattress that seemed to be the only thing in the room. Linc glanced at the expanse of tufted satin with a flash of regret.

"We should think about it, you know," she said. "We can't just tumble into bed."

"Oh." He didn't need to think, he *knew*. He wanted her. Bad. "Kenzie . . . you can call the shots. Just tell me when."

Her mouth curved upward in an indescribable smile Linc would never forget. "Okay," she said.

After he'd gone, she flopped down on the bare bed, still vibrating from that incredible kiss. She hadn't planned to jump him.

But standing there in front of her, Linc was irresistible.

Kenzie indulged herself in a full-body stretch, trying to reach all four corners of the new mattress. She relaxed and curled into herself contentedly, daydreaming about Linc for a long while.

The memory of being in his arms was healing. There was no other word for it.

And, funky though it was, the little apartment was a safe haven. It wasn't wrong to withdraw and remember what it felt like to be peaceful.

She couldn't allow the stalker—or her thoughts of the stalker—to control her every waking moment. That would be like giving him uncontrolled power over her.

The sound of car doors opening and closing in the Hamill parking lot snapped her out of it. Everyone was back from the show.

She got up and went to the window, waving at Norm and Carol.

"Did the Sleepy-Bye guy come?" Norm hollered.

Kenzie raised the window to reply. "Yes. I'm all set," she said. "Got new sheets and everything. Nice colors, no flowers. Just in case your son wants his room back."

"Good work," Norm said.

Carol looked up. "Kenzie, you can put the new sheets through a couple of washer cycles. They're always so scratchy right out of the packaging."

"Thanks. I'll do that."

The Hamills got back to taking their purchases out of their car and Kenzie began to open the sheet sets. Staying here was a lot like living at home. But without parents. Speaking of that, she thought, she owed hers a long-overdue call.

Beebee padded into the downstairs room that held a washer and dryer after she entered. She spent some quality time with him and wrapped it up with a professional belly rub. The big dog couldn't get enough. Then he heard Norm whistle to him from the shop and got up with a sigh.

"See you around," she said. Off he went.

When the sheets were tumbling, she returned to her room and reached her parents in Germany. They were upset by what had happened to Christine, even though Kenzie left out a lot. Feeling a little guilty, she told them the same broken-plumbing fib she'd used on Norm. They were glad she was with the Hamills.

She promised to call more often. The last thing she wanted was for them to worry.

Evening was shading into night when she finished settling in. Kenzie made her bed neatly, even though she would be between the new sheets in another hour or so.

She'd gone out to pick up instant coffee and milk, and a few items for a light breakfast. Right now she was heating a cup of water in the microwave to make herb tea. Kenzie sat down at the small table and waited for it to beep.

Her cell phone rang first.

She rose and looked for it, checking the screen. It wasn't a number she had in her contacts. Hesitating, Kenzie answered on the last ring. The caller was gone.

The little screen went dark, then flashed again with an incoming text.

Randy here. Meet at Ridgewood Diner 10 am tomorrow?

Oh. The medic. He must be using a prepaid phone. That was why she hadn't recognized the number. She texted back.

Sure. See you there.

Kenzie went to the microwave, taking out the cup and dropping a tea bag into it. Her uneasiness didn't entirely go away. It couldn't be a trap, though. There was no place more public than the Ridgewood Diner.

She would get there first, request a booth, and face the entryway.

At 9:55, Kenzie was waiting at the Ridgewood Diner. She looked up when a young, slightly built soldier in fatigues pushed open the door of the crowded eatery, then was distracted by a waiter handing her the two menus she'd asked for.

"Thanks," she said absently.

"You must be Kenzie," a feminine voice said seconds later. "I'm Randy Holt."

"Ah—" Kenzie did a double take. The medic was clean-scrubbed, pink-cheeked, with straight hair pulled back into a regulation bun and big blue eyes. "I didn't realize you were—"

"Female. Yeah, sometimes I forget it myself. It's Miranda, really." She pointed to the block-lettered name on the front of her camouflage jacket. "The guys call me Randy."

"Got it." Kenzie felt a certain kinship, given her own spin on her real name. "Please sit down."

Randy slid into the opposite side of the booth and accepted the waiter's offer of a cup of coffee but handed the menu back.

"Nice to meet you. I can't stay too long, though."

"Sorry to hear that. I was planning on buying you breakfast."

Randy held up a hand to forestall her. "I just finished chowing down. The grits and gravy are talking back."

Kenzie laughed as she asked for plain toast to go with her coffee. The waitress nodded and left them alone to talk.

Randy dumped two packets of sugar into hers and stirred.

"I've been trying to reach you ever since Frank died. I, uh, don't really know what kind of relationship you two had, and the guys didn't know either . . ."

She paused, waiting for Kenzie to fill in the blank.

"We were friends," Kenzie said. "That was all. I couldn't say if he had a girlfriend." There was no need to mention Christine.

Randy looked surprised, then recovered. "I'm sorry. I guess I got the wrong idea. I was told he was separated from his wife and they weren't on good terms. That's why I didn't contact her."

"That's okay." Kenzie registered the concern on the young woman's face and took a chance. "Look, Randy, you can tell me anything. I won't spread it around."

"Maybe a friend would be better than a girlfriend." The medic hesitated but not for long. "I'll get right to the point, if you don't mind."

"Of course not."

"Look, there's no way I can be one hundred percent sure, but it's possible that Frank Branigan didn't have to die," Randy said bluntly.

Kenzie didn't flinch. Donna had said the same thing. They weren't here to talk about the nice weather this time of year. "Wasn't it insurgent fire?"

"Their MO. Hide and wait in an abandoned village. You know what the houses look like: mud walls, narrow doors back and front, no windows sometimes. His buddies said he went in first, a little too fast. Too dark to see. They got him first and escaped out the back. There's no question he took multiple handgun rounds right in the chest, probably from several shooters. I saw the wounds."

Randy's voice was unemotional. Her eyes told a different story.

"I cut a double-layer tactical vest off him in the helo when he was airlifted, tried to keep him from bleeding out. The surgeon was the one who noted a sniper shot in his back when Frank was on the table in the FOB operating room," the medic continued. "Long story short, that vest failed."

Kenzie swallowed hard. "Tell me more. I never wore one. I never got off the base."

Randy nodded. "Combat vests have the same basic design. Two layers." She used her hands to demonstrate. "Next to the body you have bullet-resistant fiber, Kevlar or something like it. That blocks handgun bullets, shrapnel and bomb frags. Basically, it works by absorbing the projectile's energy over a wide area."

Kenzie knew that much, but the review was useful.

"Over that are armor-plate inserts that can handle high-velocity ammo like rifle bullets—to a certain extent, depending on the caliber. And over both layers is a camo covering and webbing straps to hold gear. You know what I mean."

"Yes," Kenzie said.

"But Frank's vest was something different. Supposedly improved."

"Oh."

"When it came off, the fiber was hanging in shreds and more than one armor plate had cracked."

"Did you—were you able to keep it?"

"No. We don't, as a rule. And his was soaked in blood. It got tossed in the medical waste."

Silent, Kenzie pressed her lips together.

"Sorry," Randy said after a minute. "There isn't a nice way to tell the story."

Kenzie collected herself. "I know. I want to hear it."

"Gear fails aren't that common," Randy said. "But it does happen. A few years ago the army refused to send over a batch of sixteen thousand vests that didn't meet standards. Someone did their damn job that time," she added.

"That's good to know, but I—I honestly don't know how I could help," Kenzie answered.

Randy's blue eyes stayed on hers. "Someone has to. Donna spoke very highly of you."

"You met her?"

"Not exactly. She's a friend of a friend. We Skyped before I flew out, not through a military server. I used a computer at a foreign aid place. Neutral non-combatants, medical support. She went off-base."

"Oh," said Kenzie. "You were careful."

"Sometimes you have to be."

Kenzie nodded. She knew what Randy meant. Internet connectedness and social media were part of the army now, but soldiers didn't always want the brass looking over their shoulders.

"Some other medics have been seeing the same thing happen. Different places, other situations. Not that frequently. But often enough that it looks like a pattern."

"Is it the same brand each time?"

Kenzie knew there was rarely just one supplier for any military need. Requirements changed constantly, and contract specs varied from supplier to supplier. Her boss had taught her something on the subject.

"Yes and no," Randy said. "The failed vests are the same brand, but they don't always fail. Word is that a grunt who took a much worse hit than Frank survived. The fiber worked right and none of the armor plates cracked. Luck of the draw."

"And you don't know why."

"No. And that guy wasn't the only one who walked away. We can't figure it out and we don't want to start going up the chain of command until we have some facts."

"I understand."

"Just to clarify, the vests are army issue but not army-made. Frank's gear was tagged X-Ultra," she added.

Kenzie thought. That didn't ring a bell at all.

"There's a limit to what we can find out from over there," Randy persisted.

"I don't doubt it," Kenzie replied.

"I'm heading back tonight. So I was hoping—well, you knew Frank."

Randy was obviously determined to play the cards she held.

"Not that well." Kenzie met her gaze. But he had said her name when he was dying. The medic was nice enough not to remind her of that.

"Someone stateside is what we need," Randy said calmly.

Kenzie thought of Christine suddenly. It might be months before her friend knew about Frank's death. But she would.

"That's true." Kenzie faltered. "Although right now—is not a good time. I can't really explain why."

Truthfully, she wouldn't even know where to begin. But she understood the army creed that had driven the medic to find her. Her dad had lived by it; she'd always known it; Jim Biggers had it framed on his office wall. Since Christine's accident, she truly understood what it meant.

Never abandon a fallen comrade.

Randy Holt wasn't alone in her suspicions. She and the other medics didn't have enough facts to make a stink. The young woman had risked a lot by contacting her.

Kenzie, on the other hand, had nothing to lose. She pushed her coffee cup aside and looked straight at Randy. "I'll do what I can."

The medic seemed surprised. Her mouth curved up in a crooked smile. "You sure?"

Kenzie nodded.

CHAPTER 7

Linc looked at himself in the motel's bathroom mirror. Scary. He had overslept and he desperately needed a shave.

What a night. He hadn't fallen asleep until after four A.M. He rubbed his eyes hard and opened them all the way.

No female had ever given him a kiss like that. He hadn't been able to stop thinking about it. About her. Kenzie had rocked him down to the soles of his shoes.

Linc picked up the spray can of shaving cream and shook it vigorously, squirting a huge dollop into the palm of his hand. He slapped it on and looked around for his razor.

Not where he had left it. Maybe it ran away with the toothbrush. He didn't see that either. The housekeeper might have tidied up a little too much.

Linc hitched up the boxers he'd slept in and conducted a search. For some reason known only to housekeepers, she had moved the razor and the toothbrush to the side of the TV, where his cell phone was.

He picked up the razor just as his cell phone rang. Linc squinted at the number. Gary Baum. He answered the call.

"Hey. Did you get anything?"

"Yeah. Where are you?"

The reporter laughed when Linc gave him the address and name of the motel. "What's so funny?"

"That place is hooker heaven."

Linc didn't want to know. "Seems quiet to me."

Baum chuckled. "It used to be nice. But you know, new owner-ship," he said vaguely. "We did an exposé on it last month. *Knock, Knock, Who's There?*"

"I missed it."

"Too bad. Cops, CEOs—you wouldn't believe who we caught on tape. So when do you want to meet?"

Linc looked at the digital clock provided by the motel, then picked up his watch. They didn't sync. "In an hour."

"You got it." Gary hung up.

Linc had time to grab breakfast in a bag from somewhere after he got through the rest of his morning ritual. Good enough.

He had finished eating and was scrolling through the news on-line when Gary's loud knock resounded through the room. He left the page up when he went to the door.

The reporter stood there with his hands in his pockets again, looking a little chilly. "Got any coffee?"

"I didn't drink mine. You can have it." He indicated the capped takeout cup he'd left on the table.

"Thanks." Gary sauntered past Linc and looked at the counter-man's marks on the lid. "What have we here? Black, two sugars? How I like it. Great minds drink alike."

Linc managed a half-smile. He had to be nice to the guy. So far no money had changed hands.

Gary sat down in the chair Linc had just left and tapped a key on the laptop, glancing idly at the headlines. "Big day, huh? Flamingo escapes from the zoo. That's the kind of story I usually get."

He fiddled with the tab on the cap and took a slurp.

Ugh. Linc looked elsewhere, then busied himself picking up clothes while Gary drank his coffee.

"Thanks. I felt like I was in a frat house," the reporter observed.

"I wasn't doing it for you," Linc said. He tossed the balled-up clothes into a corner.

"Whatever." The reporter leaned forward and eased out of his jacket. He slipped a hand into an inside pocket and pulled out two silver discs. "Here's the accident footage, hot out of the sta-tion computer."

Looking for a CD drive, Gary set down one of the discs and gave Linc's machine a half turn with his fingertips. It bumped into Christine's closed laptop. The reporter looked at it and smirked, fanning himself with the other CD.

"Kittycats, huh? That yours?"

"Shut up, Baum."

Linc picked up the CD on the table. He set Christine's laptop aside and touched the button that opened the right drive on his.

The reporter watched him insert the disc and tap the keyboard to get it started. Linc adjusted the screen for a better angle to where he was standing.

"I can't see," the reporter said.

"Tough," Linc replied. The footage began with a herky-jerky pan around the accident scene. EMTs, highway patrol. Screaming sirens and shouted orders.

The cameraman had tried to get in closer, immediately pushed back with curses not aired on family-slot news shows.

Then Linc saw the part he remembered. The victim that he hadn't known was Christine, being lifted up on a spine board with a head stabilizer.

He could see how he'd mistaken her for Kenzie. The footage was blurred and her features weren't clear. But the long dark hair and her small size had been enough to mislead him.

It was amazing how different unedited footage looked. The station producers had to work fast with only seconds of lag time. He watched in silence.

There was the license plate. KENZYZ. The dark blue uniform of the angry officer who manhandled the cameraman away from the wreck filled the screen again.

"I cut out the Suds-Up spot," Gary said, yawning.

Linc kept watching.

The reporter and the cameraman had been forced back to the accident perimeter, where cars were slowing. A different officer made them move on. Linc hit Pause for each one, looking at the drivers and the passengers.

Bored, Gary put in his two cents. "The usual. Housewife in curlers with dumb dog. Traveling salesman. Two goobers in a pickup. Teenagers—now, they should let them learn what a nasty accident looks like."

"Just let me watch."

Gary shut up again. Linc saw nothing that set off alarms in his mind, and no one out of the ordinary. The CD drive stopped with a faint whirr.

"Ready for disc two?" the reporter asked.

"Yes."

Gary smirked again. "It'll cost ya." He rose and tossed the empty coffee cup in the general direction of the wastebasket. It landed on the floor. "You can keep that one. Nothing on it that everyone and his cousin hasn't seen."

"Listen, Baum—"

The reporter was moving toward the door, opening up his folded jacket. Linc could just see the curved edge of the second disc in the inside pocket.

The other man stopped as if he'd just thought of something. "Hey, you never did tell me why you're so interested in that accident."

"I don't have to."

"Is she your girlfriend or something?"

"No."

Gary shrugged. "I looked you up online. Some mentions but nothing much. No full-face images of you. Just a couple of crappy distance shots from your brother RJ's wedding and a ridiculous yearbook picture from Acne High. Nothing in between. Why is that?"

Linc curbed his temper. "I don't control what's online."

"Wish I could." The reporter put his jacket back on. "The accident didn't get a lot of page views either."

"Why should it? Something like that happens every day."

Gary Baum looked at him shrewdly. "I was thinking maybe that lady was married or something, heading home after a hot night with you. Then—crasho. Husband found out and now he's after you. Am I getting warm?"

Linc scowled. "Not even remotely."

Gary Baum looked steadily at him. "Huh. You're telling the

truth. Too bad. I liked my version. Well, see you around." He put a hand on the doorknob and turned it.

"How much for disc two?"

The reporter opened the door. "A thousand. There's an ATM right around the corner. Want me to wait in the area by the front desk? I could make myself a waffle."

"You do that."

Deal done. Linc was lighter in the wallet but not broke. Gary was gone and he was reviewing the second CD.

He'd taken the precaution of taking both laptops with him when he'd gone to the ATM. He'd also affixed a little gadget to the motel room door that would let him know if anyone went in while he was gone.

The reporter seemed a little too interested in who Linc was. Sneaky as Baum was, he still wasn't likely to find out why Linc barely existed online. The agency took care of stuff like that.

He'd come back with the money and found Baum munching a waffle in the parking lot.

Linc kept on pausing the CD on each car. He almost missed Baum's capsule descriptions from the chair he was in. At the sound of the reporter's voice, Linc sat up straight.

Not in the room. Baum had recorded his own comment over the on-scene audio for the next frames.

"Hey, Linc. How about him? Dresses like a fed, looks like a fed. Dark suit, forgettable face. You're not supposed to notice those guys. That's why he stands out."

Linc hit pause. Gary Baum was right. The cameraman had captured a neatly dressed man. Not old, not that young. Full head of tawny hair. Regular features. Sunglasses.

Unfortunately the shot was from the side and slightly blurred.

Linc let it run at normal speed. The man not only slowed his car, but pulled it over and got out.

For less than two seconds. Triggering an explosion of wrath from the cop he'd disobeyed, who stood in front of him. The man got back in his car, black but otherwise as nondescript as he was, and drove on.

Linc put the brief sequence on slo-mo and watched it again. And again.

The Maryland license plate had fall leaves, dull gold and brown, covering nearly all of the number. Strategically glued or a gift from Mother Nature, Linc couldn't tell. The car itself was medium-sized and boxy, the type purchased by the freighter load for government fleets. He could find out the exact model and other details when he dissected this image down to the pixels.

Kenzie took the time to visit the hospital's garden, dropping a coin in the donation box at the entrance and glancing at the sign. She followed a winding walk planted on both sides with fragrant flowers just past their prime.

Fortunately many of the shrubs were evergreens, carefully clipped. The garden would have been too depressing otherwise, she thought, once autumn was over.

The sign had mentioned that the garden was maintained by volunteers. One, an older woman in a canvas smock, looked up from her energetic digging as Kenzie passed, murmuring a hello.

There were patients on benches, soaking up the sheltered garden's sun. Some walked with relatives or nurses. In bathrobes and pajamas or wearing regular clothes, they had the same wan look from spending a long time indoors.

She nodded at a frail, stooped man, guessing that he'd once been strong and tall. He lifted a hand to take the arm of the woman who walked beside him, the wedding band he wore catching a spark from the sun. They both smiled at her and she smiled back. His wife, providing discreet support, guided him to a bench.

Kenzie found one for herself. In the shade. She figured no one else would want it and she could think.

She had said yes to Randy Holt's simple request, knowing full well that it was going to complicate her life, and without the slightest idea of how she could find out the information the medic wanted.

She leaned back and looked up at the brown leaves rattling on the sycamores. Kenzie told herself to just start somewhere and do something.

Besides, she had other things to do besides worry. Right now the Corellis were expecting her.

The elevator was full of white coats. She moved to the back into a corner, listening to them talk shop, not understanding some of the medical jargon. A lot of people exited on the cafeteria floor. She looked out at the large, tiled room as she moved out of the corner, taking a few steps forward. Absently, she recollected not wanting to go into it with Linc the night of the accident.

It didn't scare her now.

She was alone when the elevator stopped at the neurology floor, which had its own ICU. The complexity of brain trauma and disease made it necessary.

Kenzie saw Alf Corelli at the end of the hall. She went toward him and walked beside him the rest of the way to Christine's room.

"We have a surprise for you," he said in his rumbly voice.

She looked at him, startled by his words. Mrs. Corelli hadn't said anything about it. "You do?"

He nodded, exchanging a word or two with the nurses and medical staff they passed in the corridor. Everyone responded, even when they were in a rush.

"Looks like they all know you," she observed.

"Oh, I'm memorable," he said with a wry smile. "Must be the beige windbreaker."

Kenzie gave him a pat on the back. "It's a very nice windbreaker, but I don't think that's why."

She was sure that the older man's devotion to his daughter had earned him the admiration of the ICU staff, along with his wife. Between the two of them, Christine had never been left alone. They spoke to her, because they knew she could hear, even if she couldn't respond. And her mother sang to her every night as the late shift began, soft lullabies in her native Italian that Christine had loved as a child.

"How's Christine today?" Kenzie asked. They were nearly at the door of the private room.

"The last nurse I spoke to said she's holding steady. I missed the neurologist this time around. But Minerva said she took notes."

Kenzie managed a faint smile. Christine had sometimes complained about her mother's ability to keep track of everything. "That's a good idea. It's easy to forget what a doctor said."

"Minerva keeps them on their toes."

He pushed down on the lever that opened the door, moving ahead of her into the room. The shades were drawn and the overhead lights were switched off, with soft illumination provided by sconces. Kenzie took a deep breath and looked at Christine. Her head was nestled sideways into a comfortable pillow and her eyes were closed. If not for the medical gear connected to her, she could have been simply asleep.

But she wasn't. Kenzie moved carefully around tubes and wires, and pressed a kiss to Christine's forehead. Her friend opened her eyes.

Kenzie gasped.

When she straightened, Alf Corelli was smiling at her. "Second time today."

She looked at him, speechless, and back into her friend's hazel eyes and saw confusion and—she was sure of it—a flash of recognition.

"Chrissie, it's me. Kenzie." She slipped her hand into Christine's and had the odd sensation of the two of them being little girls again. Best friends forever. Maybe the forever was back.

Christine's eyelids drifted down. Kenzie let go right away. She could have sworn she felt a slight, very slight pressure against her palm. Christine was still here. Very much alive.

"I'm so glad you got to see that," Alf Corelli said quietly. "First time, her mother and I did. We almost didn't believe it. It happened right when the neuro team was in the room. Big moment. No cheering allowed. We all wanted to."

Kenzie could only nod. Christine's hand went limp and she gently withdrew her own.

"Thank you for coming so often. It's been very good for her. I'm sure she knows we've all been here, off and on."

Kenzie swallowed over the lump in her throat. "I plan to keep on doing just that." She took a moment to compose herself. "Where is Mrs. Corelli?"

Her husband shrugged. "Dunno. But she's never far away." He moved to Christine's bedside and began to stroke her hair.

Minerva Corelli came through the open door with a warmed, folded blanket over one arm and greeted both of them in a gentle voice. "Alf, there you are. The nurse at the desk said she saw you go by. Kenzie, how are you?"

"Fine, thanks, Mrs. Corelli."

The older woman waved the formality away. "I think you're old enough to call me Minerva, don't you?"

"I couldn't," Kenzie said, laughing. "Don't make me."

"Good heavens, we're more than family by now." She looked at her sleeping daughter and the two happy people that stood beside the bed, setting the blanket down at the end. "Alf, did Christine—"

"Yes. Again. She looked right at Kenzie."

"Oh, honey."

Kenzie went into her open arms for a mutual hug.

"It's a great day," Mrs. Corelli whispered. "For all of us."

She let go of Kenzie and went to her daughter again, spreading the warmed blanket over the lower half of Christine's bed, pulling it up as far as she could.

"Kenzie, I almost forgot to thank you for the photo CDs. I had some printed. They're over there on the wheeled table if you want to look at them."

"I'd love to." She moved aside to give the Corellis room and lifted up the first photo, of Alf and Minerva, beaming at the person behind the camera. Kenzie happened to know it had been Christine.

She was in the next one, laughing. Then there was one of her and Christine together. More friends. Pets. Happy times. A party she'd forgotten going to, with a lot of cheerful guests. Frank Branigan was among them.

With care, Kenzie put the photos into a pile and turned around again. A nursing assistant had come in to take away a tray of half-eaten sandwiches that Kenzie knew had been provided for the

Corellis. Tidying up, she picked up napkins and added a few fallen petals from a bouquet of deep red roses.

Mrs. Corelli noticed, and thanked her. The young woman smiled shyly as she left with the tray.

"Kenzie, I would swear Christine saw those when she opened her eyes." She waved at the vase and its lavish silk bow. "She loves roses."

"Yes, she does. That color especially."

She went over to see who had sent them, looking for the card. It was inside an envelope stuck into a little plastic holder, almost hidden inside the arrangement.

Nosiness got the better of her. She took out the envelope. It wasn't sealed. She opened the card inside.

With love. From Kenzie to Chrissie.

An icy chill seized her heart.

The Corellis were paying attention to their daughter. Christine's father had turned her head on the pillow so that her mother could brush her hair. They spoke to each other in low murmurs. Her mind awhirl, Kenzie scarcely heard them.

She slipped the card out of its envelope and studied the feminine handwriting. The florist had probably made it out.

The vicious bastard who'd run Christine off the road was playing a bizarre game. He'd paid for the flowers and ordered them delivered. She still knew nothing about the man, other than that he had to be watching both of them, had to know she would be at the hospital. Kenzie's whole body tensed with rage—and fear.

"So nice of you to send them."

She looked up, startled, at Christine's parents. "I should have told you right away."

"What's the matter, dear?" Mrs. Corelli picked up instantly on the change in her. "Told us what? You're shaking all of a sudden."

"Am I?"

"We felt shaky too, right after she first looked at us." Alf smiled understandingly. "It was almost too much to comprehend that Christine is on the mend. She may even be out of danger."

"No." Kenzie's voice was laced with fear. "Not yet. Please, I have to talk to you. Separately or together. But not in here."

Alf was alone with Kenzie in a room set aside as a quiet sanctuary, meant for families of patients. It was simply furnished, with abstract paintings in soothing colors and wide windows that looked out above the trees.

The urgency of her request had compelled both Corellis to leave Christine's room at the same time, but Mrs. Corelli had returned there, though not before giving Kenzie a hug.

She didn't think she deserved it.

Alf turned to talk to Kenzie. "I want you to understand something important."

Inwardly she braced herself.

"From the moment we knew how badly Christine had been hurt, Minerva and I never talked about how the accident might have happened or who was responsible," Alf said. "That was for the future. We knew that Christine needed us and that was all that mattered."

"I still should have told you something," she said stubbornly.

"You made a decision that you believed was right. We can't fault you for that. Not after all you've done for Christine and us."

"Do you think it was right?"

Alf heaved a sigh and clasped his hands loosely in front of him. "You were terrified. And if you assumed my wife and I were too overwhelmed to deal with something like that—well, you weren't wrong."

"I believed Christine was safe here with you two and all the nurses and doctors."

"She was. Nothing happened."

Kenzie fell silent. That was true.

"We assumed you'd met with the police and that there'd be an investigation into the crash sooner or later. Someone did call yesterday, by the way."

"Who?"

"A lieutenant. I think his name was Mike Warren. My wife was going to call him back."

"Let me talk to him first," Christine begged. "I wish I hadn't touched the card. It is something they can trace. I didn't get a screen grab of the man I saw in the laptop or even a good look at his face."

But what he'd said about the Corellis' daughter was seared in her mind.

Is that bitch Christine still on life support? Too bad.

The serene family room had seemed to echo with the words when she'd repeated them. Mr. and Mrs. Corelli had said nothing at first.

"He needs to know everything, from start to finish," Alf emphasized. "Write it down if you have to. Make sure it's all there. The vase and bouquet could be just as important." He rose to go back to his wife and daughter. "We didn't touch the flowers."

But she had. The nursing assistant had too. Still, the florist's envelope and the little card inside it connected to someone.

Mike Warren's business card was at the bottom of her purse. She dialed his direct number, hoping he wasn't out of the station. He picked up after several rings.

"Ridgewood PD. Lieutenant Mike Warren."

His tone was nonchalant. Just another day for him.

"H-hello," she began nervously. "This is Kenzie—Christine Corelli's friend. I need to talk to you."

He seemed to go on instant alert. "Do you want to come in? Where are you?"

"At Guilford Hospital. I think you need to come here. And bring an evidence kit."

She told him why, from beginning to end.

Linc arrived shortly after and stayed with Kenzie in the sanctuary.

"Best to stay out of the way," he said to her. "The room's getting crowded."

The staff members who had to be informed of the officers' visit to the ward didn't know exactly why the lieutenant and patrolman were there. No one seemed to think much of it. Cops were a familiar sight around hospitals.

But maybe not one wearing rubber gloves to carry a vase of roses with a plastic bag over it.

Through the glass doors, Linc saw him pass and head for the elevators. Lieutenant Warren walked by next, but he stopped when he saw them and came in.

"Hey. Just wanted to say thanks," he said to Kenzie. His manner was utterly unemotional. "We'll see what we can get from the florist's card and that envelope."

"My fingerprints," she said dully.

"Yes. And others. I'm going to talk to the owner today. I know the shop. I buy flowers for the wife there sometimes."

Kenzie nodded.

"What's going on with the car?" Linc wanted to know.

"It's still in the impound lot. We don't have the paint analysis back yet."

"Anything else?"

Mike Warren took out a small notebook with a pencil slot on the side. "Actually, yes. Kenzie, someone from SKC returned my call—Melvin Brody was the name. He left a message with the deputy on the night desk. It didn't get routed to me until this morning. Something about a company laptop missing from the office. It had been assigned to Christine. Know anything about that?"

"If she had an SKC laptop, I didn't see it," Kenzie said, adding indignantly, "and she wouldn't take one from work without authorization."

"No one said she did." The lieutenant flipped to the page he'd been looking for and tapped it with the pencil. "Tell me again. Exactly when were you in her apartment? I want to be sure I wrote down the right time."

Linc noted the other man's casual tone. Mike Warren knew what he'd written. He was making sure the details of Kenzie's story were consistent. Big cases got built on little things that jumped out at you.

"Monday afternoon," Kenzie replied. "I only went there because Mrs. Corelli wanted me to pick up insurance paperwork for Christine."

"Right—and she said she also asked you to find Christine's personal laptop, a white one, and bring it to the hospital. Where is that now?"

"With me," Linc said. Eventually he was going to have to explain a little bit about where he worked and say even less about what he did, then whip out the problem-killer government ID.

The lieutenant cast a brief but curious glance up at him. "Both of you handled it?"

"Yes," Linc replied. Mike Warren would be interested to learn that he'd worn gloves. And why Linc had them in his toolkit in the first place.

"I'll keep that in mind if I can get a look at it later."

Subtle. Neither Linc nor Kenzie chose to take the hint.

"There's a possibility the man you saw was actually in Christine's apartment and got to the laptop before either of you did. We need to dust it for prints—cover, keys, everything. Sometimes we can pick up a DNA bonanza just from the crap that gets into the crevices."

He seemed to assume they would just hand over Christine's laptop. Linc looked at Kenzie.

"Let me ask her parents if it's okay. And I can look for the SKC laptop at her apartment," she volunteered.

"All right," the lieutenant said. "If you want to drop it off at the station, I'll see that it gets to that Brody guy."

"We can take care of that," Linc volunteered.

"Great. Thanks. By the way, I don't think I gave you my card," the lieutenant said to him. "Give a call whenever."

"Sure." Linc's tone of voice was neutral.

"You going with her?" Warren asked Linc. "I mean, to the apartment."

"Hell yes," Kenzie said.

"That's a good idea," the lieutenant said. "If you're leaving now, I'll walk out with you two."

"Kenzie?" Linc asked.

She gave a slight nod. "I'm ready."

CHAPTER 8

Linc escorted her to his car after the lieutenant left in an unmarked SUV. She stayed closer to him than she usually did. He
liked the feeling of having her near. Too bad it took a second
shock to make her do it. He wished to God the stalker would
show up and get what was coming to him. So far, the bugged shell
of Christine's laptop in the back footwell—the Not Serviceable By
User insides carefully removed by Linc and hidden next to his
toolkit—hadn't attracted the stalker. Obviously he preferred the
weaker sex for his degenerate games.

Too bad mind control didn't work from a distance. If Linc had a
way to make the psycho flame out and self-destruct, it would save
a lot of trouble.

He opened the passenger door for Kenzie and shut it when she
slid in. He got in on his side and put the address she gave him into
his GPS. The moving road appeared on the screen. He shut off
the annoying voice.

They drove across town, silent at first. She stared ahead, lost in
thought.

"Anything else happen today?" he finally asked.

"What?" Kenzie turned to look at him. "Oh—yes. I was going to
tell you. I finally met Randy Holt. We had breakfast."

"What's he like?"

Kenzie smiled wryly. "She. Randy is short for Miranda. She's
great. Good-hearted. And tough."

"Medics have to be. What did she want?"

"I—I don't want to talk about Frank and all that right now," Kenzie answered. "Maybe later."

"Not a problem." He thought better of telling her about the arrival of the flag-draped coffin at Dover that he'd seen on TV. The Branigans would probably contact her and let her know about the funeral or memorial service.

Linc turned down the street that led to their destination. "That guy Baum sold me some of the outtakes from the accident video."

"Sold it? Is it his?"

"No. He's a two-bit reporter. It belongs to the TV station. I couldn't get it any other way. Not that quickly, I mean."

"Is that what he does on the side?"

"Sometimes, I guess."

Kenzie scowled with disapproval. "I'm not going to ask how much it cost you."

"Kenzie, it's not like I could get a court order and make the TV station give it to me. I'm not Mike Warren. We need a visual on the stalker any way we can get it, and I didn't feel like waiting."

"I can relate to that," she said ruefully.

"Same kind of thing happens with the good old military chain of command. Put in a request or make a complaint, and nothing happens."

"Randy said the same thing."

"Yeah? Why?"

"Later. Like I said."

"Okay. When you're ready I'd like you to look at some still frames from the video." He glanced at her set profile. "Not the accident itself. Just the people who drove by, gawking."

"Wouldn't Mike Warren want to see that too?"

"Maybe," Linc replied evenly. "I'm not done with it yet. You okay with that?"

"It's up to you." She was silent for a little while. "He's all right. Doing his job, I guess. By the way, I picked up some brochures about SKC when I was there. Not to be rude, but he could probably answer some of his own questions if he read them."

Linc smiled to himself. "Maybe so."

"It's a monster conglomerate," she said absently. "Lots of subsidiaries. I didn't get a chance to read the material myself." She looked into her purse. "And I forgot to give him the brochures."

"Don't worry about it."

She heaved a ragged sigh and clutched the purse, rolling the soft leather band that closed it nervously between her fingers. "What a day. I'm glad it's almost over."

"Do you feel better now that the Corellis know?"

"I wish I did. Maybe I will."

"You did the right thing."

"That's what they said." She sat up straighter. "I almost forgot to tell you. Christine opened her eyes today. Just for a few seconds, when I walked in—but I knew she recognized me." Her voice was threaded with joy.

Linc could guess why she'd forgotten. The innocent bouquet of roses. It amounted to a second message from the stalker. He'd hit closer this time. Linc didn't like it at all.

"You didn't forget, Kenzie. You just needed the right time to remember, that's all. That's great news."

Her mood brightened and she seemed a lot happier, talking to him about what Alf had said about it being the second time that day and how Christine was on the mend.

Linc turned the steering wheel to move the car into a parking space half a block away. He followed her into the building, scoping out the area. Nothing to see. His instincts told him their man was far away at the moment. Biding his time.

The same closed-in smell permeated Christine's apartment, slightly stronger this time. Kenzie hesitated on the threshold, letting Linc go in ahead of her.

He strode through the rooms, banging doors and making noise. "No one here," he called to her.

"Unless they're deaf."

Linc came out of the bedroom and stood in the middle of the living room. "Nice and neat. Except for that thing."

He went to the hutch, looking down at the tumbled papers and files Kenzie had left behind twice. "Is this where the laptop was?"

"Yup. In the bottom cabinet, charging."

Linc squatted on his haunches and used a stray piece of paper to move the doors. She'd left them both open. The second time, when she'd grabbed the laptop and cord, even more paper had tumbled out.

"Then maybe the other one is in here too."

Kenzie walked over and bent down to look. Linc tsked and waved the protective paper at her. "My prints are all over everything in this place," she told him. "There's no point in my being careful."

"Okay." He smiled easily. "Then start going through this stuff. There might be something worth keeping."

"Don't you want to find the SKC laptop first?"

"Not necessarily."

She sat down cross-legged and leafed through miscellaneous papers and files. "What a mess. She has her college essays in here. *The Dichotomy of Quotidian Experience.* What does that mean?"

Linc got up and began to look elsewhere. "Exactly nothing." He let his gaze roam over shelves and tables and furniture, doing a purely visual sweep. He was trying to get a deeper sense of the place, guessing who might have come and gone, not really looking for the laptop. Kenzie could find it if it was here.

He heard her stuff the papers back into the hutch and the sound of a cardboard box being dragged out. It landed with a thump.

"Here it is," she said. She kept the box flaps parted and looked down into it. "There's the SKC logo right on the cover. Should I open it? Does it matter if I get my fingerprints on it?"

"Hard to say. Mike Warren isn't going to return it right away."

She looked at him quizzically. "How do you know that?"

"Because this is a stalking case and that's a company computer and he has to check it. I think the police know how to do a little hacking."

"But not at your level," she said.

"Well, no," he conceded.

They exchanged a glance. She got to her feet and lifted up the box. "Let's fire it up and see what you can find out."

Linc used paper to lift the laptop up at a diagonal, keeping it in the box and looking underneath. "There's the cord." He stopped.

"Um, I think Christine keeps rubber gloves under the kitchen sink."

He went to look and returned with a pair of hot pink, nubbly-fingered dishwashing gloves. "Better than nothing." He drew them on one by one, stretching the rubber thinly over his large hands. "Actually, they're not too bad. Not really my color, though."

"How come you're so careful about not getting your prints on things?"

He smiled as he flipped the laptop open. It was a solid machine, sheathed in matte black metal. "Sometimes it's not a good idea. They're not on record or anything. I'd like to keep it that way."

Linc pushed a button and it started up. He took out the gizmo on his keychain and hummed as it did its thing, watching the changing screen.

"Lot of firewalls," he commented. "Nothing special, though." His tone was casual but his mind had switched into high gear. A giant military supplier wouldn't let a laptop just walk out the door.

Icons began to pop onto the screen. Documents with titles enlarged themselves as he stacked them like index cards, alphabetically.

"Looks routine so far. Purchase orders, spec sheets, production runs."

"Is it classified?"

"Not seeing the big black stamp."

"What about Christine's work e-mails?"

"Stored on SKC servers." He sometimes forgot that Kenzie didn't spend her workdays staring into a screen like everyone else. "But she did save some, I just caught a glimpse of that file. Hang on—I want to look at these."

He meant the alphabetized documents.

Kenzie waited while he flipped through them. "And . . . R. S. T. U. V. And . . . X. Y. Z. That's all."

"Wait a minute. Go back to X. Put that one on top."

Linc tapped.

Kenzie studied the document, not reading it but looking at the title. "X-Ultra. That's what Randy was talking about. I didn't know SKC owned the brand."

She went to get her purse, searching for the brochures she'd forgotten to give to Mike Warren, opening two before she said, "Bingo. New product. There's the logo."

Linc glanced at it and enlarged the document even more. "It's not on here. This is just text and half of a schematic. Care to enlighten me?"

She seemed as baffled as he was. "Frank Branigan was wearing X-Ultra body armor when he was shot. Randy said it failed."

Interesting. And noted as an open circle on an important intersection of his mental grid. "Why?"

"She didn't know. Some of the other medics in country confirmed other instances in the last few months. X-Ultra is a new product." Kenzie stopped talking for a minute. "I think Frank was wearing it in a photo he posted. I thought there was something different about it."

"You'll have to show it to me. Not on this computer."

She gave a brief nod. "Randy said the armor apparently does work sometimes. Just not all the time. Which means—"

"Bad design. Shoddy testing. A couple of extra dead soldiers here and there. But who's counting?" he asked grimly.

Kenzie took a step back from the laptop. The room was growing darker and they hadn't turned on any lights. It glowed, emitting a faint hum.

"She wanted me to help her find out why."

"And why you and not someone else?"

"Because she thought I knew Frank better than I did." Kenzie looked up at him with troubled green eyes. "And it seems that Donna sort of recommended me, if that's the right word. I got the feeling no one knows the whole story, but Randy seemed sure of what she was saying. She's keeping her head down, though."

"So should you." He turned the laptop on its side, looking at the bottom.

"Mind if I ask what you're looking for?"

"Location transmitter." He investigated the plastic feet. "Not in these, but there could be one inside the case. I'm going to make sure."

Turning the laptop right side up again, he tapped into a program stored on the gizmo and started a bug scan. "Nothing," he said a few minutes later. "SKC must really trust Christine. Or else they're just lazy about security."

Kenzie began to pace, then stopped when she came to the window, peering out through the gap between the side edge of the curtain and the frame. She turned to look at Linc. "Just checking. It's getting to be a habit."

"Good. We still don't know what he looks like."

They exchanged a long look. "Christine does," she said after a while.

"Don't be too sure of that," Linc pointed out. "She may never remember who hit her or anything else about the accident."

"What if she knew him before it happened? Christine and I were super close, but that doesn't mean she didn't have a few secrets."

She was finally thinking in shades of gray. Linc suppressed a smile. It didn't come naturally to her.

"That was always a possibility, and he could work at SKC. But keep in mind that the X-Ultra problem isn't necessarily linked to what happened to her."

"I wonder if Frank contacted her on that."

"He wasn't a whistleblower, he was a soldier—lived by it, died by it. Sounds like only a few medics were aware of problems with the armor."

"I don't think it's a coincidence," she said with a trace of heat.

"One way or another, we have to have proof."

He clicked out of the files and shut the laptop down, removing the gizmo from the USB port and reattaching it to his key ring. "You can carry it to the car. I'd have to keep the gloves on, and I don't want to be conspicuous."

He began to peel them off.

"Are you going to keep it?" she asked.

"For now."

"But what about—"

"The lieutenant can wait. It'll take me several days to copy and analyze everything on it—files, drives, hidden stuff."

"Is that legal?"

He went into the kitchen to put the gloves back.

"SKC doesn't know where it is and Mike Warren doesn't have to know," Linc said when he came back.

"What if he asks me about it?"

"Stall. Say you couldn't find it. He can't confirm that. The Corellis have a lot of other things to worry about, and he's not going to ask them to retrieve it."

"So he asked us. On behalf of Melvin Brody, who is not a nice guy," she warned him.

"Warren is making nice. He has to go to SKC to question her coworkers—that's routine. Returning this thing would give him a reason to be there."

"Just so long as it gets returned, Linc." Kenzie hoisted the box.

He only shrugged.

"Tell me one thing. Are you going to hack into SKC servers with this?"

"It's an option."

"You could go to jail for that."

He smiled. "They would have to catch me."

"And that would never happen," she said with a dash of scorn.

"I don't make too many mistakes, Kenzie."

"Sometimes I wish you would," she sighed. "Let's get out of here."

"Where are you headed?"

"Back to Hamill's," she answered curtly. "I have to talk to Norm and Carol. Then I'm going to grab Beebee and go for a long walk."

"Is that smart?"

"I can't stay cooped up. I'm going nuts as it is. He's good protection. Don't forget that I trained him."

"Right. You mentioned it." He looked around the empty apartment. "Are we done here?"

"I hope so," Kenzie said, heading for the door with the box cradled in her arms.

Chapter 9

A week later . . .

L inc heard a vehicle pull into the parking lot of the motel and
waited for the sound of a car door opening and closing.

Nothing.

Mildly curious—and bored with wading through the technical
files on the SKC laptop—he got up for a stretch and moved to the
side of the window to look out without being seen himself.

A sport ute. Vaguely familiar.

He was surprised to see Mike Warren finally get out and head
for the motel office.

No call, no contact. Why was he here?

He picked up the phone by the unmade bed when it rang.

"Hello," said the woman at the front desk. "There's someone
here to see you. Mike Warren."

"I'll be right down." Linc didn't feel like inviting the lieutenant
in or cleaning up. He looked at himself in the mirror and frowned.
He had a habit of running a hand into his hair when he was concentrating hard, which made it spike. Right now he resembled a
pissed-off cockatoo.

Linc couldn't find a comb. No time to shave.

The room was too warm and he hadn't added anything to the
jeans he'd thrown on first thing. He was bare-chested and bare-
footed. He grabbed yesterday's polo shirt and yanked it over his
head, then located his sneakers.

Good enough. The process of making himself presentable was

irritating. Even though he'd been forcing himself to keep reading the endless files, he still didn't like being interrupted.

Warren turned as Linc came into the lobby area. "There you are," he said pleasantly.

No apology for showing up unannounced. Linc didn't extend a hand for a shake. "What's up?"

"Nothing much. Just wanted to talk."

The woman behind the desk got busy with whatever it was she'd been doing.

Linc nodded toward the door. "We can go somewhere."

"Lead the way."

Out in the parking lot, the lieutenant stopped by his SUV.

"Let's take my car," Linc said. No way was he going to get into an unmarked. He had no idea why Mike Warren had showed up out of the blue, but it wasn't a social call.

"No problem."

Something about the lieutenant's manner was different. He couldn't put his finger on it.

"Mind if I ask why you're staying here?" he asked.

"It's cheap. And it's reasonably close to Kenzie's apartment."

Warren nodded. "Quieter than it used to be. We raided this place a couple of times last year. Still keeping an eye on it."

Gary Baum had been truthful.

"And you happened to see my car, so you just stopped by," Linc said.

"Not quite. I'll explain."

Linc unlocked the car and they both got in, making small talk as he drove to a park by a river, one that he'd scoped out several days ago. Not too many people and it had exercise structures and a running track—he'd hit it a few times to blow off steam and get some exercise.

The frustration of the task he'd assigned himself had been getting to him. So far, the SKC laptop didn't seem to hold any secrets, and the clogged hard drive was excruciatingly slow.

He glanced into the rearview mirror, not seeing anything that bothered him. There had been nothing from the stalker since the roses.

"How's Kenzie?" the lieutenant asked.

"Fine. She spends a lot of time with Christine," Linc replied.

"I understand from Mrs. Corelli that she's improving."

"So I hear." Kenzie had kept him posted on that.

He pulled into a parking space and indicated a bench under a willow tree.

It was right by the river, per training that had long ago turned into reflex. Electronic eavesdropping would be tough for anyone listening in, though not impossible.

The lieutenant matched him stride for stride as they walked to the bench.

"Nice day," he said affably.

"Yeah," Linc replied, irked by the other man's seeming assumption that he had nothing to do. But then, he couldn't explain to Warren that he had been dissecting the SKC laptop and was getting nowhere.

They sat down and watched the river flow for an idle minute.

"Guess you're wondering why I wanted to see you," the lieutenant said.

"A little, yeah." Linc didn't bother to ask how Warren had gotten his address.

"I realized last time we talked that I didn't know your last name."

"That would be because I never mentioned it."

The other man chuckled. "Right. And I didn't want to ask the Corellis. So, I, uh, ran your plates."

That was why he'd walked them to the hospital parking lot.

"I was curious. No offense, but in this type of case you cover all your bases."

Linc knew what was coming. He folded his arms over his chest, listening more to the birds in the willow tree than to the lieutenant.

"I got the basic screen. Full name, address, date of birth. You're an organ donor. After that, nada. Level Five block. Access to subject information restricted."

Linc sighed.

"That's federal, isn't it?" The lieutenant looked over at him. "But not the FBI. Those guys comb their hair. You with the agency? The army?"

"Want me to lie?"

"No, of course not." Mike Warren seemed awfully pleased with himself. "I did get your last name. Nice to meet a real Bannon."

Linc braced himself, prepared to field irrelevant questions about his brother RJ and the Montgomery case, but the lieutenant seemed inclined to stop while he was ahead.

"Look, I know your connection to Kenzie is personal. But that doesn't mean you have nothing to contribute. Going forward, if you can help, it would be just between you and me. Totally off the record."

Linc knew what Mike Warren was getting at. Different databases, different protocols. Not a lot of sharing. The lieutenant was way out of his league, but he had the guts to ask. Linc respected that.

"Happy to," he replied. "But there are limits."

"I understand." Mike Warren got up and looked toward Linc's car. "Okay. I have to get back to the station. I'll let you get back to whatever you were doing."

"Sorting socks."

The lieutenant grinned. "My apologies for the interruption."

"Christine . . . look at me," Kenzie said gently.

The dark-haired girl rolled her head on the pillow. She concentrated on focusing, mostly on Kenzie's face.

"Hey," Kenzie said with a smile. Christine responded with a soft sound. "Do you want to see more pictures?"

A nod.

It seemed to Kenzie that they were making progress—it had been six days. They were halfway through the photos Christine's mother had had printed from one of the CDs. Looking at them seemed to make Christine happy. But she tired easily and sometimes cried.

Mrs. Corelli held up another. It was the photo of the two young women out for a day on the water, paddling toward whoever was taking the picture.

"What do you see?" Kenzie asked.

Christine studied the picture, her lips moving without a sound. Her eyes brightened as she suddenly answered. "You. Me."

Mrs. Corelli's eyes widened over the top of the photo. "Very good. That's right."

Kenzie wanted to shout, pump her first in the air. Real words—the first Christine had spoken since they'd started.

Dr. Asher had told them not to expect much at the beginning. But he'd been all for it. In less than a week, Christine had improved enough in other ways to leave the ICU soon and transfer to a neurological rehab center.

Recovery from brain trauma was a complex process that involved the help of many. Basics first.

With the help of a physical therapist, Christine had managed to get out of bed and find her balance. Then she'd taken a couple of wobbly steps before sitting back down, exhausted but triumphant.

Kenzie had watched, desperately wanting to help, not knowing enough to do it right until her next try on the following day. Slowing down to Christine's pace made Kenzie stumble sometimes. Mrs. Corelli was a lot better at it.

The number of steps increased each day. The therapist explained that walking was critical to avoid muscular contracture. They'd taken turns massaging her legs before those first steps.

Fine motor control was aided by allowing her to feed herself when the nutritional IV was removed from her arm. They improvised and they figured things out. Small chunks of cheese beat pudding when it came to getting a grip. Liquids—milk, juice—really did find their own level. Spoons flipped like acrobats and landed on the floor. But Christine was getting the hang of it, little by little.

The mental exercise of image and word recognition was by no means the easiest of all.

Mrs. Corelli was still holding the photo so her daughter could see it. Kenzie looked at Christine, who'd sat up straighter, leaning forward.

"Canoe," she said suddenly. The word came out a little garbled.

"Yes." Kenzie fought to keep from bawling. "That is definitely a canoe. And you and me. On the river a year ago. We can go again."

Mrs. Corelli put down the photo and took her daughter's hand. "You are amazing, do you know that?"

Christine yawned, her eyes half-closed. Her mother and Kenzie had to smile. A few seconds later, the nurse came in, glancing at the chart and making a note on it.

"Hello, everybody. How are we doing today?"

Kenzie looked toward her friend. Maybe, just maybe, Christine could answer that for herself.

"Fine," she said clearly. The single word echoed in the quiet room. Christine nestled back into the pillow and closed her eyes again.

"How about that." The nurse looked from Kenzie to Mrs. Corelli with a pleased expression. "Keep it up, you two."

They got Christine settled in for the night and were packing up to go. Alf was on his way.

The Corellis felt a little easier about leaving their daughter these days. But Kenzie knew they still coordinated the times of their departures and arrivals carefully. There was never more than half an hour between one leaving and the other arriving.

Mrs. Corelli picked up a tote bag stuffed with unopened cards and letters. "Oh my. I was going to put these around the room. Maybe we should save them for the rehab center."

"Good idea. I can open them," Kenzie volunteered.

"Would you? Thanks so much." She handed her the tote bag.

"There must be a hundred letters in here," Kenzie said.

"I didn't count. But maybe there are."

They both paused in the doorway of the room for one last look at Christine, who had been sleeping through their low-voiced conversation. Then they moved down the hall to the elevators.

"She's really doing well, Mrs. Corelli."

"I know. But she's not out of the woods yet."

The elevator arrived before they even pressed the button and Dr. Asher got out.

"Hello, ladies. Heading home?"

They didn't answer, but launched into an immediate report on Christine's progress instead. He laughed.

"That's wonderful news. Thanks for filling me in. I'll stop by and see her."

Mrs. Corelli warned him that Christine might be asleep as they got into the elevator. They rode down to the lobby and parted affectionately, heading for different parking lots.

Home was still at Hamill's. Kenzie hadn't worked up the nerve to go back to her own place yet. She'd had the mail held at the post office and she could pick it up anytime.

She hadn't for the last three days, just too busy.

Back at her room, she greeted Beebee, who grunted in his sleep, blissfully happy that he was allowed on the new bed. She had bought a fuzzy blanket for him to protect the coverlet.

Kenzie gave him a pat and reached for a DVD. The movie was lightweight and forgettable, exactly what she needed. She slid it into the DVD reader of the funny little TV she'd bought for herself. Jim hadn't been kidding about keeping the direct deposits going.

She clicked the remote and watched for a while, then dozed off.

Beebee's dog dream woke her—he must be chasing flying hamburgers, his legs twitching in his deep sleep. She moved, realizing she'd been lying on the remote. The movie was over and the TV screen was blue. Kenzie switched it off.

She was definitely awake. But it was too late to call anyone, even to chat.

For something to do, she reached for the tote of get-well cards for Christine. It was better than opening real mail. No bills, just good wishes.

Most of it had come to the Corelli house, though a few had been sent directly to the hospital. She would save the envelopes. She wasn't sure which addresses Mrs. Corelli had.

She'd opened at least twenty when she came to one with something in it about the size of a credit card. But the envelope was the square shape of an expensive greeting card and addressed by hand. Probably someone had sent along a refillable coffee card or something like that as a gift.

The handwriting was a little hard to read and feminine—it was from someone named Mary Dee. She glanced at the return address somewhere in Maryland. Kenzie didn't know the person or the town.

She opened the envelope and a small laminated card with rounded edges fell out onto the bed.

Christine's face was on it, smiling in a small photo next to gray block letters that Kenzie had seen before. SKC.

Had she left her ID at a friend's house? Nervous, Kenzie pulled out the greeting card the wrong way, looking at the empty white back with puzzlement before she turned it over to the front. The art was tasteless. The words *Let's Get Wrecked* danced beneath a drawing of a smashed-up car.

Feeling sick, Kenzie opened the card.

> *Give the ID back to the bitch. She should be more careful.*

Carefully, she closed the ugly card and set it aside even though she wanted to rip it to shreds.

She and the Corellis had agreed not to talk about the stalker unless it was absolutely necessary. For nearly a week after the roses there had been nothing.

Not that long, she thought. The letters must have been in the tote bag for a couple of days. The stalker had sent the card a day or two before that. She looked at the return address. Mary Dee. M.D.

MD was the postal abbreviation for Maryland. The street address wasn't legible and the town was probably bogus. Dropped in a box somewhere in the state. The postmark was real. The whole thing looked believable enough to get someone to open the envelope without thinking.

He had sent it to the Corellis' home address. The stalker seemed to know more and more about where to find anyone who was close to Christine.

She curled over, her stomach in a knot of anger and fear, clenching her fists. Beebee, still half-asleep behind her, was aware that she'd moved, and he shifted position. Kenzie collapsed next to him. His broad back was warm against hers. The sleeping dog felt like an island of safety.

Kenzie didn't want to turn off the light. She wouldn't sleep. She stayed right where she was.

Linc woke up late, feeling groggy. The SKC laptop sat on the desk where he'd abandoned it after midnight, its screen dark. He was half-tempted to give it back.

Let Mike Warren take a crack at it. But, he thought irritably, he would have to tell him about the possible SKC connection to X-Ultra if he did. The lieutenant didn't have the clout or the manpower to investigate a company that size. By Linc's guess, Warren was about five years away from full retirement. Figuring out what the hell was going on at SKC could take ten.

The accident scene tape hadn't generated anything he would call solid data. Kenzie had said she'd look at it, but he didn't have particularly clear images yet. He'd picked it completely apart, retrieving the embedded geotag coordinates to identify the location of the wreck. But after this much time, he knew investigating the site of the accident was a lost cause.

Why in hell had he thought he could do it by himself? He was going to have to rethink his strategy.

He pushed the coverlet halfway down his body and crossed his arms behind his head. Linc stared at the overhead fixture, his new best friend for the last several days—he'd actually felt like talking to it a few times.

Kenzie had called but she hadn't come over.

During the day, she was at the hospital a lot, and she was needed there. Christine was making real progress. Linc felt guilty for not being able to do more.

The evenings were another story. For the last week, Kenzie had headed back to the shooting range and disappeared behind its high locked gate. To see her, he would have to be let in, get the once-over from Norm—and she and that dog were now best buds.

Worse, she hadn't invited him there. The promise of the sensual kiss they'd shared still tantalized him. She had seemed so willing, so open. He'd responded, that was for damn sure. And stopped. He hadn't wanted to take advantage just because she needed him.

Being a gentleman was driving him crazy.

Linc flung the covers completely away and headed for the bathroom to soak his head, disgusted with his own self-pity. He stepped into the shower and turned the water to hot. When he got out and got dressed, he reached for his phone and called her.

He wasn't going to mention one word of what he'd been thinking. Right now he wanted to hear her voice more than anything. Somehow that was what he'd missed the most.

She picked up after several rings.

"Hey, Kenz. It's me."

"Hi, Linc."

He heard a background clamor that didn't make sense. She was someplace that echoed. He heard a few shouts and yelps too. "What are you doing?"

"Climbing the walls."

"Kenzie, you need to take a break and calm down. I keep telling you that."

"Hang on," she said. "I'm sending you a picture. Wait for it."

She hung up. Linc looked at the screen in frustration. A few seconds later, the photo arrived. Kenzie had held the phone above her head with one hand while she clipped a safety rope to a climbing harness that strapped around her hips and thighs. There was a vertical rock face behind her, dotted with colorful hand grips and toeholds.

He studied the picture. The harness was interesting—could be well worth his while to get a closer look. Been a while since he'd rock-climbed anything, real or fake. It was big fun. But she wasn't smiling. He called her back.

"I get it," he said. "Guess we can't talk if you're heading up."

"Nope. That's the idea."

He frowned.

"All I want to do is crawl up a hundred feet. Inch by inch. You can't think about anything else. Clears the mind."

"Yeah, falling off cliffs will do that."

She laughed without humor. "Don't worry. This place doesn't let anyone climb without a safety rope."

"Good. Mind if I stop by?"

There was a pause. "It's a public place."

He grimaced. Not exactly a *sure-I'd-love-to-see-you*.

"I'm on my way." Linc knew something was the matter with her. Just not what.

When he entered the climbing gym and walked to the railed side area outside the towering walls, he saw her on the floor.

The harness looked even better in person, cupping her curves from the waist down. Improving them, even. She unclipped the safety rope and handed the business end of it to an instructor to use for someone else.

Linc's gaze followed the rope to its secure fastening on a steel beam high above, then moved down to her as she walked over.

"Hi," she said tonelessly, adjusting one of the gloves that covered only her palms.

"Good climb? You sounded like you needed a major workout."

"I'm not done."

"Mind if I watch?"

"You're here. Why not?" She wiped sweat from her face with chalky fingers that left traces of white. Her body was tense. Rock climbing tightened everything.

He hadn't been expecting a flirty conversation. Kenzie's ability to focus was intense to begin with and all-consuming when she was doing this. She wasn't thinking about him.

So be it. He liked looking at her.

The instructor came back with a different rope.

"Want to go up again?" he asked her. He didn't even look at Linc. Kenzie moved away from him, clipping the rope on.

"See you in a bit," she said over her shoulder.

Linc waved.

She pulled herself up with grace and strength to a double handgrip and went from there. The small bag of powdered chalk at the back of her harness bobbed as she found footholds, then began to climb in earnest. Shifting her weight. Bending her body backward to tackle a difficult overhang.

He was mesmerized.

Kenzie reached the top in her own sweet time. He had a crick in his neck from watching. Rappelling down, she bounced lightly off the wall to slow her speed. Enjoying the free feeling.

But she still wasn't smiling.

When she landed again, she bent over with her hands on her knees, easing her lower back. Then she straightened and un-clipped the rope for the instructor to take, strain evident on her face.

More slowly this time, she walked back to Linc, taking heaving breaths that hollowed her midsection.

"That was ten," she announced.

"You went up the face ten times?"

"Maybe it was twelve."

"Take a break."

She nodded. "I guess I should. Nothing like going up a fake rock and coming back down. Over and over again. It's just like life. Only here I get to be in control. Not the stalker." Her voice cracked.

"What the hell happened?" he asked in a low voice.

Kenzie smacked the chalk off her hands before she wiped the sweat from her forehead. There was still a residue that left a mark. He wanted to reach out and take it off himself with a wet thumb.

Then he realized the mark was partly smeared blood.

She was inspecting her palms. "I didn't even feel that."

Linc looked over the railing and saw the split in the skin as she flexed her fingers down. She'd come here to push herself past her limits.

"Enough. Get out of the rig. Are you trying to kill yourself?"

"No. I had someone else in mind."

He knew who she meant. "Go change. Let's go somewhere else."

Kenzie didn't argue.

They stopped at a drugstore first, to buy salve and a roll of gauze for her palm. Back in the car, he wrapped it deftly and man-aged a decent-looking flat knot to hold it in place.

"Thanks."

Then she told him about the card.

"I let myself think he was gone for a while, Linc. He's never going to be gone. He won't stop. I was terrified. I still am."

At least she was able to say so.

"You can't take it out on yourself."

She turned her eyes, intensely green, to him. "I feel a little better."

"Don't say that. Your hand is a mess."

"It will heal."

Linc gave a sigh of pure frustration. "Kenzie, listen. And don't swing at me if I ask you a question—"

She cut him off instantly. "I haven't told anyone besides you, but I will. Mike Warren can have the card to keep with the roses."

"And the Corellis?"

She reached for her purse. "I'll call them right in front of you. Is that enough?" Her bandaged hand snagged on the strap of her purse and she flinched. "I wish I didn't have to."

He could see blood beginning to seep through the white gauze. Linc caught her wrist as gently as he could, but she pulled it away with a low cry.

"Listen to me, Kenzie. You're not a human shield. You can't protect the Corellis or Christine by putting yourself in harm's way."

"That's not my intention. Not anymore. I admit I did try to do that at first, but—"

"But what?"

Her eyes shimmered with unshed tears. "Now you're here."

Kenzie twisted herself into his arms and stayed there, her face buried in his shirt. He stroked her hair and soothed her as best he could. "Yes, I am," he said softly. "For as long as you want me."

CHAPTER 10

Linc slid a zip-locked baggie across the diner table to Mike Warren. "There's the card and the envelope. Kenzie's fingerprints will be on both. She didn't realize what it was until she opened it."

Mike read the words on the front through the clear plastic. "Looks like the bastard's having fun."

"In his way."

The lieutenant turned the baggie over to get a look at the back. "Did he sign it?"

"No. The envelope had a fake name."

"You said she found it in a tote bag that Mrs. Corelli gave her. I assume the other cards were legit."

Linc nodded. "I think so." He took a smaller baggie out of his shirt pocket. "Almost forgot. Here's Christine's missing ID."

"Another piece of the puzzle." The lieutenant slipped the baggie into the inside pocket of his jacket before the waitress came over. The place was quiet. In fact, they were the only patrons.

"Menus for you two?" she asked.

"No thanks, Louise," the lieutenant said. "Two javas will do it."

She gave him a smile and went off to fill the order.

"She knows I tip the same for a steak dinner or a cup of coffee," Warren explained.

"Nice of you," Linc said.

The lieutenant grinned. "I believe in good community relations."

And he was wearing a wedding ring when he said it, Linc thought.

Warren waited for the two coffees to arrive before he spoke to the business at hand. "I'll have the lab dust the envelope and the card, check the flap glue for spit and shed cells, see if we can pull some DNA. He's starting to leave a trail we can follow."

"Speaking of that—did you ever get out to the scene of the accident?"

"Yeah, as a matter of fact."

"Find anything new?"

"Not at the site. The detective and I decided to walk north and south of it, a half mile each way."

Linc raised an eyebrow. "And?"

"Nothing to the south. But we found an area on the shoulder to the north that was interesting. This would have been about a quarter of a mile from where the accident happened. I took a bunch of pictures."

Linc had noted the lieutenant's roundabout way of making a point before. He sipped the coffee, which was strong but fresh-tasting, and let the other man talk.

"You might not know what I was looking for," Warren began.

"Try me."

"Ha. I didn't delete them off the camera, got it right here." He patted the pocket of his jacket. "My wife looked at them, wanted to know why I took so many. I told her, you know, art shots, fall colors."

Linc nodded patiently.

"Anyway, the area caught my eye because it was shaded by maples, but only in that one place. South of there, toward the accident site and after, it's mostly scrub oak and pine. Looks like hell. The vines are choking it all to death."

Linc was familiar with the rampant greenery along I-95. The highway maintenance crews didn't whack it back until it started to grow over the signs.

"The maples caught my eye because they were so yellow, but they still had all their leaves. We got closer, I could see they were the Norway type—they grow close together. Like a giant umbrella, know what I mean?"

The botany lesson had to have a point. "Tell me," Linc said.

"The ground under Norway maples generally stays fairly dry, even in heavy rain. So we found some deep tire tracks. A double set, side by side. Not that recent."

"Okay."

"We figured two cars had swerved off there, one right behind the other." Mike Warren stirred his coffee. "I photographed the treads first. Then my guy measured and plotted the distances in a sketch—photos distort information like that."

"Makes sense." Linc thought of his struggles with the digital video.

With an appreciative audience, Mike Warren was warming to his subject. "We took soil samples to compare to the dirt we scraped out of Kenzie's tire treads. There's a lot of reference points: type of soil, seeds, vegetable matter, dead leaves, mud—we can match it all."

Linc was impressed. "You think Christine was forced over more than once?"

"No. I didn't say that." The lieutenant looked at him levelly. "It could be that she pulled over first."

Linc was a lot more interested now. "Why?"

"Because she knew the other driver. Let's say he honked and she looked into her rearview mirror and thought, oh him. He's a casual acquaintance, a coworker—someone she isn't afraid of. He honks again and points to the shoulder of the road and she pulls over. Doesn't get out, though."

Linc got the idea. "No footprints under the maples."

"Not a one."

Linc leaned in, pushing his cup of coffee aside before he folded his arms on the table. "Go on."

"They talk for a bit. But for some reason she's picking up a weird vibe from the guy. Christine takes off. He follows."

"And then he forces her off the road."

"That's what I was thinking. If the soil analysis confirms a connection, it's something to go on." The lieutenant patted his jacket over the inside pocket. "So is this."

Linc leaned back, thoughtful. "Are you thinking coworker?"

"Yeah. Because of the ID. That didn't fall out of her wallet—I saw the wallet before we returned her effects to her parents, looked inside. It was the kind with plastic slots for credit cards and her health insurance and store discount cards. All of them tucked in nice and tight."

Linc felt compelled to play devil's advocate. "Really? Kenzie told me that Christine wasn't that organized." He didn't have to mention that he'd seen her cluttered paperwork for himself.

"She worked at a company with serious security," Warren said. "She had to keep track of her ID."

"Granted. Could be, though, that her ID card was stolen from her purse at SKC and she didn't notice it was gone."

"Maybe," Mike Warren sat back with a dissatisfied look on his face. "But so what. We still have no clue as to who the guy might be and no evidence to help us get an arrest warrant if we find a likely suspect."

"You might. Soon."

"I'll let you know about the soil samples. Helps us with probable cause and judges like that kind of stuff. Conjecture, not so much."

"That's your department," Linc said.

The lieutenant groaned theatrically. "Last time I winged it, I got told to take off the tinfoil hat and stop talking about my imaginary friends."

Linc thought of something else. "What about the wreck? Forensics find anything useful yet?"

Mike Warren finished his coffee and set the cup down with a clink that resonated in the empty diner.

"We got the paint analysis back. The other car was black—it's a type of paint that's been used on, oh, about ten million vehicles in the last fifteen years."

"That narrows it down," Linc said dryly.

"Yeah," Mike replied. "But it kinda fits the profile for our guy when you think about it. There doesn't seem to be anything too different about the stalker. He just doesn't stand out one way or another."

Linc shifted in his seat, feeling a little frustrated. "He'll trip up sooner or later."

The lieutenant nodded. "Maybe he already did. Want to see the photos from the shoulder?"

"Sure."

Mike Warren pulled out the digital camera and turned it on. He handed it over to Linc with the first frame in the viewfinder, then turned to look for the waitress and get the check.

Linc studied each image. Dirt. Mud. Crushed leaves. Tire tracks squeezing it all into rippled patterns. A measuring tape stretched out on the ground for size reference.

There was a skyward shot of the maples with crowded, skinny trunks, growing like weeds. Then a close-up of the thickly clustered yellow leaves that had blocked the rain.

For the finale, a wide shot of the tracks on the shoulder with the detective in it. Linc used the zoom function to look at the tracks again. Definitely from two different cars.

To his eye, they had been made at the same time. Lieutenant Mike Warren was onto something.

Kenzie continued the work of packing up, filling a paper shopping bag with get-well cards and trinkets. Mrs. Corelli was chatting with Christine. Her outward manner was cheerful, but Kenzie knew how frightened the older woman was inside.

Alf was too tough to show much emotion. But even he was shocked that the stalker knew their address, had dared to send the trashy card. At the moment he was in the parking lot, moving things around in their car to find room for everything they were bringing home and the few items that were going to the neuro rehab center.

The outpouring of love and support expressed in the many cards Christine had received didn't negate the one from the stalker. She'd handed it over to Linc hoping it would be the last.

Maybe, maybe not. They both knew that.

She added a small stuffed bear to the shopping bag. "This is full."

Christine looked her way and said something that wasn't clear. More and more words seemed to be coming back to her, almost by the hour, but putting them into sentences gave her trouble.

"I think you said to bring everything, honey. Is that right?" her mother asked.

Christine nodded eagerly and Kenzie smiled at her.

"I will," Kenzie said softly. "Don't you worry."

Now more than ever, the vulnerable look in Christine's eyes made Kenzie want to be strong for her. The transfer to the rehabilitation center would happen in the next few days, which intensified her feelings of protectiveness.

Christine would ride with her parents in a patient transport van, not an ambulance. But it would be the first time she'd been outside of the hospital.

They had been told that she might become disoriented, even difficult, in the new setting, but not for long. Dr. Asher had explained there were bound to be a few setbacks, but that Christine was making steady progress toward recovery.

The rehab center was homelike, Mrs. Corelli had said. Families and friends were encouraged to visit. Kenzie hadn't been there, but she had a feeling the place was more open than an ICU.

She quelled her nervousness as she picked up the file of printed photos. There was just room enough in the shopping bag to slide them in.

Christine waved a hand to get her attention. "Photos," she said.

Kenzie stopped what she was doing at Mrs. Corelli's approving nod. "Do you want to look at them before they get packed?" she asked.

"Yes." Christine scooted over in the bed and patted the empty space beside her. "Come here."

A big smile brightened Kenzie's face. That counted as a complete sentence. "You bet."

She scrambled onto the bed and opened the file. The idea was to show the same images each day and add in different photos as well.

The party picture with everyone in it was one Christine hadn't seen yet. Kenzie hesitated. Frank Branigan was in it. So were a whole lot of other people, having a grand time in colorful party hats, blowing on horns and teasing each other with feathered roll-ups.

Christine leaned over to look at the photo before Kenzie could decide whether to show it. "New Year," she said. Then she began to slowly name the guests.

Mrs. Corelli beamed at both of them. "Look at you two. I wish I had a camera."

Kenzie smiled at the suggestion. Christine nudged her with an elbow as she pointed to the photo. "Lisa," she said. "Molly. And Frank."

"Yes," Kenzie said. "That's him. He looks happy. It was a great party."

The cemetery was quiet and well-maintained. She walked through it, her face somber, looking now and then at the tombstones to either side. The military graves had flags, and sometimes a memento left by a surviving buddy.

She spotted a full bottle of beer, cap on, propped against a tombstone next to a spray of silk flowers. The flowers and the label on the beer bottle were sun-faded. Both had been there a while. She hoped whoever had left them knew that the offering was untouched.

She stopped in front of Frank's grave. The earth over it was fresh, without grass, a temporary marker in place.

Kenzie had attended the funeral a few days ago without telling Linc. She'd kept her distance, standing at the edge of the crowd, not knowing, for the most part, who was family and who were friends and who were simply respectful or curious. She recognized his parents and ex-wife from his Facebook page, and that was about it. But there had been a lot of people to pay their last respects to him.

She had murmured the responses of the funeral service with everyone else, echoed the final amen, but she wasn't done—and she wouldn't be until they found out why his armor had failed.

Kenzie knew it was a tall order. But she had to try. She also knew Linc wasn't going to quit.

She stood looking at the rectangle of earth, leaves drifting down from the trees around her. The afternoon sky was cloudy and the air was cool. She put her hands in her pockets, wishing she had some small thing to leave to mark her visit, but both were empty.

Impulsively, Kenzie bent down and pressed her hand against the earth in an inconspicuous place. The light imprint barely showed.

"That's from me and Christine," she whispered. "She'll visit on her own some day. Not just now."

She straightened and offered up a silent prayer that it would be soon if all went well. But it was a reality that Frank's tombstone might be installed and grass grown over the dark earth before her friend was able to walk here on her own.

Kenzie tried to shake off a sudden sense of foreboding. If Linc were here, he'd guide her back to the wandering path that led out through the gates.

But he wasn't. She turned and walked away, alone.

When she had gone through the stone gates, a man stepped out from behind the thick trunk of a gnarled old tree. He walked to Frank Branigan's grave and stood near the spot Kenzie had pressed.

Looking down at it, his eyes glowed with hatred. He set his heel where her hand had been and obliterated the mark she'd made.

"I'm glad that Christine is doing so well. She's lucky to have you around."

Jim Biggers was sitting behind his desk, his gaze on Kenzie, concern in his eyes. His directness was comforting.

"I owe you for that," she replied. "Thank you again for the time off."

"Not a problem. We all miss you, but that doesn't mean I'm asking you to run back."

Gruff. Unsentimental. Kind as could be. That was Jim.

"It's hard to believe I've been out for a week and a half—and you all survived," she said lightly.

"Seems longer."

It did to her too. A thorough explanation of everything that had happened wasn't possible. Christine, Frank—she'd gotten that far and stopped. Then there was Linc. She wasn't going public with the particulars of that relationship—or her feelings for him—just yet.

Kenzie sighed inwardly.

The training sessions for the day were nearly over. She listened to the familiar commands coming faintly through the office windows without paying much attention to them.

Jim cleared his throat. "I didn't know him, but I'm sorry to hear about Branigan. Sounded like he died for no damn reason."

"I didn't tell Christine that he had."

He drummed a pencil on the desk, then stopped suddenly. "I almost forgot to ask—any leads on the accident?"

"No. It's still listed as a hit-and-run." That was true. "They're investigating." That was true too. She wasn't sure how to tell Jim about the stalker. He would go ballistic and she might just break down a second time.

There were other things she wanted to talk to him about first.

The clock ticked in the quietness between them. Kenzie watched the hands move to five on the dot.

Jim got up.

"I'm off duty." Leaning over his desk, he switched off his computer and shuffled his paperwork into rough order.

"I won't keep you."

She knew he was expected home for dinner with his family at six o'clock. He rarely missed one.

"Spit it out, Kenzie. I know there's something else on your mind."

Silently, she chose the lesser of two evils: SKC.

Jim sat down again. Truck trotted after him, lying down next to his master and resting his big head on his paws. His soulful eyes moved from Jim's face to Kenzie's. The barks and yelps that reached his ears from the training yards outside the office windows didn't seem to distract him.

Kenzie got to the point. She had told Jim something of what she knew about Frank Branigan's death. Now she filled in the background, from the meeting with the medic to Linc's involvement.

He sat back, drumming the pencil again.

"You're up against a huge company. SKC snagged hundreds of millions in government contracts."

"X-Ultra is a subsidiary," she said. "It's small."

"Not for long," Jim replied. "Better body armor is a critical priority for the army."

"But theirs isn't reliable."

Jim scowled. "Take it from an old supply sergeant: They cut corners to meet production deadlines and skipped the testing to get the goods out the door."

She could sense the anger behind the clipped words. He did know what he was talking about. She wasn't going to argue.

"So should we start with SKC or X-Ultra?"

Jim thought for a few more moments.

"Okay. I'm going to give it to you straight."

She braced herself. Truck's ears went up in twin points as Jim took a deep breath and started over.

"Someone at the parent company, meaning SKC, is directly responsible for a screw-up of that magnitude. I say go for the top guy. And aim right between the eyes."

That was heavy-duty, even for Big Dawg Biggers. He really was furious. She had never seen him like this.

"Could you be a little more specific?" she asked. "I'd like to stay out of jail. Just a thought."

"First of all, you two aren't going to get an invite to waltz in and look around the factory."

"Agreed." She waited.

Jim rocked back in his chair, balancing on the back two legs. "I'm thinking congressional hearing, media firestorm—a CEO under the hot lights—"

"Aren't you getting a little ahead of yourself? We know hardly anything for sure." If her boss had a vice, it was his addiction to CNN and C-SPAN.

"You have the beginnings of a good story. Throw in a few hard facts and you have a great story."

She was irked by his single-mindedness. "The medic didn't give me too many details."

"Know any reporters? Let's raise some hell."

"No."

"You'd need a major name," he mused. "Someone with a big mouth, a popular blog, and connections."

"It can't be that easy."

He gave her an annoyed look. "This is the golden age of round-the-clock news, in case you haven't noticed."

Kenzie hadn't expected him to go down this road. She'd been looking for tactical advice. "Sorry I asked." The comment wasn't intended to be sarcastic.

Jim studied her for a long moment. "What do you have to lose, Kenzie? Not this job."

"Thank you." She knew that he meant it.

"How scared are you?"

"Not too."

"Then get on it. Ever heard of something called asymmetric warfare?"

"Yes, but—"

"You're the flea and SKC is the elephant. That doesn't mean you can't win."

"I'm not following you."

"You're a helluva smart flea, Kenz. Hop to it."

CHAPTER 11

Kenzie agreed to meet him at the park in the morning. Early. Linc sat in his car, waiting for her and watching the sun come up. She pulled in less than five minutes later.

They ran some laps, and she told him what Jim had said. Then she ran ahead. He lengthened his strides to catch up, concentrating on the running so he could think.

She outpaced him several more times.

Feeling frisky. She seemed to have bounced back from her near breakdown at the climbing gym over that ugly card.

He caught up again and flung himself across an imaginary ribbon. "And the winner is!"

"Cheater," she yelled, laughing.

He loped off the track toward the exercise structures and she followed.

Linc grabbed the pull-up bar and swung himself up, doing several.

"Jim's not crazy, Kenzie. Five."

The pull-ups hurt his arms, but it felt good. He'd been spending too much time sitting in front of laptops.

Kenzie leaned against the metal frame of the structure, looking around absently at the small park.

"I guess he was just thinking out loud. I never saw him get that steamed, though."

He let himself down with excruciating slowness and went up again. "Six. You can understand why."

"Yeah, I do."

"Seven." He went for some fast ones. "Eight. Nine. Ten." He sucked in a breath, tightening his abs, and let it out with a whoosh. "Going to the media is an idea. I considered it myself. But—eleven—it won't work for us. Not at this point."

"Don't forget about Randy Holt. She didn't want to go public."

"Twelve." His biceps bulged as he stayed up, swinging a little in midair. He thought he detected a flicker of interest in Kenzie's eyes. About time. He was killing himself.

She swung her arms to warm up. "Are you done showing off?"

"Are you impressed yet?"

Small smile. Okay, she had a lot on her mind. He wouldn't push it. Then—Linc almost lost his grip when she walked over and put a hand on his chest.

"Don't forget to breathe," she said mischievously.

Linc gasped. He wasn't sure whether to drop to the ground and take her in his arms, or lose the challenge.

"Thirteen. Fourteen. And . . . fifteen." He dropped to the ground with bent knees, more winded than he expected. "Your turn."

Kenzie reached high to grab the bar before he could grab her and did several without breaking a sweat, her ankles crossed. Perfect form. In more ways than one.

"I thought about Randy," he said. "She's the main reason I shelved it. Once the spin starts, it gets hard to control."

"Didn't you tell me once that you know some big-deal reporter?" She breathed in rhythm with her efforts. "Hell. I forgot to count. What am I up to?"

"More than me," he said. "And yes. Not Gary Baum. Someone else. A friend of my older brother."

"Name?" She kept on doing pull-ups, her trim arms working hard. "He? She? Why are you being so cagey?"

He thought about stalling her a little longer and decided against it. "She. The one and only Kelly Johns. If we ever need her, she can command a three-ring media circus."

Kenzie swung down. "Absolutely not. The stalker is still out there."

"We may be a little closer to him." They walked over to the bench by the river where he'd sat with Mike Warren. He told her about the double set of tire tracks, the forensics reports, and the lieutenant's new theory.

"So now we're waiting for fingerprint reports and envelope licks."

"Don't forget microscopic mud analysis."

Kenzie nodded. "That's interesting. Hadn't thought about that when I went to look at my car."

"Warren is methodical. He has to start building a case before he can get a warrant."

"How is he going to get that with no name and nothing to go on?"

"Perseverance. And luck."

She wasn't buying it. "If the stalker never committed a crime, his prints and DNA aren't going to pop up."

"The DNA, no. But lots of people have prints on file somewhere. Not in law enforcement databases, though," he conceded.

"I saw him. I wish there was a way to extract the memory from inside my brain. It must be in there. Right?"

"I guess so."

"Every time I think about it, there's less to see. I know it's a face, but it's mostly a dark blur."

"Then don't think about it." He put an arm around her shoulders. "Your mind is protecting you."

"Screw that," she said vehemently. "I want to be able to recognize him. Did you boost the pixels on the video? Is that the right term?"

Linc inclined his head in a nod. "More or less. I'm not ready to have you look. It could be clearer."

Christine held the key. If she had pulled over before the accident, she would probably recall the other driver, even the conversation. Eventually.

The accident, no. He knew from his long-ago motorcycle smashup that practically no one remembered being hit or careening off the road. He hadn't. The detailed police report on the incident had seemed to be about someone else entirely.

If the stalker really was someone Christine knew, then she very likely would remember him in time.

He didn't want to press the point. Kenzie was edgy enough, what with Christine moving out of the ICU to a rehabilitation center. He reminded himself to scope out the place.

"You know, it wouldn't hurt to talk to a police artist," he suggested. The lieutenant had mentioned it in passing.

"What's that going to accomplish? His face was in shadow. I couldn't say if his nose was long or short or even if he had a nose. Just that he was ordinary. Except for his eyes."

He rubbed her shoulder and she drew close to him under his arm. "Then start with those. Worth a try, Kenz."

"It's a waste of time."

His tone was level. "I don't agree. But I can't make you."

Kenzie fell silent for a few moments and gazed at the little river flowing by. "Look at that beautiful water," she murmured. "I wish I could just jump in and float away."

She broke off, lost in thoughts she didn't seem to want to share. Even so, she stayed where she was, warm against his side.

It felt so good just to hold her. It felt right.

Kenzie straightened away from him. An ache replaced her warmth. Linc leaned forward to ease his overworked muscles.

She didn't seem eager to leave the serene park, he thought. Her present accommodations at the Hamill shooting range probably had something to do with that.

The medic would be the first one to tell her she had a touch of PTSD. Banging guns and muzzle flashes didn't cure that.

She changed the subject. "So what have you been up to? You never say."

"Slogging through every damn X-Ultra document on the SKC laptop."

"And you're not finding anything."

"I'm finding too much. It's like going through nine thousand filing cabinets. I thought about writing filtering software to process the docs and PDFs, but that would take two more weeks."

"Wish I could help."

"You can't," he said, raking a hand through his hair. "It's an exercise in futility. I need actual X-Ultra vests, not schematics and spec sheets."

"More than one?"

"A statistically significant sample would be best. Like a hundred."

"Why so many?"

"Target practice."

Her eyes widened. "Let me make sure I have this straight. You want to blow holes in one hundred bulletproof army vests."

"That's correct."

"Where do you plan to do that?"

He looked at her.

"I'll ask Norm," Kenzie said.

"If it's not too much trouble. What if he tells you no?"

Kenzie shook her head. "He's ex-army."

"Should have known. He never shaved again," Linc said.

"Shut up. He's a ZZ Top fan. Be glad he won't mind. He might ask you not to be too conspicuous about it. There's a smaller range off to the side. You haven't seen it."

"If he has the right targets, I can pay him," Linc offered.

"You should see what's in the basement. Everything from paper thugs to wooden dummies. I'll borrow a gun from Norm. I want to get this done and over with."

Kenzie was military all the way, but he hadn't noticed her having much interest in hardware. "Mind telling me why you're so gung-ho?"

"Because sooner or later I'm going to be the one to tell Christine that Frank Branigan died. And I don't want her to think I had a chance to help find out why and did zip."

"Okay. I understand. But I'm the one who has to get the vests. You can't do that. They know who you are."

She conceded the point with a nod.

"How are you going to get in?" she wanted to know.

"Right through the front gate."

Kenzie shot him a curious look. "Let me guess. You aren't going to explain how you're going to do that because you would have to reveal your secret identity."

He chuckled at her reply. "You're not that far off."

"Thought so," she said with satisfaction.

"And," he went on, sobering, "there is one more thing I have to do."

"Let's hear it."

"Mike Warren and I noticed that a lot of lines are starting to converge on SKC. While I'm inside, I want to take video."

"Of what?"

"More like who. As in everyone I can get on microcam."

"How micro is it?"

"About as big as a button." He rose and stretched, rubbing his back. "Which is good. I may not be able to carry anything ever again."

"Tough workout?" she teased.

"Let's just say I had more fun watching yours."

Linc was back at the motel, showered and shaved. He was going through files on the clogged SKC laptop again. There had to be something in them, but he had no way of understanding the office codes on the documents relating to the X-Ultra vests.

Some codes repeated frequently, some didn't. He cut-and-pasted them for later sorting out. It was tedious work.

His cell rang and he recognized Mike Warren's number.

Then he noticed the time. He'd been at the desk for three hours. His back hurt. One ring before the call went to voicemail, he snapped out of it and answered. "Mike? Where are you?"

"In the motel parking lot. Ah, the memories."

"Shut up and come up."

A minute later there was a knock. Linc closed the file he was in, not wanting Mike to know everything he was up to. They weren't exactly in the same patrol car or on the same page. He went to the door.

"Come on in," he said to Warren. "Wish I could offer you something, but I'm out of snack-packs and the vending machine is busted."

"Got any ice? I'll have water."

"You don't want what the ice machine spits out, believe me. Besides, it's in the lobby."

Mike laughed. "Skip it. I'm not staying long. How's Kenzie?"

"Did I tell you I was meeting her?"

"No. I just didn't think you'd spend a beautiful day with an ugly laptop." Mike had known for a while that Linc had the SKC machine and wasn't ready to return it.

Linc took a few seconds to shut it down all the way. "I'm sick of staring into the thing. Also, I'm getting nowhere. So why are you here?"

The lieutenant found a chair. "Got some updates for you."

"That was fast."

"Slow week otherwise for forensics."

He took out a small notebook from the inside pocket of his jacket and flipped through its pages, then looked up at Linc.

"You know something? It's going to take us an hour to get through all this," Mike said cheerfully.

Linc knew he'd been had. "Okay. Get started."

"The vase and the roses," Mike began. "We powdered like girls at the prom."

"What?"

Mike held the notebook open with his thumb as he gestured with it. "There were no prints on either. Not so much as a smudge."

"Really? Seems hard to believe," Linc said.

"It's an expensive shop," Mike explained. "I know the owner. His employees wear white gloves when they do up a bouquet and deliver it. Everything has to be sparkling for the prices they charge."

"Other people touched it. A nurse, one of the Corellis, maybe."

"Mrs. Corelli told me she wiped off the vase because water spilled out. Too bad she's so neat, huh?"

"What about the little card?"

"The assistant wrote it out. The order came over the phone and the customer used a credit card number. Which the florist was nice enough to give me—I buy flowers there all the time for my wife."

Linc hoped he wasn't going off on another tangent.

"We traced it to an online racket," Mike continued. "They sell numbers before the original owner even knows they're stolen. So that was a bust."

"Moving right along. The greeting card that was sent to the Corellis?"

"Nothing on that, either. And we checked the envelope flap for saliva. Not a trace."

"I'm going to guess that Christine's ID was completely clean."

"Yup. Like it was just laminated."

"All right," Linc said, disappointed. "Well, I'm working on other things." He explained briefly about the codes on the documents.

Mike Warren nodded. "You never know what's going to help." He snapped his fingers. "Almost forgot. A call came into the station from someone who used to work at this motel."

"As a—"

"Not a housekeeper. Same profession as a couple of women who disappeared from here a year ago."

Linc got the idea. "Do I need to know their names?"

"Jill and Jane. How's that? The one who called today is, uh, Jeri."

"Good enough."

"Anyway," Mike went on, "back then Jill and Jane were one step away from moving their business to the street corner. They could barely afford the hourly rate at this joint."

Linc cast a glance at the bed. And he'd let Kenzie fall asleep on it. Once. Never again.

"I know what you're thinking," Mike said. "Don't worry. They preferred the ground-floor rooms."

"Good to know."

The lieutenant dialed down the smile. "Tough way to make a living, but they kept at it. Then one night someone decided they were better off dead."

"Who found them?"

"I did. Not here, in a ditch by the highway. In pieces. For some reason that doesn't scare the public until a cheerleader gets whacked."

"So I hear. But what does it have to do with—"

"I'm getting to that. This woman who just called, Jeri, told one of my detectives that they'd been soliciting clients using the on-line lists."

He paused and patted his jacket pocket, as if he was feeling for a cigarette box. "Hell's bells. Forgot to bring the nicotine gum."

"Chew your nails."

Mike returned to his story. "Anyway, Jeri suddenly wanted to tell us Jill said she was being stalked."

"After a year?"

"There's a reason she waited. Don't distract me."

"Sorry."

Mike collected his thoughts. "Jill told her the guy had, quote unquote, evil eyes. He liked to talk dirty online, keep his face out of the light. His big thrill was to come in close and make her jump. Then he'd show up in person for, you know, the finale. Last video chat happened a week before Jill's body turned up."

Evil eyes. Kenzie's exact words.

"Seems that the guy recently contacted Jeri, mentioned Jill. You following this?"

"Yes."

"Jeri thought it over, made the call to us, and the detective who took it remembered that I worked the case. Didn't Kenzie say the same thing about the guy who scared her?"

Linc felt cold in the stuffy room. "Evil eyes, yeah. Could be a co-incidence, though."

Mike Warren nodded. "Just figured you'd want to know."

Linc thought about it for a few moments. "So Jeri spoke to him? I guess she didn't get a screen grab."

"She didn't mention it or the detective didn't write it down. Take your pick."

"Did she leave a number?"

The lieutenant gave a resigned shrug. "Caller ID pegged it as a pay phone. She didn't want to get that close."

"Hmm. So we can't follow up. Sounds like a long shot anyway."

"Agreed," Mike said. "But it's interesting. Sometimes you get a random thing like that and isolated facts hook up, boom. You can get warrants, make arrests, charge someone. Build the kind of case that a prosecutor likes."

"How close are we?" Linc asked.

"Not very. Right now this is still tagged as a hit-and-run. You're the one who sees a connection—" Mike held up his hands when Linc opened his mouth to protest. "Hey, don't get me wrong. I'm inclined to agree with you. But I can't prove a damn thing yet."

Linc fell silent.

"There's only one witness to that accident besides the perp," Mike went on. "Christine. The victim. And she can't tell us anything yet."

"She worked at SKC. There are X-Ultra files on this machine." Linc rapped his knuckles on the black metal cover.

"Which reminds me—it is now officially a stolen laptop. Reported to us, serial number and all."

Was that the real reason Mike was here? Linc didn't ask.

"By, um . . ." The lieutenant flipped through his notebook. "Melvin Brody. Christine's boss."

"Give him my regards."

Mike ignored that and pretended to read other pages.

"I'm keeping it," Linc said. "Kenzie and I heard from a reliable source that there are problems with their armored vests. Serious problems. Christine had to have known."

"That's a guess."

"There has to be a connection," Linc insisted.

Mike groaned. "Pretend you're me and you're talking to the DA," he said. "There's a bad accident, looks like a hit-and-run. A woman who works for SKC, the biggest employer in the county, was in the car. You believe that an SKC subsidiary is making defective gear and wants to shut up anyone who says so."

"That about sums it up, yeah."

"Conjecture. Not evidence."

"I'm looking for more of that. So are you. So is Kenzie—I mean, she's going to check out photos and video footage, try to ID the guy she saw. What I have so far isn't as clear as it could be. And we're going to test the vests."

"Go ahead. You can do things I can't and you have connections I don't. But stay on the right side of the law."

Linc shot him a questioning look.

"No hacking into SKC servers," Mike clarified. "Unreasonable search will get the case thrown out of court."

"If you're so worried about that, why not just give the laptop back to Christine's boss?" Linc asked.

"Ah, Melvin Brody wasn't too polite to me. And I'm pretty sure you can get into their system without it anyway."

Linc grinned. "You're right."

"Don't."

"I heard you, Mike."

"Just trying to do my job, pal. I can't decide if you're my secret weapon or my worst nightmare."

"Mike." He paused. "I don't work for you."

"No, you don't. But we have to work together." The lieutenant eased down in his chair, stretching out his legs. "I'm really glad we're having this talk."

Patronizing comment. Linc wished he hadn't invited Mike in, even though he liked the guy. He just hadn't been expecting a lecture. To be fair, he'd given Mike an opening. The man wasn't wrong.

"You mentioned video footage."

Linc thought back. He had. Throw him a bone, he told himself. Then you can get back to the SKC stuff.

Or better yet, lie down. The hard workout with Kenzie was still echoing in his muscles. Or maybe it was the brief moment of physical reconnection between them at the park that was doing that.

"Linc?"

He came back to his senses. "Uh, yeah. The reporter on the scene, Gary Baum, was very helpful. But like I said, the footage isn't that clear."

"Let's look at it anyway."

"I figured the other driver might've come back, so I concentrated on that activity around the accident and after."

"Sometimes they do." Mike Warren straightened up in his chair.

"You want to see it?"

"Yes."

Linc pushed the SKC laptop aside and moved to his own, booting it up. "The driver that stopped is—well, take a look at his car yourself. I didn't see any damage."

He showed Mike the freeze-frames from the video and then let the footage run in slo-mo, then at normal speed.

The lieutenant got up and dragged his chair over to the table, sitting in front of the laptop. "Can I see the first part again?"

"Here ya go." Linc remained standing, reaching out to tap the keys. "What do you think of this guy? You didn't say."

"The one in sunglasses?"

"There's something about him. Can't say what exactly. Half the time he's turned away or his face is in shadow. Then that cop has to go and stand in front of him."

Mike didn't seem to care. "Look at that. You got a nice clear shot of the back of the car. Can you enlarge it?"

"Sure." Linc tapped a key for a close-up. "Notice the leaves on the license plate? Probably glued on."

Mike shook his head. "I was checking out the tires."

Linc swallowed a fly. He knew what Mike was getting at. Hadn't occurred to him.

"Go bigger. And bigger than that."

Linc clicked the Command key and the plus sign several times. The tread pattern filled the screen.

"Very interesting," Mike said. "Could be identical to the tread marks from the second car that pulled over under the maples."

"I didn't think of that," Linc muttered.

"Well, I do have to check this freeze-frame against the tread photos from yesterday. Routine. For a detective. I was good at it. That's why I made lieutenant, in case you were wondering."

"I wasn't."

Mike chuckled. "Now, if you could do the same thing for the front right fender—that's it. Great. A little closer."

He peered at the image. "I'm seeing evidence of a dent there.

It doesn't take much of a hit to make another car swerve out of control. He could have pulled over to bang out the worst of it."

Linc grudgingly conceded the point. "But the finish looks okay."

Mike put his index finger on an imaginary nozzle. "*Shpzzz.* Spray paint. Black on black. Who's going to notice?"

"I should have."

"You got the footage, pal. Good work. We make a great team."

Linc could hear his father's voice in his head. *Don't ever think you have nothing to learn.*

"Can you copy it for me, Linc?"

"Sure." He had some blank discs left over from making the photo CDs for Mrs. Corelli. "Maybe you'll find something else I missed."

It only took a few minutes. Mike didn't talk, just watched.

"Should be useful," he said when the CD ejected. "Solid evidence like this is what we need. As far as the guy in sunglasses, he's going to be tough to ID. He could be wearing a rug, you know."

"Have to ask Kenzie on that. Women can spot fake hair from a mile away," Linc said.

"Even if she did, eyewitnesses get things wrong. Best to get something that can be scientifically proved to have come from the individual, something unique. Fingerprints are still good. DNA is even better."

"The creep's ahead of us," Linc pointed out. "He doesn't even lick his envelopes."

Mike sighed. "Let's see what I can find out about the tire tracks." He put his notebook and the CDs in an outside pocket. "Thanks. Sorry if I interrupted you. Looked like you were working."

"I never stop."

"Keep it up." The lieutenant clapped him on the arm and left, closing the door behind him.

Linc headed for an armchair, wishing he could stop. His cell phone rang. He couldn't ignore it.

He looked at the screen, not recognizing the area code or the number. What the hell. Maybe he'd just won a cruise or a couple of free daiquiris at the local tiki bar.

"Hello."

"Guess who this is. Guess where I am."

Deke. Linc heard reggae music thumping in the background.

"You there, Linc?"

"Yes."

"Did you guess?"

The music got louder. Deke hummed along with it. Linc wondered if the brunette from the wedding was there with him.

"No idea," Linc said.

"I'm at a top-secret location in the Caribbean at a highly classified party. Having a wonderful time. Wish you were here. What are you doing?"

"Working hard. Knock yourself out." Linc hung up on him.

Linc cracked the door of Office 25, prepared to be chewed out by Chet York, the nominal head of the project he was supposed to be working on.

Unless he got lucky.

If his CO, Dana Scott, had sent Chet to a far corner of Fort Meade for the day, Linc had nothing to worry about. She'd cleared Linc to work off the base in the first place.

Dana firmly believed that tech wizards needed time off now and then to keep their heads from exploding. She should know. She was married to one.

He opened the door all the way.

"Hey, Dana." He gave her a huge smile.

"Come on in." She didn't look up. "Don't tell me where you've been. It doesn't matter." She pulled up a document that he recognized. He had coded it. Dana pointed to the screen. "Nice work. Where are you going with this?"

He told her, and added a few brilliant suggestions for improving his contribution that made her smile back. Finally.

It took him an hour to get around to the most important reason for his return.

"You want more time off?" She pushed the laptop away and made full eye contact. Dana didn't do that often.

He explained why, down to the last little bit of information.

Dana Scott lived and breathed information. She liked data she could really crunch, just for the sheer pleasure of crunching.

"SKC, huh? The name came up in a meeting at the agency. But I didn't hear anything about defective gear."

Linc explained more. He'd cobbled together PDFs and documents to add substance to his formal request to proceed. Chet York would have asked for the file and stuck it in his in-box. Dana Scott actually read everything in it with blinding speed.

"Not much to go on, Linc," she said after a pause. "You need to run some tests on a statistically significant sample."

Those were her favorite words. Dana liked data but she loved statistics.

He told her how much one vest would cost. No discount for buying in bulk. Not sold in stores. He didn't want SKC to know that he was a designated secret shopper for the government.

She did the math and sat back. "Are you kidding me?"

"No. It's a lot of money, I know."

"For cripes sake," Dana groaned. "Where am I going to hide an expense like that? I've got a congressional committee that wants to play Twenty Questions with me, and I have to justify every nickel we spend on Project 25. This has nothing to do with it."

"I need a new identity too."

Dana scowled at him. "It isn't Halloween yet. And Bob and Betty Taxpayer don't want to foot the bill for your cute costume."

"This is important. Maybe more important than Project 25."

Dana read through his formal request again. "Yeah. It is. All right. You know the drill."

"Refresh my memory."

"Have Andy write up a bio for you and design a fake website. Check the beta before it's up, please, so he can make corrections. And memorize it. We'll goose the page rankings so it looks like you're legit."

"Great."

"He can set you up with new ID and business cards and whatever else you need. Buy a good suit." She looked with distaste at Linc's jeans and jacket.

"I need an advance."

Dana took a platinum credit card out of a slim folded purse on the table. "Put it on this. Same goes for the vests. Get a car and driver too. Don't use ours." She handed over the card. "There's no limit. Go to town. But get receipts."

"Is my new name Dana Scott?" Linc asked.

"Why not? You know it's not really mine. No one outside the agency and the man I love knows who I am."

"Thank you. Very much."

"Don't grovel," she said absently, pulling her laptop back in front of her. "It's a giveaway. Act like you could buy SKC if you felt like it. For cash."

"I will."

She took the trouble to give him one last look. "Buy a *really* good suit. So good your own mother wouldn't recognize you."

"You don't know Sheila Bannon."

"All right, whatever. We're not trying to fool her, are we?"

Kenzie had missed his call. The message Linc had left baffled her.

"Hey. I have to drive out to Fort Meade and show up at work before they forget what I look like. Next time you see me I'll be a new man."

A day had passed before he'd called again. And now she was meeting him for lunch at a nice restaurant down the road from Hamill's. He'd said something about the fast food place, which was closer, being nowhere near good enough.

Carol let him through the gate. Kenzie, preserving her dignity, didn't look through the windows of her second-floor room. But she heard Carol's squeal and the other woman telling Linc how good he looked.

She went down the stairs and opened the door to the outside.

He did look good. In fact, he looked amazing. The dark suit he wore emphasized his powerful frame and height, and fit him perfectly. This was a new Linc. She almost wanted to sniff him to make sure it was the same Linc.

An expensive aftershave wafted her way as he strode toward her. She noticed the haircut. Just right.

He grinned at her. There was something about the conservative suit that brought out a touch of the devil in his grin.

Kenzie felt a little underdressed. She had put on a pretty dress,
just in case, but she didn't have heels to go with it, only flats in a
matching color.

"You look gorgeous."

He was being a sport. "I think the word applies to you, Linc."

"Is it too much?"

She looked him up and down. He seemed to enjoy her scrutiny
tremendously.

"No. You got it just right."

"I had help."

Of course, she thought with annoyance. Feminine, sophisti-
cated help. A sales associate to adjust the jacket across the broad
shoulders with manicured hands. Another to kneel with needle
and thread, to make sure the break of the pants hems over the
black shoes was just right. A hairstylist clipping and snipping and
tenderly brushing the back of his neck. She disliked them all. No
one was going to get next to Linc Bannon before she did.

"Ready to go?"

Kenzie nodded. "Is there a coach and four on the other side of
the fence?"

He grinned again and took her arm. The car was dark cobalt, as
conservative as the suit, with a daringly low chassis that had been
designed for high speed.

"My boss told me to get one with a driver," he said. "I settled
for this."

"Very nice."

He escorted her to the passenger side and helped her in. At
the restaurant, he did the same thing. She counted the stares they
each got, somewhat mollified that she was slightly ahead by the
time they were seated.

Settled at a table in a back corner per his request, they consulted the menus.

"I assume I can order anything," she said.

"Absolutely."

The food was quite good, simple fare with a touch of elegant inventiveness. She kept looking at him and he didn't seem to mind.

"These are my work clothes, you know," he said, halfway through his steak.

"Oh."

He slipped a hand behind the front of his jacket and examined one of his buttons.

"Is it loose?" she inquired. "Can't fix it, sorry. I forgot my sewing kit."

Linc smiled. "It's working fine. I just took a five-second video of you."

"Oh." So that was the microcamera he'd mentioned. Kenzie was too curious not to look at it more closely. The button looked like any other button. "I didn't hear a click."

He held up his hand. A heavy gold ring set with a flat stone caught the light. "You press the stone. Done."

That hadn't been on his hand until a second ago. He must have had it in his pocket and slipped it on. "Seriously?" Her tone was faintly mocking. "I don't believe you."

"Wait for the download."

"Oh, okay. Whatever you say."

Linc shrugged. "This gear is for real, Kenzie. And it's not that expensive or unusual. Anybody can buy it at a snoop store in a strip mall or online. Good guys, bad guys—we all use the same stuff."

She had to laugh. "Whose side are you on again?"

"Yours."

"I guess I should be grateful. But no more candids of me, please."

"Not a problem."

The food was great, but she didn't request dessert and neither did Linc.

When the check arrived in a leather fold, he didn't even look at it, just took out a wallet and slipped in a credit card to cover the tab.

Not quite fast enough. She saw the name on it. "Dana Scott?"

"My new identity. But only for a day. Don't get used to it."

Kenzie shook her head regretfully and folded her arms on the table as he glanced around for their server. She'd never been a fan of men in suits until now, but he looked fantastic. The easy knot on the million-dollar tie made it clear he didn't take himself too seriously in it. As far as the suit—the drape, the natural shoulders—it was perfectly tailored for a man who liked to move.

He put his wallet back into the inside pocket and adjusted the lapel. It didn't need adjusting.

"Do you get to keep that?" Kenzie asked.

He winked. "Yes I do. Everything but the car." He brushed a nearly invisible crumb off the jacket. "Hey, I don't know when I'll ever wear this again, but it's definitely getting a closet of its own."

"I see." Kenzie surveyed him with a wry smile.

No question that he had dressed to kill just to get inside SKC, not to impress her. But the fine clothes had done something for his attitude. The final touch—that cocky grin—beat a pocket square any day of the week.

The bill taken care of, they left. Kenzie did her best to ignore the admiring glances Linc "The Suit" Bannon got from the women in the restaurant.

He didn't take her back to the shooting range right away. There was a lookout point between here and there. Linc swerved the dark cobalt car into it, pulling alongside the rock wall and switching the engine off. They had the lookout to themselves.

"Why are we stopping?" she asked. Rhetorically.

"Great view."

She glanced at the distant DC skyline, seeing the dome of the Capitol to the east and the tip of the Washington Monument. The Mall, its grassy expanse invisible from where they were, stretched to the Lincoln Memorial at the other end. Its blocky rectangular top appeared through the bare-branched trees.

"Sure is." Kenzie tossed her handbag into the footwell and turned to him. That grin on his handsome face was not about sightseeing. She allowed herself the pleasure of looking him over one last time. He pretended not to notice.

Even looking straight ahead through the windshield, his dark eyes had a knowing glint. It was arrogant of him to assume that he knew what she wanted, even though he was right. And annoying of him to wait for her to make the first move. One strong hand rested on the wheel and the other on his thigh.

Kenzie unbuckled her seat belt and leaned over. Two could play that game. She put her lips against his ear and he stiffened visibly. "What's on your mind, Linc?" she breathed, teasing him.

She was amused to see his eyes close with pleasure. Maybe he hadn't been expecting her to say something like that. Too bad. She'd said it.

Kenzie slid her hand over his smooth-shaven jaw and turned his face to hers. Wow. His gaze burned with passion. She'd never seen Linc like this. He was all man and then some.

Hard to say who began the kiss, but it went on for a while. She didn't remember taking the knot out of his tie, which hung open. A couple of buttons had parted company with the buttonholes on his shirt.

Linc sat back when she did.

"Wow. I mean, maybe you should take me home," she said. "Not that I don't want more, but—"

Linc nodded, turning the key in the ignition until the engine revved. "Tell me when, Kenzie. That's all I ask."

Some minutes later, good-byes exchanged, he forced himself to think. Next up, SKC.

Linc's first call to the company on the previous day had gone straight to the phone on the CEO's desk, thanks to a personal recommendation from a higher-up at the agency.

After a kiss like that, it was a miracle he remembered so much detail. Kenzie was capable of shredding his concentration with a few soft words. He told himself not to fall into the tender trap a second time and concentrated.

He and Lee Slattery, the CEO, had chatted for an hour. Linc had his talking points memorized: He was a CEO himself with a strategic materials business. Overseas factories to keep manufacturing costs low and profits high. He was looking to buy SKC vests for a hundred-and-fifty-man security team.

Lee had been very friendly on the phone—the man was a serious talker who followed the news of the day, especially stories with a military slant. He had a tendency to name-drop, Linc noticed.

He'd dropped a few of his own—mostly agency names who would instantly vouch for him. But he had thought to mention Kelly. He couldn't pretend he hung around with movie stars, but she was close enough. On the East Coast, she was famous.

Kenzie beat her for beauty, though.

The lookout had proved to be an excellent strategic move. He watched her trim frame walk away from him behind the chain-link fence of the shooting range. The dress looked like it was made out of handkerchiefs, pure white with lace points. The fluttery hem revealed just a little more than she probably intended, now that a breeze had kicked up.

Nice. Unbelievably nice.

In person, Lee Slattery matched his online image. He was the silver-fox type, dressed with impeccable taste.

Slattery extended his hand, shaking Linc's with a firm grip. "Welcome. Pleasure to meet a friend of Kelly Johns. I'm a big fan of hers."

And a few other blondes, Linc thought, surveying the framed photos on the wall. He didn't see one of Kelly, with or without Slattery, but there were several of the CEO standing next to well-known actresses and TV personalities with highlighted hair and legs that didn't quit. He reminded himself that Slattery was divorced and no one cared.

The photos of Slattery with various politicians were more telling. Linc was pretty sure that the jowly guy with his arm around Slattery's shoulders was the head of a military appropriations committee. And he recognized a senator or two in the mix.

"So," Slattery said affably, "I understand you'd like to tour our operation. Some of it is off-limits, you understand," he added with a wink. "You would need a classified clearance and—well, you're the new kid in town."

"I'm working on that," Linc said casually. Slattery was never going to know that Linc's clearance was several levels above his own—but that was beside the point.

"Let me know how it goes. I may be able to help expedite it." Slattery gave a meaningful nod at one of the photos, with a different politician.

Linc smiled. "Great. No rush, though."

Slattery came around the desk and clapped him on the back. "You just say when and I'll make a few calls."

"Thanks. Much appreciated."

The older man went to his office door and gestured for Linc to follow him. "Let me show you around. At the end you get to walk down my favorite street. I don't do that for everyone."

Linc managed a smile, not sure what Slattery was talking about. "I'm honored."

They toured the main building first. It was new and smelled new.

Slabs of acoustic ceiling tile alternated with fluorescent fixtures. No windows, just walls that seemed to run for miles. The worker bees kept their heads down, their faces tinged with blue from the glowing screens in front of them. Men and women both.

Lee Slattery kept right on talking in a somewhat lower voice, proud of his hive.

From time to time, a high-level manager appeared from an office and greeted Slattery with some surprise. Linc guessed that he didn't walk around too often. There was a lot of glad-handing and introductions to this sub-chief and that division head and a couple of veeps to finish up.

A man around his own age came and went around the edges of the group, but Lee didn't bother to introduce him right away. Linc wondered who he was. His recent crash course in good suits told him that the man's had cost more than his own.

Okay. An exec. But young to be on Slattery's level.

He had a dark buzz cut that showed a fair amount of scalp and an athletic look. Not the weekend warrior type—kind of military. His eyes were dark too—oddly flat, almost black.

The man fixed his gaze on Lee Slattery. Linc noted his expression of contempt, wondering what that was all about.

The silver-haired CEO turned to the man as if he'd been

tapped on the shoulder by him. "There you are, Vic. When did you get here?"

"About ten minutes ago."

Slattery didn't really listen to the answer, quickly handling the introductions in his usual breezy way. "Dana, this is my right-hand man and second-in-command, the one and only Victor Kehoe. We call him Vic."

The contemptuous expression didn't change—Slattery didn't seem to notice or care—but Kehoe extended a hand to shake, gripping Linc's with noticeable force.

"Dana Scott is in the market for our new bulletproofs," Slattery added. "Someone at the agency sent him to us."

Kehoe gave a curt nod, taking in the information. Linc guessed he'd just been added to a file marked Nobody Important.

It would be interesting to find out why Vic Kehoe disliked his boss. Linc made a mental note to cultivate Kehoe as a contact at SKC.

Slattery could be as crooked as he was smooth. The second-in-command was likely to have the goods on him.

But Kehoe wasn't exactly warming up to him, though he condescended to make small talk for a minute or two. Linc let it go, focusing on being Dana Scott, foreign-based businessman with money to burn.

There was another greeting from another head of something before Linc could take in any more details. Vic Kehoe excused himself.

Leaving, Linc noticed, with a smaller entourage of his own, which broke off from Slattery's gang and regrouped around him.

SKC was big on hierarchies. That fit. Plenty of ex-army people went through revolving doors to companies like this when they left the service or retired. That was where the money was.

Some fact-finding mission, he thought with disgust. He was never left alone for a second. He couldn't ask random questions.

Did you work with Christine Corelli? What department?

She hadn't been a cubicle cutie, but an assistant to someone fairly high up.

Doing . . . exactly what, he still didn't know.

It almost didn't matter. SKC had to be raking in millions. The business of military supply generated enormous profits, no matter what soldiers might have to say about the quality of the goods.

According to his research, the company had been on a hiring spree since this new group of buildings had gone up. Slattery was saying something about his plans to expand. The area was relatively near DC but still uncrowded, ripe for development. Other companies were following SKC's lead, gobbling up farmland and chewing up trees.

Linc half listened. He managed to start the miniature camera on his jacket button. He could just feel the infinitesimal buzz.

He took video only of the men. Linc would never remember them all, but he had to try and jog Kenzie's memory.

The stalker could be any one of them. An ordinary guy. On the outside.

He wished he'd gotten footage of the men who'd left with Vic Kehoe, but it was too late now. Linc guessed that a lot of it was going to be blurred or partial anyway. The thing was tiny and he wasn't a pro, unlike Gary Baum's cameraman. He knew for sure he'd gotten several shots of shirt fronts bulging with middle-manager fat.

Someone, not Lee, finally walked him over to the X-Ultra department. Melvin Brody put down a sloppy sandwich to greet him. He invited Linc into his office for a spiel that could have been prerecorded on the merits of the new fiber in the vests.

Linc didn't like the guy. His shirt had mayonnaise on it, but that wasn't the reason. Brody was rude to the girl who'd replaced Christine. Kenzie had mentioned her. Brenda White. She kept her head down, too, involved with paperwork.

He happened to glance at the names in an appointment book on her desk, at first not recognizing the one at the top.

Dana Scott. That was him.

Brody took a call and said yes several times to whoever was on the other end. Linc waited, hands in the pockets of his fabulous suit, rocking back a little on the heels of his expensive shoes.

"Let's go. The big boss says he has a treat for you."

More corridors, more employees. Brody brought him to a

different area, not where he'd started. Ground level. Industrial-looking. Steel beams and reinforced concrete.

He wondered if he was going to be handed a hard hat. But Slattery came out, still talking a mile a minute to an underling, who gave Linc a thankful look as he disappeared.

"Ready?" the older man asked.

"Sure."

Slattery steered him around a double set of riveted beams toward a golf cart.

Linc half expected to see clubs in bags stashed in the back, but there weren't any.

The cart was new, with roomy seats. He and Slattery headed off to their next destination, with Slattery at the wheel. Whistling, the CEO negotiated through a gigantic warehouse with practiced ease for several minutes. It seemed to be all one structure, and Linc wasn't sure where it ended. Dangling from a ceiling of corrugated metal, wire-caged lights provided spots of illumination in corridors that were on the dark side.

There were catwalks way up high. And a structure that appeared to be a construction crane. Tall though it was, it still cleared the top of the enormous space. Linc glimpsed an occasional worker in coveralls here and there, checking shelved cardboard boxes with a handheld monitor, and guessed that the warehouse staff was mostly men, because they were all on the big side. The blue glow from the handheld monitors illuminated faces, but only for a few seconds at a time—and Lee Slattery was driving quickly.

He slowed and pulled the golf cart over near a wall, stopping in a pool of yellow light that made everything around them seem darker than before. He switched off the cart and turned to Linc. "Here we are."

Linc got out, seeing the same shadowy corridors stretching away on all sides. Puzzled, he kept his expression neutral and said nothing as he watched Slattery walk over to a bank of electrical switches, flipping several in succession.

Linc's eyes narrowed, momentarily blinded by what seemed to be brilliant outdoor sunshine. No shelves here. No workers either.

He took in a dusty path that wound between high mud walls. Low houses built of the same material stood to one side of the path, opposite a ditch on the other that was filled with jumbled stones.

It was a good replica of a Middle Eastern village street, right down to the *wadi*—the dry watercourse filled with stones. Nice touch.

The path ended some distance away in a wall of jagged rock that vanished into gloom as he looked up, noticing the handholds built into it. A climbing wall. He brought his gaze down to the spindly trees arching over the walls, too stiff and green to be real. He blinked.

"We're still inside," Slattery chuckled. "And yes, it's all fake. Like it? We use it for testing gear. And to demonstrate the goods, show off design upgrades, that kind of thing."

"Very impressive."

"Gotta stay ahead in this business," Slattery said, clasping his hands behind his back and rocking a little in place. "The enemy keeps coming up with new IEDs—Improvised Explosive Devices, that is. I'm sure you're familiar with the term."

"Yes, I am. But tell me more."

"Oh, there's not much to it. We bring the client here, show him the path, a warehouse guy slings a bulletproof vest and groin cup over his coveralls and goes for a stroll. Then—kaboom! Mock explosion. No shrapnel, no harm done. The gear gets peppered with dye pellets. Memorable visual, don't you think?"

"I bet it is." Linc was wondering if he was about to see it happen. But he and Slattery were alone—Linc didn't see or hear any of the warehouse workers.

"Beats the hell out of our competition. They use animated films and illustrated brochures. But we can stage our own little war games right here in the warehouse."

"I'm impressed."

"This is only one reason why we're outselling them right and left. Clients get a huge kick out of it. My second-in-command, Vic Kehoe, came up with the idea and rigged the whole thing after the walls and path were done."

"So what explodes?"

Lee Slattery waved vaguely. "I'm not sure. It's really no big deal. You'd have to ask Vic. He's the munitions man."

His casual tone didn't fit the setting. Fake though it was, the empty path was faintly menacing. Tiny particles of dust hung in the artificial light, stirred up by the golf cart's sudden arrival—or someone who had stepped out of sight. Someone who could be watching them.

Linc felt the back of his neck prickle and turned his head around, seeing nothing in the other direction but endless, shadowy tiers of shelves, mostly empty.

He looked back at the path, remembering a similar setup but much larger, built for the army. He'd stayed there for six weeks, breathing in dust just like this along with the acrid smell of explosives.

Located in a remote part of the southwest, the mock village was a training center for bomb-disposal specialists. It was riddled with hidden devices—in doorways, in the crisscrossing streets, and inside false-front houses within walled compounds.

Linc had helped to engineer the electronics that controlled the exercises. The soldiers he'd worked with joked around a lot, but they all knew the training was deadly serious. Not like this playpen.

"Did I scare you?" Slattery's question interrupted his thoughts.

Linc shook his head. "No. But the path looks authentic. Good work."

Slattery smiled proudly. "You would know. And hey, I didn't really mean it about taking a walk. I'm not sure if Vic has any booby traps set at the moment. Doesn't look like it."

He indicated the path and Linc noticed that there were no footprints in it. Or any other marks. Slattery chuckled again. "He's good at covering his tracks."

Talking further with Lee Slattery's second-in-command oughta be interesting, Linc thought. The guy could be good at covering up a lot of things, including the threads that Linc had followed to Slattery Inc. So far, he had a feeling that the silver-haired CEO was in the game for the glory, not the money.

He'd read up on him, spending a scant hour on Google, and

then going to an agency blacknet for in-depth corroboration that hadn't been supplied by an SKC publicist.

Lee Slattery didn't have to earn another dime as long as he lived, not with the fortune he'd inherited ten years ago. He'd signed on as CEO of SKC to have something to do—and rub shoulders with the brass.

Linc had run into the type several times in his own work for the military: successful men who had never served but liked people to think that they had. A toy soldier, displaying a flag that never waved in his paneled office.

Linc drove back along the George Washington Parkway. His favorite highway, if you could call it that. Built in the 1930s, it was too narrow and swooped into unexpected curves through parkland that had reverted to wilderness. You had to be alert. Especially at night, because there were no road lights on it. Low stone walls bridged certain sections over hidden gorges in the ridge. He caught glimpses of the river below, shimmering in twilight, flowing fast from the mighty falls several miles to the west.

The trees were losing their leaves rapidly, but there were a few diehards. One lifted a scarlet crown above the bare branches, defiantly red. It looked like a torch, standing sentinel over this remnant of wild land.

In another few minutes he would be in Arlington. He was meeting a friend from Langley for a beer and a platter of wings.

They had nothing serious to talk about, just a mutual interest in sports TV and maybe a game of pool. He needed to stop thinking.

SKC was somewhere out there, beyond the treetops of Rosslyn. The tall new buildings springing up were screwing up the rest of the view. He'd seen no reason to stay late. He didn't want to get asked to have dinner with the customer Lee Slattery was dragging around and subjecting to an all-out snowjob.

Must be someone rich, he thought idly. Slattery didn't turn on the charm otherwise.

He looked out at the skyline, surveying the new construction.

It seemed to him that a building started up every week. The demand was there. Temporary types. His neighborhood was new and anonymous. He liked it that way.

He leaned on the penthouse railing, looking straight down at the clean sidewalks and puny trees.

A car sped down the street, weaving around others. There were always one or two cars that went too fast with drivers hidden behind tinted windows. He didn't wonder why some didn't get stopped, even when they ran a red. The cops knew who was who.

Cyclists in spandex rolled over the Key Bridge between rows of antique lampposts, just coming on. Many would turn left for their evening ride at the liquor store, now closed, where the university students used to get their kegs and drink themselves into oblivion. The cyclists maneuvered around pedestrians and joggers and dog owners. He scarcely noticed the men.

He preferred to look at women.

Walking together. Walking alone.

He watched them come and go. The weaker sex always attracted his attention, even from on high.

Up close, the look in their eyes when they first saw him was like an electrical charge. He needed it. Craved it.

They always made it so easy.

He was nice at first, especially at work. Women employees liked the little things. A sincere hello without getting the once-over. A note of appreciation for all the work they did that didn't usually get noticed.

He didn't bother with the older ones or bored wives looking for a fling. Younger was better, but not too young. He had no respect for men who hung around playgrounds. He prided himself on fighting fair.

He did like it when his prey fought hard.

The extensive offices were an ideal stalking ground. He kept in practice. Taking them home was problematic. But he liked to think that what he needed was boxed to go in tidy cubicles. They perched on swivel chairs, stared into screens. All he had to do was stop and wait for them to look up.

They made him wait, but he enjoyed that part of the game. He liked to see how they sat. Primly, with ankles crossed tight. Hiding it. Or casually, a high heel propped on the chair support with one leg bent and the other stretched under the desk. More open.

Sometimes they were silent, attending to busywork in a tapping frenzy of fingernails. Sometimes they talked incessantly on the phone. Eventually they all decided to notice him.

He knew when they did that they were sizing him up, ranking him instantly on a female scale. One. Marriage material. Two. Single but spoken for. Three. Good only for weekend laughs and a few drinks.

Four. None of the above.

Be a gentleman—he'd been taught that, very strictly. He believed in it. But when the need grew too strong, he went elsewhere. He didn't have to be gentle where he wasn't known.

They couldn't seem to figure him out. But the reverse wasn't true. He could read their lives in their eyes. When, in due time, he sparked fear there, he was happy. Their fear made him stronger.

They were always impressed by his penthouse.

It was a duplex with an extensive terrace. From there, even with the new buildings, he could still see the river, suddenly flat and slow, a dull silver ribbon pouring into the vast bay to the south.

To the east were the white buildings and the dome that defined the nation's capital. At twilight they glowed faintly purple— the inevitable backdrop for evening news shows, a stock image for a thousand thrillers.

His mind supplied the overlay of crosshairs in a circle.

He would never go that crazy. The city fed him.

The carillon in the memorial park near the river rang out, a melancholy reminder of battlefield casualties.

The sound was annoying. War had made him millions, more money than he would ever need. The world might be running out of oil, but it was never going to run out of wars to fight for it. Wars required equipment and expertise like his.

Before he'd returned to the States to take advantage of his connections, he'd run a black op for another government.

Efficiently.

The prisoners were invariably male. They got put in boxes until they were ready to talk. They seldom did, though he got paid either way. Their silence got them carried out in smaller boxes. Other prisoners soon replaced them.

It was routine and lucrative, for such boring work.

Until the woman with dark hair was brought to the prison.

She gave up fast. But he'd had fun while she'd lived. Invented some new moves that he'd used again on those two from the motel a year ago. They made too much noise and that was that. Couldn't have the cops show up when the neighbors complained about noise.

Below him a siren screamed. Red lights revolved on the top of an emergency vehicle speeding through the streets.

Nothing to do with him. He went back inside and thought about Kenzie.

CHAPTER 12

Linc returned to the shooting range in the sleek car, but wearing his usual jeans and an ordinary shirt. The gate was open and the parking lot was full. Kenzie came out of the shop, carrying a large gun case and a squarish bag made of heavy-duty nylon. She had two pairs of goggles pushed back on her head and wore padded ear protectors on each wrist.

"Steal that car," she said. "I won't tell."

He grinned wickedly. "I don't have to give it back until tomorrow."

"Just so long as I get one more ride." She opened the car door on her side.

"My pleasure. What's in the bag?"

"Ammo. Compliments of Norm."

He looked in and saw several opened boxes of different ammunition and a few loose bullets. Interesting selection that boded well for the loaner guns. Norm hadn't just thrown in cheap stuff to get rid of it.

With a happy sigh she swung down into the passenger seat, putting all the gear at her feet.

They drove slowly through the parking lot, heading for the other side where the smaller range was. Kenzie glanced toward the main range. It was full up, with a shooter in every slot, men and a few women. Someone had rolled an awning over the long space where the shooters stood at different stages of readiness, taking aim.

Linc braked to a stop.

Gunshots burst out all at once. Then there was silence. He couldn't hear the ticking timer, but he knew there was one. "Must be cops."

"No uniforms. How can you tell?" Kenzie asked.

They were reloading. A solo shot rang out, then there were a few more. "Us Bannon boys went to firing ranges with our dad when he thought we were old enough. Cops practice like that."

"Like what?"

"They go for x shots in x seconds. Wait for it—"

There was another barrage. Kenzie covered her ears.

Concentrating on the targets, the shooters didn't see them go by. Linc raised a hand to Norm, who was visible behind the glass of the shop. "I owe him for this."

"He said you don't."

Linc waved away her reply. "This is on the agency nickel, don't forget. And we're using the expensive targets."

"Norm didn't say what they cost."

"The target dummies with layers of Kevlar backing aren't cheap. I want to dig out bullets that go through the vests if I can."

"Keeping souvenirs?"

"No. Any vest that can't absorb or deflect a hit goes straight to the ballistics experts at Langley, plus the spent bullets, chunks of the target, and unused vests for comparison."

"You have this all planned out," Kenzie remarked.

"Not exactly," Linc said. "There's a limit to what I can do—this isn't my area of expertise. But a brand-new vest shot full of holes is a very effective visual. Beats the hell out of a memo or a scientific report."

"And I thought you loved science," she teased.

"I do. But I know what gets on blogs and on the news."

"You can't go public, Linc. Not until we—well, you know what I mean." Her tone held a note of alarm.

She meant catching the stalker. He hoped that was going to happen. "I'm not going to," he assured her. "I only got my first look at the SKC operation yesterday."

"After today"—she hesitated—"it's going to take a while to get everything analyzed anyway."

"That's right."

Kenzie turned around to look at the boxes jostling in the backseat.

"How many vests did you bring?"

"Twenty." He looked over his shoulder. "They're a hybrid type. Armor plates, backed with a material that SKC recently developed. It's like Kevlar but lighter."

She was familiar with armored vests, but had never had to wear one, as she'd told Randy. Kenzie's posting to the army garrison in Darmstadt, Germany, meant she'd never heard enemy fire either. It was a peaceful place.

Kenzie counted five. "So the others are in the trunk."

"Yeah. I'll show you the removable armor plates, also new and improved. Lee Slattery had his chief of engineering give me the whole spiel and a binder crammed with fact sheets." He held his thumb and index finger inches apart. "This thick. Haven't read it yet."

She directed him to a range in the near distance. The targets were positioned in front of a high berm of bulldozed earth. "Over there."

His gaze moved over the berm and up to the high chain-link fence topped with razor wire.

"Good setup," he said.

"I think this was the original range," Kenzie told him. "Norm took out a loan to build the big one."

"Like I said, I'm paying him. Where was I?"

"Telling me all about bulletproof vests," she said.

"So," he went on, "I left with a hundred of each. Told Lee I was going to put them on my jet and fly out tomorrow. He slapped me on the back, like we all belonged to the same club."

"I'm surprised it was that easy."

"Money talks. They make millions on military contracts, but they don't only sell to the military," Linc said.

Kenzie heard a box slide forward and turned around again to push it back.

"It's not illegal to sell gear like this to private buyers?" she asked.

"No, not in this state. Not in most, in fact. But you do have to have an export license from the U.S. State Department for higher-level armor plates."

"That can't be hard for you to get."

He gave her a rueful smile. "Probably not. Lee told me that it takes three weeks to two months. He seemed to think it was a giant waste of time."

She acknowledged that with a nod, then looked back again. There were three vests she hadn't noticed, not in boxes, but folded and stuffed into the rear footwells. "And those?"

"Not SKC. For comparison. The blue one is police issue—it's Kevlar, no plates. A present from Mike. The other two are military grade. Gray camo is the Improved Outer Tactical, for just about everyone. And the brown one with a groin flap is a Modular Tactical—that's Marine Corps."

"I'm not going to ask where you got those."

He smiled slightly.

"I had to wedge them in for the drive home," he said. "The trunk was jammed. The backseat and floor and where you're sitting right now were filled to the roof."

He glanced up at it, running his right hand over the smooth interior surface. "Hope I didn't scratch it anywhere."

"Don't act like you own it," Kenzie teased him. "Where are the other sixty?"

"Mike Warren let me use a police storage area out near the impound lot, and he helped me unload."

"I'm still surprised the SKC people just let you drive off with the goods, no questions asked."

He pulled into a slot. The others were all empty.

"The warehouse supervisor didn't blink an eye when I said I'd take them to go. I got the feeling they're not too strict about who buys their stuff."

"Figures."

"I don't care. Just so long as Lee Slattery buys my story," he said with a wink. "He seemed to."

They had the alternate range to themselves. She'd arranged it with Norm in advance. The bigger range was far more popular. There was the opportunity to talk shop and socialize, and get out of the sun under the awning. And it had a soda machine.

There were no luxuries like that on this side. The shooters' structure looked a little rickety by comparison. Scrubby, low-growing plants had escaped the berm and popped up here and there, giving the area a weedy look. But the smaller range did get used. Brass casings gleamed in the gravel as she swung open her door and stepped out.

"So show me what you got," she said.

Linc popped the trunk before he got out and she went to look. The carpeted cavity was filled with similar boxes, but larger, stamped with the SKC logo next to the X-Ultra brand. The label said *Bullet-Resistant Vests*—they weren't bulletproof, she knew that. Nothing was.

He came around, opened up the top box with a swift stroke of a car key, and took one out.

It was made of standard camo material in desert tones, with laddered webbing straps across the body of the vest to hold equipment.

"Here you go." He handed it to her.

Kenzie laid it on top of an unopened box to unlatch the quick-release fasteners on the side. She flipped the vest inside out, looking at the flat pouches.

"You know what those are for."

"Yes. Small Arms Protective Inserts," she replied.

"I love it when you talk military."

He looked in the box and took out an armor plate to show her, tapping on it. "This is SKC's version. Ultra-thin and very hard."

"The design isn't that different." She took it from him and slipped it into one of the interior pouches, which were sewn into a grid, front and back. "Seems to cover the major organs." Kenzie poked at the interior seams. "It still has gaps, though."

"That's where the new fiber comes in, as backup, in case bullets or frags get through."

"No difference there, either. The IOT is made the same way."

"Not with the same materials. That plate is supposed to withstand rifle fire, super-high-velocity bullets, shrapnel, you name it."

"Supposed to." Doubt drew down her mouth.

"I'm just telling you what Lee and his guys told me. He went on and on about their extensive field testing. He told me X-Ultra was so advanced the army was begging him to manufacture more."

She set the vest down and found more armor plates in the open box. "The army runs its own tests."

"Maybe those results are in the binder." Linc's comment had a sarcastic edge.

"And maybe Lee Slattery is full of it."

Linc laughed. "We'll find out."

She moved the vest with the installed plates to one side. "Where do you want this?"

"Let's fill a few more X-Ultras and then take them all out to the targets." He moved to the car's back door and took out the police vest and the two official army-issue vests.

She held up the vest. "This isn't light."

"No? It's supposed to be."

"You keep saying that."

Linc frowned. "Sorry." He reached out for it and she slipped the wide shoulder straps over his wrists.

"See what I mean?"

"Yeah. Feels like twenty-five pounds at least. Not an improvement."

"Add in the equipment they have to carry around and you're talking fifty or sixty pounds," Kenzie pointed out.

He handed it back to her. "You're right about that."

"Make a note," she teased.

He made a *check* gesture.

"I wish we could weigh them," he added. "The testing we're doing is kind of crude."

"Tsk tsk. Did you forget your graph paper and slide rule? I bet you took first prize in every damn science fair."

"I'm proud to say I have an unbroken record of coming in second every year," he informed her. "Except for the first time. My baby brother sabotaged my baking-soda volcano and I only got an honorable mention. And for your information, slide rules went out with eight-track tapes."

"I stand corrected. So how come you never became a cop?"

"Just not my thing. I was interested in tech stuff. My big brother

RJ, now, he lived and breathed it. Becoming a cop was all he ever wanted."

"Before the Montgomery kidnapping—didn't he get shot by a drug dealer?"

"You read the papers, huh? Not just the headlines. The articles."

"All the way through. After all, I loaned him a really good dog."

"Thanks again for that." He took folded sunglasses out of his shirt pocket and slipped them on. "Feel like putting about five of these together? The light ones are good to go right out of the box. I want to check the targets."

"Sure."

He'd seen the demonstration at SKC. It wasn't difficult to slide the rigid panels in—the vests were meant to be put together quickly. And he wanted her to look at them closely. Kenzie might spot defects he'd missed.

Linc walked out to the row of targets. There were ten. Not a type he'd seen before, tube-shaped with featureless heads. They were made of a composite material that he could barely get the point of his key into. He didn't know exactly what it was, but it looked like it might stop a slug. But considering how higher-caliber bullets cut through flesh and bone and vital organs, maybe not. The Kevlar backing would tell the true story.

He counted his paces as he walked back. The shooters' structure was actually a little too close. They needed to fire from a specific distance.

"Let's get set up farther back," he called.

"Okay. I have the vests ready." She was waving something at him. "These don't fit anywhere."

He reached her. "Those are helmet pads." He took the one she was holding and looked at it to be sure. "SKC is covering all the bases."

"They make helmets too?"

"I don't think so. But word is that some soldiers are sticking rolled-up socks in their helmets because the standard issue pads are hell on their heads. I guess these are like free samples."

"Socks? Remind me to bring extra if I ever get sent out."

"I hope not."

"Don't worry, Linc. I don't plan to re-up."

They went back out to the targets together to dress the targets in the vests, mixing up the army and police issue with the X-Ultras. Linc slung helmet pads over a couple of the featureless faces for something to aim at.

They walked back and she slipped her hand into his. He was surprised and pleased. Not about to say so, just in case she had second thoughts.

When they'd reached the car, she let go to take the guns and gear out of the footwell on her side.

Out of habit, he looked at what was behind them. The chain-link was just as high on the side opposite the targets, but there was a fair amount of overgrowth sticking through the diamonds. There were tall milkweeds, sumac, saplings, weeds. More than enough to hide a man.

The cooler weather had taken its toll, and some of the vegetation was turning brown and keeling over. Besides, the plants filled the shoulder of the busy road just behind the fence. He could see and hear the cars and trucks whizzing by. It wasn't a safe place to stand, if anyone wanted to watch, and whoever tried would be seen from the road.

Not just the road. Linc spotted a slow side-to-side movement at the highest corner of the fence. A cam—a small one, but where it should be. Norm had every inch of his operation under active surveillance. The older man had seen combat, according to Kenzie. He didn't fool around when it came to safety, period. And she had told Norm what was going on.

He or someone in the shop was keeping an eye out for trouble on an inside monitor. Linc told himself not to worry. And he didn't want to worry Kenzie.

Linc turned his attention to getting ready, exchanging his sunglasses for goggles, but waiting on the ear protectors until they'd chosen their weapons. She opened the case.

There were three guns. A Desert Eagle and two smaller guns, plus clips.

"Nothing's loaded." She hoisted the ammo bag and set it close to him. "Take your pick. Norm keeps trying to interest me in that."

She pointed to a Ruger Mini-14, next to a box of .223 ammo.

"Good little gun," Linc said.

"Well, I prefer the Ruger Target with a seven-shot clip," Kenzie added. "And there it is." She picked it up. "I heart Norm. He listens."

He didn't want to use his own gun. Just in case anyone was going to analyze bullets. "I'll take the Eagle," Linc said. "And Gold Dot JHP. Let's see how the armor plates hold up against that."

"Fine." She put on her goggles, then handed him a set of ear protectors. Absently, she whipped her long hair into a ponytail with a scrunchie she pulled from a pocket.

For a second he stopped what he was doing to watch her. The action had an unconscious grace and her lifted arms showed her slender figure to advantage.

Linc swallowed hard and began to load his gun, mentally going over the reasons why he was here. To protect her. To catch the evil bastard who dared to threaten his beautiful girl.

Not yours yet, bucko, he reminded himself. But holding hands was a start. Or maybe second chance was a better way to put it. He thought of that hot and tender kiss she'd given him. It seemed like a long time ago. He looked around the weedy field and out at the targets. Not exactly a romantic setting.

Kenzie attached a loaded clip to the Ruger target pistol and set it aside, pointing the muzzle carefully away. Then she put on her ear protectors and picked up the semiautomatic again, nodding to him.

They moved a comfortable distance apart. Like her, he took a braced stance. They exchanged a look that held determination, a serious commitment. Git 'er done.

Then they turned to aim and take their first shot. After that they fired and reloaded repeatedly, in a random way.

Like combat, more or less, he thought. Where you didn't know what was coming at you, luck or death. You didn't get to choose.

It had been a while since Linc had done any target shooting. He hadn't lost the knack. The vests were taking a beating. But that didn't mean they were defective. They were too far away to see.

They stopped to reload.

Kenzie matched him round for round. He had one bullet left,

and stopped to watch as she squeezed off the final shot in her clip. She aimed for the helmet pad on her chosen target and hit it dead center. The impact was visible but the pad remained intact.

He did the same thing to another target. The pad blew away from the head, in pieces.

It had been penetrated. The thing was crap. Some soldier would have had the back of his head shot off if he'd had that inside his helmet.

He lowered his gun and looked toward her. Kenzie nodded. They checked the chambers to make sure there were no bullets in either of the guns and set them in the case.

"Let's go look," he said.

She lifted off the ear protectors. "Okay."

They kept the goggles on as they walked across the open area to the targets.

Kenzie rubbed her nose. A burned, acrid smell got stronger as they got closer. "Ugh. Chemicals. That's not just the camo."

"Probably the new fiber inside. I don't know what's in it. Could be the plates too."

She and Linc inspected the vests, starting at opposite ends of the lined-up targets.

Elastic webbing dangled from all of the military jackets, torn apart by the force of repeated shots. The single civilian model from Mike showed bullet damage in multiple places on the blue covering. But the yellow Kevlar was intact.

He took a close look at that one and felt it for good measure. There didn't seem to be a single hole, yet he had no way of knowing where all the bullets had hit.

The ballistics lab would have to figure out the details. A high-velocity projectile didn't slam to a stop without leaving a calling card.

He spotted a bullet on the ground below the vest and picked it up. The nose had mushroomed into a dish shape. He stuck it in a pocket.

"See anything?" Linc asked her. He'd moved on to one of the military vests, the IOT, standard army issue. Outside of the shredded webbing, it seemed to be all right.

"This is a fail." Kenzie stood in front of an X-Ultra, jabbing a finger in a burn hole.

The hole was center front. Right where a soldier's heart would be. Linc shook his head, his mouth tightened in a grim line.

Without commenting, he checked the others from SKC.

"These seem to have held up. Wait—no. Something loose in this one." He released the side fasteners and pulled out a cracked piece of thin ceramic plate. "Also a fail. Two out of ten."

Kenzie, gun in hand, had stepped behind the target to pick up the pieces of the helmet pad he'd shot. She handed them to him without saying a word and he stuffed them into his shirt pocket.

He was looking at the featureless face of the target next to it. "Hm. There's a hole here. I don't remember shooting this one in the head. No helmet pad on it."

"So? You missed." She sounded tired. "Everyone misses now and then."

"I didn't miss." He took his car key and began to enlarge the hole, flicking away bits of composite material. "Damn. In deep."

"Bang bang. That's what bullets do." Kenzie slipped a hand into the pocket of her jeans and pulled out a penknife. "Try this." She handed it to him.

After a minute, a large chunk of the target face fell off. He swore, frustrated, and pushed at the head. It thumped into the grass. Separated at the neck, the multilayered Kevlar backing went with it.

"We should set the bad stuff aside," he said. "I'm going back for a box."

Kenzie wasn't paying much attention to him, studying the damaged vests with a fierce look in her eyes.

Linc knew what she was thinking. Frank Branigan had gone out for a routine patrol. He'd known the dangers, stayed alert. Before he'd been shot, he was walking through an orchard or cutting through a field, avoiding the roads. There were too many concealed bombs under soft dust.

His buddies had been with him. From all reports, it'd been an ordinary day and a routine patrol. Branigan was only a few weeks away from coming home.

Now he was back for good. For the wrong reason.

Linc began to remove the vests. He slung the two fails into the box and bent down to pick up the chunks of the target's head, throwing both in.

Kenzie trudged back across the field with him to get more vests out of the trunk. They went through the same drill, reloading, firing, and resetting the targets.

The rest of the X-Ultras passed with flying colors. So to speak. All of it looked like it'd been caught in a firefight. Linc got two more boxes and piled the rest of the twenty into them.

Kenzie carried one, he carried the other. They put them into the open trunk, on top of the two vests that had failed completely.

"Let's get inside," Kenzie muttered. "I can't stand any more of this."

He nodded and went around to his side. "Thanks for helping," he said.

"I didn't want it to be true about the vests. I can't handle any more responsibility for anything."

"I'll take care of it. We're done with this."

She didn't get in the car, just walked away, her back ramrod straight.

He followed her at a short distance, looking to see if the squad had left. The officers were gone, replaced by casual shooters and not many of them.

Linc parked closer to the shop and got out. Kenzie walked past him and up the stairs. He locked the car and followed her.

They hadn't noticed his contribution to their research. Eventually they would.

The rifle bullet was essentially untraceable. He machined his own and he would take the ejected casings with him when he left. Even if he left one or two, there was no manufacturer's mark, nothing to identify.

The distance hadn't been that great. He'd made kill shots at 700 yards. From where he was to where they were was a lot less than that.

Wind scoured the high roof again, scattering bits of gray over the black surface. The sound reminded him of being in the desert. The roof was a barren place, just as lonely.

Fortunately, the wind had died down a few minutes ago and not interfered with the shot. No humidity, no smoke. Nothing to affect his accuracy. The clear, dry fall weather was a sniper's dream.

Best of all, the building on the opposite side of the road had a perfect line of sight to the back of the Hamill shooting range. Its ornamental cornice removed long ago, there were slots in the roofline to rest the SR-25. The rifle was semiautomatic, not bolt action. He could have taken several shots. But he hadn't wanted to or needed to.

He began to break down his weapon, collapsing the bipod and removing it. The S&B sight was next. Hadn't failed him. Excellent glass and quality optics.

Then the suppressor, a plain-looking tube of dark metal. It worked. With that and the noise of the busy road, he hadn't heard the shot at all. The man and woman at the back range hadn't either.

He set the sight and the suppressor within the interior padding of the case.

The routine was soothing. He brushed a speck of grit off the stock, running his hands over its hard smoothness.

In parts, in place, the sniper rifle was ready for the next time. He closed the cover of the aluminum case with a soft click.

CHAPTER 13

Kenzie stretched out on the bed in her room above the gun shop, lying on her side, her leg thrown over one pillow and her cheek resting on another. She was deep in thought, not asleep.

He wasn't going to ask dumb questions and get snapped at. He knew by now that when she was motionless, her mind was racing.

She'd dropped off the gun case and the almost empty ammo bag with Norm. The old guy had seen the test shooting on the shop monitor from the security cam. He didn't know the results, but he didn't ask questions.

Linc had brought up his laptop. She still hadn't seen the dissected shots from the accident video—he had wanted to wait until he had more from the microcamera and show them to her simultaneously.

One slide show, coming up.

It took less than a minute to download the SKC video. The Quicktime software stopped on the opening frame, giving him a brief glimpse.

Linc blew out a disgusted breath. "Bad," he said, clicking keys, issuing commands. *Heighten contrast. Fade shadow. Reduce noise.* None helped.

"Really bad?"

"Not quite. Better than nothing."

"What did you expect from a button-size camera?"

He clicked on a key to start the show. "More than this." Blurry images from his visit to SKC floated into view. He frowned.

He rotated the laptop so she could see. Kenzie stayed sprawled on the bed, but she lifted her head a little. "Sorry," he said. "Nothing I can do about it now."

"I see what you mean."

"The fisheye lens takes in a lot, but it distorts."

"The close-ups aren't too bad," she said.

"Yeah, but I didn't get too many of them. Not like I could stick out my chest whenever I wanted."

She sat up, swinging her legs off the bed but remaining seated on it. "Put it on my laptop with a USB cord so I can really look. Slow it down."

He complied. "Holler if any faces look familiar."

She looked at the video. "How about big guts?"

Linc gave up. "You okay with looking at the freeze-frames from the accident footage? The guy who shot that was a pro."

Kenzie seemed to be bracing herself.

"There are no shots of Christine in it," he promised her.

"Even if there were, I would look," she said. "I have to. She might never remember."

"See anything?" he asked after a while. He'd looked over her shoulder. Kenzie had clicked on the Quicktime rewind button several times. By now Linc had reviewed the footage so many times it no longer made sense. He had hoped her fresh eye would make the difference.

She shook her head slowly. "No one I recognize."

"How about the guy you saw on Christine's laptop?"

"I barely got a glimpse of him. I guess he could be in there." She nodded toward the screen, her mouth set in a tight line. "Hiding in plain sight."

Linc sighed inwardly. So much for all the money he'd spent. Gary Baum had made out like the bandit he was. He closed his laptop and set it aside.

Kenzie pushed her laptop away and stretched out on the bed, her back to him.

Linc waited a few minutes before he joined her, curling around her. Keeping her safe. She let him, but she wouldn't turn around. They lay that way for a while, until her laptop gave a soft chime.

There was more than one way to be saved by the bell. He

rolled over and watched her struggle up to a half-sitting position to look at her laptop.

She checked her e-mail. "Hey. One from Randy." Kenzie read aloud. "Can we Skype at 1800 hours—I think she means today. That's an hour from now."

"Want me to leave?"

"No." She seemed surprised by the question. "I don't mind if you listen. You can say hi if you want to. You're the reason I have something to tell her."

"All right. Okay with you if I grab a bag of burgers before then?"

"Please do. I'm starving."

Linc scooped up his car keys and left. He ran a couple of errands before he got in the drive-through lane at the burger place. When he returned, Kenzie had connected with the medic. He'd figured on giving her time to talk without him there.

Kenzie waved at him without looking away from the screen when he entered.

"Linc just came in," she said. "He's the friend who helped me with this. Want to say hi?"

Linc heard a friendly laugh coming from the laptop. "Sure."

He moved around so he was in view, holding up the bag. "Hey, Randy. Want a burger?"

Randy laughed louder. "Hell yes. We can get them here, but it's not the same. The pickles are weird. You can pass one right through the screen." She reached out.

Linc reached into the bag and held out a wrapped burger, but Kenzie swiped it.

"Not fair," Randy complained.

Kenzie unwrapped the burger and took a big bite. "Mmm. Sorry," she said when she swallowed. "Seriously, I could airship you some in a cooler."

"Thanks. I'll live. So tell me what you guys found out."

Linc sat on the bed next to Kenzie. "Not much so far." He noticed how Randy's gaze moved from him to Kenzie. She had to be thinking that they were a couple. He didn't mind.

He looked at what was behind her, seeing low plywood walls and USB cables draped over them. Not a military setup. He saw signs in French. *Médecins Sans Frontières*. Doctors Without Borders.

Neutrals, Linc thought. Randy Holt was being careful.

"I latched onto some X-Ultra vests," he began. "Plus a standard Improved Outer and a Modular Tactical for comparison."

"Don't forget the cop vest," Kenzie reminded him.

"That too. Kenzie and I used up a lot of ammo. The army stuff held up. So did the cop vest. There were two fails out of twenty X-Ultras."

"Got it," the medic said. Her clean-scrubbed face looked suddenly older. "Thought so. I guess I should tell you guys that we're talking to a colonel sometime in the next couple of weeks. Me and two other medics," she clarified.

"That's great," Kenzie said.

"Maybe he'll listen to us. Maybe not."

"He should," Linc said.

"Ya think?" Randy asked tiredly. "Gee, maybe something will happen before the troop drawdown we keep hearing about."

Kenzie and Linc exchanged a look. Randy Holt was on the front lines in more ways than one. She had reason to be suspicious of empty promises.

"But keep on with what you're doing."

"We will," Linc said.

"Is there anything else you think we should do?" Kenzie asked.

"Your call, people. I'm in Afghanistan."

Kenzie looked to Linc, then back at Randy. "Um, he's going to bring the vests we shot at and new ones out of the box to a ballistics lab."

"Where?" Randy asked.

Linc shot her a look that he hoped the medic would get across five thousand miles. Neutral connection or not. "Take a guess."

"I think I understand," Randy said. "Keep me posted any way you can. I'd like to be able to hand an official report to the colonel."

Kenzie took a deep breath. "I wish we had more to say," she began. "I guess I was thinking we could solve it just like that. Wave a sword, go for the glory."

"Yeah? Watch out for glory. It can get you killed." The medic's words were blunt and friendly. "Listen, you guys did great. Above and beyond."

She didn't have to say *the call of duty*. Linc and Kenzie knew what she meant.

"You still there?"

The call began to show interference. Zigs and zags. Static crackling.

"We're losing you," Kenzie said.

"Yeah." Randy's voice faded. "Same here."

The screen froze but they could still hear her garbled voice. Then she came back, clear and strong. "Reminds me of my grandma's old Philco. She doesn't want a new TV. I guess she likes the special effects."

The screen went black.

Later that night, Linc called Mike from his car.

"We tested the vests. Two fails."

"Out of how many?"

"Twenty." Linc was pushing the point. They hadn't tested them all.

"Two out of twenty is ten percent," Mike said.

Linc resisted the temptation to tell the lieutenant he was a mathematical genius. "Yes it is. So?"

"That could be manufacturing error."

"Error? On the extreme end of what scale?"

"Mine."

"No way," Linc argued. "I would say one percent is reasonable for manufacturing error. If that."

"Ten, one—there's no such thing as one hundred percent perfection," Mike said dismissively. "So you and Kenzie shot up a couple of vests and they look like swiss cheese. That isn't proof that someone forced Christine off the road because of it."

Linc was irked. "And there's no such thing as one hundred percent proof either."

The lieutenant interrupted him again. "Equipment fails all the time. Companies recall it, issue a fix or make good—"

"I don't think SKC operates that way," Linc said, exasperated. "I just toured the place and I saw too many people who looked chained to their cubicles. Most of them wouldn't even glance my way."

"Your point?"

"They're scared to death. The place had a bad vibe. I didn't like it."

"Vibe, bad. Let me make a note of that," Mike said.

Linc told him where to put the note and his notebook. The lieutenant only laughed.

"I walked through a room where you could smell the fear. The drones are afraid of management and management is afraid of the execs. Guess who's raking in the big bucks and doesn't care."

Mike coughed. "Show me the tax returns."

"Come off it, Lieutenant. You know how big corporations work. SKC is getting bigger and richer every day."

"A military supplier is going to make hay while the sun shines. There is a war on. When it ends, there will be another one."

"It's not right."

There was a pause.

"You vote, Linc?"

"Yeah. Hell yeah."

"Then that's about all the say you have. It's a free country. SKC and Lee Slattery are allowed to get rich."

"Not for the wrong reasons."

"You have to prove wrongdoing. I keep saying that. And then you have to prove they meant to do wrong."

"The ballistics lab will—"

Another bark of laughter cut him off. "They will get back to you. In, what, weeks? Months?"

"I don't know."

The lieutenant shut up for a few seconds. "I'm trying to keep you on the straight and narrow, Linc. Call me back when you find some evidence."

Linc ended the call with a push of a button. He longed for the old days, when telephones were heavy enough to kill someone. Slamming down a receiver would have been a lot more satisfying.

CHAPTER 14

The rehab center was a low structure comprised of several buildings joined by glass-walled corridors. Kenzie walked down one with Alf Corelli, holding Christine's bags and carrying a hand-crocheted blanket over one shoulder. They had arrived ahead of Mrs. Corelli and Christine, who were coming in a patient-transfer van that had one other stop to make.

Colder weather had arrived in the area and both of them wore heavier jackets. Alf had added a snap-brim hat to his outfit and Kenzie had a muffler wound around her throat. The sun-splashed corridor was a pleasant place to walk, if too warm for what they had on.

The center was a lot more open than the hospital. A little too open, though she didn't want to say so to Alf or his wife. She pushed aside her feelings of uneasiness. They couldn't live in bunkers. It was bad enough that she hadn't been back to her apartment even once.

Besides, there were a lot of people around. Staff. Patients—it was center policy to get them out of their rooms at least twice a day. She noticed that the corridor was more than wide enough to accommodate wheelchairs going in opposite directions or side by side.

Several patients were strolling or being pushed in wheelchairs between one building and another. A few people were making their way using walkers. Most wore regular clothes. Kenzie was very glad that Christine was out of the baggy-gowns-and-shuffling-slippers stage of her recovery.

Alf tipped his hat to an elderly lady who was going slowly and not without difficulty. She brightened and gave him a little smile, walking just a bit faster.

Kenzie wished that men still did things like that. It was a shame that being gallant was considered old-fashioned. Then she thought about Linc and smiled to herself.

It took a while to get Christine settled in her new surroundings, and she seemed irritable. She knew she was somewhere different but she didn't seem to know why. The jiggly suspension of the van had made her doze off and she'd been groggy when she awoke. Dr. Asher had warned them that it would take her time to adjust to a change of this magnitude.

It occurred to Kenzie that Christine had never quite seemed to know that she was in a hospital. Her room here was a lot more homelike.

Her parents had left to complete the paperwork for the transfer, and Kenzie was in charge.

"It's nice here," she said encouragingly. "What do you think?"

"There's too much light," Christine said in a low voice. "I can't turn it off."

Kenzie looked toward the picture window and the clear fall sunlight streaming through it. At the hospital, Christine's room had beige curtains that were often drawn over the one small window. The ceiling fixture was usually dimmed, unless the doctor was there. She understood why Christine would feel uncomfortable at first.

She went to the picture window and fiddled with the pull cord until a pleated drape lurched forward, stopped, and got stuck for good halfway. Kenzie was afraid of breaking the cord. She would have to call a nurse assistant or wait for Alf.

Christine turned her back to the window and stared at the wall. There was no picture on it. Kenzie thought of the bright posters framed behind plastic that she'd taken down the last time she painted her apartment. One or two of those would add a cheerful note if the rules allowed it.

Right now there wasn't much she could do. She heard the familiar but unexpected noise of scrabbling nails on a smooth floor and turned to look a moment before a brown-and-white dog entered the room.

A red service-animal jacket was strapped around the dog's plump midsection, but Kenzie could see that she was a female and young. The dog seemed to be in charge, tugging at a leash held by a smiling young woman with curly hair.

Kenzie glanced at Christine, who was sitting on her bed, still withdrawn. "Look who's here. Did you ask for a visit?"

Christine shook her head and turned away slightly, as if she didn't want to look at the dog or her handler.

"I'm sorry. Peach is new here and she tends to just charge in." The volunteer took a step backward and looked at the room number. "No, my fault. I have the wrong room. Well, my name is Ginny. It's nice to meet you, Christine."

Kenzie hesitated when Christine didn't reply.

She'd sat in on the team meeting with Mr. and Mrs. Corelli. A social worker had emphasized that neuro-rehab patients were expected to speak on their own without being urged to do so, or worse, interrupted by well-meaning people speaking for them. A psychiatrist made sure they knew the move to rehab might cause Christine to regress to some extent or behave strangely at first.

They got the idea: The recovery process was never easy and cognitive therapy was unpredictable. Kenzie could see that for herself right here and now. Christine talked more, but she sounded uncertain and very young. She got stuck on some subjects and then forgot about them in the next second.

It was something new to worry about. But everyone on the staff seemed genuinely involved and concerned.

Ginny didn't seem at all fazed when Kenzie introduced herself but not her friend.

The dog came forward and got busy sniffing Kenzie's ankles, circling around slowly. Kenzie laughed, pinned to the spot.

"This is her first week," Ginny said. "She doesn't know the rules. Peach, behave."

The easygoing handler wasn't making a point of it.

The dog tugged her over to the bed and set her front paws on the edge, peering curiously at its occupant.

"Now, that's not good manners," Ginny began, unsure of Christine's reaction. Christine remained indifferent.

Both she and Kenzie smiled with relief when Christine reached out a hand and began to stroke Peach's head. The dog let her tongue loll to one side, giving Christine a comical grin of enjoyment.

"She has pretty eyes," Christine said in an almost inaudible voice.

"Yes, she does. She gets those from her mama," the young woman explained.

The dog made the most of her moment in the spotlight by gazing soulfully at Christine. Then she stretched up another inch, bracing herself with her paws, and licked the tip of Christine's nose.

"Hello," Christine murmured, "you're sweet."

The ice broken, she invited Peach up on the bed by patting it. The plump dog was happy to oblige, sniffing at the blankets and getting her nose into the folds.

"What is she doing?" Christine asked. She still asked questions in a tentative way, as if she was afraid she might not understand the answer.

"Oh, she's wondering if you have a treat for her. But she's on a diet right now. Peach is a little too fond of food," Ginny said. "She gets that from her mama too."

Kenzie chuckled. "Her mother must be the beagle part."

"That's right," Ginny said.

"Kenzie knows everything about dogs," Christine said. She adjusted her position so that Peach could come onto her lap. The dog settled down and the red service jacket scrunched up around her neck as she gave Christine another adoring look.

"Not everything," Kenzie said. "But a lot."

"Oh, do you work with dogs?" Ginny asked.

Kenzie explained briefly.

"That must be so interesting." Ginny seemed eager to hear more, but she didn't ask, returning her attention to Christine and the dog in her lap. "Look at you, Peach Pie. You're so silly."

"I think she wants to take a nap," Christine said softly. The dull expression on her face had been replaced by one of interest. She rubbed the dog between the ears until Peach closed her eyes in bliss.

Ginny smiled and shook her head. "How did you know? Napping is her favorite thing besides food. But she has friends to see."

Christine lifted a floppy ear and pretended to whisper in it. "I need a nap too. But come back."

She rumpled the dog's fur under the jacket to rouse her. Peach opened bright brown eyes and grinned again.

"Faker." Ginny laughed. She gave a slight tug on the leash and the dog left Christine's lap, pausing on the edge to gauge the distance to the floor from the bed.

"Go." Christine gave her a light pat on the rump and Peach made the leap. Christine looked up at Ginny with a wistful smile. "Can she come back? Today?"

"Of course. She really likes you. We'll stop by on our way out."

"Thank you," Christine said simply.

The dog's nose moved to the floor and she followed it.

"Peach Pie," Ginny called. "Let's go."

The dog strained against her collar in the opposite direction. Kenzie suddenly saw what Peach was after: There was a black disk lying in the corner.

Her heart tightened. She had one thought—it was a transmitting device. Not here. Not in this safe, sunny place.

But anyone could walk in here. Ginny had.

"Hang on." She forced herself to stay calm as she moved the chair that held it in place out of the way. Then she bent down and picked it up. It was the top to a condiment cup from someone's takeout meal.

"Just an old lid. The cleaning service must have missed it." Kenzie smiled and tossed it in the trash, earning a mystified look from Peach. "Not for you," she chided.

"If it has something to do with food, Peach will find it," the handler joked.

"We'll remember that." Christine smiled again and waved as Ginny left with the red-jacketed dog. "She was nice," she said to Kenzie.

"Yes. And Peach looks like a lot of fun. Better hide your lunch when she's around."

Christine sat back in the pillows.

"How are you feeling?" Kenzie asked.

"Better. Hope it lasts."

Kenzie collapsed into a chair. She was so tired she was seeing things. A little piece of trash seemed suspicious. Linc had something to do with that.

"You okay?"

She nodded, propping her chin on her hand. "Sure. Just frazzled. It's been a long day for all of us."

The routine hubbub of a medical-care facility echoed in the halls. Kenzie heard the clank of trays being delivered to individual patients from a food cart. Judging by the sound, they had a little while before it reached them.

"Kenzie, tell me something," Christine began. The brief happiness of meeting the friendly little dog had worn off fast. She seemed low again. "How long will I be here?"

"For a while. We all want to get you home." Kenzie kept her replies simple.

"I know I was in an accident," Christine blurted out.

Kenzie sat up. "What?"

Had the Corellis told Christine that? Kenzie seemed to remember that they'd planned to before the move to rehab. But she hadn't been at the hospital every hour of the day.

As far as she knew, Christine had never asked. By unspoken agreement, there had been no photos of the black-and-yellow sports car among the others they'd shown her. One thing at a time. That was a big thing.

Christine reached under her pillow and pulled out a thick folder. Her medical file, Kenzie saw at a glance. "Mom left this at the front desk."

"How do you know that?" Kenzie asked, startled for the second time.

"Someone brought it by when you weren't here and said so. Stuck the whole file in that thing." She gestured. "Some papers fell out, so I read them."

Kenzie turned that way to glance at the clear plastic document holder attached to the door. It was empty. She looked back swiftly, suddenly afraid. "Who was it? A woman or a man?"

"A woman," Christine added. "She was old. Not like Ginny."

Kenzie extended a hand. "May I see the file?"

Her friend wrapped her arms around it. "No."

"All right."

Christine relaxed after a few minutes. "I know it's about me. I can read some of it, but the words don't stay still."

"That's okay. It's really good that you can read."

Kenzie was heartened, but Christine's wavering voice gave away how she felt.

"I want to know what happened to me."

Kenzie heard a quiet exclamation coming from the doorway. The Corellis had returned. She murmured a quick explanation of the file.

"Oh—I forgot to take that," Mrs. Corelli whispered.

Their daughter stared at them with troubled eyes. "Why didn't you tell me?"

"About what, honey?" her father asked.

"The accident."

"It wasn't time yet," Mrs. Corelli answered straightforwardly. "And now—I guess it is."

"I don't remember anything about an accident." She stopped, thinking. "I woke up in the hospital and you were all there."

"That's right," her father said. "You were in the ICU for more than a week and we stayed with you."

"What happened—well, it's over." Kenzie left it at that. She couldn't think of the right thing to say. It was hard to bear the idea of Christine reliving a nightmare.

"I want to remember some things," Christine said. "I think I do."

"You will." Again Kenzie hesitated, looking at the Corellis. "When we were looking at the photos, you knew the people. Where you were and who was with you—"

"Not the accident. I want to know." Her insistence made her voice rise.

"Christine, do you mind if I go outside with your mom and dad?"

She shook her head, still hanging on to the file. Kenzie and the Corellis closed the door behind them and conferred in the hall.

"I wish I could talk to her doctor first," Mrs. Corelli said worriedly. "But it's the end of the day. He must be gone."

"If you're worried about what she knows, the file doesn't give particulars," Alf said. "I read through it, made sure everything was in order."

"Thank heavens for that," his wife replied.

"For now Christine doesn't need to know anything other than that she was in a wreck and suffered a head injury," Alf replied. "Agreed?"

He looked from his wife to Kenzie. They both nodded. No one spoke as they went back into the room.

Mrs. Corelli sat by Christine's bed and tried to explain. Finally, she let go of the file with some reluctance.

"Do you want to eat something?"

The tray of food that had been left on a side table for her hadn't been touched.

"No," Christine said. "I'm tired."

Kenzie stayed near the door. Her mind was racing. In the last several days, she'd learned an awful lot about brain trauma. Recovering her full memory could send Christine into emotional shock. Kenzie didn't need a social worker to explain why.

She thought again of the man's eyes. Mesmerizing her with the power of his hate. Had Christine seen them up close?

If she didn't remember him, that was a mercy. They had to do more to catch him. Not the Corellis—she and Linc.

Kenzie would go to the police sketch artist as Linc had suggested. She had to try. Not that seeing the stalker's face on an eight-by-eleven-and-a-half sheet of paper would cut him down to size. He'd terrified her on a laptop screen.

She was afraid that the sudden knowledge of the accident would make him appear in Christine's dreams.

Her sleep had never been peaceful once the drugs were withdrawn. But Christine had never seemed to remember if she'd had a bad dream.

It bothered Kenzie beyond belief that family members weren't allowed to stay the night here—the rehab center had different rules on that. Tonight, Christine would be alone for the first time since the accident.

Kenzie saw the social worker and psychiatrist, a young woman and a gray-haired man, heading down the connecting hall, coats on.

"Excuse me," she said quickly and dashed after them, out of earshot of the Corellis.

She literally took them both by the sleeve, pleading to break the rules.

"Just once. For tonight. Not the whole family—one of us. She's upset—please."

The rest of the conversation was hushed, but the two others finally agreed. Dr. Liebling left written orders at the front desk for the night staff.

Kenzie went back to tell Mr. and Mrs. Corelli.

Alf went out around seven P.M. to buy an inflatable mattress. He drove to the nearest gas station and took it out of the box, attaching it to the nozzle of the air pump and feeding in quarters. No one there looked twice.

He returned to the rehab center and managed to get it through the door. The nurse at the front desk looked up from her magazine as he approached.

"Evening," he said.

She kept a straight face. "Hello, Mr. Corelli. I saw the doctor's orders. Go ahead."

"Thank you." The air mattress wobbled under his arm as he walked away. She looked after him, smiling faintly, and went back to her reading.

Christine laughed when he entered her room, then clapped a hand over her mouth. "That looks like the one we took to the beach."

"It's firmer than that," he said.

"Let Kenzie stay," his daughter begged.

That hadn't been decided.

"Please." Christine's voice was shaking.

"All right," the older Corellis said in unison.

Kenzie couldn't sleep. The air mattress had a soft, flocked

cover, but it smelled strongly of new vinyl. There were no sheets. She didn't give a damn. Christine had drifted off, but not before giving her a blanket from her bed.

There had been no more talk of the accident before her parents left for the night. But Kenzie's fears on that score were realized hours later. Her friend began to thrash, crying out as if someone was attacking her.

Kenzie struggled up from the sliding mattress on the floor and went to her. Christine's eyes were wide open, gleaming in the darkness just before dawn.

"Shh," Kenzie soothed. She put a hand on her friend's forehead. Not hot, but beaded in sweat. "Shh. I'm here. What's the matter?"

"Bad dream."

"It's over."

Christine sat up in bed, clutching the covers and burying her face in them. "It seemed so real."

"It wasn't. Dreams are only dreams."

"No, Kenzie. He was there."

"Who?" She knew the answer before Christine said it.

"The man who hit me. When I was in your car."

CHAPTER 15

Another session with the SKC laptop yielded nothing. Linc was done with cudgeling his brains and was about to switch on the television when his cell phone rang.

Good old Mike. He debated the wisdom of answering, then told himself that something could have happened to Kenzie or Christine.

"Hey. What's up?"

"Got the soil analysis back."

Linc drew a blank for a second. "Huh?"

"From the double set of tire tracks we found north of the accident site," the lieutenant said patiently. "Under the maples."

"Right. They were Norway maples."

"Awww. You remembered," Mike said.

"So what did the lab say?"

"Got a pencil?"

Linc looked around. "No."

"I'm at work, Linc. I can't drop off a copy. There's three new cases on the board, and one is a double homicide. The chief's breathing down my neck."

He clicked some keys, opened up a new document on his screen. "Okay. Blank doc ready to go. I'm putting you on loudspeaker."

"You can touch type?"

Mike's voice sounded tinny but he could hear him.

"Yeah."

Mike read from the lab report. Linc got the gist of it down.

"So the tires on the wrecked car had dirt, seeds, you name it, from both places."

"That's right," Mike replied. "But keep in mind that the dirt and road grit samples from both were very similar. There's only a half mile between the accident site and the spot north of it, under the maples where the tire tracks didn't get washed away."

"Got it. Go on."

He could hear Mike rattle the papers he was reading from.

"However, the vegetable matter in the samples—seeds, like you said, leaves and that kind of stuff—was very different."

"So it looks like Christine did stop under the maples first. Before the car crash."

"Yes. And don't forget the tracks. Not fresh, not perfectly clear, but we were able to identify the type of tire on the other car."

"Nothing that would be unique to those tires? You know, like wear patterns, tread damage?"

Mike sighed. "No. Just the type." He told Linc what it was. "You can look it up online if you want."

"I will. Anything else?"

"Backtrack. You told me about the vests but not the visit to SKC. So tell me. I promise not to insult you."

Linc stopped typing and leaned back in his chair, picking up the cell phone and taking Mike off speaker.

He took a few minutes to fill him in on his visit to SKC. "I tried to get video with a microcam, but it didn't work too well. Bought a bunch of X-Ultra vests for my nefarious purposes, and listened to Lee Slattery for two hours. The guy's a talker."

"That's good. Keep him talking," Mike said. "Sounds like he took a shine to you."

Linc shrugged, even though he knew Mike couldn't see him. "I had someone at the agency call and vouch for me before I showed up. He was impressed. And I spent a lot of money."

"Not yours."

Linc laughed. "You know where I'm living. I got a grant, put it that way. My boss okayed it."

"All right. Don't tell me more."

"I wasn't going to," Linc replied.

"Any other breaking news?"

"Uh, besides that, I've been hanging out with Kenzie."

"Keep an eye on her. Someone has to. How is Christine doing?"

"They moved her to a rehabilitation place," Linc said. "Kenzie said she's adjusting pretty well."

"At some point she might start to remember the accident."

"Not yet. When Christine came to, her mom and Kenzie started using pictures to help her talk. As in one word at a time. I understand she's making progress, but she has a long way to go."

Mike was silent for a few moments. "Give my regards to the Corellis when you see them. They're good people. Can't wait to catch the bastard who did that to their daughter. We are going to catch him."

"Damn straight," Linc said.

Mike didn't say anything more. Linc could hear the everyday noise of a police station in the background.

He came back. "Gotta go. Thanks for the update."

Mike hung up before Linc could say good-bye.

The information on the tires and what had stuck to their treads was good, a few more pieces added to the puzzle. But there were still an awful lot of gaps.

Linc thought for a few minutes and started a new search online.

It was time to go back several years, find out more about how the huge SKC complex had been financed. Transparency wasn't a mandate in the closed world of military contracting. Despite Lee Slattery's backslapping friendliness, Linc suspected that SKC followed the same unwritten rules.

By the fifth page on Google, he came across an unflattering article from years ago on the company that would become SKC. He glanced at the reporter's byline and then at the thumbnail photo.

Linc hooted. Gary Baum had written it.

So that was what he looked like before he got bitter and cynical. Baum must have been right out of college then. Eager. Young. So young that Linc could picture him with freckles and a bowtie, holding his journalism degree rolled up with a red ribbon. Ready to go forth and fight injustice.

Linc was chuckling when he picked up his cell phone. He tapped Gary Baum's number, listening to the ring.

Could be an easy way to get more information on Lee Slattery and a couple of the names he remembered from his tour of the factory. If Gary had kept his notes.

Gary answered and said hello in a surly voice.

"Hey. Linc here. How are you, Gary?"

The reporter seemed taken aback by the warm greeting. "Fine. You?"

"Bet you're wondering why I called," Linc began.

"I'm not giving the money back."

"That's the last thing on my mind," Linc assured him. Not strictly true—he'd just checked his bank balance, surprised by the precipitous drop in available funds once all the checks cleared.

"So what can I do for you?" Baum asked in a slightly less nasty voice.

"Well, I just happened to come across your name online. You wrote an article about SKC. A colossus in the making, you called it."

There was a pause.

"That was a thousand years ago," Baum said.

"Doesn't matter. I thought it was very well-written," Linc said. "Seriously."

Gary gave a snort. "It was all right. Not my best." He paused again. "So why were you interested in it?"

"I'm getting to that. There's a connection to—"

"The accident," Gary crowed. "You know, once you paid me all that dough, I really started thinking. The station researcher happened to mention that the girl in the wreck worked for SKC. So let me take a wild guess. She was having an affair with the smooth talker, the big boss with the silver hair. Lee. Right so far?"

"No."

The reporter was on a roll. "I bet it gets worse. Lee didn't want wifey to know and there was an argument. Her parents hired you and you're looking to take Slattery down. Am I warm? Am I hot?"

"Not even lukewarm."

Gary Baum swore, very creatively. "So enlighten me."

"I can't tell you that much. Actually, I'd like to interview you for a change."

The reporter cackled. "That's a switch. Okay, the motel again?"

"Come on over."

"Just because I have nothing else to do, I will. You don't even have to pay me for my valuable time."

"See you." Linc rolled his eyes as he hung up.

Gary arrived about an hour later with a file folder under his arms. He held it out. "Clippings. That's how long ago it was."

He walked to the table Linc had turned into a desk, glancing— not idly—at the open laptop.

Linc was ahead of him. He'd set the screensaver to a happy fish swimming around, followed by a lady fish with pouty lips who bumped his fin and gave him a big fat fishy kiss.

"I like your aquarium," Baum commented.

"Thanks. So what's in the file?"

Gary pushed the laptop to the back of the table and opened it. "First draft to the last. Notes. Some photos they didn't run. Knock yourself out."

Linc sat down and indicated that Gary should do the same.

"That's Slattery," Linc said. "Not quite so silver."

"Correct. I'm surprised I remember those guys as well as I do."

"I just met them myself," Linc said. He intended to keep his comments on the safe side.

Gary flipped through a few pages and photos that were jumbled together. "I bet Lee Slattery hasn't changed much. The Great Introducer, right?"

"He was a glad-hander, no doubt about it."

"The other guy, Vic Kehoe, had just joined. He was ex-army, if I remember right. Or ex-something-like-the-army."

Linc looked more closely at the picture. "I met him. I thought he was military." He raised a questioning eyebrow.

"No big surprise. A lot of execs like him and Lee are. Even though a lot of their products are outsourced. These days, military supply is like any other business."

Linc let him talk.

"I mean, there are plenty of reputable companies," Gary conceded. "They have, like, a mission. Quality is a big deal to the best of them."

"What about the rest?"

"Look, there are a few operating on the cheap in countries where laws are a joke. Ship it back and sell it for top dollar to

Uncle Sam. Just so long as you stay within a procurement budget, everyone's happy."

"So are you saying that's how SKC got started?"

"They cut a few corners. Rumors were flying about kickbacks, internal corruption—there was an investigation."

"Police? Federal?"

Gary snorted with contempt. "In-house. Slattery got it hushed up fast—apparently the corruption was high up. As I remember, a couple of execs got the boot and that Kehoe guy took over for them."

"Do you mean he took over where they left off?"

The reporter chuckled. "Two sides to that question, aren't there?"

"Maybe."

"I couldn't say. Their black-ops materiel support was what put them on the map. Slattery and Kehoe both got rich."

"How rich?"

"Very," Gary said. "That's a booming business. Mobile prisons—they invented those. Bring 'em in to remote locales by helicopter, take them out the same way. That's how they got started. Or that was the scuttlebutt, anyway."

"Interesting."

The reporter nodded. "Kehoe had the know-how and he hired out as a consultant. Still does, I guess."

"How about Slattery?"

"He liked to hint that he hung out with tough guys who got the job done and to hell with due process."

"I didn't get that impression."

Gary Baum snorted. "Mr. Chamber of Congress never met a colonel he didn't like. SKC's been awarded one fat contract after another. About the only thing they don't make is guns and ammo. Everything else, oh yeah. Corned beef hash to chemical toilets. One-stop shopping for all your army needs."

"Didn't they just start making body armor?"

The reporter gave him a shrewd look. "You asking me or telling me?"

"Asking."

"I heard that they were, yeah. Sounds like their kind of deal. Let's say sixty thousand units at eight hundred per—what is that?"

"About five million."

"And that would be only one order." He sighed, gathering up his papers. "I don't know why I thought journalism school was a good idea."

"So," Linc began, "do you have negatives for these photos?"

"No. They're digital."

"Even better."

"Want a disc?" Gary asked quickly.

"How much is it going to cost me?"

Gary grinned. "Not a cent." He looked through the material in the file. "There's a couple in here. Aha."

He pulled out a square envelope with a silver disc inside and handed it over.

"One for you and one for me."

"Thanks."

Gary scowled at the photo of Lee Slattery. "I can't stand that guy. I was in the running for a byline at a national paper, and he called the owner, told him that he thought I was, quote unquote, a weasel."

"Really."

"That was the end of that job. And that's how I ended up covering the blood-and-guts beat for W-K-R-A-S-H."

Linc didn't think that was the name of the TV station, but it was close enough.

"You can have his picture for nothing. And I'll throw in the other guys as a bonus. If you don't mind my asking, what did Lee Slattery do to you?"

Linc only shrugged. "I hardly know the guy. I just needed more info on his background for my, uh, client."

"I see," Gary said. "Clear as mud. But I don't care." He closed the folder and shoved it over to Linc. "You can have my notes too."

"No charge?"

"Nope. Maybe I'll need a favor someday."

"I'll keep that in mind."

CHAPTER 16

Christine's new laptop was on her bed, resting on a book. The Corellis felt the same way as Kenzie about the old one: that it was somehow tainted. They'd bought a pearl-white model that looked like the first, except that it had no stickers. Kenzie had stopped at the dime store to pick up a few packets, but Christine didn't seem interested.

Right now she was on Facebook, scrolling through messages from friends.

"Wow. Look at my wall. Hundreds of get-wells and luv-yoos and hang-in-theres. I can't answer them all."

"You don't have to. Your mom posted daily updates from the beginning."

"I guess I wasn't ready for visitors. I'm still not," Christine said.

Kenzie nodded. Christine had more good days than bad, but neither was predictable. "That's up to you. Neuro rehab is no party."

Christine laughed a little. "My therapist says it's a challenge. If I get any more challenged, I'm going to run away."

"You'll get through it. One day at a time." Kenzie took out the shopping bag from the dime store and pulled out skeins of yarn and two thick plastic needles. She cast on a row and added several more before Christine noticed.

"I didn't know you could knit."

Kenzie smiled. "Just the basics."

"Are you making a potholder?"

Kenzie held up the rows with the knitting needles. "I'm hoping it will turn into a scarf. Give me a year."

"When did you learn?"

"In Germany. A buddy had some extra yarn and needles. She was really good—she could do Fair Isle patterns."

"Oh. I had a Fair Isle sweater once." Christine smiled again. "Somehow I never pictured you knitting."

"You know, it calms me down," Kenzie said. "Oops. Dropped a stitch." She picked it up. "I don't even care when I make mistakes."

Christine glanced outside, distracted by a group of men in the courtyard. They wore coveralls and carried buckets. One pushed a round contraption that held squeegees and, Kenzie figured, the cleaning solution. Another dragged a very long hose.

Kenzie went back to her knitting. "The windows could use a wash."

She'd seen them unloading their van when she arrived. The window cleaners had been moving from building to building in the rehab complex.

"Guess we're last," Christine said. She returned to her Facebook session.

It was another hour before the cleaners set up outside their window. They sloshed detergent-laden water over the glass before they got to work.

Christine looked on, absorbed in the rhythmic motions of the squeegees mounted on long, flexible poles. She still did fall into short trances now and then.

Kenzie found herself doing almost the same thing. "It's almost like being in a carwash."

Christine giggled. "I know what you mean. Hey, I just remembered something. Frank kissed me in a carwash once. He said he didn't want anyone to see. It was a great kiss."

Kenzie dropped another stitch and didn't bother to pick it up. Christine turned back to the laptop as the cleaners wiped off the dirty water with practiced strokes, leaving the window sparkling clean. They set down their gear and headed back for the van.

"That was so nice of you and Mom to make that slide show for me," Christine said. "Frank was in it, wasn't he?"

"Yes." She steeled herself for the next question, putting down her knitting.

Christine hummed as she scrolled through photos. Kenzie didn't know if she was looking at the slide show or Facebook pages.

"There's Frank," Christine said happily. "In his new bulletproof vest. He looks proud. Did you know I took that picture of him?"

"No." That particular photo was on Facebook. Kenzie dreaded what was next.

Kenzie hadn't touched a computer for months after Dan Fuller's death in Afghanistan, not wanting to see his smile or read the kind tributes. His parents and his stateside friends hadn't known who she was.

It didn't take Christine long to find the memorial page. Kenzie saw her eyes widen and fill with tears. "What?" The single word was a painful whisper. "Those are—his boots. And his rifle and his tags. That's a battlefield cross."

Kenzie bit her lip as Christine pushed the laptop violently away. She rocked back and forth, hard. Her mouth opened but not a sound came out. When Kenzie rose to go to her, she waved her off.

"Stay away from me."

"Christine—"

"He's dead. I didn't know. No one told me."

"We couldn't," Kenzie whispered. "We just couldn't."

Her friend curled into a ball around a pillow and hid her face, racked with grief. Kenzie stood there. There was nothing she could do.

Outside the room, the ebb and flow of the center's afternoon routine continued. Kenzie went to the door and closed it most of the way. If she'd shut it completely, someone on staff would have come in.

It was dusk when Christine stopped crying. Kenzie sat on the edge of the bed and touched her shoulder. Christine didn't shrug off her hand, reaching out instead to cover it with her own.

"I know you couldn't tell me," she said softly. "I just wish—I never got a chance to say good-bye."

"No one did. It happened very suddenly."

"Tell me how," Christine said in an almost inaudible voice. "Tell me everything."

Kenzie didn't. But she told Christine what little she knew about the firefight and about his buddies risking their lives to try and save him. She told her about the medic who'd been with him at the end.

"Where is he buried?"

Kenzie told her that too. "There's no tombstone yet. But his grave has a marker. I visited the cemetery when you were in the hospital. I told him that I was there for you and me—and that you would come soon."

"I want to go." Christine's voice was low and raw. She sat up.

"We'll go together," Kenzie whispered.

The two friends held each other until the sky outside the window darkened into night.

CHAPTER 17

Linc was waiting outside the rehab center in response to her text. Kenzie gave him a wan smile as she opened her door and slipped into the front seat.

"We don't have to talk about it," he said.

"Thanks. I had to tell the Corellis. They came right away."

"How's Christine?"

"Quiet. But she's okay."

Linc didn't ask any more questions, but drove through the streets. She seemed preoccupied, but that was to be expected.

After a while she spoke again. "Just so you know," she said, "it wasn't like Christine and Frank were madly in love. But I think she had her hopes. His side of it—well, that was complicated."

"You told me that. It's okay. You don't have to explain."

She looked out the window. "Turn left here."

He recognized the street. It had been a while since his mad dash to get to her apartment building that rainy night.

"What is that?" She leaned over the dashboard to see better.

"Looks like scaffolding."

Her building was half-concealed by metal bars that connected at every corner. Long planks were slung between them for walkways.

"I didn't know they were painting the exterior," she said.

"Looks like they're just getting started." Linc found a parking space a safe distance away. He was back in his regular car, but that didn't mean he didn't care if it got spattered with paint or dented by a falling bucket. Though it did look like the painters were done for the day.

He went around to help her out after he'd switched off the ignition, but she was way ahead of him, reaching to open the front door of the building as she kicked aside a drop cloth. Linc clicked the key to activate the door locks and followed her.

"So tell me why you wanted to come here," he said, watching her unlock the door. She bent down to pick up the notice from the management about the painting.

"Just because," she answered.

Kenzie paused to read the notice. "We apologize for the inconvenience and assure all tenants that the painting crew does not commence work until eight in the morning. However, you are advised to keep shades down in the interests of your personal privacy." She crumpled it up and stuck it in her bag. "Thanks for the heads-up, people."

She swung open the door and both of them saw that the place was as neat as they'd left it. She breathed a sigh of relief. The amber walls glowed in the light from the single lamp they'd left on. Low watts, long life. It hadn't burned out.

She walked into the kitchen, went in and came back out, lightly touching her hands to the walls as if she was reassuring herself that they were there, this was home, it belonged to her.

"I missed it so much," she said. "It's good to be back."

Linc nodded, making a closer study of the place that had nothing to do with sentiment. He literally saw nothing amiss. The polished wood floors couldn't reveal footprints like a carpet. Nothing had been moved.

"I guess I should tell you," she went on. "Christine and I talked about getting a place together. Or maybe two apartments in the same building. Not this one. Not hers."

"Could work," Linc answered.

The apartment was quiet. Almost eerily so, without the everyday clamor of the active gun range coming through the windows.

But something was making the back of his neck prickle.

Kenzie flopped down on the couch. She stretched her arms out along the back. "If all this craziness hadn't happened, I would stay."

She smiled up at him.

"But it did happen, Kenzie."

She moved forward and lifted herself up with her fists.

"Oh, all right. Just thinking out loud. Let's get what we came for and go."

"What was that again?"

"My laptop."

He tried to remember where they'd stashed it. His mind went blank on that subject as he tried to process what his senses were telling him.

"Something the matter?" she asked.

"Can't put my finger on it."

She reached up and stroked his jaw. "Relax. For once."

Linc got distracted by that. But the tension didn't leave him. He was right behind her when she pushed her bedroom door open all the way and switched on the overhead light.

Kenzie stopped cold. He did too, looking over her shoulder. She'd made up the bed, but not with a coverlet. She'd used a blanket instead, one with a fine silky nap.

It held the impression of a man's body. A big man. He must have lain there for a while, spread out. Waiting for her to come home.

Someone's been sleeping in my bed.

Linc could almost hear the words as she thought them.

Kenzie stepped back and he put his arms around her.

"I got you," he said.

Kenzie twisted in his protective embrace and broke free, running to the living room. She stopped there, breathing hard but otherwise silent.

Linc pulled his gun from its concealed holster and slammed open the closet doors. No one. He found a broom and thrust it under the bed. Empty.

He did the same thing throughout the apartment. "He's gone."

"Just tell me one thing," she begged. "How did he know that I was coming here?"

Linc didn't answer. He holstered the gun and took a small flashlight out of an inner pocket of his jacket.

"What's that for?"

"It has a UV bulb."

"So?" She snapped out the single word.

"New paint reflects UV light. Old paint absorbs it. So if we see a patch, then it's likely there was a bug placed behind the wall."

He tapped lightly, listening for hollowness as he swept the small flashlight back and forth.

"Crap construction. You can hide a body behind drywall if you want to. A bug is nothing." The back-and-forth motion of the light suddenly stopped. "Got a glow." He tapped on the wall again. "I need something small and sharp."

Kenzie went to the kitchen to scrabble in a drawer and came back, a small tool with a triangular blade in her hand.

Linc used it to trace a large square in the wall, then carefully sawed around it. He used the blade's tip to pry the square loose.

"There it is." He pointed to a black plastic device positioned in the space between two studs, held in place with taut wires on either side.

He flicked a dangling wire. "This isn't connected. Could have been left there for me to find. This guy likes to play mind games."

"So what do we do?"

"Remove the rest of the drywall. Or you can move out for good. Take your pick."

Kenzie looked at the black plastic circle. She turned away without saying a word and went to her closet, grabbing a duffel bag and filling it until he took it gently out of her hand.

"I didn't mean right now. Let's just go."

"No. He wins if we do. I won't let him scare me off."

Kenzie rested her hands on the window and pressed her forehead against the coolness of the glass.

"Do you have a headache?"

"Yes. Pounding like a machine gun."

"I'll get you some water and a couple of pills."

She heard him leave and go into the bathroom, opening the medicine cabinet over the sink.

"Find some?" she called.

"Yeah. Where are the paper cups?"

"Next to the mouthwash."

"Got 'em," Linc said, his voice fading slightly.

She turned her head sideways, trying to take the heat out of her face by pressing each cheek against the cool glass in turn.

Left. Then right. It helped a little. She stayed there and closed her eyes, her hands still resting where she'd placed them.

"Dropped one."

She heard him curse and opened her eyes, looking absently toward her resting hand.

There was another hand on the opposite side of the window. A man's hand.

Kenzie drew back in horror.

Him. Dressed in black. A half mask—black too—covered his face from the bridge of his nose to his chin. There was an opening for his mouth.

He smiled.

There was only the glass between them.

His breath marked the window as he spoke. Sickened, she had no idea if she heard him or read his lips.

You can't hide.

He moved back, keeping himself in the shadow. She caught a dark gleam in his other hand. He held a shotgun. The double barrels were lethally short.

Kenzie screamed. Mute terror took over as the man vanished into the night.

Linc came running, catching Kenzie as she stumbled backward, away from the window.

"He—he was there," she gasped. "On the scaffolding."

Linc raced to the window, beginning to lift it when she screamed again.

"Don't look out! He has a gun!"

She grabbed both his arms from behind and held on with all the wild strength she had. Linc didn't fight her. She didn't need another dead hero in her life.

Linc returned to the apartment very early the next morning. He knew Kenzie would be holed up at Hamill's for the day.

Let in by Norm last night, she'd headed through the gate fast and gone straight upstairs, leaving him on the other side. She was as safe as she could be there.

Linc had gone shopping. The coveralls and cap he had on looked too new even with his artistic splotches from a kid's watercolor set, but he figured on the tenants not being that awake.

Per the notice, the painters hadn't started yet. The scaffolding was empty.

He walked under it, looking up. Kenzie's apartment was on the third floor. A row of planks ran right under her bedroom window.

Linc grabbed a bar and swung himself up to a connecting metal ladder. He got to the third floor quickly and walked along the planks. Someone had stashed a bucket and roller, both crusty, in a safe corner. He decided on the bucket for a prop, and picked it up by the handle.

Making very little noise, he went on, stopping to the side of her closed window.

The glass had no mark. She had said his hand was ungloved. Either the stalker hadn't actually touched the window or he'd cleaned it afterward.

He could easily have waited one floor above and watched them go. He was methodical, Linc would give him that.

He stepped in front of the window, noticing that the inner floor was parallel to the planks he stood on. His reflection nearly filled the window.

Linc did a little deduction. He knew where Kenzie came up to, standing against him. And she said she'd been eye to eye with the stalker. So the man wasn't as tall as he was, but close.

Kenzie's bedroom looked the same. He'd let her grab the laptop from its hiding place and they'd retreated.

The rising sun cast its light over the glass and made it hard to see the surface of the soft blanket. Linc set down the bucket and cupped his hands by the sides of his face, peering in.

The blanket seemed the same. He moved away from the window and rested his hand on a supporting bar. Above it on another bar was a scrap of black cloth. Very small. Snagged on a piece of sharp metal.

He examined it without touching it. If it had scratched skin, there could be DNA on it. That was for Mike.

For Linc, the scrap was a signpost that pointed to the roof. He made his way there and looked around, not seeing anything that stood out. Still, there could be latent prints—finger, palm, shoe—on a lot of surfaces.

Linc took out his cell phone and called the lieutenant at home.

"Rise and shine, Mike."

He heard a groan. Then a curse.

"Same to you," Linc said pleasantly. "Listen, can you meet me at Kenzie's building before eight?"

"Call me back at ten. I might be awake by then. *Might.*"

"Let's shoot for seven-thirty."

"How about I just shoot you, Bannon? Not fatally. I'm thinking a graze."

Linc offered a very brief explanation of why he was there and what he needed from the police.

There was a sound like a drawer opening and closing. A nightstand drawer. Just big enough for a pencil and small pad of paper.

"Give me the address," the lieutenant snarled.

Linc did. Twice. Slowly.

"See you," Mike said.

Linc leaned over the roof when he heard a car, the first to go down the street since he'd arrived himself. He could just see the lieutenant at the wheel, steering with one hand and holding a takeout cup of coffee with the other.

The car was unmarked. Mike parked it at a yellow stretch of curb, tossing a PD placard on the dash.

The door swung open and Linc pulled his head back. Ten minutes later, the door to the roof was pushed open. Mike was red in the face and breathing hard.

"This better be good," he warned.

"Give me that." Linc took the empty coffee cup from him and crunched it into one of the pockets of his coveralls.

"What, do you think I'd contaminate a crime scene?"

"No."

Mike walked out onto the roof, staying on a narrow board walkway over the asphalt. "Did you know that the security cams in the stairwell are kaput?"

"I noticed that the first time I came here," Linc said quickly.

"Standard creep trick. Who would notice? This is a small building, they don't have anyone looking at the feeds on a monitor. Those cams are up so building management is covered in case of a lawsuit."

"You could be right. The black paint on the lens didn't look new either."

"Allow me to extrapolate." Mike was warming up. "Creep did the artwork on the lenses, maybe came back to check it a few times, and figured no one knew what he looked like or suspected someone was hanging around."

"Well, now we have more to go on—or rather, Kenzie does. He was gone by the time I got into the bedroom. He had a mask on, but Kenzie saw him up close. I didn't get into it with her. She was a mess last night, in shock—"

"Linc. I saw her walk in to the station when I was leaving. Harry Cowles, our sketch guy, was waiting to meet her."

Linc wondered why she hadn't called him. Oh, well. As long as she was there.

"That's great."

"Guess you didn't talk to her about it."

"Not today. Not last night either. I was going to."

Mike smiled faintly. "Kenzie doesn't seem to be the type who waits for instructions."

"No," Linc said. "Which is good sometimes and bad other times."

Mike only nodded. He stepped on the board walkway and surveyed the roof. "Okay. We need to dust. This is a big area. I have to call a couple of my guys, get them out of bed."

"Do that. I'm going to go home and change. Meet you back here."

The words were spoken into the air. Mike was squatting down, examining the textured asphalt surface by the walkway. He picked up a few grains by pressing his fingertips against it. "Old and crumbly. I bet some of this stuck to his shoes." He looked up at Linc and flicked the grains away. "Maybe he keeps his shoes in the same place he hides his car. Haven't found a trace of the black bomb."

Linc shrugged, heading for the door to the stairs. "I doubt he took the tires off it."

"Meaning?"

"He has more than one pair of shoes and more than one car," Linc called back over his shoulder as he went down to the landing. He paused to listen to Mike's reply.

"Don't get cocky. I thought of that."

"Good thing you could come in right away, Ms. MacKenzie," Harry said.

"Call me Kenzie." She smiled, summoning up her confidence. "I wanted to do it while the memory is fresh."

Not quite the right word. *Seared* was better. That masked face was going to leave a permanent scar in part of her brain.

The police artist opened up a file on his computer. "Was there a particular feature that really stayed with you? Like, say, a broken nose or male pattern baldness? We can start with something like that and go on to the more subtle stuff."

Kenzie hesitated.

"We can go slow," Harry advised. "Getting a likeness takes patience."

"I didn't see his hair. He was wearing a mask that covered a lot of his face. It—it had an opening for his mouth."

Harry listened.

"His eyes," she said. "I saw them clearly."

"Good. Let's look at eyes." He clicked on a document. "Take your time."

CHAPTER 18

Linc met up with Kenzie at Hamill's. She was out in the parking lot, throwing a large ring toy for Beebee. The dog had boundless energy, but she looked wiped out.

The gate had been left open. There were a few shooters getting ready to fire at the range and a customer inside the shop. He returned Norm's wave through the glass.

From inside his car Linc watched Beebee gallop off to retrieve a wild throw. It took him about half a minute to find it and come back with the large ring hanging from his mouth. He looked like a door knocker. A very happy door knocker.

"Give it up," she told the dog. Beebee shook his head. "So much for you being an obedience champ."

The dog didn't seem to care in the least. He went to the doormat of the shop and flopped down. Then he put his paw protectively over the toy and grinned at Kenzie.

"Having fun?" Linc asked as he approached.

"Beebee is."

"He has a lot of energy."

Kenzie summoned up a smile from somewhere, but it disappeared fast. "Not me. Not after last night."

Linc gave her a reassuring chuck under the chin and she lifted her head. The vulnerable look in her eyes got to him. She had a right to be scared.

"Mike and a couple of detectives are going over the building. I gave them your apartment keys."

"Fine with me." She shrugged. "You know I'm never going back there, right?"

"No reason to. Not for you, I mean."

She thrust her hands into the pockets of her jeans, looking over at Beebee. "When I get shaky, I lean on him."

Beebee sat, still keeping his paw over the toy, surveying the parking lot. He looked even bigger at rest, muscular and heavy, his black coat gleaming in the sun.

"Good idea. He's a great dog." He hesitated for a second or two, then spoke. "I was thinking maybe you'd like to get away for a day."

"What do you have in mind?"

"You and me and a lazy river."

Her green eyes lost their vulnerable look. "Sounds nice."

"We could be there in half an hour."

She nodded. The smile came back.

"Is that the place?" she asked. "Hard to see all of it."

The boathouse was tucked under the bridge on the George-town side. A row of colorful kayaks rested on a floating dock. Several had been taken out and returned, judging by the puddles underneath them.

"It's there."

They made their way down carefully. Departing kayakers had left puddles on the steps too.

"How wet are we going to get?" she asked jokingly.

"We're ready for it."

Linc had stopped on the way at a sporting goods store and bought quick-dry tops and bottoms for both of them. She'd wanted to pay but he had waved her away from the register as the cashier was cutting off the tags. They'd changed in the dressing rooms, returning to the car with their jeans and warm jackets bundled under their arms.

The proprietor came out of the boathouse when they reached the docks. "Hiya. I'm Ted. What can I do for you?" Ted had long hair tied back in a scraggly ponytail and a relaxed grin. He wore baggy print shorts that hung below his knees and almost fell off his skinny hips.

"We'd like to rent a kayak for a couple of hours," Linc said.

"No problemo. You guys got the memo on the no-heavy-clothes-thing, I see." He looked with approval at their outfits. "I can give you a drypack for your wallets and stuff."

Linc nodded. "That would be great."

"Okay," Ted said, leading them to the kayaks. "I can set you guys up with a double. Pick a color."

"Your choice, Kenz," Linc said. "Pink, purple, yellow. There's a green, ready to go." He pointed to the side of the dock.

"Hmm." The shape of the bobbing kayak and the color put her in mind of a leaf on the water. Exactly what she wanted to be. "The green one."

"You got it." Ted walked back with them to the boathouse and Linc took care of the rental paperwork. They listened to Ted's brief spiel on safety and rules of the river, then put their personal items into the drypack he offered them and donned lifejackets.

Ted took hold of the nylon rope that kept the kayak alongside the dock and pulled it closer.

"Ladies first," Linc said.

Kenzie stepped down into the scooped-out seat and found a comfortable position against the low backrest. Then she extended her legs into a partially bent position and rested a hand on the attached paddle.

"Whoa. I'm not in yet." Linc stepped in and the kayak rocked. He took a little longer to get settled, slipping the drypack under a flexible net.

"Excellent," Ted said. "You guys look like you know what you're doing."

"Just so long as we don't have to run any rapids," Kenzie joked.

"Nah. The whitewater is way upstream. But be careful. Down here the Potomac looks fat and slow, but it can fool ya."

Kenzie looked out at the wide river. Farther out, tiny ripples met and swirled where the water was deeper and the current got stronger.

"Ready to shove off?" Ted asked.

"Yup," Linc said.

She looked over her shoulder to see him raise his paddle and use it to push away from the dock. Ted waved to them. "Have a great time, you two."

Kenzie sat with her paddle resting across her thighs.

"Might as well let me start us off," Linc said.

"But you're doing all the work."

"Feels like fun to me. Just relax."

She didn't argue.

They floated silently through the soaring arches of the Key Bridge, which seemed much higher from their new vantage point. Downriver, there was a faint mist that hung above the water, softening the stone walls of the riverbanks.

The large, wild-looking island ahead seemed lost in time. The tall trees on it had lost most of their leaves, but there were touches of rich autumn color here and there on the bare branches.

For the first time in weeks she felt free, moving through the river as naturally as the fish and fowl who lived in it. She breathed in its coolness, enjoying the play of light on the surface.

"I could do this for days," she murmured, glancing over her shoulder at him.

Linc laughed. He seemed much more relaxed himself. His dark hair was blown every which way by the light wind, and his face glowed with ruddy color.

"I know what you mean." He paddled on with strong, swift strokes, and she picked up her paddle and joined in, just for something to do.

Another double kayak headed upstream, keeping close to shore to stay clear of the current. Kenzie thought for a moment that it held three people. She squinted. There was a man, a woman, and—

"Oh, it's a dog," she said.

It was a retriever, outfitted in a canine life vest, whiffing the air and having a fabulous time. She waved to its owners as they went by.

"Can you imagine Beebee on a kayak?" Linc said with amusement.

"If he stayed still, he'd be fine."

"And if he didn't, he'd capsize us." Linc paddled closer to the island. "Want to get out? There's a nice little cove right ahead. We could tie up to a tree."

"No." She laughed. "Just drifting like this is heaven."

He whistled a song that she knew mentioned heaven in the lyrics. The kayak pointed downstream again and the island was behind it.

It was nice knowing that Linc was so close. If it weren't for the low seat, she could lean back and lie in his arms. Well, no. Not if he had to paddle.

"I changed my mind," she said. "Let's go exploring."

Linc grinned and turned the kayak in a tight half-circle. "You got it."

Closer to, the island didn't look as inviting. Maybe it was because the sun had gone behind a cloud. The tangle of dead brush under the tall trees seemed impenetrable.

She turned around and glanced anxiously at Linc. "Maybe we shouldn't. Those look like briars. And I'm sure that's poison ivy."

He lifted his dripping paddle and rested it across his lap while he looked out at the island.

Something about it didn't seem to sit well with him either. He didn't argue with her.

Two hours later they returned to the boathouse and saw Ted on the dock.

"Looks like we're the last ones to come in," Linc said.

Ted didn't seem at all concerned about it. His baggy trunks fluttered in the wind as he checked lines and got the kayaks squared away for the night.

"Hey there," he said. "How was it?"

"Great. Really great," Kenzie replied as Linc maneuvered the kayak against the dock. Ted bent over to grab the nylon loop attached to the prow and held it while they both clambered out.

Linc reached for the drypack, then handed it to Kenzie while he helped Ted drag the kayak up onto the dock. She took out his wallet and hers, and watched them at it.

It only took a couple of minutes to secure the lightweight craft with the others. Ted walked back with them the short distance to the boathouse.

"Hang on," he said. "Just want to give you guys a flyer about our weekend deals."

They went with him into the area set aside for customers and waited. Ted looked through brochures and papers and found what he was searching for. He handed the flyer to Linc. "Here ya go, dude. Starts this Friday."

"Thanks," Linc said, looking it over.

"Unless . . ." Ted's attention was distracted by a small TV tuned to a weather channel. The announcer was saying something about a big storm system headed their way. She predicted three days of rain, heavy at times.

"Yikes," Ted said. "That changes everything. We might have to shut down."

"How bad can it be?" Kenzie wanted to know.

Ted gestured toward the calm river. "The opposite of that."

"Oh well," Linc said. "There's always another weekend. Thanks, man. We'll be back."

They drove far into Virginia instead of heading back to Ridgewood. Kenzie dozed off for a while, pleasantly tired from the day in the fresh air, waking to see that they were on a two-lane road with a solid yellow stripe down the middle.

It didn't seem to matter. There wasn't anyone else who might want to pass them. Bare-limbed trees arched over the road, visible only for the brief time they appeared in the headlights. There wasn't a house in sight either. She felt almost as if they were traveling back in time.

"Where are we going?" Kenzie asked, yawning.

Linc turned and flashed a smile. "A country inn. An old one. It has a fireplace this car would fit into."

"Sounds cozy."

"You look like you need some warming up. I've been meaning to ask you out for a nice dinner."

Kenzie looked down at the clothes she'd changed back into. "How nice?"

"Don't worry. It's low-key, but the food is excellent., especially the seafood."

"Are we near the Chesapeake?"

"Between the Bay and the Blue Ridge. That's all I'm going to say."

"You are a sneak," she complained. "But I'm starving. So you're forgiven. You still haven't told me the name of the place."

He grinned. "I know where it is. Isn't that enough?"

"What's the big secret?"

He pretended not to hear her. "The inn dates from Colonial times, if you really want to know."

Kenzie reached out and messed up his hair. "Aha. I understand they didn't have combs then."

Linc laughed, not bothering to smooth it back down, and turned into a wide driveway that crunched loudly under the wheels of his car.

"Hear that? Oyster shells. This place is authentic."

Kenzie peered into the darkness outside the car window. The old inn's carriage lamps, hung on iron bars, didn't provide much illumination. She realized with a start that the small parking lot was crowded with late-model expensive cars.

The inn was a white saltbox under a low roof, with additions to either side. Diamond-paned windows glowed warm and welcoming on either side of a heavy carved door.

An older man, impeccably dressed, escorted his beautifully coiffed companion down the front stairs. Her conservative high heels barely showed under her long coat. Kenzie caught the glitter of diamonds against a fur collar. This was definitely not Ye Olde Crabbe Shacke.

"Linc—"

She turned to him, but he was already out of the car and coming around to her side to open her door.

"Welcome to the Greenwood Inn," he said, offering her his hand.

Kenzie finally saw the oval sign above the front door. The Greenwood Inn only looked unpretentious. The inn's long-standing reputation for intimate dinners and excellent American cuisine attracted the elite of DC and the wealthy of Maryland and Virginia.

"I am so not dressed for this!" she hissed at him.

"Don't worry about it," he insisted. "They serve by candle-light."

Kenzie groaned under her breath. She searched in her bag for a pair of flats and changed out of her sneakers. That was about as posh as she could get. Fortunately, her clothes were dark.

She found a comb and tossed it at him. Linc didn't seem to care in the least what he was wearing. If he had the nerve to walk in to the one and only Greenwood, she would too. Besides, she really was starving.

The maitre d' welcomed them with smooth aplomb, not looking at their clothes. It wasn't as if Linc knew him or anyone else there. It was just that the place was too discreet to notice minor indiscretions.

Kenzie peeked into the main dining room while the maitre d' looked over the seating chart. Linc was right about the candles. Waiters came and went quietly over wide-planked, shining floors, serving the customers in near silence. She could swear she saw a senator or two. There were other faces she recognized, people who weren't exactly celebrities, but who were definitely powerful or renowned in some other way.

"Could we have a table in there?" she asked, pointing to a smaller room that seemed to be a bar, though with a few tables set for dinner. A cheerful fire blazed inside a vast fireplace, brightening stones blackened with age.

"Of course," the maitre d' said after a confirming look at Linc, who nodded. "Please follow me."

Kenzie slid into a chair, hiding her jeans-clad legs immediately under the white damask cloth. Linc sat down next, smiling at her. "You look gorgeous," he said softly.

"Thanks." Her irritation vanished, replaced by interest in her surroundings. Massive beams overhead and the warmth of wood everywhere made the room cozy but not stifling. The Greenwood Inn really was authentic, right down to the draft from the old windows.

Linc was examining a wine list as if he did it all the time. She wasn't familiar with the vintage he eventually ordered from a sommelier, but the man seemed to respect his choice and withdrew, taking the list.

Linc began to study the menu. "Are you hungry enough for an appetizer?"

"Sure. You pick. I'm heading for the powder room."

When she returned, there were two wineglasses on the table and the business with the cork and first taste seemed to be over with. Kenzie sat down and sipped from the glass poured for her. The white wine was delicate, almost tingly.

"Nice," she said, pleased.

"Glad you like it."

A waiter appeared with a cut-crystal bowl of crushed ice topped with six tiny oysters and thin slices of lemon. He set it in the middle of the table.

Kenzie looked at them nervously. The presentation was dazzling, but . . . the oysters were raw.

"What's the matter?" Linc asked.

She ventured a smile. "Are they dead?"

"Far as I know." He laughed. "Sorry. I should have asked. Not everybody likes raw oysters."

"I just think they look better cooked," she assured him. "With bread crumbs. A lot of bread crumbs."

"Not a problem. What the lady wants, the lady gets. And I can easily eat those by myself." He was about to summon the waiter when she put a hand on his arm.

"Really, it's okay. I'll look at the menu while you eat the oysters." She studied hers carefully. It seemed to be classic American cuisine—she chose roast chicken and Linc ordered fish.

"Well," she said, putting her napkin over her lap. "The Greenwood lives up to its reputation. See anyone you recognize?"

He glanced into the main dining room. "I do. Wish I could table-hop and make a few powerful friends. We could use some on this case."

"But you're not wearing the magic suit," she teased him.

"Nope. Guess we'll have to come back."

Kenzie moved her knife a sixteenth of an inch to the left, closer to the spoon. "Is this dinner part of a plan to distract me?"

"Kenzie—"

"It's working. I can't think about—that man—all the time. So thanks." She swallowed the word *stalker*, not wanting to say it.

"We may have something more to go on there. Mike Warren keeps the brakes on, though. He's a slow and steady kind of guy."

Kenzie looked up at him. "So is Harry—the police sketch artist," she clarified, when Linc drew a blank on the name for a second. "We're making progress."

They set the discussion of the case aside when the salad course arrived. It was a lot easier to talk about the merits of blue cheese dressing—hers—versus herb vinaigrette—his.

Both entrees proved to be excellent.

She had more of the wine than he did, because he was doing the driving. In fact, she was pleasantly tipsy by the time the bill arrived, presented and taken away as quietly as everything else.

Kenzie rose when Linc had signed the final slip of paper. Her face was glowing from the fire and the sparkling wine—she could feel it.

"Thank you," she said simply.

"My pleasure."

He escorted her to the outer room, and stopped off on the way. Kenzie made a beeline for a comfortable-looking armchair and plopped down to wait.

A glossy folded card on the small table beside it caught her eye. Idly, Kenzie opened it.

A photo of a lavish four-poster bed made her sigh. Below it, discreet small print advertised the room rates. The Greenwood really was an inn.

What an incredible bed. The canopy was trimmed with hand-knotted lace and the coverlet looked soft as a cloud, with a deep ruffle that brushed the carpeting.

It was easy to imagine herself in a bed like that. With Linc.

Kenzie thought back to the time she'd put a blanket over him, sleeping as best he could on her couch. When he'd lugged the new mattress upstairs to her room at Hamill's, she'd almost given in to temptation.

It would be heaven to spend the night with him here.

She heard him coming and hastily closed the card and put it back.

Linc walked over to her. Kenzie got up a little unsteadily and allowed him to take her elbow. The night air was cold and refreshing when they went out the front door, stirred by a brisk wind that rattled the branches.

They walked the few steps to his car and Kenzie rested a hand on it, glancing up at the midnight sky and then at him.

"I don't want to go just yet," she whispered.

He turned her around to face him, holding her close. The dark gleam in his eyes held a tantalizing promise. "All right. There's nowhere else I'd rather be."

The vibration of his deep voice made her more giddy than the wine. Without hesitation, Kenzie slipped her arms around his waist and lifted her lips to his.

Linc didn't wait to kiss her hard and deeply, his hands running over her pliant body as if she wore no clothes at all.

The wind whirled around them. The carriage lamps swayed on their mountings, casting flickering light that didn't reach them in the shadows.

She wanted to stay in his arms forever. It was the only place where she felt truly safe.

The storm came and it stayed. By the second day, Kenzie was convinced it would never stop raining. The remembered sensation of Linc's kisses warmed her for a while, but frustration got in the way eventually.

She wanted him. The desire was mutual—and intense. But there was just too damn much going on for that to be anything more than a highly sensual fantasy.

She helped out in the shop at the shooting range, but there weren't very many customers. Norm told her she might as well skedaddle back upstairs. She was happy when Mrs. Corelli called to chat and even happier when the older woman accepted her offer to be with Christine for the rest of the day.

The other alternative was returning Harry Cowles's call, which she wasn't ready to do. None of his sketches so far resembled the man she'd seen. She was frustrated by her inability to remember him—and angry at herself.

Christine still didn't know about the stalker. Kenzie's instincts told her that he was concentrating on her at the moment. Maybe she was more fun to hunt. He didn't seem to be as interested in wounded prey.

Kenzie could defend herself. And she intended to protect Christine.

She shook the thoughts away.

Christine would be glad to see her. Kenzie got ready to go and made a mad dash to her car.

Peach was curled up on Christine's pillow, the picture of contentment.

"Ginny stopped by at the end of her rounds," Christine explained. "She had errands to run, and she didn't want to take Peach in the rain."

The dog gave a sleepy sigh.

"Tough life, Peach Pie." Kenzie laughed.

"I like having extra time with her." Christine stroked her ears. "She's one popular dog."

They chatted for a little while about nothing in particular; then Christine asked an unexpected question. "Don't you miss the dogs at the kennels?"

"Ah—yes," she replied. "But I know they're going away. So I try not to get too attached."

"Oh."

Kenzie wondered something. "Would you like to visit the kennels with me? We could, you know. Any time."

Christine shook her head. Her face was turned slightly away from Kenzie, who couldn't read her expression.

"Is something the matter?" Kenzie asked gently.

"I'm not sure I'm ready to go anywhere just yet."

"Didn't your mom and dad take you out?" Mrs. Corelli had mentioned something about it.

"We went for a drive. And I—I just got so scared."

Kenzie came over to sit on the bed by Christine.

"You don't have to tell me why if you don't want to."

Christine hesitated. "I don't even know what road it was. We didn't go far from here, though, I'm sure of that."

Then they hadn't been anywhere near the site of the accident. That made sense. Kenzie couldn't imagine the Corellis taking her there.

"I was up front and my mom was in the back. My dad was driving."

"Was there a lot of traffic or honking?"

She'd noticed Christine's sensitivity to loud noise and how much she disliked feeling crowded. Chalk both up to brain trauma.

"No. The road was clear and it was sunny. But the signs went by so fast. I got disoriented."

"Was that your first time outside the center?"

"No," Christine said, then amended her answer. "I mean, yes, if you mean in a car. I went walking with my parents and the physical therapist lots of times. Just not with you."

Kenzie nodded. "Go on."

"I couldn't help thinking that something bad was going to happen."

Agitated, Christine shifted position, twisting her hands in her lap.

Peach picked up on it. She raised her head and then got all the way up off the pillow, moving to Christine's side and settling down again.

Absently, Christine began to pat the dog's rounded side, and her agitation seemed to lessen.

Peach Pie was pure, warm comfort. Better than anything Kenzie could think of to say.

"I asked them if we could go back, but I didn't say why. We weren't out for very long. When I got back here, I felt okay again."

"Your mom and dad didn't know how you'd react," Kenzie began.

"Sometimes I wonder if they're sick of taking care of me," she blurted out. "Or if you are."

"Christine, you know that's not true."

Kenzie was concerned, but that was beside the point. The important thing was that Christine had to be able to say what was on her mind.

She patted the dog, lost in thought.

"I'm sorry," Christine replied after a while. "Maybe it's just that I don't like having other people take care of me."

Kenzie smiled. "Me neither. I totally understand why that would bother you."

"And I wish that I could do something besides walk around the center and back to my room. And I want my words to connect with what I think. They don't always. I get so mad when I make mistakes."

"Patience is beautiful."

"Stuff it," Christine said with spirit. "I'm tired of being patient too."

Kenzie had to laugh. "Sounds to me like you're getting better, even if it doesn't feel like it sometimes."

"Am I? Do you think I'll ever be able to go back to work?"

Another unexpected question. "Of course you will."

"You know something? I miss it. I never thought I'd say that in a million years. Not about SKC."

"Oh. Um, they are keeping your job open," Kenzie said tentatively. There was no way she was going to explain about the defective SKC vests anytime soon.

"They'd better. The outdoor company must have hired someone else by now."

So Christine remembered that detail. Good sign.

"They probably did," Kenzie said. "Let's talk about something else."

Christine looked out the window at the rain. "What? Like how cranky I am?"

"No. Don't be silly."

"Well, books then. Except I can't read for longer than five minutes. There's always movies. Seen any good ones?"

"I stopped on the way and got a couple of comedies."

Christine made a funny face. "Are you trying to distract me?"

The dog at her side woke up and stretched, then yawned.

"Yes, I am." Kenzie turned when she saw Christine look toward the door.

Ginny had come back. Peach jumped down to the floor and trotted over to her mistress.

"Hi, you two," Ginny said. "Did Peach behave herself?"

"She lived up to her name," Christine said affectionately. The dog wagged her tail in agreement. "Yes, I'm talking about you."

"Glad to hear it. Take care, Kenzie. And you too, Christine—thanks so much for watching her."

The three exchanged good-byes and the handler left with her dog. Kenzie took the two DVDs out of her purse and handed them to Christine.

"You pick. I don't care which one."

Christine looked absently at both. Then she made her choice and took out a DVD from the case, getting her laptop from the bedside table.

She opened it and stopped.

"Kenzie," she said, "I just remembered—there was an SKC laptop at my apartment. Did they ever ask for it back?"

Reported stolen. Kenzie didn't say the words. She wasn't inclined to do SKC any favors, for that reason and a few others she wasn't going to tell Christine.

"I think so."

"Maybe I should ask my mom," Christine said. "She told me you went and got mine before it broke down."

White lie of the week.

Christine slid the DVD into her new laptop.

"I'll ask her," Kenzie said quickly. "If it's there, I'll find it."

"That would be great. There's a lot of stuff on it that I was working on, but I'm not sure exactly what. If I do go back, I'd like to be caught up." She frowned. "If that's even possible. My boss Melvin is a forward-march type. Did you ever meet him, Kenzie?"

"No." That was absolutely true.

"I don't feel like giving it back to him," Christine confessed. "Sorry. I ask you to do so many things for me."

Kenzie waved that away. "What color is it?"

"Black. It's chunky. Not like this one. I think I left it in the hutch."

"I'll look there. Did I tell you that your mom tidied up your place?"

Christine groaned. "I'll never be able to find anything ever again."

"Do you want to go back?" Kenzie was risking a lot by asking the question, but Christine might think it was strange if she didn't.

Christine stopped looking at the movie menu. "Not yet. Not for a while. It's like—" She hesitated, searching for the right words. "I was someone else when I lived there, put it that way. It seems like a very long time ago."

Good enough. Kenzie would have been hard put to come up with a reason for Christine not to go back to her own apartment.

She called Linc once she was ensconced in her rooms above Hamill's. He was out somewhere. Sounded like a bar full of loud guys.

"What are you doing?" she asked.

"Watching sports on TV, playing foosball, and having a beer," he said cheerfully. "What's up?"

"Just wanted to ask you something."

"Okay." The background noise diminished. "I'm someplace quieter. Go ahead."

She heard a tremendous crash and then his yelp. "Dropped tray," he muttered. "No major damage—to me, anyway."

Kenzie rolled her eyes. "Do you want me to call you back?"

"No. You said you were going to ask me something. I want you to ask me something."

Maybe he'd had more than one beer. He sounded a little too cheerful all of a sudden.

"I spent the afternoon with Christine," she said.

"How is she?"

"Doing okay. She asked me about the SKC laptop."

"Oh?" He sounded more serious.

"She just remembered that it was in her apartment. She wants it."

"What for?" Linc was totally serious now.

"I think she has some vague notion about getting caught up with whatever she was working on at SKC. Just in case she goes back or something like that."

"It is hers. Or theirs. Not mine, anyway."

Kenzie knew he'd copied what he might need from it. "I think you should just keep it for now. She's apt to forget that she asked for it—she still does do that."

"You sure?"

"Yes. I think so." She paused for a moment. "You didn't ever find anything on it that would scare her, right?"

"No. It all seemed fairly routine. I hate to admit that most of it confused me, but that may be because some of it was in code."

"I think I'm following you."

She heard a faint sound like a heavy door swinging and realized he'd gone outside.

"Hear that?" he asked.

Kenzie was silent. "No."

"It's a cricket. The rain's stopped. It's chirping up a storm."

"Don't say that word. I don't believe you anyway. It's under a little umbrella."

Linc laughed. "No, it isn't, and neither am I. I can see a couple of stars too—right there, where the clouds are opening up. One for you and one for me."

"That's nice." Kenzie hoped her smile was in her answer. She missed him.

"Okay, nature girl," he said. "I had another idea for something to do. Want to see where the river gets wild? Great Falls is amazing after a storm. We could go tomorrow."

She wanted to see him right now. But she heard one of his buddies come out and start joking around. Another joined them.

"Sure," she said. "Text me a time. I'll be ready."

Kenzie leaned against the flat side of an enormous boulder, using it to brace herself as she watched the river below her, at near-flood level after two days of ceaseless rain. It raced and smashed over rocks that were barely visible in the dark water and

white foam. The wind whistled through the gorge, the last reminder of the storm front that had stalled and finally blown
through.

Linc was somewhere behind her. He'd stopped to help a group
of hikers find their bearings on a map they'd unfolded. She'd
gone ahead, a little annoyed by their endless questions.

The storm-swollen river captivated her. Jagged rocks, danger-
ously slick, crowded closer together at the falls. The river boiled
over, a white torrent. The churning water below became a trap
that no one could escape.

The warning signs made the danger very clear, but there were
those who didn't take them seriously.

Kenzie kept a safe distance. But she still enjoyed the beautiful
display of nature's power.

By chance—she hadn't heard them—she turned to see an elderly couple. They were dressed alike in khaki, both with binoculars around their necks. Slowly but surely they made their way up
the path behind the rock, and paused to talk to her.

"Isn't it amazing?" the woman asked.

"That's the right word. Yes."

"Hope we didn't startle you," the man said.

"No, not at all. I saw you before I heard you."

"Well, I guess you found a safe perch." He smiled at her.

She indicated their binoculars. "How's the birdwatching?"

"Oh, we saw a few," the woman replied. "Nothing unusual. Our
friend the heron must be hiding from the storm. Perhaps he hasn't
woken up yet."

Our friend the heron. They were so sweet.

"Maybe so." Kenzie laughed. "Best of luck. I think we're seeing
the last of the storm."

"Let's hope so," the old man said.

"Now you be careful, dear," the woman said to Kenzie. "You
wouldn't want to slip. Not with the river so high and wild."

They went on. Helping each other over rough spots.

How it ought to be. She looked sideways and down, not seeing
Linc. Where was he?

Wild as it was, the park always had visitors, and they were generally quite friendly. Some were from out of state or even other countries. But a large number of them were from right around here in Virginia and Maryland.

She went on a little farther, going the opposite direction from the old couple, keeping her hands on the rock as she moved along the increasingly narrow trail.

Someone spoke to her. Kenzie didn't look around. She couldn't.

"You're very near the edge." A man's voice. Not young, not old.

She gritted her teeth. "I'm being careful."

"That's good. The water is dangerous."

There were a lot of well-meaning people in the world, she thought. "Yes, I know."

The pleasant voice paused. Maybe because she was acting like someone who didn't want to listen.

"River and rock." He sounded like he was hypnotized. "Do you know what happens underneath a waterfall?"

Kenzie kept moving. She didn't answer.

"If you get swept over, the water rolls and rolls—and traps you. Forever. They call it a drowning machine."

She turned to stare at him.

There wasn't much to see, except that he was solidly built. He wore a fleece parka with a collar that was part of the hood, zipped all the way up.

Not because it was cold. Because he wanted to conceal most of his face. He wore sunglasses, which he lifted to the top of his head.

Those eyes. She had seen them before. Twice.

It was him.

Kenzie pushed herself off the rock and ran down the path, little rocks skittering. She was losing her footing, her body tilting from side to side as she struggled for balance and ran on. She didn't care if she twisted her ankle. She only wanted to get away. She didn't look to see if he was behind her.

CHAPTER 19

Linc took the path along the river, looking for Kenzie. He'd sent the hikers on their way, map and all. Sometimes being nice didn't seem worth it. Where was she?

The turbulent river sent spray flying into the air as it rushed past him. A floating tree, muddy roots in the air, smashed against a rock and splintered into pieces which the water swept away.

There was no sign of her.

Uneasy, he went faster, edging through a part of the path that was so narrow he had to use his hands to move along. He looked ahead and then down, seeing no one but an elderly couple, binoculars raised. The last thing he wanted to do was startle a couple of birdwatchers. But they might have seen her.

He made his way down to them.

"Hey there," he said. "Sorry to interrupt, but—"

They both lowered their binoculars and turned to look at him.

"Not a problem," the man said. "There's nothing to see out there. The birds all flew away home. I'm thinking me and Agnes should do the same."

"Speak for yourself, Earl. I haven't given up," she said.

Oh boy. Linc didn't want to get stuck in another conversation. He got right to the point.

"Did you happen to see someone go this way? A woman, not very tall, with dark hair?" He described what Kenzie was wearing.

"Oh yes. We certainly did. She seemed like a very nice young lady," the woman answered. "She didn't come down here, though.

She went a different way. I think she wanted a clearer view of the river."

Linc felt his pulse jump. Kenzie knew better than to get too close to the banks—what was left of them—when the river was like this.

He took a deep breath. These folks didn't seem at all alarmed, so that was something. At their age, they had to be careful of every step.

"How long ago was that?"

"Oh, I dunno," said the old man. "Probably about ten minutes. Is that right, Agnes?"

"I think so," she chirped. "Do you want us to tell her that you're looking for her? What's your name?"

"Linc. And her name is Kenzie."

"Okay. If she comes back this way, we'll stop her. I hope you two don't end up going in circles."

"Me too. Thanks." He started off with renewed energy.

Then the old man spoke again. "I almost forgot. I looked behind me to adjust the focus on these things"—he patted the binoculars—"and I saw another person going the same way as her. A feller in a parka. I didn't get a good look at his face."

"He was walking with his head down," his wife added.

"And no wonder," Earl chuckled, "considering how dang slippery the path is. But he was moving kinda fast. Does that help?"

Linc didn't stick around to answer the question.

He was out of breath and crazy with worry when he finally spotted her a half mile down the path, where it took an abrupt turn inland. Kenzie was under the massive trunk of a tree that the storm had blown down, crouching with one hand clutching a broken branch.

"Kenzie!" The wind swallowed his voice. She didn't even look his way. He came closer, slipping in the soft, damp earth. He reached for her, getting a grip on her arm. "What the hell happened?"

She twisted free without answering and came out from under.

"Why did you go so far ahead of me?"

"I was hiding," she gasped.

She turned her face to meet his gaze. Linc saw the streaks of dirt under the tumbled hair.

"He just doubled back and went by. He didn't see me."

Linc knew who she meant.

"Tell me exactly what happened. What he said."

In a halting voice, she did.

"But he never touched you?"

"No." She shivered. "It almost didn't matter. The way he looked at me—I felt like I couldn't move. Then he blinked and I ran."

Linc gently drew her close. He rubbed her arms, trying to warm her up. It didn't work. She wasn't shivering because the air was cold.

"You did the right thing."

Kenzie nestled against him and he wrapped her in the circle of his arms. He lifted his head, still keeping watch. The trees moved in the wind that whistled through them. The sharp crack of a falling branch made her flinch.

"Linc . . . how does he keep finding me?"

"I don't know." He stroked her tangled hair and held her closer. "But we have to work harder on finding him."

Harry Cowles let Kenzie go ahead of him into his office. It was small, with no windows and muted lighting. A large monitor dominated the desk, as before. There was a chair that she knew was his, and others along the wall, in different positions from what she remembered.

Kenzie reminded herself that she wasn't the only one who came here. Cowles spent hours each day with victims of much worse crimes than stalking.

She'd gotten off lightly. So far.

"Good to see you, Kenzie. Thanks for coming back."

"I wanted to try again. We didn't get too far the first time."

"You did fine. Don't underestimate yourself. We ended up with a good preliminary sketch."

Cowles was half shrink and half artist. "Can I see it again?"

He leaned over the desk and touched a key. "I left it pulled up—there you go."

She didn't want to see the man again, didn't believe she'd gotten anything right. Though she didn't want to admit to it, her fear
distorted her memory of him.

"Would you like some coffee before we get started again?
There's a brewing machine down the hall that uses those little
cups. You can pick your flavor."

Caffeine was something she definitely didn't need. Her nerves
were stretched to the breaking point.

"No thanks," she replied. "But water would be good. Is there a
vending machine in the hall?"

"No."

He moved to a small refrigerator that she hadn't noticed her
first time here and opened the door. The sudden bright light from
its interior startled her for a moment. The glass shelves held bottles of water and cans of soda.

"That's convenient."

"Okayed by the chief. I keep it filled. People who come in here
are stressed as it is. As you're finding out, getting an accurate
drawing can be a time-consuming process."

"It shouldn't take two visits. I'm sorry."

He smiled. "Don't be. And please sit down." He handed her a
bottle of water. "Which chair would you like?"

"That one." She pointed and he moved it closer to the monitor.

"I understand you saw him again. Up close."

She nodded. The memory made her gut tighten. "He had on a
hooded parka with a high collar. It was zipped up over his mouth.
But I did see his eyes. Very clearly."

Harry Cowles nodded. "You gave me a good general idea of
what you saw through the window." He sat down in front of the
monitor.

She forced herself to look at the drawing on the screen. It
seemed flat and lifeless. The man could be anybody.

Harry used a trackpad and a thing like a pen to highlight the
contours of the face in the half-completed drawing from the first
session.

"Does that still look right to you?"

"I—I can't be sure. I only saw him for a few seconds that time."

"Let's go with it for now. We can always make changes."

She knew that. And she trusted Harry to do his best. It wasn't his fault that the image of the man was so hard to pin down.

The coordinates linked to an address. She was at the police station. Not for the first time, either. It didn't matter. He had covered his tracks and his face. He was fairly sure they wouldn't figure out who he was until he'd left the country.

There was nothing they could charge him with. Connecting him to the accident was next to impossible. And, tempting as Kenzie was, he hadn't done anything to her.

Yet.

It wasn't as if she had full-time police protection. And her boyfriend wasn't always with her.

He assumed that Linc Bannon had found the first bug under her car and removed it. The others were still there.

He'd had to remote-activate the second bug sooner than he'd expected. There were several others left. Someone would have to crawl under the car to find them one by one.

That didn't matter either. He'd found the right place for the prototype device a business associate had given him. Microchips got smaller every year. The circuitry in the device was impossibly small, but it worked. It excited him to know exactly where she was twenty-four hours a day, in or out of a car.

Kenzie was not always careful. She'd handed him his chance the same day he'd sent the roses, from Kenzie to Chrissie.

He had still been physically following her at that point, had parked near her at a convenience store by the hospital. The tears she'd cried privately in the car left gleaming traces on her cheeks that he found very satisfying.

Too upset to remember to push the button that rolled up the window, she'd even left her purse on the front seat of her rental car, grabbing only her wallet.

He hadn't waited. No one noticed him. The other drivers in the lot were screaming at kids to shut up or digging for change in the cup holder.

Her purse held a jumble of necessary things and odd items. No cosmetics case. She didn't wear much makeup.

But he'd found something—a small compact with a magnifying mirror and a regular one. He'd popped out both and added a few improvements underneath, then put the compact right back into the purse.

He'd watched her come out of the convenience store and drive away, giving him a chance to test the mike.

The sad song on the radio came through fine. She didn't talk to herself as she drove. After that, he picked up Linc Bannon's voice and her replies now and then.

Funny that he'd never seen the guy. He sounded young—younger than he was, anyway. Army but not old school army. Some kind of hotshot in CyberCommand.

Lucky that Linc hadn't found the beacon, which was a cut above the bugs. Precise coordinates in real time, jiggleproof.

The camera came on when she opened the compact. Kenzie used it only to put on lip gloss, never a full face. He loved the way she looked with her lips parted. Smacking them to spread the gloss. Trying out a pout. Running her tongue over them for extra shine.

She didn't use it often. Which meant that every time she did—and snapped the compact shut—the desire to hurt her was unbearably strong.

Linc headed for the Ridgewood police station. The front desk cop buzzed Mike Warren's office and waited for an affirmative reply, then waved him in.

"You said you would call me back and you didn't. She hasn't checked in." Linc pushed open the unlocked door. "Last I heard she was coming here."

"Settle down. She's still here. With Harry Cowles." Mike Warren looked tired.

"Why? It's past seven."

"Harry's the kind of cop who stays late when he thinks it's necessary. And you don't get to interrupt her." Mike pointed to a chair. "Sit. And shut up. You already explained what happened, and I took notes. My turn to talk."

The lieutenant gave him a friendly smile and folded his hands on top of the paperwork on his desk. Linc glanced and took in the words *Double Homicide*. Mike had mentioned that. He swallowed what he was going to say.

The lieutenant didn't seem to notice that. "Unfortunately, we still don't know who the stalker is. Even if we ID him, we can't charge him with anything—"

"Not even breaking and entering?"

"No," Mike said. "Can you prove the man she saw made the impression on the bed? We took lots of pictures, for what they're worth. Someone lay down on a fuzzy blankie. That's all we know about that."

"How about forcing Christine off the road? Any progress there?"

"The tire treads we found in the mud north of the scene and the tire treads on the car in the accident footage do match. Which proves . . . not a lot, without the car. And let's hope those tires are still on the car when we find it. If we find it."

Linc knew the lieutenant was doing what he could with scant evidence and no manpower. That didn't keep him from seething inwardly.

"By the way," Mike continued, "both you and Kenzie should stop in at the night clerk's and get inked, so we can sort out the prints we picked up inside the apartment. The roof, nothing. The scaffolding, forget it. Painters were swarming up it by the time we were finished with the roof."

"I forgot to tell them to take the day off."

"Don't be a smart-ass."

"Sorry."

"This is a priority." Mike picked up the homicide paperwork on his desk and waved it at Linc.

"I understand that."

"Look, I want to protect Kenzie and Christine just as much as you do. But there are limits."

"What are you saying? That he has to hurt her first?"

"As far as Kenzie is concerned, he has to take it up a notch. Staring in the window is a peeping-tom offense. A wrist slap from the judge, one night in jail for a naughty boy."

"If I catch him, I'll—"

"I can imagine. Maybe you should line up a good lawyer in advance."

Linc leaned forward. "What's the plan?"

"Besides you and me winging it, there isn't one. Kenzie doesn't qualify for police protection."

"Mike, he's out there. Getting closer. He may be focusing on Kenzie right now, but that could be a way to throw us off the track so he can get to Christine. Can't we protect her?"

"Maybe." Mike looked thoughtful. "There are rookies the chief wants out of his hair. As in assigned to easy duty. One is the son of a state representative and the other is a reporter's daughter."

"I'm not following you."

"Add two more patrolmen to babysit them, and we can station unmarked cars at the front and back entrance of the rehab center. No further incidents involving Christine since the roses, right?"

Linc shook his head. "Nothing. Kenzie would have told me. She goes to see Christine a lot."

Mike raised an eyebrow. "You should go with her."

"I will. She's going to get sick of looking at me. Get back to the unmarkeds."

"Hypothetically speaking, the officers would be there at night, not during the day."

"Okay. Do what you can."

"Everyone will be briefed on the stalker." He paused to think. "Too bad Harry hasn't finished the drawing yet. But we know he's white, we have a build and a height for him, and a few other visual facts. Wears black clothes and a mask when he goes window-shopping for victims, has been spotted in a parka zipped up over most of his face. Not much to go on, but it's something."

"My guess would be that he's ordinary otherwise."

Mike nodded. "You're probably right. Which is not a crime. Keep in mind that we can't stop everyone."

Linc would take what he could get. "Just get your officers

there. It's not like there's a lot of people hanging around a neuro rehab center at night. Anyone walking by is going to stand out."

"I promise you they'll do their best."

"Too bad you can't send big guys with guns."

"The rookies have guns. And the ponytail is actually a crack shot."

Ponytail. Linc sighed inwardly. Slang for a female cop, back in the day. Mike Warren's day, not his.

A knock on the open door got their attention. It was Kenzie. She had a file folder in her hand. "Hi, guys. We're done. Harry printed some out for me."

"I'd like a copy," Mike said.

She extracted one and handed it to him.

The lieutenant glanced at it and then laid it flat on his desk. "Look familiar, Linc?"

"I never saw the guy." But he studied the copy of the drawing. The eyes were intense. The face had the flat look and pieced-together quality of most police sketches. "What do you think, Kenzie?"

She shrugged. "It's okay. We had to guess at a lot of things. Better than nothing, right?"

There was no way to answer that forlorn question, so Linc didn't. He put an arm around her shoulders.

"Let's go home," he said quietly.

"Two cars?" She asked the question without thinking first.

Mike Warren looked up. "You can't leave one here."

"Two cars," Linc said. "But I'm staying at Hamill's. I don't care if I have to sleep on the floor."

It was too late to explain the latest developments to Norm or Carol. The lights in their part of the building were off. Kenzie led the way up the staircase, with Linc and Beebee behind her.

"He usually sleeps in the yard. His doghouse is heated. But tonight I want him closer than that."

Linc patted him on the head. "Beebee, you rock."

There wasn't much space on the landing for the three of them. Kenzie unlocked the door and they sort of tumbled in.

The dog went to his accustomed spot on the floor of the kitchen area. Linc stood there, looking around. He was prepared to sleep sitting up if the floor was taken.

Kenzie seemed to have read his mind.

"Oh, just get in the bed," she told him. "There's plenty of room for both of us. Just don't—"

"I wouldn't."

Kenzie seemed okay with that short answer. "All right, then. I'm beat. Let's turn in."

She touched the wall switch and they undressed in the dark. There was a faint glow in the room from the perimeter lights that Norm kept on at night.

He didn't look her way, just got down to his T-shirt and underwear, slinging jeans and shirt over a chair. She slipped in first, disappearing into the big bed.

Then he realized that she was holding the covers back for him. Linc eased his tired body down on real cotton sheets and under a comforter that hadn't been used by ten thousand truckers.

The bed smelled like her. Sweet woman.

She turned and stretched out of reach. Linc saw that she was wearing a tank top. Or maybe it was a cami. Could be a touch of lace on it.

He caught a pungent whiff of sulfur. Kenzie had struck a match. She touched the flame to the wick of a large candle.

"Just for a little while," she said.

The candle's flickering light cast a golden line over her shoulder. More than anything he wanted to trace that line with his lips, caress the sleek softness of her skin.

She kept her back turned to him, curling up halfway. Her long hair streamed over her pillow.

Just don't. He wasn't going to. He knew what she meant.

But they could still cuddle.

He moved closer. She didn't pull away and she didn't look over her shoulder. Linc stopped. One inch closer and the position would definitely count as a cuddle. He went the extra inch. Then he put a protective arm around her.

Kenzie stiffened.

"I'm not trying anything," he said softly. "Seemed to me you could use some holding, that's all."

Some of the tension eased from her body. He wouldn't go so far as to call it relaxation.

He was surprised when Kenzie's hand slipped over his. "You're right about that."

That she trusted him to get next to her was a revelation. To be this close to her was bliss. And torture.

She turned in his easy embrace. The change in position meant their bodies were no longer touching, but to be able to look in her eyes and simply lie next to her was all he wanted.

Without thinking, he reached up and stroked her cheek. She accepted the intimate gesture without flinching away.

"So when do I get my life back?" Kenzie murmured.

"I'm working on that," Linc replied.

"Is it okay to just hide? Right now I don't care if I ever look out a window again."

She could hide in his arms for as long as she wanted to. Knowing her, that wouldn't last.

"Every time I open a door, I imagine him on the other side."

"He's not here, Kenzie. You have me and Beebee for tonight."

"I won't sleep, Linc."

"The trick is not to try to."

She fell silent. In the candlelight, her eyes were large and dark.

"If I could move away from here, I would," she sighed.

Linc didn't comment. It wasn't a solution unless she really went into hiding.

"I can't leave Christine," she said softly. "Mrs. Corelli wanted to thank Mike for all his help, by the way."

"I'll pass that on."

"How long can he have the unmarked cars out there at night?"

"I'm not sure." Linc stroked her hair and lifted a wayward lock away from her face. Then he put his hand back at his side. Kenzie smiled at him. "Mike will do his best. Just like all of us."

"I know."

He didn't say anything more. And he respected the slight distance she silently insisted on. The candlelight cast a spell that made her drowsy after a while.

She slept. He stayed awake. The candle's flame began to jump as if there was a breeze coming from somewhere.

He turned to look. Beebee had come into the room. The big dog's hackles were up, as if he sensed or smelled an unseen danger.

Linc wasn't going to leave Kenzie and go looking for trouble. Beebee rested his head on the edge of the bed and Linc patted him until the fur on his back was smooth again.

"I got this covered, pal," he said in a low voice. Beebee lifted his head and turned away, but stayed in the room. He found a fresh spot to sleep, settling down with a sighing whoosh.

The candle had burned low. Linc rose halfway on the bed and leaned carefully over Kenzie to blow it out.

When morning dawned, Kenzie was refreshed. Linc seemed groggy.

She got up and headed to the bathroom for a quick shower, dressing there with the clothes she'd brought in.

Beebee stood by the door, looking at her expectantly.

"You want out, don't you?"

She went with him down the stairs, pressing a towel to her un-combed wet hair.

The dog trotted out, heading in the direction of the shop and breakfast with Norm. The two had a routine.

So had she, once upon a time. Kenzie went back up the stairs, holding the towel and thinking hard.

She needed to be hyperalert from now on—and also keep on going as if nothing had happened. If her life as she knew it had changed forever with Christine's accident and the stalker, her life still had to be lived.

But no matter what, Christine still had to come first. Kenzie wasn't ready to believe that the stalker had given up on her.

Linc was up and making coffee when she came in. His T-shirt was a mass of wrinkles, but the jeans he'd donned looked reasonably okay.

"I never knew you were so domesticated," she teased him.

"Just the basics," he mumbled. He stood back to watch the aromatic brew drip, rubbing sleepy eyes and then dragging a hand through his hair. "Sorry. Haven't washed up."

"Nothing to be sorry about. I was in the shower."

He yawned. "I'll take one back at the motel."

"I'm coming with you."

"Really?" He looked pleasantly surprised.

Kenzie laughed. "Um, not for that. Christine wants the laptop back, remember?"

"Oh." He looked disappointed.

"That's not a problem, is it?" she asked.

Linc took down two cups from a cabinet. "Look, it's not mine. But it's not exactly hers either."

"SKC will get it back eventually. In the meantime, it is hers."

He put the cups by the coffeemaker and held up his hands in surrender. "Okay. Just let me make sure it's good to go. Give me a half an hour when we get to the motel."

Kenzie waited in the dingy room until he had looked it over hurriedly, then left with him. He dropped her off at the rehab center. They set a time for him to pick her up. She seemed resigned to that.

Laptop in her tote, she arrived at Christine's room to find her gone. Kenzie checked the written-out schedule for the day.

Therapy, physical.

She put the SKC laptop on the table, closed. Let Christine decide whether she wanted to open it.

She looked for the bag that held her knitting and settled down with that. The simple task had lost its power to calm her nerves. After a while she rested the needles and yarn in her lap and folded her hands over them.

Christine appeared in the doorway.

"Hi." She gave Kenzie a bright-eyed smile. "I wasn't expecting you so soon. Mom left very early. She said to give you her love."

Kenzie missed the Corellis. But being with Christine in shifts at the rehab center meant they saw each other only infrequently.

"I just thought I'd come now. Is later better? I can come back if you want."

"No, stay."

Christine studied her. Kenzie fumbled with her knitting.

"You seem different," Christine said. "Did something happen?"

"Oh—I'm okay. It was too humid last night. The last of the storm, I guess. I didn't sleep too well."

"Tell me about it. I almost never do."

Kenzie swiftly changed the subject. "So how was therapy?"

"About the same. Paula said I'm doing really well on fine motor skills. We played pick-up sticks."

"You and I used to play that all the time," Kenzie said.

The memory seemed to cheer her up. She even smiled. The uneasy mood between them vanished.

Christine grinned. "That's right. And I usually won. I don't think I would now, though."

"I'll get a set at the dime store. If they still sell them, that is."

"They do. But the points aren't as sharp as they used to be. For safety, I guess."

"Makes sense."

Christine spotted the SKC laptop and walked over to the night-stand. "You brought it. Thanks. Was it in the hutch?"

"Yes."

That was true. It had been.

"Where's the cord? As I remember, the battery didn't hold a charge for very long."

"Linc gave it to me—I think it's in my bag. Hang on." She reached for it and found the neatly coiled cord, the prongs tied to keep it that way. "Here you go."

"Linc. Is he your new guy? My mom mentioned him."

Yikes. Kenzie hadn't until now. "He's a good friend. He brought me to the ICU that first night."

"You never told me about him."

"I was going to," Kenzie said.

"Is he a friend with benefits?"

"No!"

Christine looked at her steadily. Kenzie felt color rise in her cheeks.

"Sorry. I didn't mean to embarrass you."

"You didn't." Kenzie's denial was unconvincing, but her friend didn't press the point. "I guess I should have said something. He's really helped me out during all this."

"So why did he have the laptop cord?"

"He was—he coiled it for me, that's all. He's particular about things like that sometimes."

"What does he do?"

"Linc is a tech specialist. Based in Fort Meade."

"Last question. When do I get to meet him?"

"Soon."

Christine slid her hands over the laptop as if she was trying to remember how it opened. She left it closed, then uncoiled the cord. She turned the laptop around, attaching the prong to it and plugging in the other end to the wall outlet.

"What a clunker," she said. "Built like a tank. I didn't take it home too often."

"It's a lot heavier than yours."

Christine set her thumbs to either side and clicked it open. "Here goes. I wonder if I'm going to remember my password."

Kenzie didn't feel like telling her that Linc had figured it out right off the bat.

Christine typed slowly. "Cat-five-kitty-seven. Got it the first time." She looked up with a proud smile.

Kenzie didn't want to breathe down her neck. She went back to her knitting. Minutes went by. Every now and then she cast a glance at Christine, standing up to tap at the keyboard.

Her friend's face was a study in concentration. After a half hour she picked up the laptop and got comfortable on the bed, resting it on a large book.

"This is amazing," she said after a while. "I actually remember a lot of this. Of course, I was working on these files for months before the accident."

Kenzie nodded and picked up her knitting again.

"So why can't I remember how that happened?"

"I don't know. I'm not a neurologist."

"Put in your two cents anyway."

Kenzie took a deep breath. Christine's need to understand what had happened to her had to be balanced against the facts coming to light about the accident. What they knew and didn't know had the power to hurt her.

"I think you just answered your own question," she said casually.

"How?"

"You said you worked on those files for months. But the accident only took a few seconds. So it stands to reason that you would remember the work and not the crash."

Christine heaved a sigh. "But I want to remember both."

"Give it time."

Her friend grew thoughtful. "How much longer?"

"I don't know the answer to that one. Probably best not to worry about it."

"What if I never remember the accident?"

Kenzie could only shake her head. "If you can't, you can't."

"My therapist says that brain trauma is kind of like an eraser, one you can't control. It takes away some things but not all."

"Makes sense."

"When she told me that I thought of school chalkboards."

"How so?"

"You could erase them, but not completely. There were words and numbers you could still see. Like ghosts under the dust."

Kenzie bent her head down. A ghost was nothing. Everything she'd seen had been all too real.

Christine misinterpreted her reaction. "Hey, don't get upset. Paula thinks that nearly all my memory is intact," she said.

"That's good."

Christine was looking into the laptop screen but no longer typing. "Computers don't forget. Everything that happens on them is somewhere on the hard drive."

The thought was depressing. Kenzie knitted quickly and badly. In another minute, she heard the clicking of keys as Christine went back to looking through saved files.

For an hour, they stuck to their busywork in companionable silence.

"Huh." Christine looked up at Kenzie, her brow furrowed.
"Something's wrong here."

"What?" Kenzie dropped a stitch and swore under her breath.

"Mel Brody sent me a file to download the day before the accident. I did and I saved it in my docs, but I didn't open it."

"Until now?"

"That's right. The file is for X-Ultra—wait a sec, you don't know
what that is. Want me to explain?"

Kenzie wasn't ready to tell Christine that she and Linc had
begun an investigation on their own. "Sure."

"X-Ultra is military body armor, a new kind. My boss was supposed to head up production for it—we got cc'd on every stage of
production—but Lee Slattery gave the project to someone else."

"Oh."

"I guess that's why I parked the file. But I don't really remember."

Kenzie lifted her knitting and frowned. It was hopelessly
snarled. She would have to unravel it and start over. "So what
caught your eye?"

"The codes."

Linc hadn't been able to understand them either. Kenzie had
not expected Christine would be able to pick up where she'd left
off. Not this fast.

"I think this set of numbers—347889—indicates failed components. Which means those vests should have been pulled. But it
looks like they were packed and shipped."

"Are you sure?"

"No. But I do remember that new gear had to undergo a lot of
testing to meet standards. Codes got assigned for different parts
of the process." Her voice was threaded with anxiety. "I don't
understand how any of this passed inspection."

Kenzie just looked at her. Now or never. She couldn't pretend
she didn't know a thing about X-Ultra.

"I have to explain." She rose from her chair and went to sit by
Christine on the bed.

Christine set the laptop aside. "What's going on?"

"For starters, I don't know everything. Just a little."

"What are you talking about?"

Kenzie swallowed hard. "Right after your accident, I was contacted by a medic. Some of those defective vests *were* packed and shipped. To the front lines."

She told Christine the whole story, not leaving anything out, not sparing her.

"That's what Linc has been helping me with." Kenzie was nearly finished. "A police lieutenant is investigating the crash. His name's Mike Warren—your parents met with him a few times."

"They didn't tell me any of this."

Kenzie bit her lip. "I hope they're not angry when they find out I did."

"They won't be. My mom and dad think you walk on water."

Sinking fast, Kenzie thought.

She summoned up her nerve. "Do you remember anything at all about the accident?"

"No. Not a thing."

"How about right before it?"

Christine got up to walk around. She seemed agitated, but Kenzie couldn't take back the question.

"Nobody's asked me that yet. I was driving down the highway and there was someone behind me—that's no help, is it? Sorry. Blank-out. I don't know who was driving or what kind of car it was."

Kenzie kept quiet.

"Do you think someone at SKC is trying to hurt me?" Christine blurted out.

"Maybe."

"Why? Because they thought I knew something about these vests? Joke's on them," she said bitterly. "If I ever did, it got knocked right out of my head."

"It might come back to you."

Christine heaved a sigh. "Looking at the forms and codes is a start. But in five minutes I know I'm going to forget. What I knew—and who I used to be—all that is still in pieces. Sometimes they come together—"

"That's good."

"Sometimes they don't. Like you don't know that."

Christine's eyes were shadowed with confusion. Kenzie knew that her erratic reactions and blunt way of talking were aftereffects of the accident. She hated asking about it.

"Kenzie, when I was looking at the spec sheets, I thought the vest looked familiar. So I checked the photo Frank posted—him showing off his new gear."

"I know the one you mean," Kenzie said.

"Do you? He was wearing an X-Ultra vest. Was that what got him killed?" Her voice was raw with pain.

"We don't know that for sure," Kenzie said quietly.

"Maybe I tried to tell someone that the vests were defective. I just don't remember."

"Just let it be," Kenzie pleaded. "What happened to Frank just—happened. You couldn't have prevented it."

The haunted look on her friend's face was heartbreaking.

"I want to do something to help," Christine said slowly. "But I can't. Was he the only one?"

Kenzie hesitated. "No."

Christine stared dully at the floor. "Any other things you haven't told me?"

Kenzie fought off a feeling of guilt. "No. That's it. You weren't in any shape to hear the whole truth. So I'm not going to apologize."

Christine smiled faintly. "Same old Kenzie. You're tough."

"I used to be."

Christine didn't respond to that, just got up and went to the window.

"So what happens next?"

"We—meaning me and Linc and Mike Warren—are trying to keep you safe."

"How?"

"Mike arranged for two unmarked cars to guard the front and rear entrances here."

"I think I see one."

"Don't wave," Kenzie said wryly. "Seriously, they can only be here at night."

Christine thought that over. "But what about you? Who's guarding you?"

Kenzie sidestepped the question. "You're a lot more vulnerable than I am."

"Should I give back the SKC laptop?" Christine looked at it like it might blow up.

Kenzie didn't smile. "Not just yet."

By nightfall, Christine was back on the laptop again, her curiosity piqued by her earlier look at the work files on it.

It held a lot more than that. She clicked into the miscellaneous files that she'd kept on it, looking for one with pictures that had been forwarded by someone in publicity.

Lee Slattery was big on company get-togethers. Besides the balloons with SKC printed on them, there were always motivational signs over the real draw, a catered buffet.

She might be able to pick out a face that would jog her memory.

Christine found the file and opened it. Vaguely aware that the hallway was quieter, she studied one photo after another. Everyone had posed, from the top—Slattery, Kehoe, and a few other execs—to the thickly populated ranks of middle management, including her boss, Melvin Brody, right down to the janitorial crew.

Smile big for the camera, she thought. Which one had tried to kill her?

The footsteps of the night nurse stopped at her door. The woman peeked in. "Don't stay up too late, Christine. You know the rules."

"Oh—I didn't realize what time it was." She sat up straight on the bed and looked at the digital clock. "Almost midnight."

"That's right. Time to turn in. Want me to turn off the overhead for you?"

"Thanks." Christine didn't object to the gentle reminder. Her sense of time was definitely altered.

The night nurse flicked the switch and Christine realized how tired her eyes were. The darkness was soothing. Listening to the footsteps walk away, she looked at a few more photos, then gave up.

She shut down the laptop and moved it to her nightstand. After a while, she fell asleep.

Two hours later, she awoke, gasping for air. A nightmare had seized her brain.

Some of the accident came back to her again. Not in sequence. More like jagged pieces of glass.

In the dream she had reached out to touch a stop-motion image of herself, screaming. Her hand went through the window of the car to touch her badly wounded face. Christine pulled it back covered in blood.

Awake now, she looked at it. It was just her hand, the same as always. Irrationally, she wanted to scrub off the imaginary blood on the sheets that covered her. Then she realized that the damp feeling on her skin was sweat.

A cold sweat.

She sat up, feeling sick and weak.

Christine looked around for something to write on. She might not remember in the morning. Kenzie would want to know what she had seen.

The man's face was familiar. That was all she knew.

She couldn't find a pen or a pencil. Her reaching hand knocked her cell phone to the floor. The little screen glowed. The hell with it. She was going to tell Kenzie right now.

Christine tapped the number to speed-dial her.

After several rings, Kenzie answered, her voice fuzzy with sleep. "Christine? What's the matter?"

"I think I'm starting to remember."

There was silence, then a faint sound of movement on the other end of the call. She could imagine Kenzie throwing back the covers and grabbing a robe.

Christine knew her friend would take the nightmare seriously.

She did her best to describe it. "I saw myself in the car," she began. "Like I was outside and inside at the same time."

"When?"

"After the crash." Christine suppressed a shudder. "My eyes were closed but I was screaming. I wanted to help myself—I tried to reach in the window and I cut myself. Then I saw him."

Kenzie waited for her to compose herself.

"There was a man in another car right near mine. He was so close I could see his tattoos—big thorns, dripping blood. He wasn't wearing a shirt."

"Did you see his face? In the dream, I mean."

"Yes," Christine said hesitantly. "But not his eyes. Just his smile. It was so evil. Oh, Kenzie—I'm so scared."

The hand holding the cell phone shook and she dropped it into the bedcovers. Christine scrambled to pick it up, hearing Kenzie reply before she brought it to her ear again. "It was a dream. Just a dream."

Christine shook her head. "Yes and no. It's the first time anything's come back to me."

Kenzie was quiet for a few seconds. "Okay," she said finally. "Let's talk about something else for a little while. When you feel calmer, you might remember more."

"I hope so. I'm sorry to wake you up, Kenzie."

"It's all right. I'm not going to go back to sleep. If I could come over right now, I would."

"I know, Kenzie. But don't."

CHAPTER 20

"What's going on?" Melvin Brody pointed a thick finger at Vic Kehoe. "Your signature was on the original X-Ultra production runs. But not anymore. Mine is. And it's on the official okays too. I never signed off on either."

"Close the door." He waited for Brody to obey. It was important to establish who gave orders and made demands. Not middle-level managers in short-sleeved shirts.

Brody came back, looking around the austere office. Vic got brisk with him. "What are you talking about?"

"The vests, what else? I never okayed all the lots. Several should have been scrapped."

"You mean they went out?" Vic asked blandly.

"Yeah. Some did. Months ago. Then we got that order for ten thousand units and ramped up production. I didn't realize the problems with the fiber and the plates hadn't been resolved, so I didn't follow up when Lee Slattery pulled me off X-Ultra."

"That can't be. Let me look at the okays." Vic had to soften his tone or Brody might run screaming to Lee Slattery. "We can figure this out. Does anyone else have duplicate files, by the way?"

Brody pulled out a crumpled handkerchief and mopped the sweat off his face. "The laptop Christine Corelli used has the production run documentation for last year and this year."

Vic frowned. "Was that necessary?"

"She needed some of it for cost analysis," Brody said defensively. "Most of what was on those docs was too complicated for her to actually understand."

"You hope."

Brody caught his breath and rested his hands on the belt slung below his gut. "I'm still trying to get that damn laptop back. I finally reported it stolen. Her mother swears she doesn't know anything about it."

"And?"

"Who knows? Haven't heard a word from the cops."

The reply made Vic sit back and think. "Could be a lost cause," he said after a while. "All right. Don't worry too much about it. Like I said, I have your back on this one."

"Really? You going to explain to Lee Slattery that I didn't do anything wrong?"

"Sure. Not a problem. Sit down, Brody."

The other man looked around the office. "On what? You have the only chair."

Vic chuckled in agreement. "There are a couple of folding chairs in that closet." He pointed. "It's my office. I like to work alone."

The door swung open again. Vic looked up, a flash of anger in his black eyes. He calmed down when Lee Slattery stepped into the room. Jaunty as ever. Another five-thousand-dollar suit on him.

"Vic—what are you doing here, Brody?"

"Just, uh, chatting with Vic."

"How about that." Lee held up a folded letter. He tapped it against his palm. "I wanted to talk to both of you."

"What is this, a firing squad?" Brody joked. He was sweating harder than before. "What's the severance?"

"Brody, don't say things like that. You're a valued employee," Lee said. He could have been talking to a kindergartner. "Read it, Vic."

Lee Slattery didn't bother to unfold the letter he tossed on Vic Kehoe's desk. If it had been in an envelope, that wasn't attached.

Vic looked up at him with annoyance.

Lee liked to play at being CEO. He expected a certain amount of deference from everyone, which was why he wasted so much time strolling around the buildings. SKC employed over a thousand people, not all of them in this complex. He didn't have time to visit everyone. But Lee sure as hell got his required daily allowance of sucking up from those who were interested.

Vic excepted himself. "Can I read it later?"

Lee thrust his hands in his pants pockets, buckling his suit jacket across the middle just so. He liked to pose too. Most days he looked like an ad for men's fine tailoring.

"No. It came registered mail, return receipt requested. From a government agency I never heard of."

With a sigh, Vic rotated his leather swivel chair, turning sideways to the desk as he unfolded the letter.

"Material and Supply Testing, Military Division," he read aloud. "I never heard of them either."

"Maybe that's because we don't make a lot of mistakes at SKC. I run a tight ship."

Vic's mouth tightened. That was another annoying habit of Slattery's: assuming that he ran anything. He was a useful figurehead—a rich guy with extensive connections on the Hill.

Vic was the one who had arranged for the financing of the vast complex when their business went global, put his own fortune on the line when Lee came up short. They'd recouped his investment ten times over.

However, due to a couple of undue-force incidents in a dusty, violent outpost several years ago, Vic still had to keep a low profile.

Lee was the face of SKC. He liked everybody, cranked up the charm for one and all. He was as happy with a hundred-unit order from a businessman like Dana Scott as he was with a ten-thousand-unit order from the army.

Vic set aside the opened letter, but he kept his hand on it. "They want more information on X-Ultra components. And they want to know if we use an independent testing lab."

"Do we?" Lee asked breezily.

Melvin Brody looked a little shocked. Good old clueless Lee. Vic shook his head. "No. We do our own."

"Oh, right. And pass along the cost to customers." Lee grinned. "We get the goods out, don't we? And fast."

"That seems to be a concern." Vic read aloud again. "Preliminary studies indicate an unacceptably high rate of failure for the X-Ultra vests. This may or may not indicate inadequate testing and below-standard manufacturing. Please forward information as specified below on original components, and country of origin."

"Oh no," Lee mocked. "Sounds like we might have violated a regulation or two."

"The letter doesn't cite any," Vic said. "What do you want me to do?"

He refolded it and put it as close as possible to where Lee Slattery was standing. Maybe he would take the hint and answer it himself.

"You'll think of something," the CEO said cheerfully. "Check in with me when you do. And Brody, better print out all the relevant documents and get them into binders by month."

"Okay," Brody said.

Lee snapped his fingers. "Wait, you have a temp. What's her name again?"

"Brenda White."

"Nice girl. Seems competent. Be sure to tell her Lee Slattery will be stopping by."

He nodded to both of them and pushed the folded letter back across Vic's desk.

"Take care of that, Kehoe. What you get paid for, right? I gave you the X-Ultra project for a reason."

Vic watched him go. He had a short fuse, and Slattery had just lit it. Having Brody as witness to his humiliation didn't make Slattery's condescension easier to take.

"You didn't exactly get me off the hook," Brody snapped.

He looked up at him. "I didn't have a chance."

"Listen, Kehoe—"

Vic stuck the folded letter into a drawer. "Don't take this too seriously. It's not a subpoena. We can stall them."

"Are you going to take my signature off the okays? That's all I want to know."

"I said yes, didn't I?" Vic lowered his voice. "Don't make yourself crazy over nothing."

The balding man cast a cynical look at him. "Hope I'm not being set up," he said.

Brody wasn't stupid. Of course he'd been set up. And when the printouts were analyzed, Brody wouldn't look good.

Vic guessed the man would raise an unbelievable stink. He could almost smell it now. A muscle ticked in his jaw, but he kept his expression composed.

"Just so you know," Brody said, "I did a little research."

Vic forced himself to look interested. "Did you? On what?"

"I'm sure you remember that kickback investigation a few years ago." Brody smirked. "Did any of that money land in your bank account?"

"I don't know what you're talking about."

SKC had grown so fast since then that the investigation had largely been forgotten. The recent reports on the defective X-Ultra fiber were buried deep. No reason to screw up the bottom line over them—soldiers got shot no matter what. Vic wondered what exactly Melvin Brody had found out.

The other man gave him a sly look. "You had your hand in the till. My guess is that you still do."

"Actually, I don't," Vic finally replied. "But I think you and I need to discuss this."

The other man's smirk widened into a triumphant grin. "Now you're talking. But don't take this for a blackmail attempt. Let's just say I believe in sharing the wealth."

Vic fiddled with a pencil and finally snapped it. It occurred to him that he could snap Brody's neck just as easily. The cracking sound didn't seem to register with the other man.

"So, drinks and dinner? I assume you're paying."

Vic looked at him calmly. "Fine. But let's go somewhere we won't be overheard."

"All right," Brody said expansively.

The man was a fool. "Tell you what," Vic said. "Let's leave early today. You don't get seasick, do you?"

Brody shook his head. "Not if the water's calm."

"Up for a cruise to Virginia Beach?"

His motorboat was docked at a marina a few miles away. Thirty feet of white fiberglass with a modest flying bridge, like thousands of others between here and the Chesapeake Bay. Essentially invisible, right down to the forgettable name. He changed the vinyl lettering on the stern now and then. Like the barnacles gave a damn.

"Hey, you heard Slattery. He told me to—"

"He won't care where you are. Tell your temp to get started."

"Poor Brenda." Brody shook his head. "She's going to have to stay late for a week. I miss Christine."

"Is she able to talk yet?" Vic knew that she was. The purse bug had picked up her voice too. He hadn't listened to the feed today, though.

"I guess so. They moved her to a neurological rehab place about a week ago."

"Remind me to send flowers." Vic couldn't help but smile.

"What for? You barely know Christine. I didn't send anything when she was in the ICU."

Vic tsked.

"I didn't want to be a hypocrite," Brody pointed out. "It's not as if she likes me. I think she was ready to quit."

No loss to the company. Although Vic had Christine to thank for leading him to Kenzie. Inadvertently, of course. But she was no longer useful, when you got right down to it.

"But Brenda is okay, for a dumb bunny," Brody was saying. "If I'm going to stick her with that much work, I'd better buy her a box of chocolates at the drugstore."

"Sure. You do that. I'll pick up beers and fresh burritos so we don't get too hungry before we get to Virginia Beach."

"Sounds like a plan."

Vic set the hook. "We'll dock by sunset, go out to eat and sling a few, then head back. Think of it as an advance vacation. I don't think you've used your vacation days this year."

Melvin Brody pulled out a handkerchief and blew his nose. "No, I haven't. All right. Sure. Not like I have anyone expecting me at home."

Vic knew Brody was divorced, with no kids.

"Meet me in the parking lot around three," he said. "Let's kick back. Screw Slattery."

Melvin grunted his agreement.

*   *   *

Vic changed his clothes on the boat. White ducks, striped polo, and a white canvas captain's cap with braid trim. Just like all the other jerks. It was important to blend in.

They pulled out of the Columbia Island Marina right on schedule.

Melvin Brody had put on a sweater. He was sitting at the stern, spread out on a seat with a waterproof cushion, his arms resting on the rail. He looked like he couldn't believe his good luck.

He even waved to a couple of cute girls coming in.

What a jackass. Vic steered clear of the smaller craft, turning the wheel and throttling down to minimize the wake as he swung the boat into the channel.

He heard Brody whoop. "This is the life!"

"There's beer in the galley," Vic called to him. "And you can warm up the burritos right now."

"A galley. That's a kitchen, right? I'd love a burrito. Hell, I could eat two. Spicy if you have 'em," Brody joked.

"Then you'll love these. I added a little something to the filling."

The other man heaved himself up from his seat and walked uncertainly to the ladder leading down into the cabin.

Vic slowed the engines so Brody wouldn't stumble. They were well under way. At some point he turned to see the other man chomping on a burrito and swigging a beer.

A few minutes later the paper wrapping floated past Vic, caught in the updraft. He turned around and saw Melvin toss the beer bottle overboard. What a pig.

His passenger went back for seconds, hollering, "Want a burrito?"

"No." Vic turned around, looking out at the water again. A lot of pleasure craft were out at the close of day, but keeping a good distance.

Melvin Brody belched so loudly Vic heard it over the low engines. Your last meal, he thought. Enjoy it.

He gave the throttle a hard shove and they picked up speed. He had no reason to dawdle. Two burritos laced with crushed downers ought to do it—the spices would cover the bitterness of the pills.

The bay was flat and he didn't see too many other boats. None were close enough that anyone waved.

An hour later Mel fell out of his seat with a heavy thump.

Vic cut the engine and jumped down from the bridge. The unconscious man's head rolled on the textured fiberglass of the inside deck, his body limp. He shoved him under the seat and used a bailer filled with heavy tools and a thick coil of rope to keep him there.

The water was calm. They hadn't passed the Cape Henry lighthouse yet. They might hit some chop beyond it, in the open ocean.

Vic returned to the bridge, taking the boat through the buoys with no problem, doing a visual check on Brody now and then.

With the lights of Virginia Beach dwindling behind him, he idled until nightfall, bobbing on the calm sea. He stayed far away from the fishing boats, tiny bright spots on the water.

Brody didn't stir. Vic killed his running lights fore and aft before he moved farther out and switched off the engine. He left the bridge again and went down into the galley, opening a cabinet where he'd stowed duct tape and a spool of thin, strong rope. Below that were flat weights left over from a training machine. There were several ten-pounders and some fives.

The moon was a sliver in the dark sky. It was all the light he needed. He stripped Brody in seconds, setting aside the wallet and watch and putting the clothes in a pile. The man groaned, his flabby chest heaving with the effort to breathe. But his eyes stayed closed.

Vic threaded the thin rope through the heavy weights, tying them at the ankles and Brody's neck, double-wrapping everything with duct tape. He'd use the lighter weights to sink the clothes and the emptied wallet separately.

Best to burn the credit cards and ID, he thought. He had a steel bucket and lighter fluid on board. He could make a small bonfire safely enough and get it over with. He hated the nasty smell of burning plastic.

He pulled out the gangplank next to the cleats and set it next to Brody. With one shove, he rolled him onto it and stood, rubbing his back.

He was a little out of practice.

Brody didn't move or make a sound although he was still breathing. Barely.

Vic lifted one end of the gangplank, dragging it to the rail and resting it there at a low angle.

Then he moved back to lift the other end and tip it toward the sea. It didn't take long. For a heavy guy, Mel didn't make much of a splash.

He put the gangplank back and went to get the bucket. The weights were coated with plastic—he might as well burn the cards into one. He tossed a five-pounder into the bucket, adding the cards, and squirted lighter fluid over everything, standing back when he threw in the match he'd scratched. The cards melted quickly into a twisted black glob as the fluid burned out, adhering to the weight.

Good enough. The bucket needed to cool. He bundled the clothes and wallet with a weight and tied it. Then he went back up on the bridge.

He headed back to the channel, going slow, stopping twice before he reached it to throw in the last of Brody's personal items.

The buoys blinked as he passed between them. It would be another hour before he turned north into the Lower Potomac. Not a problem. The boat had enormous gas tanks, more than enough for the round trip to the ocean and back. He wouldn't have to refuel.

Vic had time to think.

He was getting sick of SKC and Slattery. And he was aware that killing Brody might backfire, even though it would be days before anyone missed a loser like him.

Maybe it was time he left the States, period. He'd had offers. There were laws against U.S. citizens helping to train foreign armies. But he didn't care about his citizenship. He knew several countries that would issue him a new passport and provide him with a new identity. He could live like a king wherever he wanted to.

All he had to do was choose. He would make a couple of calls next week, explore his options. He didn't have to get on a plane. A launch or some other small craft could meet him outside the territorial limit and take him to a waiting ship. It was no big deal to blow up a fiberglass boat like this one.

If not for a certain green-eyed vixen, he would go.

He wanted to finish with her. Kenzie took up too much of his mental energy, more than any other woman he'd ever wanted. The others were merely all right. None had sparked his imagination the way she did.

He wanted to see how far he could go with her and find out what really made her scream. He wondered what she was doing right now.

The checked tablecloth was set and the covered platter in the middle smelled like fried chicken, the kind that was made in a skillet, not the kind that came in a paper bucket.

"Sit down, honey," Carol invited. "It feels so nice to have three at the table again. I miss Adam."

"He's your one and only son," Kenzie said,

"And he took full advantage of that fact sometimes," Carol remembered with a laugh. "I don't think he ever set the table or picked up a plate in his life. It's my own fault."

"What goes around comes around," Norm said, coming into the kitchen. "He just got a job as a busboy." He kissed his wife on the cheek.

"He didn't tell me that."

"You were out when he called." Norm lifted the lid off a pot of green beans. "Don't overcook these," he said.

Carol handed him a long-handled spoon. "You watch them."

Norm grinned at Kenzie and stirred the pot.

She looked around for a serving dish and found one on a shelf at eye level. Carol kept an old-fashioned kitchen, with lattice-look wallpaper and open shelves with scalloped trim. Everything was at hand and easy to find. Kenzie set the serving dish by the stove to warm.

"Oh, no!" Carol grabbed a pot holder and opened the oven door, quickly pulling out a baking sheet dotted with fluffy biscuits. She set the sheet on a wire shelf over the stove to cool.

"Good save," Norm said. He left the spoon in the pot and grabbed a hot biscuit from the sheet, tossing it from hand to hand.

His wife intercepted it. "You'll burn your mouth." She put it in a napkin-lined basket on the table and picked up the baking sheet again to slide the others in with it.

"It smells a little like Thanksgiving in here," Kenzie said happily.

"We may do a chicken this year instead of a turkey," Norm said. "I mean, if Adam decides he wants to celebrate with his friends."

Kenzie laughed. "He'll come home, with seven bags of laundry."

"I'm sure you're right about that," Carol said.

Neither of the Hamills said anything about where he would sleep if he did. Kenzie thought it was nice of them. They were nothing but nice to her.

Earlier that evening Carol had come upstairs to apologize for not inviting her to dinner in the time she'd been there, and insisted she join them.

The issue of where she would live next wasn't ever mentioned. They knew something about the stalker, of course, and a little about the possible SKC connection. Norm had been fine with the vest testing. But that didn't mean they expected her to stay indefinitely.

"You know, I'll probably have a new place of my own well before Thanksgiving. I might even share an apartment with my friend Christine."

"Now, how is she doing?" Carol asked warmly. "That poor girl. I feel for her parents, I really do."

Kenzie updated them before they sat down, and both Hamills were glad to hear of Christine's improvement.

Then Carol said grace and three amens resounded.

They tucked into excellent fried chicken and green beans that were only slightly overcooked. Norm made sure everyone had a biscuit before he took two.

Kenzie helped Carol clear away and wash up while Norm brushed Beebee's glossy coat. The kitchen was clean in no time.

"Mind if I go along when you take him out?" Kenzie asked Norm.

"Of course not."

She went to get the leash, handing it to Norm to clip to the dog's collar.

The night air had a hint of a nip, but it was refreshing after the hearty meal. She'd walked these streets plenty of times, but only during the day.

"I love these little brick houses," she said. "They're alike but all different too."

Windows golden with warmth shone out into the darkness. She could see lamps, the occasional picture, and once in a while a person moving around the interior.

"This neighborhood went up right after World War Two," Norm said. "Returning GIs bought most of 'em."

Norm was walking beside her with Beebee out in front.

"Look at the pumpkin cut-outs," she said, pointing to a picture window. "Some kids are having fun."

"Halloween is a big deal around here. It's a family neighborhood, always has been."

The children were all indoors now. She and Norm turned down a different street, keeping a companionable silence. She was content to wander. Norm's burly presence kept thoughts of the stalker at bay.

They went around a corner and a roar of voices startled her. Kenzie stumbled against him. It was like walking into an upholstered wall.

"Easy there." He laughed. "It's only a party. College football, I guess."

She looked where he pointed and glimpsed part of someone's back deck crowded with guests. The bluish light of a television she couldn't see flickered over their watching faces.

They continued on, matching Beebee's pace. He stopped now and then to sniff favorite spots, then kept on moving. Orange streetlights came on, but there was nothing warm about their odd glow with so few leaves on the trees to soften it.

The silence seemed to thicken, until the sound of running footsteps behind them made her move closer to Norm. She realized he was on alert too, looking quickly around.

A jogger passed them, white earbuds preventing him from hearing their hello or saying one of his own.

"Sorry," she said. "I'm kind of jumpy."

Norm sighed. "You have reason to be."

"I wish I didn't think so much about—something happening."

She figured he would understand what she didn't say. Carol had told her a little about his years on active duty and how long it took after that for him to feel halfway normal.

"I guess it depends. Once you get scared deep down, the feeling stays with you. Doesn't take much to start it up, either."

Kenzie nodded. She took his arm and he patted her hand.

"Give it time, Kenzie."

"How long?"

"I can't say, not for you. For myself, well—my war ended before you were born."

CHAPTER 21

Linc padded barefoot across the threadbare carpet of his motel room, cup in hand. The new coffeemaker he'd bought worked okay. Throw in a milk cow and a sandwich machine and he'd be set for another day of slogging on his laptop.

Superheroes had all the luck, he thought. Swinging on spider-webs, saving the day with a few punches, and wrapping it all up in thirty action-packed pages. Plus the love interests tended to be easy to impress. Unlike Kenzie.

He put down the cup and slung his long frame into his chair.

He had to tighten the parameters to keep on searching. Gary Baum had inadvertently given him a tip that should help. SKC upper management was mostly ex-military or former military contractors once deployed overseas, according to the reporter. That meant he could pull up a lot of information.

The Department of Defense issued Common Access Cards to allow authorized military personnel and certain civilians access to its computers and systems worldwide. Whether they were still entitled to use them didn't matter.

The Active Directory recognized his laptop. It shouldn't take him too long to get into the mother lode of data—the CAC database—and get to work. Linc had never done it, but he was counting on his high-level security clearance. If he was denied access, he could call Dana Scott and ask her to patch him in.

Gee whiz, Mike Warren would be proud. Linc didn't have to hack into SKC servers.

Common Access Cards had photos for general ID, so sharp that the eyes on the enlarged original could be matched to an iris scan. They were packed with encrypted data for each holder. And there were a lot of them—he had one—with about three and a half million active and unterminated cards in circulation.

Piece of cake.

He had copied a company phone list from Christine's computer to obtain names, company titles, and departments. He'd start with Melvin Brody, her boss, and check every name in her department.

Compare names to faces, and faces to the drawing Kenzie and Harry Cowles had come up with. The only part of the stalker's face she'd seen clearly every time was the guy's eyes.

Linc found his photocopy of the police sketch and propped it up next to his laptop.

Then he headed into the CAC database and got through the SSL handshake to verify his identity. The security clearance confirmation took longer. That didn't rely on passwords.

In fifteen minutes, he was in. Linc entered Melvin Brody's name in the search slot and sipped his coffee.

He looked at the face in the photo. Too old and too heavy. Brody had jowls and a tired look. His eyelids drooped and his eyes were watery blue, with none of the intensity of the sketch.

His bio seemed routine. A stint right out of college in the National Guard, never called up, but then there had been no need. A veteran of manufacturing management jobs around the Midwest, with better titles and salary boosts as the years went by. Married, divorced, no kids. He didn't live too far from Christine or Kenzie. Employed by SKC since the company was founded at twice the money of his last job. A step up for him.

Linc clicked out of Brody's file and entered the next name on the phone list for the same department.

Nothing panned out. Not everyone had a CAC card, though. Christine Corelli didn't. The military connection seemed to be limited to higher-ups.

He decided to do the same thing with them. The problem was that SKC had a lot of chiefs of this and vice presidents of that.

After a few hours of reading dutifully through their data, he was losing hope. Linc checked the phone list. There were only ten top execs left.

His cell phone rang. Restricted number. Linc picked up.

"Linc Bannon."

His boss said hello in a dry voice. Not Chet. His lady boss.

"Dana! Pleasure to hear from you."

She ignored his attempt at manly charm. "Do you plan on visiting Fort Meade ever again?"

"Yes."

"I mean in my lifetime, Linc. It's been days. Project 25 can't move forward without your input."

"Nice to know I'm needed."

"I don't have to pat you on the head, you know. I can fire you."

Linc tried to think of a reasonable, logical way to stall her. There wasn't one. Dana was smarter than he was anyway. He gave up.

"When do you want me back?" he asked.

"Right now, actually. Don't forget your pencil case." Dana hung up.

He walked through a Fort Meade building, feeling somewhat ill at ease. He really hadn't been gone that long, but the orderliness of the place seemed unfamiliar to him.

Here, he had defined responsibilities and a measure of control over the project he'd been assigned to. In the real world, trying to protect Kenzie and Christine from the crazy who was stalking them both, he had neither.

He took a moment to compose himself before he knocked on the door of Dana's office.

"Come in." The voice was distant but authoritative. That was Dana.

Linc put a hand on the doorknob and turned it. "Here I am."

She peered over the top of her monitor. "Guess what I'm looking at."

"I don't know."

Her finger stayed on a key. He could see the scrolling screen reflected in her eyeglasses. "The ballistics report for those vests. It's twenty pages long."

"Is that why you wanted me to come in?"

"That's one reason," she conceded. "Also because you are paid to be here. Your permission to work online, outside, is now, um, up for review."

"You told me to take as much time as I needed."

"I don't remember that."

He was pretty sure she had said something along those lines, but he didn't want to argue the point. Linc took a seat. "So what did the report say?"

"That some of the SKC vests are faulty. Some are apparently fine. The fiber is different in the faulty ones."

"Did they figure out why?"

"The chemical analysis isn't complete. A lot of things can degrade bullet-resistant material. Bleach. Humidity. Ultraviolet light. Age—none of the stuff lasts forever."

"So I understand."

"The preliminary conclusion is that some of the fiber was defective to begin with. The problem began with the manufacturer. SKC buys the raw materials in lots. One lot apparently was garbage."

"Sounds conclusive to me."

"It isn't. Not yet. The problem is picking it all apart. There was some debris in the box, by the way." She looked at him questioningly. "Not vests. Chunky stuff."

He remembered what he'd thrown in. "That was part of a target dummy. I think there was a bullet in it."

Dana made a note of that. "I'll let the lab know. I don't want anything to compromise the report."

"Sorry. I just tossed it into the box. My methods are not exactly scientific."

She raised an eyebrow. "But your suspicions have been confirmed. I'm not sure how you stumbled onto this, but it's important."

"That's why I bothered." He was leaving Kenzie out of it.

Dana continued. "There doesn't seem to be anything wrong

with the vest design per se. The side clasps release as they should. The camo material and webbing straps meet army standards. The problem is figuring out which vests have the defective fiber inside."

"What about the armor plates?"

"The lab reached similar conclusions, although that's totally different material. Some—not all—of the ceramic-type armor plates showed microscopic inclusions that could cause them to shatter, even from small arms fire."

"They're supposed to protect against rifle shots."

"Some do."

She looked at him.

"And some don't," he said. "What's the percentage?"

Dana returned her gaze to the screen. "Remarkably consistent and statistically significant. Fiber or ceramic, the fail rate is about ten percent."

One in ten. The medic had guessed as much, and so had he.

"So where does that leave us? What can we do?"

"It's enough to issue an official request for more information. I contacted the right agency."

"That's not good enough."

Dana regarded him calmly. "Do you have a personal stake in this?"

"Maybe."

She frowned. "Keep it to yourself, please."

"Will do."

"You should know that an official letter went out—on our recommendation but not from us. It ought to stop the next shipment."

Should. Ought. He didn't like the qualifiers, but this wasn't his call. "Good. Thanks. Is that all?"

"Hold it, cowboy. You're not going back to whatever it was you were doing at the—" She consulted a memo next to her. "At the D-Light Inn. Is that really the name of the place?"

"In neon. The e is missing."

"Not a chain, is it?"

"I don't think so."

"I see that it offers hourly rates." She glared at him. "Linc, this has to stop."

"Ah, I'm paying by the week."

Dana pushed aside the laptop. "I'm giving you one more week. After that you are expected to be back in Fort Meade, keeping normal hours."

"Okay."

"We're getting somewhere."

Kenzie had driven up to Fort Meade to meet him. "Sounds good," she said absently.

They were in a restaurant. Kenzie had headed straight for the back booth despite the hostess politely trying to guide them to an open table. Linc pretended he was only along for the ride and let Kenzie do what she wanted.

Her instincts were right.

At some point he stopped recounting the story of his meeting with Dana Scott, distracted by the way Kenzie drank through a straw. The cold soda made her lips wet. He fiddled with the salt and pepper shakers.

"Does she know about me?" Kenzie asked, slurping up the last drops.

"Not by name."

"Good."

"You wouldn't have to worry either way, Kenzie. She's a cool lady."

"Well, I'm glad to know she's concerned about the X-Ultra vests."

"More than concerned. She took the investigation to a level that we can't."

"Does that mean we should stop what we're doing?"

Their burgers arrived. Kenzie extracted a slice of pickle and nibbled on it thoughtfully. Then she helped herself to a french fry.

"Ah, Dana didn't say that," Linc hedged.

"Okay. I can keep on risking my life." She pointed the french fry at him. "That is a joke."

"Yeah, well—it's not that funny."

Kenzie shrugged. "I signed up for this. I'm committed to it."

"So am I, but—"

She picked up the burger and held it between them like a shield.

"Linc, I know you'd like to take over, but I won't let you. And you can't follow me everywhere."

Kenzie took a big bite. He upended the ketchup bottle and whacked the bottom.

She finished chewing. "You might want to take the cap off."

"Oh—right." He did and gave his burger a liberal dollop of ketchup. "The thing is, this guy isn't giving up."

"I noticed that." She finished her meal and he got a good start on his. Several minutes went by before either of them spoke.

"What I meant was—" he began.

She interrupted. "I don't know what stalked women do. You can't just kill the guy, right?"

"If your life has been threatened, you can get a permit for a concealed carry."

"Takes ninety days in Maryland."

So she'd looked into it. And her comment underlined the fact that she wasn't going back to her apartment in Virginia. Linc started in on his french fries. He sometimes wondered why he bothered to give her advice.

"Mike will vouch for the threat to you, pull some strings—he's got your back on this. He can push it through if you decide that's what you want."

"I'm not sure."

A waiter came over and offered dessert menus.

"I'll have the double chocolate cake," Kenzie said.

"Coffee for me," Linc told the man. He watched until the man was out of earshot. "You're hungry today."

"Yup," Kenzie said. "Life is short. I want cake."

He had to laugh. He waved to a busboy who came over to clear the booth's table, making short work of the task before heading away.

"Anything else on your mind?" Linc asked.

"Christine had a nightmare."

"Oh?"

"It was about the accident. She had one before. The details aren't that clear."

"Tell me."

Kenzie looked in her purse and took out a folded piece of paper. "I wrote down what she said. You can share it with Mike if you want."

She unfolded it and read aloud. "Christine was driving my car. Her hand was covered with blood. The other car came closer. The man behind the wheel had no shirt on. His upper body was covered in tattoos. Twisted black thorns, red drops of blood."

"What did he look like?"

"Sunglasses. Evil smile. She couldn't see his eyes."

"Kenzie—"

Linc didn't get a chance to finish what he wanted to say.

"I'm not going to promise to stay in my room. I never was too great at being a good little girl."

"I'll talk to Mike about the permit."

A slab of chocolate cake arrived, piled high with whipped cream. She dug in.

Linc picked up a six of longnecks on the way back to the motel. She had cake. He had beer.

Mike called before he popped the cap on the first one.

"What's up?"

"Just wanted to see how you were doing."

Linc blew out a breath. "I'm all right. The word from on high is that I have to go back to work in a week."

"We're going to miss you."

"Not that much. Listen, I wanted to ask you about a gun permit for Kenzie."

Mike listened. "Not a problem, but for what state? I have connections on either side of the river, but she has to apply herself, go through a background check. Tell her to come in."

"Will do. And I have something else for you. Christine is beginning to remember a few things about the accident."

"That's good. Like what?"

Linc took out the piece of paper Kenzie had given him. "She had a nightmare. Don't laugh. There could be something to this."

"Dreams aren't evidence."

"But it could be a thread to follow. Just listen, will you?"

"Okay, okay. The folder on this guy is getting fat. We have a lot of data. But still no one to hang it on."

Linc read aloud. Mike didn't interrupt for once.

"Thorns. Blood. I wrote it all down," he said. "Did you know there is a new nationwide database just for tattoos?"

"No."

Mike had bragging rights, Linc knew he'd use them.

"Still getting the bugs out, but it's coming along. We can pull up an image by design and type, sometimes by the artist who did it. Black ink, blue ink, full color. Arms, chest, back—one guy even had his crime scene done, starring himself. Charged with murder in the first degree, in part because of that. The DA got a conviction."

"Nice."

If Kenzie's stalker landed behind bars for a few years they'd be lucky.

"And that guy originally was picked up for something else, not the murder. Cops take photos of tattoos now. Some detective remembered a few of the details."

"Score one for the police."

"Damn straight. Okay, I'll ask for a database search on what you said," Mike said. "Like everything else, not instantaneous."

"Right."

"If our creep committed a crime or got hauled in somewhere for reasonable cause, and got a souvenir photo of tats or gang marks, he could be in there." Mike paused to take a breath. "No words, huh?"

"Kenzie didn't mention anything but the thorns and the blood drops."

"Too bad. Every little bit helps. Thanks, Linc."

It was worth putting up with the lieutenant's casual abuse to find out everything they could. And Mike Warren really was a good guy.

"Hey," he was saying, "guess what the most common word is in criminal tattoos."

"I have no idea."

"*Love*. Hands down. They love their mothers, they love some girl, they love Jesus. And they keep right on doing wrong."

Kenzie was stretched out on her bed with Beebee in attendance. "You shouldn't be up here," she told him.

The dog gave her a blank look.

"Don't act like you have no idea what I'm talking about."

Beebee yawned. She rumpled his ears.

"You're worthless, you know that? I can't believe I trained you."

A ringtone drew her attention elsewhere as the dog settled down again. Kenzie arched her back to reach for her cell phone, glancing at the number.

"Christine? What's up?"

"Nothing much," her friend said. "But I was wondering—Mom, no. I don't want you to go."

Kenzie listened to the brief argument on the other end of the call. She gathered that the black laptop's cord had somehow been caught in a piece of furniture and that a new one was needed.

Christine was too tactful to play the younger-generation card with her mother. Besides, Mrs. Corelli knew plenty about computers and laptops.

"The electronics shop at the mall should have one. If I go online, it would have to be shipped here."

Kenzie got the idea. "Not a problem," she said. "I'll stop by tomorrow morning on my way over, okay?"

She smiled at Christine's sigh of relief. "Mom, it's right on her way. But thanks."

They made small talk until Christine said her mother was leaving.

"Give her my love," Kenzie said. "And your dad too."

"He's not here."

"Tell him when he is."

She hung up after saying good-bye, smiling to herself.

*   *   *

"She's been a true friend, Christine." Mrs. Corelli was getting ready to leave. She'd already said hello to the night nurse.

"I know."

"Alf and I believe there isn't anything she wouldn't do for you."

"Don't make me feel guilty."

"I'm not trying to," her mother protested. "But she was at the ICU every minute she could get away."

"I barely remember. Which is probably a good thing."

"I don't think we'll ever forget it. All we ever thought about was whether you were going to live."

"News flash. I did. So you don't have to talk about me as if I were still unconscious."

"You really are on the road to recovery." Mrs. Corelli smiled. "Rude as ever."

Christine went to the window.

"What are you looking at?"

"Kenzie told me they'd be there."

The rear entrance to the rehab center was visible, illuminated by discreetly placed outdoor lights.

"Who?"

"The police. See that car? It's unmarked."

Her mother peered out. "Oh—yes. I do see it. Well, that's something." Her face became serious. "So long as you feel safe here."

"Sometimes I do."

"You're not ready to come home, honey." Her mother turned her way again. "Although there's nothing I want more. I talked to Dr. Liebling about you this morning."

"What did he have to say?"

"That you're coming along."

Christine leveled a look at her mother.

"Which means I'm stuck."

"For a while longer, yes," Mrs. Corelli admitted. "All right. I'm on my way. Alf made fettuccine."

"Bring me some tomorrow."

"Of course." Her mother brushed a kiss against her cheek. "You can warm it up in the microwave in the nurses' lounge." She smiled. "I guess I've been here too long if I know where that is."

They said their good nights and Mrs. Corelli left.

Christine went to draw the drapes closed over the window. The headlights on the patrol car weren't on, just the parking ambers.

She did feel safer now with them there. She just wished Kenzie had the same protection.

Linc took his time to finish off two of the longnecks, assessing the situation thus far. He could sum it up in a couple of sentences.

One. They were in a holding pattern if they didn't find the stalker. Two. That gave the psychotic bastard the advantage.

He hadn't failed, but he hadn't succeeded either.

The hour moved past midnight while he went over everything that had happened, moving the new facts around his mental grid.

Nothing connected.

The burger hadn't been enough. He ordered a pizza over the phone. The greasy wheel of cheese and pepperoni cost him a twenty with the tip and required two more beers to wash it down.

He regretted every bite after he'd finished it.

Linc fell out on the bed, too tired to finish going through the CAC database, although there was no one left but the top execs.

Long shots, all of them. He had a feeling he'd walked right past the guy, literally and metaphorically.

Dreaming of vengeance, he went to sleep.

It was five past nine in the morning when he awoke, feeling lousy.

So much for his plan to work into the wee hours. He took a shower that was penitentially cold and brewed some coffee. Last night's binge took care of morning hunger. He swore to himself that he wouldn't stop to eat again until midafternoon.

Linc scalded his tongue on the first sip of the too-strong brew in his coffeemaker. He made a face and set the cup aside. It took him the rest of an hour to rip through the remaining candidates, right down to their iris scans.

The next-to-last one stopped him cold.

Vic Kehoe.

Wasn't he the second-in-command at SKC?

Linc remembered the guy only slightly, but he was sure he had very dark eyes.

Seemed that he didn't. He must wear colored contacts. Black or close to black. Opaque.

The real color on Kehoe's scan was mixed. Brown and green with odd sparks of gold. But it wasn't the color that got his attention.

He dug deeper, pulling up a video of the scan, wanting to know what the man's eyes looked like in motion. A really good scan showed that. Eye tracking was as individual as the complex pattern embedded in each iris.

Vic Kehoe's eyes moved rapidly, as if bothered by the camera, wet and weirdly alive. When they looked straight into the lens, the lids narrowed with suspicion.

It wasn't just the algorithm that proved identity. The look in the eyes conveyed the truth.

Linc sat back. The magnetic intensity of Kehoe's gaze felt like he was being pushed back.

He knew he was looking at a video, but he had a feeling he was seeing exactly what Kenzie had seen. He grabbed her drawing and held it next to the screen.

The resemblance was startling. Linc was sure of it—Vic Kehoe was their stalker.

Linc clicked out of the iris scan. He didn't know who to call first—Mike could do something. Kenzie had to know. He punched the speed dial for her cell phone, frustrated when the call went straight to voicemail. He wasn't going to tell her over the phone. If he had to, he'd go find her.

He kept the message he left brief. "Call me. Like right away. I have to talk to you."

He'd be out of here in fifteen and searching for her. Mike wasn't so easy. The lieutenant would demand more than a visual comparison.

Working like a madman, Linc dredged up documents from different databases and stacked them like big index cards on the screen.

He started with a read-only PDF tagged with a red bar.

**Victor Kehoe. Age: 31. U.S. citizen.
Freelance agent from Gulf War onward, supporting
black-op teams on clandestine missions abroad.
Wide skill range. In-depth knowledge of
weapons, explosives, and all intel practices
including psychological warfare. Specialist in
close confinement and intel extraction. Quasi-
military clearance. This individual operates
under special-order rules for non-combatant
contractors and cannot be held accountable
under military law.
Kehoe displays mental toughness far above
normal limits and a markedly high tolerance
for physical pain. High IQ coupled with extreme
focus.**

There was more. He read quickly. The final paragraph offered a final chilling detail.

**Mental breakdown of unknown cause ten years
ago. Kehoe taken from posting for treatment at
base hospital. Released six months later.
Removed from active service, reasons
unspecified.**

Linc knew he was looking at the profile of a killer.

His phone rang without his hearing it as anything more than background noise. He grabbed it on the last ring.

Blocked number. Dana Scott again.

He had to answer the call.

"Didn't I just talk to you yesterday?" He forced a lightness into his voice.

"Yes. I just wanted you to know that I heard from the ballistics lab again. About that chunk of stuff you threw in with the vests."

"What about it?"

"The Kevlar backing on one of those dummies stopped a rifle bullet. Not the most powerful, but even so—"

Linc's memory provided a picture of himself and Kenzie shooting handguns at blank-faced targets. Where had the unknown bullet come from?

"It was sniper grade," Dana continued. "What was behind you at the shooting range?"

The question wasn't hypothetical.

"A high fence. A busy road."

"Think," she said.

"There was a building on the other side," he said slowly. "About five or six stories high. Not right on the road. Set back, oh, several hundred feet. Maybe more. The total distance could have been half a mile."

He could almost hear Dana frown. He took her meaning.

"Watch your back, Linc." She didn't say anything else.

CHAPTER 22

The mall parking lot was filled with cars by 10 a.m., and people coming and going. The sun shone brightly. It looked safe enough.

A heavyset attendant in an orange safety vest and ball cap jumped out of nowhere and made her slam on the brakes. She was about to roll down her window and yell at him when she realized he was waving her into a really nice space.

It wasn't too far from the entrance, in an area framed by evergreen hedges. Prime territory.

The attendant seemed to take his job seriously. The mall's logo decorated the ball cap jammed down over his pudgy forehead. She could just hear him muttering into the walkie-talkie in front of his face.

"Roger that. Over and out."

Give me a break, she thought. But she drove where directed beside a brand-new van with large windows. A sign with sucker cups in the corners displayed the name of some daycare center.

Kenzie got out, careful not to swing her door into the side of the new van. It was fairly close. She locked her doors, glancing inside the other vehicle. The parking attendant was busy directing other cars elsewhere with the same self-important gestures.

She glanced inside the van. There were several seats and a few scattered toys, but no driver and no kids either. They'd probably gone inside to enjoy the pint-size rides in the mall's atrium while their caregivers watched and relaxed with coffee.

The space on the other side of her car was empty. She wondered why it hadn't been filled. Maybe the attendant was saving it for a friend.

Kenzie slung her purse over her shoulder and headed in to get the USB connector cord that Christine had asked for. Finding a store in a large mall was always a pain. She tended to lose her sense of direction in places with no windows.

The electric doors pulled apart well before she reached them, then closed behind her.

The parking attendant made sure she was inside before he peeked into his pocket to look at the wad of bills he'd stashed inside.

He had no idea why the man in the buttoned-up overcoat had paid him to be on the lookout for her, or why he wanted her in that particular spot. They could be lovers, meeting in secret. Or maybe the lady with the long dark hair was also getting paid.

The attendant looked around for him. Gone. He hoped he would see him again, then realized he didn't have much of an idea what the guy looked like.

The wide-striped tie was brown with purple stripes. The sunglasses, brimmed hat, and camel overcoat sort of matched. He remembered enough.

All three items were being stuffed in the back of a car some distance away. The man the attendant had seen straightened, now down to a dark suit with a different tie in a subdued color.

Another clip-on. He hated the way it felt, but it was the fastest way to switch.

He got in to the driver's seat of the car and waited. This was the only mall near the rehab center, and Kenzie had visited it before. Stood to reason she'd come here for a replacement cord.

He'd picked up the late-night conversation. Nothing else to do at the time. He had been restless. His constant thoughts of Kenzie had awakened his blood lust. He couldn't control it. He didn't want to.

Not with a beautiful, fiery-tempered victim in his sights.

He had been waiting too long. She would be the last before he left the country.

After he was gone, Slattery would find out what he'd done. It was over. He was tired of pretending he was anything but a killer.

And his final kill would be spectacular. His hard-earned expertise would pay off.

He didn't know how he'd managed to hold back so long.

The first time he'd followed Kenzie here, alerted by the bug she didn't know she was carrying, she had bought a reading pillow with padded arms and a cat figurine, then gone back to the rehab center.

Then there had been the window.

Hand to hand. He loved the terror in her eyes.

The encounter at the falls hadn't scared her that much, he guessed. He'd startled her but he hadn't touched her. And he'd pretended not to see her hiding under the tree.

Maybe she was willing to go out alone for her friend. Or maybe she was too tough to be scared for long.

He'd done a couple of practice runs to test his idea yesterday, choosing women not entirely at random. They had to be pretty and they had to be silly.

Kenzie fit the first requirement but not the second.

The attendant had been happy to accept a fat bribe. If for some reason it hadn't worked, he would have tried something else, somewhere else.

It wasn't the first time he'd hung around the mall. It was a magnet for pretty women—the shopping attracted them in droves. They generally cooperated with the parking attendant, pulling into choice spots the goofball saved by the simple expedient of standing in them. The men ignored the guy, driving past, occasionally flipping him the bird.

He took note of the details of the attendant's outfit. The orange vest and padded sweater and ball cap made him into a nobody.

Always useful. People saw only what they wanted to see.

He might just buy the orange vest off the guy, keep it with the hiking parka and fake cop uniform. The color was as distracting as the whirling blue light he slapped on the hood of his car. That and the uniform had helped him pull over those two hookers who worked out of the D-Light a year ago. One had been ready to trade favors.

They'd died anyway. Cold case homicides, no grieving relatives.

Kenzie—well, someone would come looking for her. The geotag bug he had on her beeped. He checked it on the screen of his smartphone.

It was easy to follow her on a downloadable map of the mall. The geotag circle moved at a walking pace, then stopped at an information icon.

You are here.

With relief, Kenzie saw the mall map on a kiosk about fifty feet away. She studied it, getting her bearings. The computer store was one flight up and directly across from the escalator.

Two friends, dolled up and made up, were riding down as she rode up, checking their reflections in the mirrors to one side.

Kenzie smiled to herself. She didn't think she'd ever dressed up just to go shopping. But there was no harm in it. Maybe it was something Christine would like to do.

She nodded to the women when they were level with each other. On the second floor, she passed the merry-go-round. There were several small children on it, waving to their moms and, she assumed, a few daycare employees.

The sales assistant looked up as she entered the computer store. She took the damaged cord out of her purse and showed it to him.

"I'll see what we have," he said politely and disappeared into the back room.

Kenzie waited. The ambient noise of the mall drifted in. Kids, parents, friends chatting—it was Main Street without cars.

"Looks like we don't stock that one. It's an unusual type. You should try online, or order direct from the manufacturer if the laptop's still under warranty."

"Oh. I don't know if it is or not," Kenzie said.

"Sorry," the sales assistant said. "Is there anything else I can help you with?"

"No. Not today. Thanks, though."

She kept her frustration out of her voice. Without the cord, Christine wouldn't be able to work on the SKC computer.

Kenzie rode back down the escalator. The food court was serving late breakfast customers—she caught a pleasant aroma of coffee and cinnamon.

Not right now. She was too nervous to eat, even though she knew she needed to. Later she would have to go somewhere else, maybe with Linc.

Kenzie went out through the same doors she'd come in, then realized that they weren't the same.

Turned around again, she thought. She walked through the parking lot, which was nearly filled, looking for the daycare van, which was taller than her car. The parking attendant in the orange vest was nowhere in sight.

She spotted the van's white roof and went that way, taking out her car keys in advance.

Kenzie squeezed through the high evergreens to get between her car and the van. The engine was running and there was someone at the wheel. She couldn't see his face. He was wearing sunglasses that strapped around the back of his head.

The driver must have come back to get it started and move the vehicle nearer to the entrance so the children didn't have to walk through the parking lot.

Something was wrong with the muffler. She wrinkled her nose when the foul-smelling cloud coming from the van reached her.

A second later, Kenzie crumpled to the asphalt. The cloud of gas dissipated into the air.

The van doors slid open when the driver turned around. He had on a lightweight gas mask. He hauled himself out of the seat and dragged her in.

No one was watching. He'd paid the attendant even more to direct everyone away.

He hauled her up and lifted her unresisting body into the back. Then he got in and ripped down the daycare sign.

In another second, he was in front again, removing the mask.

He pressed a button that pulled shades down over the rear windows. .

He headed for the exit, blocked at the turn by a fluffy-haired woman in a convertible. The ragtop was halfway lifted but stuck, jerking up and down.

Fuming, he glanced in his rearview mirror. A circling vehicle, a real beater, had just claimed the empty spot he'd vacated next to Kenzie's rented car. The teenage driver pumped a victorious fist in the air, showing off for his buddy in the front seat.

Stupid punks. They had to be headed for the video arcade or the pizza palace. Either way, they were clueless.

He noted the make and model of the teenager's banged-up car in his wide-angle rearview. He'd phone it in to the police hotline tomorrow.

With a lurch, the convertible got going and he zoomed past it in the left lane, glancing at the malfunctioning ragtop. The driver was jabbing at the button that controlled it, cursing a blue streak.

Even if she did remember him, there was always a white van somewhere around at every crime scene. It was like there was a law.

He was as good as invisible.

He heard a muffled ringtone coming from Kenzie's purse. He'd look at the number later. He made a mental note to keep track of the cell phone. It was her only connection to the outside world. He would take it from her. She no longer needed it.

CHAPTER 23

Kenzie regained consciousness, but not completely. There was something heavy on her chest. She struggled to breathe.

The thing pressed against the center of her rib cage. On the edge of blacking out a second time, she tried to move it away.

Her hand moved over a foot encased in a heavy boot.

"Feeling better?" a man's voice asked.

She closed her eyes against the tears. They were burning hot, but they cleared her vision.

Kenzie opened her eyes and looked up. The man's face was one she recognized, but she did not know his name.

The boot pressed down.

"Who are you?" she whispered. Her throat was painfully raw. She remembered the van suddenly. And the cloud of toxic gas. Last of all, falling to the pavement.

"Don't you know? Allow me to introduce myself." His weird politeness made her more afraid. "My name is Vic Kehoe."

Kenzie knew she'd heard the name. He had something to do with Christine—with SKC—it came back to her.

Why was he playing with her? Why hadn't he just killed her?

He took his booted foot off her chest. Kenzie gulped in air, in agony, writhing on the floor. She was too weak to fight.

Kehoe lifted her top and took a long look. "Quite a bruise. Sorry about that."

She sat up halfway and he slapped her back down.

Enraged, Kenzie went for him. She clawed at the man who had

her in his grip, no match for his superior strength. But her nails ripped through the fabric of his shirt, baring his chest. She drew blood when she dragged them tightly over the skin of his iron-hard biceps.

Then she saw the tattoo she had revealed. Thorns twisted in a malevolent design, dipped in red blood. Not all of it was ink.

Kenzie heard him swear. Strong fingers closed punishingly around her upper arms. He pushed her to the floor and followed her down, holding her pinned with the weight of his body.

He let go of one arm. His hand circled her throat. He squeezed.

Kenzie woke up on a smooth floor, lying in darkness. Very slowly, her surroundings became clear. She couldn't determine the source of the indirect light.

She rolled over, looking at the ceiling. It was much too high for her to reach if she stood up. The cell, if it was one, had nothing in it. Nothing to stand on. Or sit on. Or lie on, besides the floor.

The walls were white. She crept to the nearest one and ran her fingers over it. Whatever it was made of was as smooth as the floor. Some kind of high-impact plastic, she thought. Heat-sealed seams.

Part of the wall above her glowed more brightly. But there was no fixture that she could see—just a translucent white square. Kenzie made a fist and banged on the wall. There was no echo. The plastic surface or something behind it absorbed the sound. It didn't give at all. She was locked in a high-tech prison. She tried to remember what little she knew about them.

Her head hurt.

Then it came back to her. Mobile prisons looked like boxes. Big boxes. Ten feet in height. Five deep by three wide. Outer walls of metal, sandwiching the soundproofing material with the smooth plastic. The whole thing was light enough for a helicopter to lift.

Ten feet high outside, she told herself. Eight feet inside. At least she would be able to stand up. Although at the moment she couldn't.

She dragged herself over to a corner and sat with her arms folded over her bent knees, resting her head. Her mind was still foggy. Blearily, she noticed a drain set into the floor. Not a way out. It was no wider than a jar lid and its perforations were too small to get her fingers into. She knew what it was for.

In the opposite corner was a bottle of water and a trail bar. No labels. A snack for her. How very thoughtful.

The stalker was either coming back soon or wanted her to die slowly. The bottle and the bar could keep her alive for a few days. Thirst would get her before hunger did.

Kenzie looked up. There had to be ventilation. The air didn't stir, but it didn't seem stale. She focused on a faint pattern molded into the plastic ceiling. A grid of dots. Something that let air in.

She let her head loll against the wall. It was warm. There was no way of telling if the cell that held her was outdoors or indoors. The light from the square seemed to grow faintly brighter one minute, then dim again. Like the pulse of something living.

Then she saw the camera tucked unobtrusively into a corner. A triangular bracket as smooth as the walls held it in place.

The lens had a milky look. Like an eye with a cataract. But she knew that the lens—and whoever was using it to watch her—saw her clearly.

Kenzie waited for the audio part of the creepshow to kick in. Commands. Taunts.

The silence was almost peaceful.

She placed two fingers on her wrist. Her heart rate was slow and her breathing irregular. An aftereffect of the black cloud of gas, she thought dully.

She could scream. But it would only make her head hurt more.

Kenzie staggered to her feet, using the wall to brace herself. The smoothness gave her nothing to hang on to.

She sank back down. There was no vent, no way to crawl out. This wasn't a movie with a grand finale.

She would die in silence.

Linc was in his car when his cell phone rang. He saw Kenzie's number. Thank God. He picked it up. "Where are you? Did you get my message?"

He heard a man's voice. "Don't hang up. She's with me."

"Who is this?"

He already knew. Vic Kehoe hadn't waited. He might have been monitoring Linc on the net, could know exactly what Linc had been reading—Linc hadn't been careful enough.

"Tell him, Kenzie," the other man urged. "Say hello."

He heard her get the word out. Her voice sounded far away. It echoed as if she were walled up.

"That—that's Vic," she confirmed.

"Good girl," he said.

Linc's hands tightened on the steering wheel. "Where is she?" He didn't waste energy on cursing Vic out.

"Didn't you geotag her phone?" the other man asked.

"No."

"Then I'll tell you. She's at SKC with me."

Linc was sickeningly aware that Kenzie had become the bait in an unknown trap. He didn't care. He was on his way. "That's a big complex, Kehoe. Where exactly?"

He couldn't call Mike. He had to stay on the line.

"Go around the back of Building B. To the village. The door will be open. It leads right to the path you saw with Slattery. His favorite street."

"Is he there?"

"No. Slattery borrowed someone's jet for the weekend."

Linc heard Kenzie moan.

"Don't hurt her," he said. He turned onto the road that led to the blocky buildings and vast warehouse. He couldn't see them yet.

Kehoe only laughed. "I'm going to let you do that."

Linc stepped hard on the accelerator. Almost there.

"Are you alone with her?"

"Yes," Kehoe assured him. "There's only a skeleton staff here on weekends. There is a guard at the gate, though. Probably asleep. Wake him up and ask for the pass I left for you."

"Okay." He knew better than to say anything to the guard. He knew who would suffer. He just had to get there.

There was a pause. He heard Kenzie cry out and then a thump, as if she'd been hit. Linc gritted his teeth.

"Go ahead," Kehoe taunted her. "Make all the noise you want. I haven't even started."

Linc slammed to a halt in front of the gates. He would have blown through, but the tire spikes had been reversed.

The guard, a shuffler with bad eyesight, peered at him through the glass of the little enclosure. "There's only one pass," he said. "You must be the Bannon fellow."

He held it out. Linc wanted to snatch it and roar on to Building B, but he had to wait for the spike shift.

Vic Kehoe. The man was certifiably crazy. He didn't look it. But when did psychos ever look it? They all lived on quiet, tree-lined streets with neighbors who never saw a thing.

The spikes rolled in reverse and he was through. The parking lot was empty.

The noonday sun shone on the back wall of Building B. He screeched to a halt in front of a small open door, grabbing the phone. The call was still connected.

"You there, Kehoe?"

"Tell him, Kenzie," the male voice said.

She screamed.

"Does that answer your question?"

Linc ran inside. He had to stop to let his eyes adjust to the dim light. The vast structure looked the way he remembered it. There were a few things that seemed to be different.

A construction crane had been moved to a flat field of dust behind the village. Ramps connected its highest section to the catwalks near the ceiling.

"Where is she?" He fought the shaking he could hear in his own voice.

"Take a guess. And be quiet, Kenzie. Or I will shoot him."

Linc fell silent, looking around. He was well aware that he was an easy target.

"I'm waiting," Kehoe said impatiently.

Linc's gaze moved over a steel box about the size of a small truck trailer. At first he'd thought it was attached to the warehouse wall, but on closer look he realized that the crane supported it.

Two giant prongs like a forklift were under its floor.

Very faintly he heard a switch click somewhere. With a jerk the steel box began to move. He could just hear Kenzie cry out again.

"Sit down," Kehoe told her. "In the middle."

She was in that thing. Linc recognized it as a mobile prison. Used, by the looks of it. Not shiny enough to impress clients. Maybe Vic Kehoe's résumé was enough to do that.

Wide range of skills. Specialist in close confinement and intel extraction.

The box stopped its downward trajectory.

Linc turned, startled when a large flatscreen, the type used in arenas, came down from the ceiling. It flickered to life.

He saw Kenzie. If she was in that box, it was pure white inside. But it was still a cell.

"There you go. Now you can see her. I dumped her there. And I can see both of you."

Linc kept his gaze fixed on her. He knew Vic Kehoe didn't care if he did. The bastard was bent on playing his sadistic little game for a good long time.

Her face filled the screen. Then the camera on her pulled back. She was sitting in the corner of a white space, a square of light to one side above her. He could just see a bloody handprint. Her mark.

He knew she'd left it on purpose. Just in case no one found out where she was in time.

"She fights hard," said Kehoe's booming voice. He was having fun with the sound effects on the PA system. He even experimented with a laugh.

The sound died away as the steel box continued its slow descent. The landing platform of the crane was suddenly illuminated. The spotlight beams moved over the fake street lined with mud houses.

Then the steel box hit the platform with a jolt.

Linc saw Kenzie's head bang against the cell wall. She came up, looking dazed.

"I'm out of practice," said the deep voice. "Maybe I should try again."

An invisible button was pressed and the steel cell rose several feet. Kehoe took his time about lowering it. It came down again, hovering several inches over the floor. Then he dropped it. The impact was less—it startled Kenzie instead of making her crack her head. Linc saw her hand rise and move over the wall.

Maybe she was looking for an inside opening that he could see from his outside vantage point. The platform rumbled and the giant tractor belts began to move.

Kehoe controlled it with skill.

The door to the cell lined up perfectly with the end of the fake street.

"Slattery showed you this, didn't he? And all that paintball crap he thinks is so much fun?"

Linc nodded.

"There's a real mine in it now," Kehoe said. "Spits nails and shrapnel. I rigged it myself. Spotted it yet?"

Linc looked. "No."

"Do me a favor. Walk down Mud Street and help her out of the white room."

The door swung open. Linc saw Kenzie drag herself toward it. Had she heard what Kehoe just said? He had no way of knowing.

Linc held up a warning hand. He willed her to understand the words his lips formed. *Stay where you are.*

She shrank back.

"And now the moment has come," Kehoe announced. "You actually don't have a choice about taking that walk. If you don't do it, I'll raise the box."

Linc waited, trying to hold Kenzie's gaze.

"The door is open. If I tip it, she falls out."

Linc obeyed the silent command from his invisible enemy and took a step.

"That's it. Keep going. One hint to make it fair—there is only one real mine. The others just look real. You can tell the difference if you kick them."

Linc hesitated.

"The real one can blow off your legs. Maybe not both. Get going."

Linc walked slowly, step by step. Kehoe hadn't told him to run.

Linc studied the dust on the path, looking for a trace of the buried mines. There was one area where the light reflected differently.

"I said get going." The flat voice was laced with anger.

Linc looked to his right, at the dry watercourse filled with stones. He searched with his eyes for two flat ones and picked them up. In another fraction of a second, he skipped them like stones over water. He used to be good at that. The heavier one hit the patch that reflected.

He turned his head away and prayed Kenzie would have the sense to do the same.

The shock wave deafened him. He didn't hear the fake mines pop. He looked back when the shrapnel stopped pinging off things.

A nail had hit his calf. He pulled it out of the muscle right through his jeans and ignored the blood running down into his shoe. Only one. He'd gotten off easy.

There was a huge hole midway down the path. The hidden mine would have blown off his legs and some other body parts he valued, and fragged the rest of him.

Kenzie cowered in the cell. There was shrapnel stuck in the steel and cracks in the plastic interior. Miraculously, none had hit her. He ran toward her and dragged her out.

"Good aim," Kehoe said nastily. "Now what are you going to do with her?"

Linc didn't know. She shook uncontrollably.

He searched the dark, echoing ceiling of the warehouse, scanning every inch of it for the other man. Kehoe stayed out of sight. He knew the layout. Linc didn't.

Linc could sense the depth of Kehoe's training in war games. Keep the enemy off balance. Take advantage of overconfidence.

Strike at close range.

CHAPTER 24

There was a rattling noise too loud to comprehend. Linc saw the source of it.

"Don't move," he said to Kenzie. "He wants to isolate us."

Steel cage doors were unrolling, coming down with lethal speed from high above. It took only a few seconds for the first to reach the cement floor. They would be pinned and killed if they ran for it.

"They keep the employees out," Kehoe's voice explained. "Slattery gets a little carried away sometimes. War games can get crazy."

"Linc," Kenzie whispered. "We can hide."

"No." He didn't want to die like a rat in a trap. She let go of him and ran through a mud doorway. The darkness inside swallowed her.

He had to follow. Then a bullet rang out, burying itself into the path a foot in front of him. A plume of dust rose and he coughed, trying to see inside the house.

"Run, Linc, run," the voice mocked. "You have to save her before you can save yourself. If you don't try, then you both die. Kenzie first," Kehoe added. "You get to watch."

Linc hesitated, listening for the actual location of the voice. He could just hear the delay between it and the PA.

"Leave her alone."

"I can't," Kehoe said calmly. "Something about her just gets to me. It's hard to explain."

Linc heard her cry out. Faintly.

"She must have touched the hot wall. Don't let that worry you," Kehoe's disembodied voice soothed. "The warehouse has a sprinkler system. We test it from time to time. Here goes."

Linc felt the first few drops. They stung his skin. Whatever was in the pipes wasn't water.

"Did that hurt? Let me switch it off. Stay still," Kehoe added.

Linc didn't hear a sound from the house Kenzie was in. But the drops from above stopped.

"Let's talk," Kehoe said. "Man to man. Although I don't mind if Kenzie listens."

For a fraction of a second, Linc glimpsed Kenzie within the house, near the mud doorway. Then she moved back into the darkness.

If Kehoe was focused on him, she might be safe.

"Remember when you joined the army, Linc? They took blood, so they have your DNA on file. One drop on a three-by-five card."

Kehoe knew what he was talking about.

"Yeah. So?" he said to the ceiling. At least this weird conversation gave him a reason to look up.

"That's all they need to identify your remains. Except there won't be any. You'll be vaporized. A mist of blood and bone."

An accurate description of a bomb victim, if the explosion was big enough.

Linc turned his head at the sound of a hiss. Kenzie was waving him into the house.

He heard Kehoe chuckle. "I guess she likes the layout. Want to check it out? No down payment. Quiet neighborhood."

Linc ran toward the door. The air inside was stifling. There was only one tiny window. Kenzie had backed into a corner. Her eyes glittered.

"Step away from the wall. Don't touch anything," he ordered. She obeyed.

He checked the walls and ceiling for dangling wires or a detonation cord—but not with his hands.

The imitation mud looked smooth and hard.

A square in the wall began to glow. He quickly stepped between her and it, holding out a hand to sense heat.

Kenzie coughed. "It cooled off. The light in the cell—it looked like that."

Kehoe's voice crackled loudly.

"I control that. There's one in every house. And there's a gift box in every house. Find it yet?"

Linc saw it. On the floor. The cardboard was the same color as the polymer the house was made of.

"Guess what's in it."

Another bomb. Linc wasn't going near it.

"Bulletproof vests." The voice laughed. "X-Ultra. You two get to test them. Not on a firing range. On yourselves."

Linc and Kenzie looked at each other.

"The box is open. Take one for her and one for yourself. And come out before I blow up that house."

A pause.

Kenzie dodged around him to the box and yanked out a vest before Linc could stop her. She pulled out another for him, clawing off the plastic bags.

A bullet smashed into the door frame.

One in ten. No way to tell the bad from the good.

Kenzie struggled into hers. It was loose on her. She fumbled with the side clasps.

"Got 'em on?" the jeering voice asked.

A second bullet hit, an inch above the first. Kehoe was a marksman.

"Tick-tick-tick."

Linc took a last desperate look around for a remote activator. It could be behind the square of light.

"You're running out of time."

Kenzie thrust the other vest at him. "Just put the damn thing on!"

She had snapped out of her trance. Cursing was a good sign.

Linc pulled out his gun. "Hold this."

She took it from him. "Got an ammo clip?"

"No. Just what's in it." He snapped the vest open and dragged it over his head, then fastened it. He took the gun back from her and stuck it into the back of his jeans.

Linc moved to the open doorway to show himself.

He knew Kehoe was above them, close enough to hit his targets with accuracy.

No bullets. No comments.

"What now?" Kenzie said softly.

He turned his head to the side to talk to her. "I shoot out the two spotlights over us, we run to the rock wall."

"Up to the catwalks?"

"If we can get there."

A third bullet hit the door frame. Linc jumped back. He blinked and brushed pulverized fake mud from his face.

Kenzie gave him a fast once-over. "He missed."

Linc kept her behind him while he craned his neck, trying to get a better look at the catwalks. There was a dark flash of movement. Kehoe was changing position, setting up for his next shots.

"Say when," Kenzie muttered.

One long stride took Linc to the doorway. He took aim but the lights blinded him. He missed a few shots, then made two. The spotlights shattered into sparks and went black.

"Now!"

He stuck the gun into his pants and grabbed her hand. They stumbled over the cratered path. Kehoe opened fire and missed again. Kenzie tripped and went down. Linc yanked her up.

Another shot rang out. The impact knocked Kenzie from his grip and left her rolling in the dust, stunned and gasping. He bent down and felt her legs for fresh blood, then her torso. Nothing. His hands slipped under the vest. Still nothing. The vest had taken the hit, not her. They'd picked one good one. That was something.

His vest—open question. Linc knew it was a matter of time until he was shot. A psychopath like Kehoe would want him to see Kenzie get hurt first.

Cold fury flooded him. He swept her up in his arms and carried her at a dead run to the rock wall. Kenzie had a few seconds to get her breath back. She twisted free the second they got there, grabbing the first handhold and heading up.

"Go for it," he muttered. He was right behind her, then to the side. Halfway up. Three-quarters. The darkness helped.

They reached the top of the wall and hauled themselves up and over onto a catwalk, lying flat.

Kenzie lifted her head and cursed. Linc looked where she was staring and saw Vic Kehoe. The other man smiled.

The rifle he'd used to take potshots at them was slung over his back. There was a .357 in his hand.

"Who wants to go first?" he asked nastily.

Linc put his hand over Kenzie's. He could hear her raw-throated breathing. She'd swallowed dust when she hit the path. His heart banged in his chest.

The catwalk creaked. Kehoe took a shooting stance. "Answer me." The barrel of the big gun moved from Kenzie to Linc.

They said nothing. Linc squeezed her hand.

"You must want to die together. Okay."

He kept the gun on them and took a step back. Linc saw a control console. Kehoe pushed a button on it.

There was a clanking sound. The mobile prison was coming up.

Kenzie looked down at the slowly rising box. So did Linc. It settled with a jerk at their level.

"Let go of her," Kehoe snarled.

Linc released her hand and looked up.

"Now get up. One by one. You first," he said to Kenzie.

She got on her knees, then all the way up, clumsily.

Kehoe pointed the gun at the open door of the prison.

"Inside. Be a good girl. Get in a corner."

She obeyed. Linc hadn't reached for his gun. He figured he had two bullets left. But he couldn't kill Kehoe without risking Kenzie's life. The other man was too close and too accurate.

He wasn't wearing body armor, but it didn't matter. Kenzie would die before Linc could shoot.

"Now you."

Linc rose slowly, keeping his hands up.

"Look down," Kehoe said. He cocked the trigger. "Do it."

Linc bowed his head. So he would be first. He didn't care, not if it gave her a chance to escape.

"See that? Look harder. Right below you."

There was something on the dusty cement floor that hadn't been there on his first trip to the SKC playpen. He squinted. It looked like two gas cans. Plastic. One red, one yellow.

"Tell me what that is, Bannon."

"An IED." Otherwise known as an improvised explosive device. Kehoe was a munitions expert.

"Wrapped tight and rigged right," the other man boasted. "That thing can take the roof off this building. Want to know how it works?"

"Sure." Keep him talking. Maybe Kenzie would find a way to escape. Linc hoped so.

"Two cans, two volatile liquids. No det cord, no activator. Ignites on impact."

"How?"

"Chemical reaction when both cans get pierced. Like a juice box." He looked at Linc's impassive face. "Yeah, it's that easy." He started talking faster, moving Linc backward. "All plastic too. No one can find those suckers. Except for maybe a dog."

Kehoe got him to the door of the prison.

"I used to build them and bury them just for the hell of it. I blamed it on the enemy if a soldier took a wrong step."

Linc stepped in, meeting Kenzie's steady green gaze.

"I'm going to drop you two right on it."

He pushed him in. Linc fell hard to the smooth floor.

"Prepare for blastoff." Kehoe took a last look at them both.

The door slammed. They heard the latch click.

The square of light in the wall came on.

He rolled over and crawled to Kenzie. She didn't say anything. They both listened to the faint noises coming from outside.

The prison began to rock. Kehoe had to be moving it into position above the IED. The machinery of the crane creaked and groaned. They could feel it through the floor.

He sat up next to her and put his arm around her shoulders.

Kenzie rested her head against his arm. Her gaze moved up to the high corner.

"Did he take your gun?" she asked.

"No." He felt for it and took it out. "Two shots left. I can blow off the latch with one and get him with the other. Worth a try."

"Linc—" She pointed up to a corner. "That's a camera."

He looked. "So?"

"If you miss, I don't want his eyes on me when I die."

"He's not looking now. And you're not going to die."

"Lift me up," she begged.

"Why?"

"Just do it. And give me your gun."

"Kenzie—"

"I'm not going to shoot!"

He understood. She took it by the barrel and Linc hoisted her onto his shoulder. He swayed with the force of her movement as she slammed the end of the heavy grip into the lens, holding on to her legs with his eyes closed as fine shards of glass flew outward.

They both looked at the damage as he let her slide down his body. Broken, the hidden camera dangled from the cracked lens.

He took the gun back and a second later the door to the prison swung open. They looked at each other in stunned silence.

It had to be a trick.

They stayed where they were. Then Kenzie moved forward. Linc dragged her back.

He held her so she couldn't move. She didn't fight him. He noticed that the noise of the machinery had stopped.

The silence became unbearable.

"Stay here," he whispered. "One way or another, I'm taking him down. You run for it."

She nodded.

He rose to a crouch and moved to the door. Linc maneuvered so he could see. His field of vision was cut by the half-open door.

Kenzie was on her feet but staying in the corner. He waved at her to remain there. There was still no sound from outside.

He edged into a different position and saw Kehoe in front of the console.

"Come on out," Kehoe said, glancing his way. His fingers hovered, moving in the air, about to press a button that would send the mobile prison hurtling down. He'd put on a bulletproof vest. SKC make. Not defective, Linc guessed. Playing his evil game to the end.

He didn't see the rifle or Kehoe's handgun.

Linc kept his gun out of sight, watching Kehoe's fingers play in the air as his head bobbed. He was humming under his breath.

Head or hand. Which? A bullet to the head might slam Kehoe forward, the weight of his body pressing the buttons. A bullet to the hand would be wasted. He could hit the console with the other.

Then Kehoe turned, his hypnotic gaze moving past Linc to Kenzie. "Ready to die, bitch?"

Linc heard her draw a breath. It wasn't going to be her last. He aimed between Kehoe's eyes and fired.

A gush of blood sprayed over the catwalk. The shot reverberated against the metal ceiling, deafening him. Vic Kehoe fell backward, just missing the console and toppling over the low railing of the catwalk.

Toward the bomb below.

Linc had a split second to shut the door and throw Kenzie down before it exploded. He curled around her.

The shock wave hit. The door banged open again. He lost his grip and slammed into the opposite wall.

He heard her urgent voice. Linc couldn't open his eyes.

"Wake up. Don't die, Linc. I love you. Don't you dare die."

Somehow he found the strength to smile.

He couldn't talk either. His tongue felt thick. The words wouldn't come.

Something hot and wet fell on his face. Drops of something. Blood? A single drop hit his swollen mouth. He tasted it. Not blood. A tear.

Kenzie leaned over and kissed his cheek.

Oh man.

He was alive. He struggled to speak. Three little words. Nope. One too many. He tried for two.

"Love you."

CHAPTER 25

Several weeks later . . .

Jim Biggers looked down at the puppy playing tug-of-war with one of his bootlaces. "Quit it," he growled, gently shaking it off.

The puppy yapped and scampered away, bumping into Truck's furry side and bouncing off. The big dog didn't bat an eye, but he raised his head when he heard a car door slam outside. Another puppy tumbled off his back as he got up.

Jim rose too, looking out the window.

"She's here," he announced, throwing down his pencil.

In another minute Kenzie and Linc walked in. One of the puppies ran to her and she squatted down to say hi. "Oh my gosh. You are so cute!"

"I can't compete," Jim grumbled to Linc.

The puppy yapped and ran away. Kenzie went around to the other side of the desk to kiss her boss on the cheek. "Sorry."

Jim grinned. "You're forgiven. How are you doing, Linc?"

He'd noticed that the younger man was still limping. There wasn't any need to mention it specifically.

"Better every day, thanks. How did Truck get stuck with baby-sitting?"

"I promised him half a steak," Jim said. "He fell for it."

An eager puppy chomped down hard on Truck's ear, then put his head and paws down in play position, wagging his stubby tail.

"Poor Truck," Kenzie said sympathetically. She looked back to

Jim. "Why are they here? I mean, they're cute but way too young to start with us."

"Merry Jenkins is fostering them for me. But she's gone for the next two days, so I have them. It's been fun. I'm seeing plenty of potential." He glanced at the floor, frowning. "And a few puddles."

He unrolled several sheets from the paper towel dispenser on his desk and let them drift to the floor. A puppy pounced on the white stuff and dragged it away.

Jim rolled his eyes. He unrolled more paper towels, and this time he put his boot down on them.

"I can't wait to come back full-time," Kenzie said.

"When you're ready. Not a minute before," Jim said sternly. "Everything's under control. No rush."

Linc looked down. "Am I seeing things?"

A tiny kitten was clawing its way up his jeans.

Jim harrumphed. "That's a stray. Buddy and Wells started feeding it, and now it won't go away."

"Aww," Kenzie exclaimed. "It's adorable."

Linc detached the kitten from his front pocket and held it up. The warmth of his hands calmed it, but only for a minute. The kitten stared at him, bug-eyed, then batted at his nose. "Doesn't seem to be afraid of anything."

"Reminds me of Kenzie. I guess I'll have to keep it. So where are you two headed?"

Linc put the kitten down. Tiny tail waving, it sauntered between Truck's furry legs. The dog didn't seem to mind.

"Oh—out and about," Kenzie said.

She and Linc exchanged a look. "You tell him," he said.

"We stopped by to see Christine first. You were next on the list."

"Beg pardon? What list?"

"Friends and family." Kenzie stretched out her left hand and wiggled her fingers. An oval diamond set in platinum caught the sun.

Jim's eyes widened.

"Way to go." He beamed at both of them. "That's one hell of a rock. You didn't waste any time." He gave Linc a nod of masculine approval. "So when's the big day?"

"We haven't decided," Kenzie answered.

She didn't want to say that they were keeping a low profile for as long as possible. The media furor over SKC had died down, but they were helping with the ongoing investigation.

Life went on. Love had amazing power to heal.

Truck picked up on the excitement and edged between the three of them, blocking the hug about to happen.

"Routine sniff, Linc. He has final say," Jim teased.

The black-and-white dog took his time about it. Then he sat down in front of Linc, brushing his tail across the floor in wide waves.

"He approves," Kenzie said.

"Never argue with a good dog." Jim laughed. "All right, you two. Get out of here. I have work to do."

Kenzie got a hug in before he went back to his desk.

"Congratulations." He nodded toward the picture of his wife. "From me and Josie. She'll be over the moon when she hears."

Linc and Kenzie drove away in his red pickup. The diamond on her hand caught the sun before she reached up to rub his shoulder.

"I was thinking," she began.

Linc smiled, enjoying the mini-massage. "Am I being softened up?"

"Yes."

"Just tell me what you want, Kenzie."

"Let's get away somewhere. Really away."

"Name your island," Linc replied cheerfully.

"Is there one called True Love?"

He laughed out loud. "Let's go looking. It has to be out there somewhere."